FROST

PATRICIA BRIGGS

www.orbitbooks.net

ORBIT

First published in Great Britain in 2013 by Orbit

All characters and events in this publication, other than those clearly in the public domain, are fictitious and any resemblance to real persons, living or dead, is purely coincidental.

A CIP catalogue record for this book is available from the British Library.

ISBN 978-1-84149-798-3

Printed and bound by CPI Group (UK) Ltd, Croydon CR0 4YY

Papers used by Orbit are from well-managed forests and other responsible sources.

MIX
Paper from responsible sources
FSC® C104740

Orbit
An imprint of
Little, Brown Book Group
100 Victoria Embankment
London EC4Y 0DY

An Hachette UK Company
www.hachette.co.uk

www.orbitbooks.net

To Mike, who brings color to my world

ACKNOWLEDGMENTS

Because no good book happens alone, the following people helped to get this story to print.

Mike and Collin Briggs, Kaye and Kyle Roberson, Ann Peters, Michael Enzweiler, Deb Lenz, Linda Campbell, and Anne Sowards—who read it when it was rough and helped to make it better. Thank you.

Also to Michael and Susann Bock, who fix my German and give Zee and Tad their magic. *Vielen Dank*.

If there are mistakes in this book, they are, as always, my responsibility.

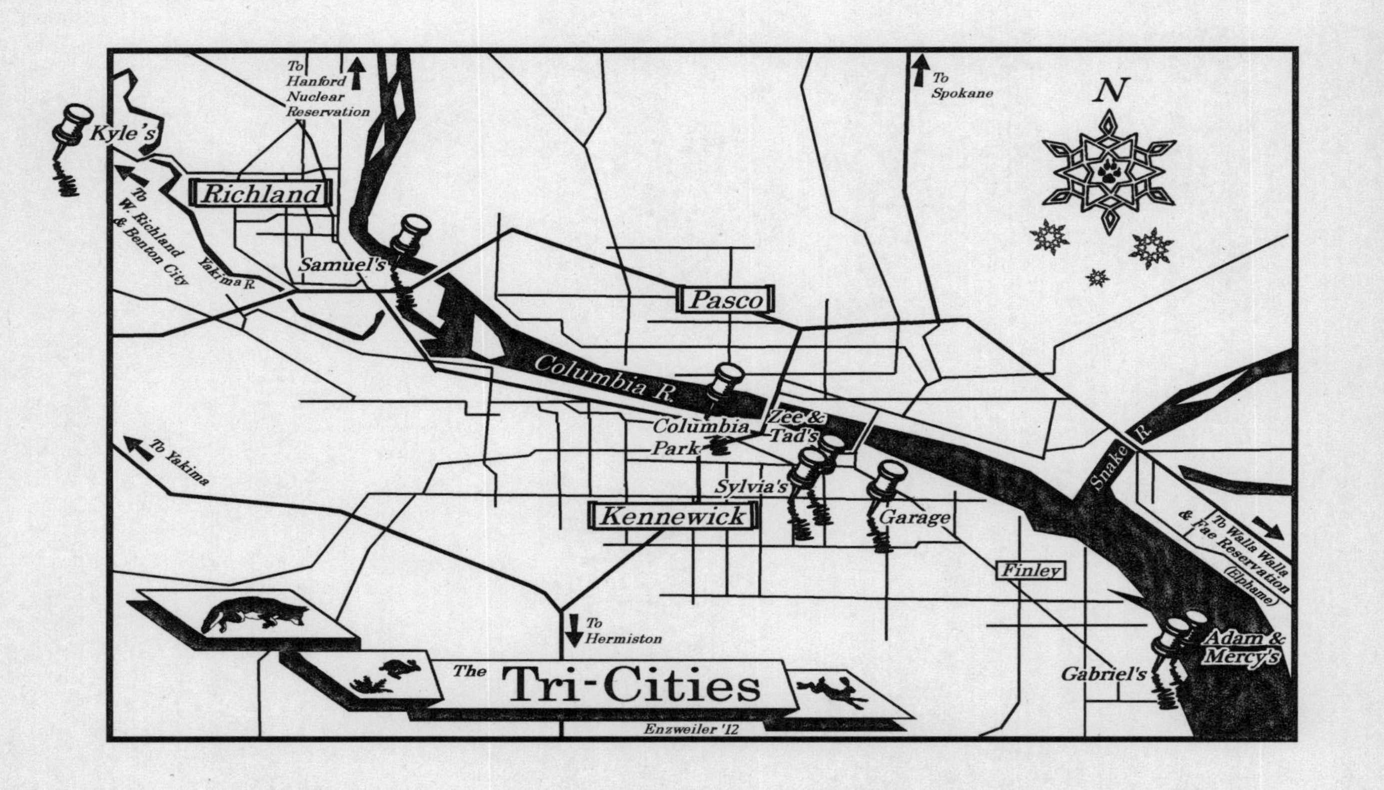
The Tri-Cities
N
To Hanford Nuclear Reservation
To Spokane
Kyle's
Richland
To W. Richland & Benton City
Yakima R.
Samuel's
Pasco
Columbia R.
Columbia Park
Zee & Tad's
Sylvia's
Garage
Kennewick
To Yakima
To Hermiston
Finley
Snake R.
To Walla Walla & Fae Reservation (Elphame)
Adam & Mercy's
Gabriel's
Enzweiler '12

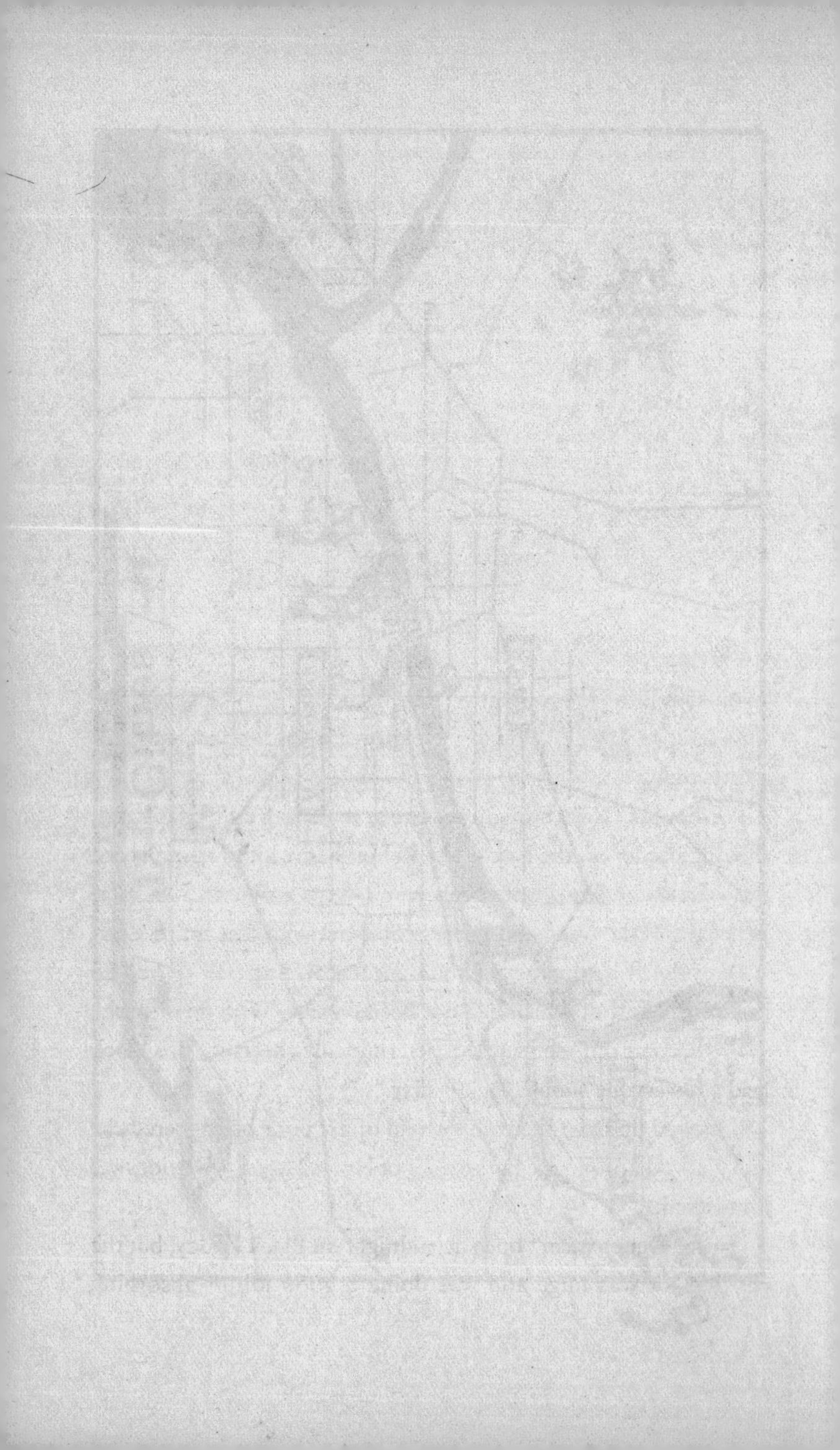

1

"You should have brought the van," said my stepdaughter. She sounded like herself, though the expression on her face was still a little tight.

"I shouldn't have brought anything, including us," I muttered, shoving harder on the hatch. My Rabbit had a lot of cargo space for a little car. We'd only been here twenty minutes. I shop at Walmart all the time, and I never come out with this much stuff. We'd even left before the big midnight reveal. And still—I had all this *stuff*. Most of which had not been on sale. Who does that?

"Oh, come on," she scoffed, determinedly cheerful. "It's Black Friday. Everyone shops Black Friday."

I looked up from the stubborn lid of my poor beleaguered car and glanced around the parking lot of Home Depot. "Obviously," I muttered.

Home Depot wasn't open at midnight on Black Friday, but the parking lot was huge and was doing a good job of absorbing the overflow from Walmart. A bicycle couldn't have parked in the Walmart lot. I wouldn't have believed there were this many people in the Tri-Cities—and this was only one of three Walmarts, the one we'd decided would be the least busy.

"We should go to Target next," Jesse said, her thoughtful voice sending chills down my spine. "They have the new Instant Spoils: The Dread Pirate's Booty Four game on sale for half off the usual price, and it was set for release tonight at midnight. There were rumors that problems in production meant before-Christmas shortages."

Codpieces and Golden Corsets: The Dread Pirate's Booty Three, better known as CAGCTDPBT—I kid you not; if you couldn't say the letters ten times in a row without stumbling, you weren't a Real Player—was the game of choice for the pack. Twice a month, they brought their laptops and a few desktops and set them up in the meeting room and played until dawn. Vicious, nasty werewolves playing pirate games on the Internet—it was pretty intense, and I was a little surprised that we hadn't had any bodies. Yet.

"Shortage rumors carefully leaked to the press just in time for Black Friday," I groused.

She grinned, her cheeks flushed with the cold November wind and her good cheer not as forced as it had been since her mother called to cancel Christmas plans during Thanksgiving dinner earlier this evening. "Cynic. You've been hanging around Dad too much."

So, in search of pirate booty, we drove across the street to the Target parking lot, which looked a lot like the Walmart parking lot had. Unlike Walmart, Target hadn't stayed open. There was a line four people deep waiting for the doors to be unlocked at midnight, which, according to my watch, was about two minutes from now. The line started at Target, wrapped around the shoe store and giant pet store, and disappeared around the corner of the strip mall into darkness.

"They're not open yet." I did not want to go where that line of people was going. I wondered if this was how Civil War soldiers felt, looking over a ridge and seeing the other side's combatants, grim and poised for battle. This line of people was pushing baby strollers instead of cannons, but they still looked dangerous to me.

Jesse looked at my face and snickered.

I pointed at her. "You can just stop that right now, missy. This is all your fault."

She blinked innocently at me. "My fault? All I said was it might be fun to go out and hit the Black Friday sales."

I'd thought it would be a good way to distract her from her mother's patented brand of guilt trip leavened with broken promises. I hadn't realized that going shopping on Black Friday (Thursday still, according to my watch, for the next minute) was akin to throwing myself on a grenade. I'd still have done it—I love Jesse, and the diversion was starting to work—but it might have been nice to know how bad it was going to be.

We drove slowly behind a host of cars also looking for parking places, eventually drifting right by the front of the store where the shoppers lurked, hunched and ready to attack the sales. Inside the store, a young man in the sadly appropriate red Target shirt walked very slowly to the locked door that was all that protected him from the horde.

"He's going to die." Jesse sounded a little worried.

The crowd started undulating, like a Chinese New Year dragon, as he reached up slowly to turn the key.

"I wouldn't want to be in his shoes," I agreed, as the boy, mission completed, turned to run back into the store, the crowd of salivating shoppers hot on his trail.

"I'm not going in there," I stated firmly, as an old woman elbowed another old woman who had tried to slip in through the doors ahead of her.

"We could always go to the mall," Jesse said after a moment.

"The mall?" I raised my eyebrows at her incredulously. "You want to go to the mall?" There are a herd of strip malls in the Tri-Cities as well as a factory outlet mall, but when one speaks of "the Mall," they mean the big one in Kennewick. The one that everyone shopping on Black Friday was planning to hit first.

Jesse laughed. "Seriously, though, Mercy. Five-quart kitchen mixers are on sale, a hundred dollars off. Darryl's broke when my friends and I made brownies with it. With babysitting money, I have just enough to replace it for Christmas if I can find it for a hundred dollars off. If we get the mixer, I'm okay with calling this experiment finished." She gave me a rueful look. "I really am okay, Mercy. I know my mother; I was expecting her to cancel. Anyway, it'll be more fun spending Christmas with Dad and you."

"Well, if that's the case," I said, "why don't I give you a hundred dollars, and we can skip the mall?"

She shook her head. "Nope. I know you haven't been part of this family long, so you don't know all the rules. When you break someone else's toy, you have to pay for it yourself. To the mall."

I sighed loudly and pulled out of the frying pan of the Target parking lot and headed toward the fire of the Columbia Center Mall. "Into the breach, then. Against mobs of middle-aged moms and frightening harridans we shall prevail."

She nodded sharply, raising an invisible sword. "And damned be he—she—who cries, 'Hold, enough!'"

"Misquote Shakespeare in front of Samuel, I dare you," I told her, and she laughed.

I was new at being a stepmother. It was like walking a tightrope sometimes—a greased tightrope. As much as Jesse and I liked each other, we'd had our moments. Hearing her laugh with genuine cheer made me optimistic about our chances.

The car in front of me stopped suddenly, and I locked up the Rabbit's brakes. The Rabbit was a relic from my teenage years (long past) that I kept running because I loved it—and because I was a mechanic, and keeping an old, cheap car like the Rabbit running was the best form of advertisement. The brakes worked just fine, and she stopped with room to spare—about four inches of room.

"I'm not the first person to misuse *Macbeth*," Jesse said, sounding a bit breathless—but then, she didn't know I'd just redone the brakes last week when I had some time.

I blew out air between my teeth to make a chiding sound as we waited for some cowardly driver a few cars ahead to take the left turn onto the interstate. "The Scottish Play. It's 'the Scottish Play.' You should know better. There are some things you never name out loud, like *Macbeth*, the IRS, and Voldemort. Not if you want to make it to the mall tonight."

"Oh," she said, smirking at me. "I only think about that when I'm looking into a mirror and not saying 'Candyman' or 'Bloody Mary.'"

"Does your father know what kind of movies you watch?" I asked.

"My father bought me *Psycho* for my thirteenth birthday. I notice you didn't ask me who the Candyman was. What kind of movies are *you* watching, Mercy?" Her voice was a little smug, so I stuck my tongue out at her. I'm a mature stepmom like that.

Traffic near the Kennewick Mall actually wasn't too bad. All the lanes were bumper-to-bumper, but the speed was pretty normal. I knew from experience that once the silly season got fully under way, a snail would make better time than a car anywhere near the mall.

"Mercy?" Jesse asked.

"Uhm?" I answered, swerving into the next lane over to avoid being hit by a minivan.

"When are you and Dad going to have a baby?"

Chills broke out all over my body. I couldn't breathe, couldn't speak, couldn't move—and I hit the SUV in front of me at about thirty miles an hour. I'm pretty sure that the Scottish Play had nothing to do with it.

"It's my fault," Jesse said, sitting beside me on the sidewalk next to the mall parking lot shortly thereafter. The flashing lights of various emergency vehicles did interesting things to her canary yellow and orange hair. She was bumping her feet up and down with excess nervous energy—or maybe just to keep warm. It was, at best, thirty degrees, and the wind was cutting.

I was still trying to figure out what had happened—though one thing I was sure of was that it hadn't been Jesse's fault. I leaned my head against the cement at the base of one of the big light poles and put the ice pack back on my left cheekbone and my nose—which had finally quit bleeding. "Captain's in charge of the ship. My fault."

Panic attack, I thought. Jesse's question had taken me by surprise—but I hadn't thought the idea of a baby scared me that much.

I kind of liked the thought of a baby, actually. So why the panic attack? I could feel the remnants of it clogging my thoughts and lingering like the edges of an ice-cream headache—or maybe that was the effect of my face colliding with the steering column.

The Rabbit was an old car, and that meant no air bags. However, it was a good German car, so it collapsed around the passenger compartment, leaving Jesse and me with bruises and bumps and a bloody nose and black eye. I was pretty tired of black eyes. With my coloring, bruises didn't stand out like they did on Jesse. Given a week or two, no one would ever know we'd been in a car wreck.

Even with the bag of ice between me and the rest of the world, I could tell that the passenger in the SUV I'd hit was still talking to the police because her voice was raised. The energy she was expending made me pretty sure she wasn't hurt much, either. The driver hadn't said anything, but he seemed okay to me. He stood a few steps back from his car and stared at it.

The younger policeman said something to the woman, and it hit her like a cattle prod. The man who'd driven the car glanced over at Jesse and me, while the woman went off like a teakettle.

"She *hit* us," the woman shrieked. That was the gist of it anyway. There were a lot of unladylike words that began with "F," with various "C" words thrown in for leavening. She had an alcohol slur that did nothing to moderate the shivery high pitch that she reached. I winced as her voice cut right through my aching skull and increased the pressure against my throbbing cheekbone.

I understood the sentiment. Even if the accident isn't your fault, there is hell to follow when talking to insurance companies, taking the car to a body shop, and dealing with the time the car is in the shop. Worse, if it's totaled, you have to argue with the other guy's insurance about how much it was worth. I was feeling pretty guilty, but Jesse's flinch made me set that aside and pay attention to her.

"Ben's better," I murmured. "He's more creative when he swears."

"He does it in that English accent, which is too cool." Jesse relaxed a little and started listening with more interest and less worry.

The woman began batting at the younger policeman and swearing. I didn't bother to listen to the details, but apparently she was mad at him now, and not us.

"*And* Ben is too smart to swear at cops," Jesse said with a sincere but misguided belief in Ben's wisdom. She had turned to look at me and got a good view over my shoulder of the only real fatality of the incident. "Jeez, Mercy. Look at the Rabbit."

I'd been avoiding it, but I had to look sometime.

The little rust-colored car was connected to the SUV in front of it and somehow had managed to ride up on something so that the front wheels, the nearest one no longer round, were about six inches up in the air. Its nose was also about two feet closer to the windshield than it had been.

"It's dead," I told her.

Maybe if Zee were still around to help, he could have done something with the Rabbit. Zee had taught me most of what I know about fixing cars, but there were some things that couldn't be fixed without an iron-kissed fae to put them to rights. And Zee was holed up in the fae reservation in Walla Walla and had been since one of the Gray Lords killed a US senator's son and declared the fae to be a separate and sovereign nation.

Within minutes of the declaration, all of the fae had disappeared—and so had all of the reservations. The ten-mile loop of road that used to lead to the local reservation near Walla Walla was now eight miles long, and from nowhere along that route could you even see the reservation. I'd heard that one of the reservations had grown a thicket of blackberry bushes and disappeared inside.

There was a rumor that the government had tried to bomb a reservation, but the entire flight of planes had disappeared—reappearing minutes later flying over Australia. Australian bloggers posted photos, and the US president issued a formal apology, so that part of the rumor seemed to be true.

For me personally, the whole thing meant I had no one to call on when I needed help in the shop or needed some time off. I hadn't even gotten a chance to talk to Zee before he was gone. I missed him, and not just because my poor Rabbit looked to be headed to that big VW rally in the sky.

"At least we weren't driving the Vanagon," I said.

The teenager I'd been—the one who had worked fast-food jobs to pay for the car, the insurance, and the fuel and upkeep—would have cried for the poor Rabbit, but that would have made Jesse feel bad, and I wasn't a teenager anymore.

"Harder to find a Syncro Vanagon than a Rabbit?" Jesse half asked, half speculated. I'd taught her how to change her own oil, and she'd helped out at the shop now and then. Mostly she flirted with Gabriel, my teenager Friday who was back from college for Thanksgiving break, but even a little bit of help was useful now that I was my only employee. I didn't have enough business to hire another full-time mechanic, and I didn't have time to train another teenager to take Gabriel's place. Especially since I thought it might be a waste of time.

I didn't want to think about closing the shop, but I was afraid it might be coming.

"Mostly, it is a lot easier to get hurt in a Vanagon," I said to Jesse. Losing the Rabbit and lack of sleep were making me melancholy, but I wasn't going to share that with her, so I kept my voice light and cheerful. "No crumple zone. That's one of the reasons they don't make them anymore. Neither of us would have walked out of an accident like this in the van—and I am very tired of being in a stupid wheelchair."

Jesse let out a huff of laughter. "Mercy, *all* of us are tired of you being in a wheelchair."

I'd broken my leg badly on my honeymoon (don't ask) this past summer. I'd also managed to hurt my hands, too, which meant I couldn't use crutches or even push myself. Yes, I had been pretty crabby about it.

The woman was still arguing with the police, but the driver was walking toward us. He might have been coming over to check that I had proper insurance or something, but I had a little warning zing down my spine. I pulled the ice bag away from my face and stood up just in case.

"Still," said Jesse, staring at the car. She didn't react to my change in position; maybe she hadn't noticed. "I loved your little Rabbit. It was my fault we had the wreck. I am so sorry."

And the driver of the other car went for Jesse like a junkyard dog, dripping words for which my mother would have washed his mouth out with soap as he barreled toward us.

Jesse's eyes got wide, and she jerked to her feet, stumbling. I stepped between them and said, with power I borrowed from the Alpha of the local werewolf pack who was also my husband, "*Enough.*"

He jerked his gaze from Jesse to me, opened his mouth, and froze where he stood. I could smell the alcohol wafting from him.

"I was driving, not Jesse," I said calmly. "You stopped—I hit you. My fault. I am fully insured. It will be a pain in the neck—for which I apologize—but your car will be fixed or replaced."

"Goddamned spic," he spat, incorrectly because I'm Native American not Hispanic, and swung a fist at me.

I might have been a mere coyote shapeshifter instead of a muscle-bound werewolf, but I had years of full-contact karate under my brown belt. The irate owner of the SUV was a lot bigger than me, but, from the smell and the lack of coordination in his movements, he was also drunk. That negated most of the advantage his size gave him.

I let his fist slip by me, took a step that angled my hips into his, grabbed the elbow and hand of his attacking arm, and slammed him face-first into the pavement using, mostly, his own momentum to do it.

Hurt me too, dang it. Car wrecks suck. Twinges of pain slid down my recently abused neck and into a hip that I hadn't thought damaged at all. I stayed balanced and ready for a moment, but the impact with the ground seemed to wipe the fight out of the big man. When he didn't immediately rise swinging, I stepped back and touched my cheekbone, wishing for the ice pack that I'd dropped.

The whole fight hadn't taken more than a few seconds. Before the downed man even twitched, one of the cops was there, putting a knee into the small of the man's back and cuffing him. The motion was smooth and practiced, and I was pretty sure the policeman had had some martial arts training, too.

"No more driving for you, tonight," the cop told the downed man cheerfully. "No more hitting nice ladies, either. It's off to the pokey to dry out."

"Pokey?" I said.

The other cop, an older, less energetic model sighed. "Nielson likes old films." He handed me a ticket for following too closely and gestured toward the cuffed man. "His girlfriend is under arrest for assaulting an officer. We got him for driving under the influence. Do you want to press charges for assault? We all saw him take the first swing."

I shook my head, suddenly feeling tired. "No. Just tell him to have his insurance call mine."

There was a loud scraping sound and a crunch. A tow truck pulled the SUV away. The Rabbit settled to the ground with a sigh, a gurgle, and a hiss of hot antifreeze hitting cold pavement as the radiator tore open.

Jesse shivered beside me. I needed to get her out of the cold.

"When's your dad coming?" I asked her. She'd called him while I'd been caught up talking to officials and people who handed me ice bags.

"I called," Jesse said. "He didn't pick up, so I called Darryl. No answer, either. I should have told you earlier."

Adam didn't answer the phone? That felt wrong. Adam wouldn't be unavailable while we were out shopping among the hordes. He'd even volunteered to come. That would have been . . .

interesting. He couldn't handle Walmart on a quiet day. That Darryl, his second, hadn't answered his phone didn't bother me as much, but it was still weird.

I pulled out my cell phone and saw that I had a new text message from Bran—even weirder. The Marrok, ruler of the werewolves, just didn't text.

I checked it and got: The Game is Afoot.

"Bran is channeling Arthur Conan Doyle," I said and Jesse peered over my shoulder to see.

I tried calling Bran back (my fingers were too cold for texting with any speed), but his phone came back disconnected or no longer in service. I tried Samuel, the Marrok's son, and got his answering service.

"No, that's fine," I told the service lady who picked up. "I'll just go into the emergency room if Dr. Cornick isn't available." There was no reason not to leave a real message with her, but the text from Bran had unsettled me. My panic attack—the cause of the wreck—unsettled me more.

I continued with other pack members: Warren, Honey, Mary Jo, and even Ben. Their cells were—in order—off, ring to voice mail, off, ring to voice mail.

I puzzled over Bran's message as I called Paul—who would as soon kill me as rescue me, though he'd feel differently about Jesse. As the phone rang without results, I remembered that the werewolves were fond of top-secret-emergency-code-word things. Nothing to do with being a werewolf and everything to do with just how many werewolves found themselves in the military at some time or other, and how that left them a particular kind of paranoid. Boy Scouts had nothing on the "be preparedness" of werewolves.

I knew about the secret codes because I'd grown up with werewolves, but I hadn't learned them because I wasn't one. Adam presumably would have gotten around to teaching me now that I was a member of his pack, but what with river monsters and broken legs and pack drama, it was no wonder it hadn't made it to the top of the list.

Paul didn't answer, either. I was willing to bet, based on the evidence, that Bran's text meant "no phones." Which was all well and good, but Jesse and I were stuck here at the mall until we found someone who *would* answer their stupid phone. If this was just a test of the emergency-secret-code system, I was going to chew on someone.

If it wasn't . . . My stomach clenched, and the panic attack I'd had that had caused the accident seemed more sinister. I was twice bound, once to Adam, once to the pack. Had something happened to Adam or the pack? I reached out for those bonds . . .

"Mercy?" Jesse asked, interrupting my concentration before I connected with Adam or the pack.

"I don't know what's going on," I told her. "Let me keep trying people."

After a moment's thought, I called Kyle. He wasn't a were-anything, so he might not have gotten the memo about the phones. *And*, as the significant other of the third-ranked member of the pack, he might know what was going on. I got his voice mail and didn't leave a message. Next I tried Elizaveta the witch. Elizaveta was under contract to the pack—I'd recently seen what Adam paid her every month and had no qualms about making her play taxi—but she didn't answer. Maybe she was in on the codes—or maybe she was shopping, and the screaming hordes kept her from hearing her cell.

Maybe the whole pack was out shopping, and I was being paranoid.

"What are the chances that the pack has joined the rest of the Tri-Cities tonight and gone out shopping in the middle of the night?" I asked out loud.

"Not high," Jesse said seriously. "Most of them are like Dad; the noise alone would give them the heebie-jeebies. Cram them in with a bunch of normal people in tight quarters and wait for the bloodbath. I can't think of any of them, except maybe Honey, who would try it."

"That's what I think, too," I agreed. "Something's up. We're on our own."

"I'll call Gabriel," she said, and did so.

Gabriel, my whatever-needs-doing man, was fighting like a demon not to be in love with Jesse. He had officially broken up with her in September, when he left for Seattle and college—though they hadn't been officially dating. But he'd sat next to her at Thanksgiving dinner a few hours ago and flirted as hard as he could given that her sharp-eyed father was at the same table.

Love doesn't wait on convenience.

When he was in town, Gabriel also lived in my very small manufactured house on the other side of the fence from the home I shared with Adam and Jesse. When he and his mother had a huge home-wrecking fight over whether or not he should be hanging out with me and my werewolf friends, he'd moved into it. He might be living mostly in Seattle—but it was there waiting for him when he came back for the holidays.

He wouldn't be on any werewolf emergency contact list so when Jesse shook her head, I started to get even more worried. Had something happened to the pack while we were gone?

"Damn it," I said, and I tried again to feel Adam through the mating bond that tied us together. The bond was strong and steady, but sometimes it took more effort to get information from it. When I'd talked to Adam about it, concerned, he'd shrugged.

"It is what it is," he'd said. "Some people have to live in their mate's head to feel secure. How did you feel when we were doing that?" He'd grinned at me when I'd tried to apologize. "Don't fuss. I love you just as you are, Mercy. I don't need to swallow you whole, I don't need to be in your head at all times. I just need to know that you're there."

There are a lot of reasons I love Adam.

I fought my way down our bond, increasing my already considerable headache, and squeezed past the barriers my subconscious mind apparently had created to keep from being overwhelmed by the charismatic Alpha among Alphas who was Adam Hauptman, and touched him at last . . .

"Hey, Mercy," said a deep voice. "You okay?"

I looked up and recognized the tow truck driver. I know most of the guys who tow cars in the area—I have a mechanic shop, it comes with the territory.

"Hey, Dale," I said, trying to appear as though I hadn't been fumbling around with werewolf magic. It would have been easier to pretend to be normal without the sudden renewal of the nasty, shivery, breath-stealing feeling that had caused me to run into the SUV in the first place. I struggled to suppress the second panic attack. Probably Dale would think that my chattering jaws were from the cold. "Jesse and I are okay, but I've had better days."

"I can see that." He sounded concerned, so I must have looked pretty awful. "You want me to tow the Rabbit to your shop? Or do you want to admit defeat immediately and I can take her out to the Pasco wrecking yard?"

I fixed my gaze on him as I had a sudden thought.

He looked down at his coat. "What'cha looking at? Is there a spot? I thought I grabbed this from the clean clothes."

"Dale, if I'm paying you to tow my car to my shop, is there room in the truck for Jesse and me, too? We can't get my husband on the phone. I have a car at the shop I can drive home."

He smiled cheerfully. "Sure, no prob, Mercy."

"That would be good," I said. "Thanks." That would work. My shop was a safe, warm place to think. I needed that, needed my Fortress of Solitude against panic. Because when I reached down the bond between Adam and myself, I could sense nothing but rage and pain.

Someone was hurting my husband, and that was all I could tell.

Dale's truck smelled like old french fries, coffee, and stale bananas. I forced myself to make light conversation, catching up on his daughter and her new baby, the rising costs of diesel fuel, and whatever else I could come up with. I couldn't let Jesse know how worried I was until I had more information.

My shop looked just as it should. The little boneyard (where the remnants of a few dead cars lingered to donate parts to their living brethren) and the parking lot were well lit. New halogen lights illuminated the four cars in the still-alive-but-need-help parking lot, and I patted Jesse's knee when she drew in a breath.

I hopped out of the truck and helped Dale unchain the Rabbit, sending Jesse into the shop. She glanced again at the four cars in the parking lot where there should have been three and ran inside without protest. She had no trouble opening the door that should have been locked—and when she went in, she didn't turn on the lights because she was her father's daughter. She knew better than to turn on lights in a room with windows when there might be something to hide.

"Poor thing," Dale said, patting my car's trunk, not paying any attention to Jesse. "Aren't many of these left running around town anymore." He looked at me, and said, casually, "I have a line on a '89 Jetta two-door with 110 on the meter. A little banged up, but nothing a little Bondo and paint can't fix."

"I'll keep it in mind," I said. "What do I owe you?"

"Boss will bill you," he said, turning my smile genuine despite my tension—Dale's "boss" was his wife.

I waved as he drove away, then sprinted for the door of my office because the fourth car, parked between a '68 Beetle and an old Type II, was a battered and worn '74 Mercedes that belonged to Gabriel.

I slipped through the door and closed it. The dark office had been enough to let me know that Gabriel knew something and that it was important to keep it quiet—otherwise, the interior would have been blazing with light. As I turned, I caught Gabriel's scent, all right, but there was also someone else . . .

Strong arms wrapped around my waist, jerking me almost off my feet. My nose told me the arms belonged to Ben of the British accent and foul mouth as he buried his face against my stomach, so I put the crowbar I'd snagged off the counter back where it belonged without smashing in his head. He moved his head until my shirt rucked up, and his beard-rough cheek was against my skin.

I'd had another werewolf do that before, felt the same tremors and ragged breathing. I was reasonably sure that Ben wasn't feeling hungry (like the other wolf had been) because it hadn't been that long since turkey dinner. So I put a hand on his head and glanced at the pair of shell-shocked teenagers standing in front of a shelf of old, mismatched hubcaps. It was dark inside the shop, but coyotes like me can see in the dark.

Ben half growled, half spoke, but I couldn't parse anything he said. From the heat of his skin against mine, he was trying to fight off the change. I made a soothing sound but didn't move my hand again because a werewolf's skin is pretty sensitive when he is changing. Ben quit trying to talk and contented himself with breathing. I looked at Gabriel.

He was gripping Jesse's hand—or letting her grip him—and didn't look to be in much better shape than Ben.

"Start over," Jesse told him. "Mercy needs to hear it all."

Gabriel nodded. "About midnight, Ben burst into my living room, grabbed me, grabbed my car keys, and dragged me out the door. As soon as we were outside, I could tell there was a lot of something going down at your house. There weren't any headlights, but I could hear cars—something with diesel engines, truck size. Ben said something about getting here and getting to you, I think. He sounded pretty odd. He shoved me into the driver's seat and hasn't said a coherent thing since. I was going to try to call you, but—"

He nodded at the floor, and I saw the scattered remnants of the shop's phone. "He didn't seem to think that would be a good idea. I am really, really glad to see you."

"Ben?" I asked. "Can you—"

He reached up and dumped a tranquilizing dart into my hand. It was about half full of something that looked like milk, but I knew better. Someone knew our secrets.

"He was drugged," I said, sniffing the hypodermic just to make sure. It smelled familiar. "It looks like that stuff that killed Mac."

Jesse inhaled.

"Mac?" Gabriel asked.

"Before your time," I told him. "Mac was a newly turned werewolf who got in the way of a Byzantine plot ultimately aimed at Bran. We've always thought that werewolves are invulnerable to drugs of any kind. But the bad guy who happened to be a werewolf himself figured out a cocktail that worked with ingredients any vet supply would have." That knowledge should have died with Gerry. "Most of the wolves who got hit with the stuff were fine, but new werewolves are more vulnerable, and it killed Mac."

We all looked at Ben, who wasn't looking too healthy.

"Is Ben going to be all right?" asked Gabriel. "Can we do something for him?"

"Burning it out," Ben growled.

I wasn't sure I heard him right, his voice was slurred and thick. "Ben? You're burning out the drug?" His skin did feel feverish. "Boosting your metabolism?" I didn't know werewolves could do that.

"Burning it good," he said, which I took to be an affirmative. "But it'll . . . a minute."

"What can we do to help?" I asked. "Water? Food?" I had some granola bars in here somewhere.

"Just you," he said. "Pack smell, Alpha smell. It helps." He shuddered hard against me. "Hurts. Wolf wants out."

"Let it out," said Jesse.

But Ben shook his head. "Then I won't be able to talk. Need to tell you."

He smelled like adrenaline and blood.

"Is it safe here?" I asked. "Do we need to move?"

"Short-term safe," Ben said after a moment. "Think so. They should be occupied with the rest . . . the rest of the pack."

"Would coffee help?" Jesse asked.

I considered it but shook my head. "I'm not a doctor. Adding a stimulant to the mixture could just make it worse."

"You could call Samuel."

I looked into her fear-filled eyes and tried to be stalwart for her sake. "Samuel's phone goes to his answering service. We're on our own."

"What about Zee?" asked Gabriel. He'd seen what Zee could do for a car and had acquired a case of hero worship for the grumpy old fae. "Couldn't he do something about the silver?"

"Zee's hidden in Fairyland with the rest of the fae," I told him, though he knew it. "He's not going to be able to help."

"But—"

"Whatever else Zee is," I told him, "he is fae, first."

"Hurts," said Ben, his voice muffled against my stomach. He was writhing against me. Silver hits werewolves like that. I wished that there was something I could do.

"Yes, you can help," he said, as though he'd caught my thoughts. Sometimes the pack bond did that—one of the things that I was still adjusting to. "You can ask me . . . that's what you can do. Ask me questions. Keep me talking so I can keep the wolf down. You need to know."

"Everyone is alive," I told him. "I can tell that much. What happened?"

"Taken," he said, then, "Federal agents."

Chills went down my spine. I had a degree in history. When

the government moves against a segment of its own population, it is bad. Nazi bad. Genocide bad. We needed the feds to protect the werewolves from the zealots in the general population. If the government had turned against us, the wolves would have to defend themselves. There was no good ending to that story.

"Federal agents from which agency?" I asked. "Homeland Security? Cantrip? FBI?"

He shook his head. He looked up at me and stared for a moment as if eye contact would let him sort himself out. He started to speak a couple of times.

"They took everyone who was there?"

"Everyone," he said. He put his head against me again. "Everyone there."

It had been Thanksgiving. I exchanged a bleak look with Jesse. A lot of the pack was at the house.

"Honey and Peter and Paul and Darryl and Auriele." He stopped naming wolves for a moment to take a breath. "Mary Jo. Warren."

"Mary Jo wasn't there," I said. "Neither was Warren." Warren and his boyfriend had put on a Thanksgiving dinner for their friends who didn't have families to go home to. Being gay meant they had a number of friends with no welcoming families. Mary Jo, a firefighter, had been on duty.

"Smelled them," growled Ben. Then he paused, his body tightening. "Said . . . they said, not Adam said. They said . . . 'Come quietly no one gets hurt, Mr. Hauptman.' Adam, he said, 'I smell blood on your hands. Warren and Mary Jo. What have you done to my people?' They said, 'Federal agents,' again. Said, 'Here's our ID.'"

He took in a big breath. "Adam said, he said, 'ID is good. But you are not federal agents.' Liars. Adam said they lied."

I couldn't tell if I was holding Ben or he was holding me.

"How did they find Mary Jo?" I asked. Mary Jo worried that she would lose her job if they knew what she was. If they knew about Mary Jo, knew about the tranquilizer, then someone knew too many of our secrets. It was a rhetorical question, I didn't expect Ben to know the answer.

"Cell phones," he told me. "Bran sent a text."

"I got it," I said. "I thought it meant that the phones weren't safe to use."

He shook his head. "Meant that someone was tracing our phones. GPS tracking. Charles has spiders." Charles was the son of the Marrok, who ruled the werewolves. Among his wide array of talents were killing people, making money, and a scarily thorough understanding of technology—but not arachnids. Not that I knew of, anyway.

"Spiders?" I asked.

He huffed a laugh. "Spiders. Bits of code out looking. Watching out for things like that. Spyware in the phone-company logs. Think he might have someone on the inside. Warning came too late, though."

"How did you escape?" I asked.

"I was upstairs." His voice was getting closer to his usual enunciation, and he sounded more coherent. "Getting toilet paper for the fu— for the downstairs bathroom." He made a noise, a half sob. I hugged him more tightly.

"Go ahead and swear," I told him. "I promise not to tell Adam."

He snorted. "Bad habit." I couldn't tell if he was talking about his swearing or me promising not to tell Adam.

"You're right," I said, because he was. "So you heard them and ran for Gabriel?"

"I heard," he told me. "I waited. Whole pack was down there. Then Adam said, 'In all Mercy, Benjamin Speedway.' Adam said that 'Benjamin Speedway' like he was swearing, but I knew. I'm Benjamin. Mercy is you. Speed meant go. He was ordering me to run, to find you. Disguised the order to give me a moment of grace before they figured it out. There were people out the back, and they saw me jump out the window. Hit me with the damned dart, and I ran for the river. Doubled back and found Gabriel. Made him drive. But you weren't here. You were supposed to be *here*."

If it hadn't been for the wreck, Jesse and I would have finished our shopping and headed home. Presumably into the arms of whoever had Adam. Luck. It made me take a deep breath, and I got a good whiff of what I'd been smelling all along.

"Blood." I leaned back, trying to get some space between us. "Ben, where are you bleeding?"

2

"Do we need lights?" asked Jesse.

"I'll get the big kit in the shop," Gabriel said, and ran for it. Night was dark to him, but he knew his way around, and the first-aid kit was on the wall just inside. He wouldn't be as fast as me, but I was attached to a werewolf at the moment.

I knew what Adam would say about turning on the lights when we were possibly hiding from some unknown group capable of taking on a pack of werewolves and coming out on top. But my night vision wasn't up to first aid in the dark.

"Flashlight," I said. "Under the counter. Also get the box cutter next to it in case I have to slice his clothes." I put my hands on either side of Ben's face and tried to make him look at me. "Ben. Ben."

"Yes?" It came out clear and crisp-upper-crust-British, as Ben, with his excellent four-letter-laced vocabulary seldom did. But he didn't let me pull his face up so I could see it.

"Where are you hit?"

"Tranq. Arse." That one wasn't as clear, but I could understand him and assumed the last word was a location and not an epithet, though with Ben it was a risky call.

"No. Not the tranq." A tranquillizer dart wouldn't have left him bleeding this much later. "Someone shot you, Ben. Where?"

Jesse aimed the flashlight. "Leg," she said. "Just above his right knee."

He wouldn't let me go, so Jesse sliced through the fabric of Ben's khakis with the box cutter. Gabriel took the flashlight and got a good look at the wound.

"In and out," he said, sounding calm, though his face paled and took on a greenish tinge.

It hadn't healed, so either whoever had shot him was using silver bullets—or the silver in the tranquilizer mixture was slowing his healing. Whichever way, we needed to get the bleeding stopped.

"Telfa pad," I told Jesse. "It's important not to use anything that might stick on the wounds." Ben's skin could grow over it if he started to heal as fast as he should be healing. "Then gauze, then vet wrap. We'll pack up, go to Samuel's, and hope that he's home."

Samuel Cornick, who was both a doctor and a werewolf, would know best what to do for Ben. He wasn't answering his phone, either, so he'd probably gotten the message from Bran. He also wasn't pack. There was a good chance that he'd been overlooked when they, whoever "they" were, had gathered up the rest of the wolves. I hoped desperately that he'd been overlooked.

I needed to get Ben to Samuel, then I needed to get help—which hopefully would also be accomplished at Samuel's. I needed to find Adam, the pack, check on the other wolves who hadn't been at Thanksgiving—and make sure that no one else had been taken or hurt, like Warren's boyfriend or Mary Jo's fellow firefighters.

If our enemies had known to find Mary Jo and Warren, then they knew more than they should about who was a werewolf and who was not. If they were humans—and Ben would have told me if he'd noticed that they were anything else—and they were willing to kidnap damn near thirty wolves, then they were either crazy, planning on killing everyone all at once, or at least armed and very, very dangerous. And they might be feds, despite Ben's recollection of Adam accusing them of lying.

"Can you stand?" I asked Ben, when Jesse had finished making a pretty good job of the bandage.

He grunted.

"We've got to get out of here. If they knew enough to get Warren and Mary Jo, we've got to assume they know about this place."

"Danger," he said, sounding bad again. "In danger. You." That thought seemed to inspire him because with a sound that was more wolfish than human, he stood up, then sort of sagged until he was draped over me.

"It's not the leg," he said, overenunciating a little. "It's the drug. Weak. Weak. Weak." He was tensing up, his eyes bright gold with the wolf's drive to protect itself. No predator likes to be weakened and vulnerable.

"It's all right," I told him firmly, because it was important that he believe me. If he didn't, he'd get aggressive, and we would have even more trouble. "You are among friends. Gabriel, grab the keys to the Mercedes parked in the garage and help me get Ben to the car."

Marsilia's dark blue Mercedes, an S 65 AMG, was parked inside my garage lest anyone walk by the parking lot and decide to key the paint or toss a rock. It was three months old, here to get its first oil change, and I could have bought a second shop for less than its sticker price.

"The AMG?" Gabriel said, though he retrieved the keys as he spoke. "You're going to let Ben bleed all over a Mercedes AMG?"

"He's already bleeding all over a Mercedes," Jesse said dryly. Then she turned to me. "Wait a minute. The AMG? That AMG? Mercedes Athena Thompson Hauptman, what are you thinking of? You can't let Ben bleed all over *Marsilia's* Mercedes."

"Marsilia the vampire queen?" Gabriel choked. "Mercy, that's just stupid. Take my car."

"She's not a queen, she's the Mistress of the seethe," I corrected him. "That car seats four and doesn't scream VW mechanic on the run with wounded werewolf." What I didn't say, because I didn't want to panic anyone, was that because the vampires were a lot like the CIA crossed with the Mob, the Mercedes also had bulletproof glass. More importantly, if we were really dealing with an attack by a government agency, this car was clean of tracking devices. Between me and Wulfe—the magic-using vampire who served Marsilia—all the tracking gadgets that were routinely attached to new cars all the way down to the RFID tags on the tires had been disabled.

And right now I had bigger things to worry about than offending Marsilia, scary though she was.

Get Ben to Samuel, who could treat what was wrong with him.

Take Jesse and Gabriel to someplace safe.

Find whoever had taken my mate and get him back.

Adam's pain was a roar in my heart, and I was going to make everyone who hurt him pay and pay.

It was like triage. Decision one—preserve those who were safe. Decision two—retrieve the rest. Decision three—make the ones who took them regret it.

On that thought, I ran back into the office. At Adam's request,

I'd taken to keeping my 9mm Sig in the safe. Being married to the local pack Alpha gained me some notoriety, and it made Adam feel better knowing I was armed. I shoved two spare (loaded) magazines into my purse and grabbed the extra box of silver ammunition. If I'd had a nuclear bomb, I'd have grabbed it, too—but I would make do with what I had.

Jesse had settled in the back with Ben. Smart girl. Ben knew Gabriel well enough under normal circumstances, but Jesse smelled like Adam. Ben couldn't sit in the front with me because the combination of drug and wound made him too volatile, and he was too strong for me to wrestle with while I was driving. Jesse had also found an old blanket to cover the seat.

I backed the Mercedes out of the garage and waited for Gabriel to close the door and get in.

"Your eyes are gold, Mercy," said Gabriel as he slid into the front seat. "I didn't know they did that."

Neither had I.

Samuel lived about twenty minutes from my garage, but it felt like hours. The temptation to put my foot down on the accelerator was strong. Marsilia's car topped out at 250 mph—I had also, at her request, taken care of the electronic governor that limited the car to more human-reflex-safe speeds. But there were a lot of cops out even at this rarefied and still-dark hour because the shopping crowds were starting to increase again. I needed to avoid getting pulled over as long as I had a man with a gunshot wound in the back seat.

At sixty miles per hour, we purred slowly along the side of the river to Samuel's house in Richland.

Before I'd married Adam, Samuel had been my roommate. He still came by to visit a lot. A wolf, especially a lone wolf, needed the presence of others. Though Adam was Alpha and Samuel was very dominant, they had a cautious friendship.

Samuel had a condo in Richland right next to the river, where land prices were at a premium. He could care less what his home looked like—he had lived with me in my elderly fourteen-by-seventy trailer for two years, more or less, without much complaint—but he loves the water. What he paid for that condo could have bought a huge house anywhere else in town.

The complex was less than ten years old, built of stone and stucco and groomed to within an inch of its life. I parked the Mercedes in front of Samuel's garage, left my comrades in the car, and knocked at the door.

No one answered. I put my forehead against the cold surface of the fiberglass door and listened, but I could hear nothing.

"Please, please, Samuel. I need you." I knocked again.

When the door finally opened, it wasn't Samuel but Ariana, Samuel's mate. She wore a sweatshirt and fuzzy midnight blue pajama bottoms decorated with white kittens playing with pink balls of yarn.

Fae have glamour—that's what makes them fae. They can take any living shape they like, and mostly they like forms that blend in. I'd first met Ariana in the guise of someone's well-to-do grandmother. I've also seen what I think is her true face and form, which is spectacular and beautiful.

Ariana's current facade was neither beautiful nor ugly, more of a pleasant average. Pale gold hair, more often found in children than adults before the advent of hair dye, framed her face and set off her soft gray eyes. Her apparent age of somewhere between twenty-five and thirty was a match for Samuel's apparent age. There were traces of her fae-self in her face, just as my old mentor Zee's fae countenance shared similarities with the human one that I was more accustomed to seeing.

Thing was, she shouldn't have been there. She was fae. She should have been at the reservation with all the others. I'd called to check on Ariana as soon as I'd found out that the fae had retreated and had gotten Samuel. He'd told me—in what I now saw was a suspiciously relaxed manner—that Ariana was safe and would return when she could. Apparently, that was a lot sooner than any of the rest of the fae.

"Ariana," I said, "I thought . . ."

"That I had retreated to the reservation with my kin?" she asked. "My mate is here. I am no follower, and my allegiance is no longer to the Gray Lords, if it ever was. They chose to allow me to stay here under the condition I do nothing to draw attention to myself." She grinned mischievously at me. "They required us to bring any artifacts or magical items we hold. I brought the Silver Borne with me—they were surprisingly eager to let me leave with it."

The Silver Borne was an artifact that she'd created long before Christopher Columbus was a glint in his father's eye. It ate the magic of any fae that went near it. Too powerful to be left where humans could get it—and too damaging to be brought to the reservation.

Her face lost its humor. "But I am chatting, and you are hurt. Come in out of the cold."

"Not my blood," I told her. "Is Samuel here? I have a warning and a patient for him. Otherwise, we should probably go."

"He's not here," Ariana said. "His father called him away a

few days ago. He said it was something to do with a meeting about 'disturbances in the Force.'"

I gave her a look, and she grinned, again. "I swear to you that was what he told me. Bring in your wounded, though. I have a fair amount of barbering experience, and Samuel keeps a very well-stocked first-aid kit."

I hesitated, and the expression on her face changed. Ariana was ancient—older than Bran, I think—but she had this softness about her, a vulnerability that allowed her to be rather easily hurt.

"I'm not doubting you," I told her. "But my wounded is a wolf. He is in human form for the moment, but he is clinging to it by his fingertips."

Ariana had a deep-seated and totally justified terror of canids, which she'd only overcome with people she knew well—meaning Samuel. Most of the rest of us did our best not to be too wolf- or coyote-like around her.

She took a breath. "I knew the patient was likely one of your werewolves. Who else would it be? Bring him in."

I gathered my people from the car, human and otherwise. I wasn't sure it was the right thing to do. I'd seen Ariana in the grip of panic once, and that was scary enough I didn't want to do it again. I'd warned her, and she thought she could handle it. Fair enough.

Jesse shoved, and Gabriel and I pulled to get Ben out of the car. As soon as Ben was up, Gabriel slipped under his shoulder and took most of his weight. I glanced around, but all the windows surrounding us were dark. If anyone was watching, I couldn't tell.

Jesse got the door. Gabriel paused in the entryway because, though the walls were painted bright colors, the carpet was white, and Ben was still bleeding.

Ariana rolled her eyes at us. "Bring him in, children; I assure you that I am more than capable of pulling a little blood from fabric and carpet."

Reassured, I waved Gabriel and Ben forward. The condo was one of those open floor plans, where kitchen, dining room, and living room shared the same space. Gabriel supported Ben through the entry hall, past the kitchen area, and into the living room, where we laid him down on the dark brown leather couch. He looked worse, if that were possible, than he had in my office. As if, now that someone else was in charge, he'd quit struggling to stay alert.

Ariana looked at all of us and frowned. "Tell me what happened."

So I did, telling the story from my point of view until we hit the garage, then dropping back to Ben's tale. When I'd finished, she put her hand against Ben's forehead.

He muttered something crude, and her eyebrows raised.

"Not fair to hold him responsible for something he says in this state," said Jesse defensively.

Ariana's lips turned up. "I've heard worse." She pulled up Ben's pant leg. The bandages we'd put on were bloody already. "Was this a silver bullet?"

"It's not healing like it should if silver wasn't involved somehow," I told her. "They definitely shot him with a tranquilizer dart that contained a mixture that included silver. Same stuff was used to kill a friend of mine a few years back. That's why we wanted Samuel to take a look."

Ariana stepped back and half closed her eyes, holding her hands about six inches over Ben. "I have an affinity for silver," she said. "I can sense it but not call it to me."

Ariana is Welsh for silver. Ironic in a woman mated to a werewolf.

"There's some silver in him," she said after a moment. "But

none near his wound, so it must be the dart they hit him with. If it was a silver bullet, it didn't leave anything behind. He'll have to wait until the silver works its way out—but I can at least treat the wound."

I kept my hand on Ben's while Ariana stripped his bandages off and coated the wounds, front and back, with some herb-and-salve concoction she kept in an old pottery jar. Ben lay on his side to allow her access. He kept his eyes closed, but every muscle in his body was tense. Ariana was the next best thing to a stranger, and he was wounded. Every once in a while he would growl quietly, and Ariana would jump like a rabbit—which made Ben tense even more.

By the time she was done, both of them were shivering like a pair of thoroughbreds before the Kentucky Derby.

"That's as much as I can do for him," she said, stepping away with a sigh of relief. She headed for the kitchen sink, regaining her self-possession with every step she took away from Ben. She washed her hands with soap and dried them on a white cloth.

When she spoke again, her voice was brisk and confident. "I don't have Samuel's expertise, but barring the threat of infection, which isn't an issue for werewolves, his leg should be fine."

If there wasn't too much silver, I thought. I couldn't tell if Ben was following the conversation or not. His eyes weren't totally shut, but now that I was the only one touching him, his body was unnaturally relaxed.

"In any case, there's nothing more we can do for him without Adam"—his Alpha, who could pour pack strength into him—"or Samuel," I said. I could borrow some abilities from Adam, but I hadn't been able to manipulate the pack bonds enough to effect healing yet.

"Let me try to call Samuel," Ariana offered, picking up the phone on the end table next to the couch. She stiffened, the phone to her ear, then dialed. "Phin. I am so sorry to wake you, but I had a dream—"

Phin was Phineas Brewster, her mostly human descendant who sold used and collectible books. Why she had decided to call him instead of Samuel was the same reason she had stiffened. I wondered what she had heard or felt that had changed her mind.

"Ari?" a sleepy voice on the other end of the phone said—I try not to eavesdrop when I can avoid it, but, like the wolves, my ears are sharp. "No," he continued foggily. Then he cleared his throat and sounded much more awake. "I mean, not a problem. Are you all right? Do you want me to come over?"

"No," she said, sounding relieved. "It was really just a dream. But it left me worried about you." The fae couldn't lie. So she had dreamed and woke up worried about Phin—but it could have been tonight or ten years ago.

"I'm fine." His voice was easy, as if he was used to having her call him in the middle of the night because she was worried.

"Stay fine." She hung up, frowning at the phone. "There was someone listening."

"The phone is bugged?" Gabriel frowned.

She shrugged. "Someone was listening. I could feel their attention. Magic or technology, it doesn't matter. If I didn't call anyone, they'd have wondered why I picked up the phone."

"No phones," I said, pulling out my cell phone. "I forgot. Jeez how dumb can I be?" Bran had sent a message that they were using the phones to trace the pack, Ben had told me that, and we carried our phones with us here. I patted Ben's shoulder. "Cell phone, Ben?"

"Crushed it on the way to you," he said, slurring the consonants. "Bran said ditch the phones."

"Jesse? Gabriel? Do you have your cell phones?"

Jesse handed me hers, but Gabriel shook his head. "Mine's next to my bed, where it won't do us any harm."

I borrowed a hammer and the garage and disposed of both phones. I was pretty sure that I could have just pulled the batteries, but pretty sure wasn't good enough, so I used a hammer.

"Who is it?" Jesse asked me when I got back in the middle of a discussion of what happened at the house. "Is it the government? The fae?" She crossed her arms and hugged herself. "The vampires?"

"Samuel told me that his father has been waiting for the government to quit screwing around with the fae and turn its attention to the werewolves," Ariana said. "The Marrok is also in the middle of delicate negotiations with the fae—negotiations that are making the vampires extremely nervous because they fear what they will face if the fae and werewolves come to an agreement."

"The men who took the pack claimed to be government," I said. "But Adam seemed to think they were lying. But they were human—which makes me think government anyway."

"Are we safe here?" asked Gabriel. "Or do we need to find a better hiding place?"

"They could have traced our phones here," I told him. "We need to keep moving. I was hoping to take a minute and see if I can contact Adam and figure out what's going on."

"You can stay here to do that," Ariana said. "I can't make the apartment disappear into a hedge of blackberries, but I can make it difficult to find for a few hours."

"Mercy?" Jesse asked. "How much can you tell?"

"He's alive," I said. I decided to trust Ariana to know her own strengths. If she could keep us hidden until I talked to Adam, it would really help. "I need to find somewhere quiet to clear my head and see if I can pick up anything more." I wasn't going to taint Jesse with the mishmash of dark and violent emotions I'd been picking up from him off and on all night. It was the off and on that really worried me.

"Take a hot shower," suggested Ariana. "Meditation is easier when you're clean. I'll bring you something to wear—and keep your flock safe."

Ben growled, and she flinched.

I tried just sitting down on the floor of the spare bedroom—but I could smell Ben's blood. My scalp itched. My right pant leg smelled of antifreeze from my poor deceased Rabbit. My shoulder ached where the seat belt had caught me, and my cheekbone throbbed. So I followed Ariana's advice and showered.

I heard the bathroom door open while I was shampooing the blood out of my hair—how had it gotten in my hair?—and there were clean clothes folded neatly on the toilet seat when I got out.

I pulled the sweats up to my nose and shook my head. If someone had come to my house, even someone I liked, I'd have been damned before I gave them Adam's clothes to wear—especially if it was someone he used to live with.

I could have blessed Ariana's generosity, though, because when I sat on the floor of their spare bedroom wearing Samuel's oversized shirt and sweatpants, I felt safe and at home. That helped while I struggled to find my way through the strong but tangled weave that was my bond to Adam, but it still didn't seem to be enough.

Frustrated with my failure, I got up. Exhaustion, fury, and

nagging pain that seemed generalized to my whole body rather than any one bruise fought with despair.

Despair won and left me muzzy and sick. I'd been so sure that I could contact Adam given just a little space and quiet. It should have been easy because his emotions were buzzing around me so strongly that it had been a strain to keep track of which were my feelings and which were his.

Only when I stood up did it become apparent that instead of plush carpet under my bare feet, there was hard-packed dirt beneath the boots I hadn't been wearing. They were a scuffed black, and the leather gave around my feet with the softness of long wearing. They weren't my boots, but I knew them.

What was I doing wearing Adam's boots? My bleary thoughts tried to figure out the logic while I became vaguely aware of my surroundings. The air smelled dry and still. It smelled like pack, my pack who were all sick and hurting. As soon as I let my awareness seek them, their pain, their sickness drifted over me.

"Mr. Hauptman," a stranger's voice said, shocking me out of my contemplation of Adam's boots on my feet.

I blinked and saw a man in dark clothes bare of any official insignia, though they had that sharpness that marked a military uniform. I narrowed my eyes and studied him more closely because something about the picture didn't match: his body was soft. Not the softness of a soldier who had retired from action and moved to deskwork. This man was soft in both mind and body—he'd never served in battle.

Paper-pusher. Gives orders for other men to die while sitting safe in home base. "We were told you'd probably be down for another hour or more. I do apologize about the restraints—rather medieval, don't you agree? But we didn't think you'd be feeling particularly happy with us when you woke up, and killing you after all the trouble that we've gone through to capture you would be unproductive. You may call me Mr. Jones."

He looked at us as he spoke. And I became aware that part of the heaviness that kept me from moving much was some sort of binding on my ankles and wrists. I couldn't really see them, something was off with my eyesight, but I could feel them, just as I could feel the bite of the silver—worse than the time I'd rushed between two trees and burst through a hornet's nest. Everything hurt.

The "Mr. Jones" made Adam think seriously about rolling his eyes like Jesse, but it would require too much energy. Jones? Did this man not know that Adam could hear every lie out of his lips? At least it hadn't been "Smith."

Adam also thought about shedding the restraints and killing the man behind the desk—but so far no one had been irreparably injured. The burn of the silver fought with the dampening effect of the tranquilizer and left his temper raw and vicious. But he had people to protect. So he held his temper and sarcastic comments and continued the parley that Mr. *Jones* had begun.

"You've gone to a lot of trouble to get us here." Adam's voice slurred a little, and he pulled energy from the pack bonds, aware that he was taking from them what they didn't have to give. But he needed to be strong and smart and able to fight for them. To do that, he could afford to show no weakness before the enemy. "What do you want?"

The power cleared his head a little—and cleared mine, too. Between my desperation and whatever they'd hit him with, I had merged myself too deeply inside him.

Experimentation had taught me that visualization worked better than almost anything for getting out of trouble when immersed in the oddity that is werewolf magic. I visualized myself stepping out of Adam's body. It tickled and made me a little nauseated.

Mercy?

Yes, I told him, and received a flood of questions that slid past me wordlessly, too fast for me to grab. He might be thinking more clearly, but he was nowhere near his usual alertness. I tried to send him power through our bond and felt him snatch it and pull. I staggered and grabbed his shoulders to steady myself. He felt solid under my fingers, but I couldn't see my own hands.

"Mr. Hauptman?"

Adam ignored him as he sent another burst of need toward me. This one was much more visceral than a simple need for strength. I couldn't tell what he wanted, but I could make a pretty good guess.

Ben found Gabriel, and they both found Jesse and me. We're all safe at Samuel's. Ben is hurt, but not seriously. I didn't tell him that Samuel was gone.

Adam straightened and took a deep breath. The pain was shivery and concentrated in his joints, making it difficult to move. He opened and closed his hands to make sure they worked. His vulnerability made it difficult to control his rage at the people who had done this to him.

I was picking up everything he felt.

I left my hand on his shoulder as I took another step back, hoping that it would give me more distance, so I could think. And then I tucked the other hand in the back of his waistband like a child in the dark—I was afraid that if I didn't anchor myself to him in some way, I'd go back to Samuel's house with no information at all.

It was better, though I could still only see what he saw, and his vision was oddly limited.

The silver, his wolf said. *Too many things not working right. My eyes see, but Adam doesn't perceive.*

I patted him on the shoulder, not knowing if he could tell what I was doing or not. Words were useless. Adam had to control the wolf, and I wasn't really there to help.

You always help, the wolf disagreed. He tugged on our bond and took just a little more strength from me. *Always,* Adam agreed, as his wolf settled around him again.

"Mr. Hauptman, am I boring you?"

Adam moved his full attention to our enemy, and Mr. Jones flinched. That flinch satisfied me and made me hungry at the same time—I liked his fear. I liked it very much.

"No, Mr. Smith," said Adam softly. "I find you very interesting at the moment."

"Jones," snapped the man behind the desk. The lie of his name smelled tainted. His angry reaction told Adam that he was weak-minded, easy prey. No less dangerous—in some ways more dangerous because he'd react with his emotions—but under real pressure, he'd break.

Someone moved to Adam's right and into his field of view. From my perspective, it was almost violently sudden. Like Jones, he wore black. His clothes weren't just a uniform, though; with Adam's perceptions I knew that he wore armor. He moved better, too. Someone had trained him for hand-to-hand combat.

I had the sense that there were other people in the room, more of the enemy, but for some reason this one held Adam's attention. He and Jones were the only ones I could see.

Soldier, Adam told me. He showed me the bulge of a second

weapon inside the cuff of the man's pants—knife or gun, and another on the outside of the opposite leg.

Adam watched the body language between the soldier and Mr. Jones. Jones was nominally in charge, but the men (the ones I couldn't see but Adam was aware of) followed the second man—including Jones. Adam had seen it in the army, when the commanding officer was green and leaning a little too heavily upon the skills of the men of lower rank. The soldier demanded respect, while Jones smelled and acted like prey trying, unsuccessfully, to be a predator.

Whatever this kidnapping was, Adam was on his feet, and the pack was okay. Not good, but alive and breathing. I was aware, because Adam was, that our pack were lying in heaps behind us. All of them chained hand and foot as he was, sick from the silver and the tranquilizer but otherwise okay. Adam thought that meant that this wasn't an extermination order. They wanted something and thought that Adam and his pack could provide it. For the moment, they were safe.

"Well?" said Jones impatiently.

Adam held his silence. They weren't friends, and Adam wasn't going to start a conversation about the weather. They had done their best to leave Adam powerless. He wasn't going to expose himself further. They would—eventually—tell him what this was about; and then he would have some leverage to move them. Until then, silence was his best defense.

The politician who was not named Jones, whatever he said, leaned back in his chair and sighed. "I was told you might be difficult. We have a proposition for you, Mr. Hauptman. Our information indicated that this was the best way to ensure your cooperation."

Adam raised an eyebrow, and the soldier smiled where Not-

Jones couldn't see him. As soon as he noticed Adam watching, the smile disappeared—but they both knew Adam had seen.

"We need you to kill someone," the politician said. "We both know you've killed for the government before, *Sergeant*." Adam had been an army ranger in the Vietnam War. Not many people outside the pack knew about it. "Don't worry. It's no one you'll feel bad about. US Senator Campbell, Republican from Minnesota." He smiled again. "I see you know who I'm talking about."

So did I. Campbell had been in office over twenty years and was one of the loudest anti-fae, anti-werewolf voices in Congress. Ever since a few werewolves killed—and mostly ate—a man in Minnesota, he had been arguing for giving law enforcement the power to kill rogue werewolves or fae with only a judge's warrant. He had a lot of bipartisan support because people were scared. He was a man with a plan, a centrist who didn't fall neatly into either the conservative or liberal camps, and so could be cheered on by both sides.

"You aren't the government," said Adam.

"I assure you, Mr. Hauptman, I work for the US government. You saw my ID."

I wrinkled my nose. He was lying with the truth—I recognized the smugness of his scent. Adam considered my conclusion.

"It will be an easy kill," Jones told Adam. "In and out, then you and yours will be free to leave."

"I have not killed for the government in a long time," Adam told him. He should have stopped there, but I could feel when the quivery I-am-prey feeling emanating from Jones and the burn of the silver that was sharpening his temper drove him further. He gave Jones a feral smile, leaned forward, and said, "Now I only kill people who deserve it, Mr. *Smith*."

Mr. Jones jerked back, and the smell of his fear made my nose wrinkle. Then he raised a Glock he'd hidden behind the desk.

Adam, slowed by silver and forgotten shackles, stumbled to his knees when he tried to move to respond. A shot rang out and the smell of gunpowder, blood, and death filled the air an instant before the earthquake in the pack bonds tried to throw me back to my own body.

I clung to Adam as tears and helpless anger wracked me, his and mine, while Honey's agonized cry rang in my ears. I didn't need to see it with my eyes because the pack bond and Adam told me who it was, told me it was fatal. By accident or design, Jones had killed Peter, with a clean bullet between his eyes, killed the heart of the pack, our sole submissive wolf, Honey's mate.

Adam's head was bowed as he absorbed the blow—Peter's death and Adam's failure to prevent it. All the other wolves in the pack were rivals, dominants who would move against the others should the wolf above them in the pack show weakness. But Peter was safe. Submissive wolves, rare, as precious as rubies, were not driven to be on top, so they could be trusted absolutely—cherished and protected from all harm.

Not your fault, I told Adam urgently. *Not your fault they brought us here. Not your fault they shot Peter.* Not his fault that he'd been hampered by the tranquilizer, the silver, and the shackles.

Adam didn't care what I thought. He was the Alpha, it was his duty to protect the pack, and Peter most of all had been his to keep safe. I could feel Adam's wild rage, Adam's desire to kill—balanced by the clear understanding that he had the rest of the pack to protect.

He swayed a little on his knees, as if his rage were a physical thing that tugged on his shoulders. I tightened my grip and felt his gratitude at my presence as he fought and bargained with his anger—and I felt his shame for the way he craved Jones's flesh between his teeth.

Jones *is dead,* I promised. *He just doesn't know it yet. But we are patient, we can wait until the time is ripe.*

Adam went still. He forgets sometimes, does Adam, that I am as much a predator as he is.

Adam looked up, and we saw that Jones looked smug, the gun still in his hand. He thought that Adam's bowed head and the way he'd not regained his feet meant that he was broken. The soldier who stood beside Jones's desk was blank-faced but more wary.

Adam sorted through possibilities before he decided that Jones needed to be a little more afraid because that fear would slow him down if he decided a second example might be needed. And if that fear made him try something, Adam would kill him sooner rather than later and deal with the soldier instead.

Adam stood slowly, which was a lot more difficult than he made it look since his hands were chained behind his back and his ankles shackled together. It required strength and balance, and he used the movement to center himself.

He let his wolf meet Mr. Jones's eyes, tensed his shoulders, and twisted the cuff on his left wrist. Metal screamed. I felt the burn as steel cut into his wrist before the joint of the cuff broke. He continued to watch Jones, daring him to do something, anything, as he repeated the procedure on his right wrist. He didn't bother moving quickly, even after the handcuffs fell to the ground. As he brought his freed hands forward, Jones jerked the gun up, but the soldier slammed it down on the desk, unfired.

"You want to shoot them all and try again, Mr. Jones?" he

said. "You aren't going to be able to get another pack the same way—and Hauptman was specifically required."

Jones fought for the gun, but the other pulled it away with contemptuous ease.

"Shut up," the soldier gritted. "You've made a proper cluster of this. Just sit there and keep your mouth closed. I told him you were the wrong choice for this."

Adam turned his attention to the manacles at his ankles. His deliberate inattention was an insult, a power play—and it scared me. *I* wanted to watch Jones and company to make sure that they didn't shoot Adam.

They won't, he assured me as he pried the manacle off his right ankle with a sharp twist of his hands. *They have gone to too much trouble to get me to kill me right now. They will wait until I kill their senator and prove that the werewolves need to be eliminated. Bran warned me that I was becoming too well-known, that someone would try to make some sort of play against me.*

And when you don't kill Senator Campbell? I asked. Adam would not do their bidding, there was no question in my mind about that.

I will do anything to keep my pack safe, Adam corrected me gently as he pulled the second ankle restraint into two separate pieces before twisting them together. *Even kill Campbell. Make sure Bran understands that when you tell him about this, so he's not taken by surprise.*

That's what Bran failed to see when he'd been worried that Adam's temper meant that he should be kept out of the public's eye. Adam had a hot temper, but he was always, always in control because he needed to protect the ones he cared about—even if it destroyed him instead.

"Understand this," Adam said in a guttural voice, staring at the soldier, though I knew his attention was also on Jones. "If another of my pack is harmed, all bets are off. You might be able to kill me, but not before I have taken care of 'Jones,' you, and a fair swath of the rest of your men."

"Understood."

Mercy, get Samuel, get Bran. Find out where they have us. Get the pack free before I have to do what they want, Adam told me, then sent me away from him and back to my own body in Samuel's guest bedroom.

I opened my own eyes and realized that there was noise downstairs—a wolf growling and a woman's singsong voice. Magic, fae magic, shivered over my skin in a rising tide.

I bolted to my feet and down the stairs, taking them six or eight at a time. Ben would have felt Peter's death. Wounded and scared, that couldn't have been a good thing.

Ariana was curled up in a corner of the room crooning in a language that sounded vaguely like Welsh but wasn't because I couldn't understand a word. Ben, in the middle of his change, was crouched on the couch, all of his attention on the stranger in the room.

Jesse and Gabriel were both standing between Ben and Ariana. Gabriel was bleeding—neither of them would be a match for Ben, three-quarters changed and raging because of the drugs in his system, the mess of the pack, Adam's rage, and Peter's death.

All of this I saw as I took the last leap that would have taken me to the floor if I hadn't altered my trajectory. I twisted in the air and hit Ben instead, and we *both* hit the floor.

I pinned him like my mother had taught me to pin calves or goats when I was ten years old, and she decided that I should follow her footsteps as a rodeo queen. Her efforts were doomed—I didn't like horses, not like she did, and she only had two weeks to visit before she had to go back to her own life. But goat tying had been fun, and I'd practiced for most of a summer. I hadn't thought about it for a decade or two, but the motions came right back to me as soon as my hands were on the enraged werewolf. Desperation is a really good way to inspire muscle memory.

"Ben, stop," I said, holding his head twisted and pressing a knee on his shoulder. "Ariana is not an enemy." I glanced at her, and added, "Not unless you scare her into doing something horrible to one of us. We need to get Jesse and Gabriel safe, then find the pack. I need you, so suck it up." He was still struggling, and I put my mouth right next to his ear.

"They killed Peter, Ben." I whispered, but I let him hear my own grief.

Peter had once charged out with a sword and saved the pack from an enraged fae that I'd brought to their doorstep. He was a great big sweetie who loved his mate and played video games with a devastating intensity and a love of planning that led his team to victory more than once, despite his disinterest in winning or losing. He left a gaping hole in the pack that had us all reeling.

"They killed Peter," I told Ben. "And we need to make them pay."

Ben stilled beneath me and started to shake. I released my hold but stayed on top of him, burying my face in his fur so I could hide my tears. It wasn't only my grief that wracked me, but Ben's, Adam's, Honey's, and that of the whole pack. We had failed to protect our heart, and now he was dead.

It wasn't fair. Ben wasn't through his change yet, maybe halfway, and at that stage, I had been assured, his skin would hurt if someone breathed on it. But I clung to him and let the wave of emotion hit me and waited for it to ebb.

"Mercy?" asked Jesse. "Mercy, what happened? Is Dad okay? Mercy?"

There was controlled panic in her voice, and it pulled me back to myself. I had no time to wait for anything.

"Ben?" I asked. "Can I let you up?"

In answer, he stood up, on four paws, shedding me as he did so. So much for my mother's tactics. He avoided looking at Ariana—I could smell her panic, too—and stared at the blinds that blocked the darkness from the room. I rolled the rest of the way to my feet and rubbed my face to clear my eyes.

I'd forgotten about the damned wreck again and yelped when I put pressure on my cheekbone. The EMTs had sworn it was okay, but it sure felt as though it might be broken to me. Bruises shouldn't hurt so much.

My left shoulder ached, along with the opposite hip and knee, but worst of all was the ache in my heart. I glanced at Ariana, who wasn't looking at any of us. She was still muttering to herself, and the smell of fae magic was growing uncomfortably strong.

"Ariana?" I asked. "It's okay. Ben's sorry. He won't hurt you or anyone else." I remembered the fae's need for truth and clarified carefully. "He won't hurt anyone here."

She didn't respond. Samuel had lectured all of the wolves about what to do if Ariana checked out and started to get scary. The artifact she'd made, the Silver Borne, kept her power muted—but she had been the last of the powerful fae born after humans began to use iron. Even muted, she could wipe out a city block or rend all of us into painful shreds if that was the form her madness took.

If she really freaked out, Samuel was worried that the Silver Borne might give her back everything it had taken from every fae for as long as it had existed. That would be bad.

"Talk," I told Jesse and Gabriel, who had stayed where they were, between Ben and Ariana. "Talk in a normal voice, it doesn't matter about what. She's not listening to what we're saying right now, just the tone of our voices. If we can keep it calm, she might be able to recover. She doesn't want to hurt us. Ben, stay quiet, stay still. We can't help anyone, can't do anything if we get wiped out by one of our friends."

"Should we leave?" Gabriel absently wiped the blood off his arm. It wasn't anything deep, and he'd been my right hand in the garage for long enough to ignore the minor wounds: old cars are full of sharp edges.

"You don't run from predators," Jesse said. "Not until she calms down a little."

"Right," I agreed. "But if I tell you to run, I want you to go and don't look back. That means all of you—especially you, Ben."

Ben glanced at me. He knew what I meant. If I didn't make it out of here, it would be up to him to keep Jesse and Gabriel safe, to let Bran know what had happened.

"Did you get in contact with Dad?" Jesse asked at the same time Gabriel said, "Something set Ben off. But it wasn't anything in the room, I don't think."

"Calm topics," I told them. "Happy thoughts." But it was too late for that now. "I talked to your dad, Jesse. Adam is okay."

"Ben?" asked Jesse. "What set Ben off?"

"Peter's dead," I told them, keeping an eye on Ariana. Jesse went white.

"Who is Peter?" Gabriel knew some of the pack, but he hadn't met Peter.

"Peter is special," Jesse said. "Dad calls him the Heart of the Pack, with capital letters, like it's a title."

"That's right," I told them. "He kept everyone centered because he didn't have to be on top. He could say things that no one else could. And it was his right to be protected by the rest of the pack."

Ben moaned, a sad, very wolfish sound.

Ariana looked up, her gaze focused on me. I had to fight to keep my eyes on hers because her pupils and irises had vanished, and her eyes swallowed the light.

"I liked Peter," she said, and my heart started beating again. If she was tracking that well, we might be okay. "Samuel asked him to help us with my fear of werewolves. Peter was . . . kind."

She wasn't all back—the smell of magic wasn't fading, and her voice sounded wrong. And her eyes were really freaky.

I didn't know what else to do, so I kept talking. "Adam and the pack, all the pack except Ben, are being held by a group of human radicals—some of whom appeared military trained. They're trying to blackmail Adam into killing Senator Campbell of Minnesota. They're still claiming government ties, but they are lying."

"Republican," supplied Gabriel, trying not to stare at Ariana's eyes and mostly failing. It was a good thing for him that the fae don't see it as an act of aggression the way the wolves do. A lot of the fae liked being stared at. When she met his gaze, he gamely kept talking. "Campbell is anti-fae, anti-werewolf, and—oddly for a Republican—anti-gun. Good speaker and a likely presidential candidate in the next election."

"Gabriel's taking a class in current events," Jesse told me. She looked away from Ariana and took a step closer to me. She didn't see the fae start forward as if to pounce, then catch herself—but Gabriel and I did. Gabriel moved a half step sideways so that he was between Ariana and Jesse.

Oblivious to her near death, Jesse asked, "*Who* are they? The National Rifle Association?"

"No clue," I told her. "The NRA . . ." I gave her a weary smile. "It seems like a lot of trouble for them to go to since there are plenty of other anti-gun senators, and none of them have made much headway against private gun ownership since the assassination attempt on President Reagan before you were born."

"Then who?"

"If Campbell died and was killed by a werewolf, it would destroy the détente between those who want to kill the wolves and those who want to see them as good people with a terrible disease," Gabriel said. "After the fae killed that senator's son who got away with murder, the only reason everyone isn't running around killing anyone who is *other* is because the fae have withdrawn and haven't done anything to hurt anyone else. Public opinion—after the first few days of panic—is behind them, even if the government is throwing fits. Freeing a serial killer because he killed only fae and werewolves wasn't justice. That the guilty man had money and political ties just made the fae's cause more righteous."

"Campbell's death would give the humans-only side a martyr," said Ariana. Her voice, still laden with magic, was not her usual one, but she was looking at me as though she knew who I was, so I thought we were over the worst. "Campbell is well liked and an obstacle for those who are more extreme. He has been a voice for moderation in their leadership. Campbell has argued against several of the more radical suggestions for how to deal with nonhumans."

"Moderate" was not a word I'd have applied to him. But there were more extreme voices, that was true.

"That answers 'why,' doesn't it," I murmured. "Ariana, are you back with us?"

"Not . . . not quite, sorry," she managed.

"Do you have a good way to reach Samuel or Bran?"

"No." She hesitated. "Yes. I know where they are—in Montana. I can drive."

"Okay," I said. "Take Phin's car, it'll be harder to trace." Phin drove an older Subaru, built before the days of GPS and electronic surveillance. Our enemy might not be the government, but they had access to government-level spy equipment.

"Is it safe for us to leave?" I asked. "Or do you need a few more minutes?"

Safe for us, not for her. I didn't want to do anything to provoke her—and Jesse had been right, never let predators think that you might be running away.

"I will go upstairs," she said. "Don't move until after I have closed the door."

Ben, who'd completed his change and stood in full-werewolf form, quivered when she walked behind him, but he didn't turn to look at her. It spoke of his willpower—it is hard to have someone who might harm you where you cannot see them. But he managed.

She stopped on the stairway. "Be careful, Mercedes. There are people who would mourn if you took hurt."

"Always am," I said, and she laughed. But she didn't look at us, just kept climbing.

When I heard the door close upstairs, I led the way out the door, with Ben taking rear guard. I eased the door open slowly, but there were no suspicious cars awaiting us.

Even so, I didn't breathe easily again until we were on the highway headed back toward Kennewick.

"Where are we going?" asked Gabriel.

"I need to stow you and Jesse somewhere safe," I told him. "There are too many big bad things out there that would love to get their hands on the two of you."

He shrugged. "Not me, Mercy. I'm just your hired hand. It's Jesse they want."

I glanced at him. "You planning on going back to the trailer and waiting to see what happens to her?"

He growled. Pretty good growl for a human.

"That's what I thought," I said. "So I need somewhere safe for you both."

"You have someplace in mind?" asked Jesse tightly. I heard the rebellion in her voice and didn't blame her—how often had I been told to take the sidelines because a coyote wasn't in the same weight class as a werewolf? It sucked. But if they took her, too—I think that Adam would sacrifice the world for his daughter.

"I have a place in mind," I said.

"Where?" asked Jesse, but Gabriel guessed.

"Oh hell, no," he said.

3

Gabriel was still arguing when we drove into the apartment complex in east Kennewick where his mother and sisters lived.

"Look," I said, not for the first time, "if they know all of the pack, then they know about you and Jesse, and they can guess I've stashed you with her. They'll also know that you and your mother haven't spoken a word since before last Christmas. They will know her feelings on the werewolves."

Sylvia Sandoval had been interviewed by the local paper when Adam and I had gotten married a few months ago because her son worked for me, and Adam was a local celebrity. She had been quite clear on how she felt about the werewolves.

"They'd never believe that she'd give the Alpha's daughter shelter," I told him.

"She won't," he said.

I smiled at him. "If I'm right, you get to clean the bathroom at the shop next. If you are, I'll do it."

He closed his eyes, shook his head.

"She loves you," I told him, getting out of the car. "Or she wouldn't be so stubborn about being mad."

I didn't need to tell him about the conversation Sylvia and I had had right before he finished high school. This was different—this time it wasn't Sylvia versus the werewolves. This time I would be more diplomatic and wouldn't leave yelling, "Fine. If you're too proud to say you're sorry—*I'll* keep him!" at the top of my lungs.

I had sent her graduation announcements. She'd been there, in the back. She'd waited until she was sure he'd seen her—then she left. She hadn't, her eldest daughter told me, wanted Gabriel to graduate without his mother in the audience. That was why I knew she'd take the kids in now.

"I don't want to cause trouble," Jesse said. "Why don't you leave me with Kyle or . . . I could stay with Carla."

Jesse didn't have a lot of close friends once the werewolves came out, and everyone learned whose daughter she was. There were rumors that some kids' parents had pulled them out of the local high school and were trucking them all the way to Richland because of Jesse. There were other teens who followed her around just to talk about the werewolves. Carla belonged to that group, and Jesse generally tried to avoid her even though they'd known each other since grade school.

"Kyle's house is the first place they'd look," I told her. And I was going to have to make sure Kyle was okay, too. "We don't have anyone strong enough to protect you from the government here—the best thing is to stay somewhere no one will look for you." I didn't even mention Carla.

"Let's get this over with," Gabriel said. He got out of the car and started for his mother's apartment with all the enthusiasm of a sailor walking a plank. Jesse forgot all about herself and the discomfort of staying where she wasn't wanted. She scrambled out of the car and hurried over to Gabriel and caught his hand.

I glanced at Ben. He lay down on the back seat with a sigh. He was right. Having a werewolf in her apartment wouldn't make Sylvia more cooperative. I shut him in before following the kids.

Gabriel stood at the door for a moment before knocking quietly. Nothing happened—it was still dark out, so presumably everyone was asleep. He knocked again, a little louder.

A light turned on, the door cracked open, and a teenage girl's head peeked out. It had been a year since I'd seen any of the girls except for Tia, the oldest, who snuck out once in a while to visit. Tia looked like her mother, but this one was a female version of Gabriel, which told me that it was Rosalinda, even if she'd gotten taller and sharper featured since I'd last seen her. She froze a moment, then the door was thrown open, and she launched herself at him. He hugged her, hard, until she squeaked.

Sylvia's apartment was clean and well cared for beneath the clutter that accumulates in a household that has children living in it. The furniture was mismatched and worn—Sylvia was supporting her family by herself as a police dispatcher. Her salary didn't leave a lot of room for luxuries, but her children grew up rich in love. They'd been a happy family until she and Gabriel had come to a place where neither could compromise.

"Who is knocking on the door at this hour?" Sylvia's voice emerged from somewhere in the depths of the apartment.

"It's *mi hermano*," the girl said, her voice muffled by her brother's shoulder. "Oh Mami, it's Gabriel." She pulled back, but latched onto his hand and hauled him into the living room. "Come in, come in. Don't be stupid. Hi, Jesse. Hi, Mercy. I didn't see you lurking behind Gabriel, come on in." Then she muttered something low in Spanish. I think she was talking to herself.

I didn't understand what she said, but Gabriel scowled fiercely at her. "Mind your tongue. Don't talk about Mamá like that. She deserves your respect, *chica*."

"Does she?" asked Sylvia. I don't think I've ever seen her with a hair out of place, and even at this unholy hour of the morning, her hair was smooth and shining. Her only concession to the time was a dark blue bathrobe. She folded her arms, her face was grim, and she ignored Jesse and me.

"Of course, Mamá," Gabriel said softly.

Her chin was raised and her mouth tight as she stared at her son. Rosa bounced a little and looked back and forth at the two of them before grabbing Gabriel's hand.

"You chose strangers over your family," Sylvia said at last. "I said, you pick. You stay here and work for Mercedes Thompson, or you come home right now. You chose her. Where is the respect in that?"

He snorted, a bitter half laugh. "I told you this wouldn't work, Mercy."

Rosa made a soft sound as Gabriel turned and took two quick strides away from Sylvia. At the door, he turned back around, and said, "Mamá, everything is black-and-white for you, but the world is gray. You asked me to abandon my friends because you thought they were dangerous. Life is dangerous, Mamá. I won't run away from my friends, who are good people, because I am afraid. Because you are afraid."

"*She* put my children in danger," Sylvia said, jerking her chin in my direction. She lost the cool anger she'd come into the room with and replaced it with heat. "She lied to me. And you chose her."

"Mercy can't tell other people's secrets, Mamá. And that wolf was more likely to dive off a cliff into the ocean than he was to hurt one of the girls. She was raised with him, she knows him." Gabriel's voice was soft, but his chin looked a lot like his mother's—which didn't make a reconciliation look likely, not if they kept talking about the incident that left Gabriel living in my house not talking to his mother, anyway.

"You were right," I broke in blandly. "Hanging around us is dangerous. Someone is after Jesse." I don't know why I said it that way, I had no real reason to believe they would go after Jesse—they already had their hands full, but my instincts were certain, and I always listened to my instincts. "They have already kidnapped her father and killed one of his werewolves."

"See, *hijo*? That's what happens when you associate with the werewolves," Sylvia said—but I saw her eyes linger on Jesse. Sylvia talked tough, but she had a heart as big as the Columbia. She also had four daughters, the oldest of whom was only a little younger than Jesse.

"Her father is a werewolf," Gabriel snapped, not seeing Sylvia's softening. "She can hardly avoid them."

I put a hand on his arm to get him to stop antagonizing her, but it was a mistake. Sylvia looked at my hand, and her face hardened again.

"The people after Jesse are human," I told her before she could say something she couldn't take back. "Not werewolves, fae, or anything *other.* They are human—and they will hurt her. And you raised a man who cannot leave someone he cares about to face that danger alone, any more than he could desert his friends just because it was the safer, smarter thing to do. Not even if his mother asked him to—because it was she who taught him how to love other people in the first place. So he is in danger, too. Won't you hide them for a couple of days so that they will be safe?"

Sylvia looked at me, straight in the eyes. Then she shook her head and gave a little laugh as her expression softened. "A compliment slipped inside a reprimand inside a request I cannot possibly turn down. Leave a child in danger? Leave *my* child . . ." And when Gabriel made a protesting noise, "You'll be my child when you are fifty and I am seventy, *hijo*, so it is better that you accept it early. I am not going to leave my son, whom I love, to face danger alone for pride's sake. Even I am not such a fool. Oof."

The "oof" was because Gabriel was hugging her hard, tears in his eyes that he wouldn't shed because he was not a man who cried in front of others if he could help it. About that time there was a squeal from one of the other bedrooms. My ears had told me that the girls were all awake and listening. They had apparently just been awaiting their mother's decision before exploding into action because the room filled with Sandovals.

I told them the whole story. If they were going to protect Jesse, they deserved to know everything.

When we were done, Sylvia shook her head. "What is this country coming to?" she asked. "*Mi papá*, your *abuelo*, is rolling in his grave. He died for this country, for good and right and freedom. He would be so sad."

"If it's the government," said Tia, Gabriel's oldest sister, "then you'd better get rid of your phones. They can trace those, you know."

"Done," said Gabriel. "Mine's back at my home, but we trashed Jesse's and Mercy's before we came here."

"Adam didn't think they were government agents," I explained again. "Even though they had proper ID."

Rosalinda got up off the floor and ran into one of the bedrooms, emerging with a cell phone encased in pink sparkly things. "Here, Mercy. You'll need a phone. No one will think to trace mine."

"Thank you, Rosa," I said.

"Thank you for taking care of my brother and giving him a place to live," she said solemnly.

"You only say that because when I moved out, the little girls moved into my room," said Gabriel. "So you don't want me to move back in."

"Well, yes," she agreed. "That was very thoughtful of Mercy."

He ruffled her hair and looked at me. "Ben's going to be getting restless."

"I need to go," I agreed.

"Be careful," Jesse said.

"I will," I said.

I got in the Mercedes and headed out to West Richland and Kyle's house. Ben stayed in the back seat, where the leather was covered. The car was an awkward fit for him. The seat was too narrow, and the floor was not big enough, either. His wound had quit bleeding, but he couldn't brace with that leg.

Warren should have been home with Kyle. Adam had smelled Warren on the men who had taken the pack. So they had taken Warren, but Kyle hadn't called Adam or me. That meant that either something was wrong with Kyle, or they had taken Warren in some way that had not alarmed his lover. Unhappily, the first was more likely.

I turned on the radio to listen for the news. It was pretty late—or rather, early in the morning—to get real news, but Mary Jo had been taken while on duty as a firefighter. If the enemy had done something to the people she worked with, doubtless we'd hear about it. It would be stupid of them, but people who attack a full pack of werewolves are either very stupid or very strong. I was betting that if someone had kidnapped a firefighter—or killed a bunch of them—there would be some sort of special report on the radio even at this hour.

While I was driving, I used Rosa's bling-covered phone and tried Elizaveta the witch's number to no avail. Then I tried Stefan's.

It said something about how ambivalent I was feeling about Stefan that I'd tried the witch, who didn't like me, first. If Stefan had still been part of the local seethe, I'd have had a good excuse to hesitate. But Marsilia had screwed him over to save her position as Mistress of the seethe. Vampire politics make the very complicated dance of manners that is werewolf protocol look like the Hokey Pokey.

She'd tortured him and his menagerie on trumped-up charges so that the rebels would approach him and reveal themselves. He'd served her for centuries, so she knew he wouldn't join the cuckoos who'd been foisted upon her by a vampire whose name had never been given to me—I called him Gauntlet Boy. Gauntlet, because the only time I'd seen him, he'd been wearing gauntlets. Boy—because vampires scared me spitless.

She'd been partially successful. He hadn't joined the rebellion—

which Marsilia quashed with his help. But he also hadn't looked upon the deaths of the people he protected as justifiable. Vampires vary a lot in how much they care for the humans who they feed from. Stefan's menagerie were his friends, or at least dear pets he cared for.

So he wasn't part of the seethe, and, vampire or not, Stefan had been my friend since I'd come to the Tri-Cities. However, thanks to Marsilia's ungentle machinations, I'd been seeing more of the vampire and less of my friend in him lately, and I didn't like it. I didn't like it enough that I seriously considered not contacting him for help.

The enemy was powerful, and we needed our allies. I was getting tired, and the weariness tamped down the anger and left me scared and alone, even with Ben stretched out in the seat behind me.

So I called Stefan.

It rang three times, and a voice (not Stefan's) said, "Leave a message." There was a beep.

I almost just hung up. But it was unlikely anyone had Stefan's phone under surveillance, and I wasn't calling from a number he would know. So I said, "Could you call me at this number? My phone is dead."

A police car had someone pulled over on the side of the road. My speed had crept up, and I slowed. The coast was not clear to speed just because one police car was occupied.

My phone rang as I passed the cop car, but the Mercedes's windows were very dark. It was unlikely that anyone could see into the interior even if Rosa's phone was so encrusted with plastic gems it ought to emit its own light. Risking a ticket, I answered the phone. "Yes?"

"Mercy?" said Stefan. "What do you need? And why are you calling me on someone else's phone?"

By the time I finished verbally reliving Peter's death, I was shaking with anger and . . . terror. So much rode on my playing the game right, and I didn't even know the rules.

At least with that much adrenaline flowing, I wasn't tired anymore—but I also wasn't paying attention to driving. Part of me, the part that remembered I'd totaled the Rabbit a few hours and a lifetime ago, tried to remind me that wrecking Marsilia's car would only make a bad situation worse. But the rest of me was focused on more immediate matters.

"Peter was a good man," said Stefan when I was finished. "I will meet you at Kyle's house."

I glanced at the sky. It was still dark, but the clock in Marsilia's car said it was five thirty in the morning. "You'll be cutting the daylight thing pretty close."

"There is time," he said, his voice as gentle as I'd ever heard it. "I can get home in very short order should I need to. Do not worry about me. We will worry about the others, yes? Hang up now and drive."

I hung up and hoped I'd done the right thing. Exposing the pack's vulnerability to the local vampires wasn't a smart thing to do. Marsilia would happily dance on our graves if the pack and I, especially I, were utterly destroyed. I trusted Stefan. I did. But Stefan was a vampire and I could never forget that.

Kyle's house in West Richland was a generous half-hour drive from Sylvia's apartment in Kennewick. I'd spent a lot of time this night traveling back and forth along the same stretch of highway. To my right, the Columbia was a murky presence as the houses of Kennewick passed by the window to mark my progress.

Had I done the right thing leaving Gabriel and Jesse? It had felt like I was getting them out of harm's way when I'd done it. But what if whoever had taken Adam did think of Sylvia? Gabriel was strong and smart, but he was also an unarmed teenage human. Had I just given our enemies more victims? I thought of the bullet that hit Peter and was pretty sure that the person who had fired it at a helpless man could shoot one of Gabriel's little sisters, too.

Somewhere nearby, Adam was being held. I had no real reason to think that they would be hunting Jesse. Not one. But I was uneasy leaving them without protection.

I called Zee. He hadn't said good-bye when he'd retreated to the fae reservation, just left a note telling me to be patient and not contact him. But he liked Gabriel and Jesse—and adored, though he'd never have admitted it out loud, the little hellions who were Gabriel's sisters.

His cell phone rang and rang as the interstate carried me past Richland. My finger was on the button to end the call when Zee said, grumpily, "*Liebling*, this is not a good idea."

"Zee," I told him, "I am completely out of good ideas and am doing my best with the bad ones I have left." I explained the whole thing again. When I finished, I said, "The fae owe us, Adam and me, they owe us for the otterkin and for the fairy queen. Is there some way you could keep a watch over Gabriel's mom's house? You probably won't have to do anything at all. I'm *probably* being paranoid—it's that kind of night. But all they have keeping them safe is my hope that no one would think to look there—and that reasoning gets weaker and weaker the farther away I get."

"I agree that you are owed a debt," Zee said heavily, at last. "There might be some who would argue that the otterkin's deaths were a tragedy. I am not one of those people. No one can argue that you were sent on an errand for us that put you in danger, and where you took much harm. And no one, not even the most anti-human of us"—the way he said it made me think that he had a specific fae in mind—"can argue you are owed for the downfall of the fairy queen, who caught so many of us in her web and might have taken us all, unaware as we were."

He made a clicking noise with his tongue that I recognized as the sound he made when confronted with a particularly difficult fix on a car. "It brings me sorrow, but at this time it would wipe the slate clean of favors owed to you if they knew that I had even answered this phone—which phone I am not supposed to have at all because it is corrupt human technology." He bit out the last part of the sentence as if he found it annoying. "If I left the reservation to help you, I would bring trouble down upon both of us." His laugh was distinctly unamused. "And if I left the reservation at this point, it might be disastrous on a much larger scale because I am trying to bring reason to chaos, which I cannot do from a distance and may not be able to do even with a sword to someone's throat. I cannot even give you advice without creating issues." He sighed but didn't hang up, so I kept the phone to my ear.

After a long pause, he said, carefully, "I could not tell you to call my house and speak to the one there. I could not tell you to think about the kinds of places that could be fortified to hold a pack of werewolves, which would not be easy. A place where people in pseudo-military garb might not be remarked upon or where they could get in and out unnoticed carrying bodies. There are not many places like that around here, Mercy. There are no peasants who are too afraid of the powers that be to speak out when men carrying guns walk where they should not be."

"You think they're being held somewhere out in the Area?" I

asked. The Area was the secured section of land surrounding the Hanford nuclear power plant.

"I am sorry, *Liebling*. I cannot help you at this time. Perhaps if the talks between the Gray Lords and Bran Cornick go well, we can discuss this again. Until that time, we are forbidden to give aid to anyone associated with the werewolf packs." Another slight pause. "This was very clearly expressed to me. Very clearly." His voice held an edge that was sharper than his knife—and his knife was legendarily sharp.

"If you know anyone who is talking to Bran right now," I said, "would you please have them tell him what's going on here? This information might not help the fae's cause with the Marrok, but you might let someone understand that *not* passing on this information will be a statement the Marrok will take very seriously. And I will make sure that Bran knows the fae were given this information."

"You phrase your suggestion very well," Zee said, sounding pleased. "I will let the ones who are talking to Bran know all that you have told me." He paused. "I will have to be creative to do it in such a way that they do not know that we have been talking on the phone." He hung up without another word.

I had missed the turn off at Queensgate and had to drive all the way to Benton City, adding more time onto the trip. Rather than travel back down the interstate, I took the back highway, where there should be fewer police, hoping I could make up some time.

As soon as I was on the right road, I called Zee's house. The phone rang and rang. After a few minutes I hung up and tried it again. Zee wouldn't have given me that number for nothing. Maybe he'd rented the house out to someone he thought could help me. Maybe there was another fae who, like Ariana, was powerful enough to defy the Gray Lords. Or maybe the fae had left designated spies outside to keep track of things they couldn't monitor from their barricaded reservations, someone who owed Zee a favor. I was still coming up with fantasy scenarios when someone picked up the phone.

"What?" he snapped impatiently.

"Who is this?" I asked, because, gruff and sharp as that answer had been, he sounded like Tad. Zee's half-human son would not have come back here without letting me know.

"Mercy?" Some of the grumpiness left his voice and I was certain.

"Tad? What are you doing home? How long have you been there, and why didn't you tell me you were home?"

Tad had been his father's right-hand man in the VW shop when he was nine, and I first met him. He'd kept on as *my* right hand and chief tool wrangler when his father had retired and let me buy the shop. Tad had left to go to an Ivy League school back East giving out scholarships to fae as a way to show how liberal and enlightened they were.

We'd e-mailed once a week since he left, and I called him once a month to keep up. Tad was the little brother I'd never had, and in some ways we were closer than I was to my half sisters. We had more in common: neither of us quite fitting in to either the world of the humans or the world of the supernatural. He because he was only half-fae and I because I was the only shapeshifting coyote in a world full of werewolves and vampires.

When the fae had pulled their disappearing act, I'd called him, both on his cell and on his dorm-room phone, to no avail. I'd decided he'd gone to the reservations with all the rest of the fae.

Apparently not.

"Tad?" I asked, because he hadn't answered any of my questions.

He hung up on me. Evidently, he didn't want to talk about it. Fair enough. I was a little short for time, too.

I dialed again.

"Go away, Mercy," he said.

"Your dad told me I should call his house for help," I said, speaking quickly. "Bad guys are after Jesse and Gabriel. I have them staying with Gabriel's mom in the hopes that no one will think to look for them there. But if they do, if the bad guys come, there isn't anyone there who can protect them."

I could almost feel Tad's reluctance to listen to me instead of hanging up again. Something must have changed in him while he was at college. I'd seen no sign of it in our correspondence or during his infrequent visits home. Maybe it had something to do with the reason that he was out here instead of in the reservation with the rest of the fae.

"You think I could protect them, huh?" he said, finally.

It was a fair question. Tad was half-fae, but I had no idea what that meant. From a few things that Zee had let slip over the years, I knew Tad wasn't one of the half fae who were as powerless as most humans. But that was all I knew.

"Your father does." I gave him the only answer I had.

He didn't say anything.

"I have to see if Kyle is okay," I told him. "Adam and the whole pack have been taken tonight, and one of the pack was killed. I'm trying to—" Do what? Rescue them? Stop the bad guys? "Check on Kyle because I think that they might have done something to him when they snatched Warren. I need Jesse and Gabriel to be safe, and I'm a little short of allies. It won't be for long. I'll come get them after I see that Kyle is okay." I recited Sylvia's address and hung up without waiting for him to say anything else.

I knew Tad. No matter how grumpy he was, he wouldn't be able to sit around while someone was in danger. He'd flirted lightly with Jesse when he'd been home last—then spent two hours under the hood of Gabriel's car helping him fix an electrical problem.

And the sooner I made sure that Kyle was safe, the sooner I could let Tad off the hook. I put my foot down and hoped the cops were out watching Walmart, the mall, and the interstate routes. The big Mercedes engine gave a satisfied purr and ate up the miles through the desert back to West Richland. The speedometer said 110, but it felt more like 60. I patted the dash, and said, "Good girl."

The eastern sky was still dark when I neared Kyle's house at a more lawful speed. Kyle and Warren lived in an upscale neighborhood where every house had ample garage space and driveways to catch the overflow. Usually, there were no cars on the street unless someone was having a party.

I passed a modest, dark, American-built car parked half a block from Kyle's house and, as I drove sedately by, I saw that there was an unfamiliar black SUV in the driveway. There were no lights on at the house. Not even the one by the door that Kyle left on all night. The SUV and the car had California plates.

I drove right past and turned the corner, parking Marsilia's dark, not-American-built car in front of a house twice the size of Kyle's, where it looked much more at home than the cars I'd just passed. I got out and opened the back.

"It doesn't look good for Kyle," I whispered to Ben. "Did you see those cars?"

His ears flattened, and he stood up in the back seat, his sharp claws digging into the leather, even through the blanket, in a way that might have caused me to wince on any other day.

"No," said Stefan, scaring me out of what was left of my wits.

If he hadn't covered my mouth with a cool hand, I would have awoken the neighborhood. He made soothing sounds until I quit struggling—which was an embarrassingly long time. I was tired and my head had just blanked out for a little bit and it took a while to realize what had happened.

"There now," Stefan said, his voice pitched low enough that a human standing next to him might have had trouble hearing. "Better? I am sorry. I didn't want to alert anyone."

Sorry for sneaking up on me or sorry for holding my mouth shut? I couldn't tell and didn't care. He was here, and I didn't feel so alone. Stefan was smart, dangerous, and *competent.* I hoped that I was the first two, but it was the third I really needed for this.

"Kyle's in trouble," I whispered back. Keeping our voices down made sense. People ignore the sounds of cars, but most of them will wake up to the sound of a strange voice. I didn't want to wake the neighborhood watch and try to explain to them what we were doing. "There is a car and an SUV parked by his house that shouldn't be there and no outside light. Kyle always turns on the porch light."

Stefan released me and took a couple of steps back, leaving me to grip the open car door for balance when Ben bumped against me as he got out.

Stefan was wearing a dark polo and slacks and I missed the Scooby-Doo shirts and jeans. I hadn't seen him wear them for a while, not since he'd left the seethe. He wasn't emaciated, but he had never regained the healthy look that he'd had before Marsilia had laid waste to the menagerie of humans he fed from. Marsilia's betrayal and the destruction of his menagerie had nearly destroyed him.

"I had a few minutes to check out the house while I was waiting for you," he said. "There are two strangers in the living room opposite the kitchen. There may be more on the upper floor because the lights are on."

Now that we were not touching, I could see the awkwardness the older vampires I'd met exhibited—as if he knew how he should act but couldn't quite feel it anymore. As if by giving up his Scooby-Doo shirts and his beloved Mystery Machine, Stefan had given up his last firm anchor to his humanity. Still, the Mystery Machine, Stefan's old VW bus with the cool paint job, remained parked in his driveway, so I had hope.

"You didn't see Kyle?" I asked.

"I didn't see him. I don't have your nose to follow a scent, and I didn't want them to know I was watching. They were just a little too alert for my comfort. I could smell blood, though. I don't know whose it was."

I would. He waited, and I considered.

"Let's go around back," I said. "I can slip in through the back porch; there's a dog door Kyle put in for Warren. I can check out the house and call you in when I find him."

"I think that sending you into the house alone is the stupidest of our many options," said Stefan repressively. "Ben should be at the front door, you should go to the back—and wait in the yard, Mercy—and I will go in."

The oldest and most powerful vampires acquire names that define their most prominent characteristic. Stefan's name among his kind was the Soldier. This was the sort of situation in which he excelled. I felt the relief of having an expert make the calls.

"They are only human," Stefan said, and there was a familiar look in his face, though I was more used to seeing it on the wolves: hunger. "I will kill them, and Ben will kill any who get past me. You can let us know if anyone tries to get away out the back, and we will kill them, too."

Stefan had always liked people. I hadn't noticed before that he also enjoyed killing them. Maybe that was part of the new, more vampiric Stefan.

So much for letting someone else make the calls.

"We don't need to kill them," I pointed out reasonably. "As you said, they are only human, and there are only two."

"That we know of," he said.

"We don't know anything about them," I told him. "We aren't even certain that the two men in Kyle's living room have anything to do with the people who took the pack."

Stefan raised an eyebrow—he was right. Who else would they be?

"We don't know who is backing them or what their endgame is," I continued doggedly. "We don't even know if Kyle is there. What I *do* know is that we can't go in to kill."

Stefan frowned at me. "I forget that you are too young to remember the lessons of Vietnam. Go in to win, Mercy, or do not go in at all. How many people are out here who could help Adam?"

"Us," I said wretchedly, then added, "Maybe Ariana, though she was pretty freaked-out when we left." I knew what he was saying. I did.

By that logic, we should leave Kyle to his fate. But I wasn't just Adam's wife, I was his mate. That made me second in rank—and that meant I had to protect the pack. It meant that I especially had to protect the weakest members first. We had already lost Peter.

Kyle needed to be protected—and we could do it without killing everyone.

"These people have taken down an entire pack of werewolves, Mercy," Stefan said coolly. "We cannot afford to take risks, or we might throw away the game trying to find out what they have done with Kyle." He lost the distant-vampire thing when he said Kyle's name. Stefan liked Kyle, who was snarky and happy to argue tactics in *Scooby-Doo* episodes as if defending a doctoral thesis. "If they are waiting at Kyle's, whom do you think they want? The only people important to Adam they don't have are you, Ben, and Jesse. And there is this: if they see me, if they understand what I am and do not die before they can tell their superiors over their communication devices, then we will lose more than just Kyle this night."

People don't know about the vampires. Oh, they know the stories—Bram Stoker and all his ilk made good use of the old legends. But they think they are just stories. The problem, for the vampire, is that now that the fae and the werewolves have admitted what they are, people are ready to believe that the old stories might be true. If Stefan was the vampire who gave those legends new life, Marsilia would kill him. I understood why he thought killing the enemy was the best way.

Part of me even agreed with him about killing them all. These people had killed Peter and taken Adam and put my world into danger.

"Kyle is human, and they were not worried about leaving Peter dead," Stefan said, saying what I didn't want to hear. "Kyle is less valuable than Peter was. He only matters to you and Warren. Adam would not kill someone, risk the werewolves' standing in the human world, for Kyle. A hostage is a lot more work than a dead body, Mercy. There is a real chance Kyle is already dead. If you aren't willing to kill—you need to leave them alone."

"If Kyle is dead"—and didn't that suck to say—"we still need to know it. I don't think he is; I think I'd feel it through the pack bonds because Warren is as mated to him as Honey was to Peter." That thought steadied me. I'd felt Honey's grief—still did, for that matter.

"We are going in after Kyle—and, Stefan, we can't leave a pile of bodies behind. We can hide your part in this. I'll tell everyone that you are a weird kind of werewolf if I have to. But people know about Kyle and Warren. Warren doesn't advertise what he is, but it will come out because he doesn't hide it, either. The bad guys—whoever they are—want Adam to kill an important man in a public way, so that the werewolves are blamed. I have the distinct impression that the last part is as important as the first. If we leave piles of dead bodies in our wake, we'll be accomplishing at least half of what the people who started this want." I sucked in a breath. "I do not enjoy helping my enemies."

Stefan frowned at me. He could just go in and kill them all, regardless of what I said. But his name was the Soldier—not the Killer or the Commander. (Yes, those are real vampires. I'm told that we're lucky they don't live anywhere near here.) Stefan had ceded me leadership because this was my problem.

So I was in charge, but I wasn't dumb enough to think that made me competent—I needed Stefan for that. Fine. I wouldn't authorize killing them all, but there should be other options.

"Could we go in quietly to check and see if we can find Kyle?" I asked. "I might be able to scent him from outside. If he's not here, we can leave them waiting for no one. If he is there, maybe we can get him out without killing people."

He shook his head. "Mercy. They have already proved themselves capable of taking a werewolf pack. Kill them or leave."

I glanced down at Ben; he was in no shape for battle. The danger wasn't just that his wound would slow him, and they could hurt him more easily, though that was part of it. If Ben killed tonight, wounded and shaken by Peter's death, he could lose control of his wolf and never regain it.

"We might be under attack by the government," I told Stefan. "We can't afford to lose the moral high ground. As long as we don't do any harm, the public will support us and force the government to back down. We're not going in to kill everyone in sight.

"You are welcome to leave, if you'd like," I said grimly, stripping my shirt off with my bra. He wouldn't abandon Kyle, I knew it. I was mad at him because I wanted to let him dictate our plan of attack, but I couldn't because I knew I was right. I kicked off my shoes. We were talking too much, and it was time to move. "I'm not leaving Kyle to rot when I might be able to do something for him. I'm going to look for Kyle. When I find him, I'll do whatever it takes to get him out. I will try to leave as few bodies behind as I can manage."

"If we fail, Adam is the one who loses," Stefan said.

"Kyle is pack," I explained. "He is vulnerable. Adam is Alpha and strong. So we need to make sure Kyle is safe first because that's what pack does, Stefan. The strong protect the weak."

Stefan's face froze. He hadn't been able to protect his menagerie, hadn't realized that he needed to protect them from Marsilia, the woman he'd given his loyalty.

I hadn't meant to hurt him.

I jerked down my jeans and underwear so I was naked on the dark sidewalk. Anyone looking out their window or driving by would get a show. I didn't care. Being a shapeshifter had gotten me over modesty by the time I was old enough to know what the word meant.

That didn't mean I was comfortable running around naked in front of everyone I knew. Once upon a time, Stefan had kind of had a thing for me. Not so much in love, but interested in that direction. I usually avoided being naked in front of him just like you don't hold out a slab of meat in front of a lion while planning on keeping the food to yourself.

"We have an opportunity to save Kyle. A chance you did not have when Marsilia took your people." I told him. "Will you help me?"

I changed to coyote without waiting for a reply and shook the change off my fur. Stefan gave an odd laugh, not happy or humorous—but it sounded like him this time and not the vampire Stefan, so it was all right. Then he picked up my clothes and tossed them into the car, his motion smooth and almost human. He hesitated with his head in the car.

My gun was under the front seat. I almost changed back to let him know, but decided not to. I couldn't carry it, and I was the only one who would be more dangerous with a gun in my hand tonight.

"Blood and humans and sweat and . . ." Stefan stood up and shut the back door. "Mercy, you let me talk to Marsilia about this before you return her car."

I gave him a brief nod and trotted toward Kyle's house. Ben was on three legs, but he had no trouble keeping up. Stefan brought up the rear.

The guy next door to Kyle had died a while ago and the house was still empty with a FOR SALE sign in the tidy front yard. The gate to the backyard was open, so I led my posse in that way.

There was an eight-foot stone fence between the yards, but someone had left a ladder next to it. Had old Mr. What's His Name been sneaking into Kyle's swimming pool before he died, or—and this was more troublesome—had someone been spying on them? In any case, it was not much effort to get over the fence. Even on three good legs, Ben didn't have to use the ladder; nor did Stefan. As a coyote, I'm outclassed by the werewolves and the vampires in everything except blending in.

Like the empty house, someone kept Kyle's yard neat and tidy so that we ghosted over grass rather than rustling through the leaves of fall. We kept to the shadows, though I don't think that anyone would have seen Stefan if he'd walked through the middle of the backyard. He was doing something, some vampire magic, that made him really hard to focus on.

I kept a sharp eye out, but I didn't see anyone keeping watch. That didn't mean they weren't there, but between Stefan's mojo and the concealing pack magic that Ben and I were pulling around ourselves, only truly bad luck would allow a human to see us anyway.

I could smell it before we hit the house. There was blood on the lawn. I abandoned the shadows to cast out until I found where the dark wet stuff splattered the grass, because it was Warren's blood I smelled.

Ben sniffed beside me and snarled soundlessly, exposing his fangs as he turned his eyes to the house. From the back, it was as dark as the front, but this near the house, we could both hear the murmuring of voices from inside. They were being quiet, and had we been human, we would not have heard them at all. As it was, I couldn't hear what they were saying, just a rumble of men's voices.

They'd taken Warren here, in the backyard. He'd been in human shape—a werewolf's scent changes when they are in human form, becomes diluted. That they took him in the yard was good. That I smelled only his blood was also good. That meant that all of Kyle and Warren's friends who'd come over for Thanksgiving probably weren't in the middle of a firefight. That was good news, and not just for Kyle and Warren's friends. Once these people began killing innocent humans, there was no way back. Their only survival path would then be to kill everyone who knew about them—including Adam and the whole pack.

As long as the dead were werewolves, it was unlikely that they had to worry much about the consequences as far as the human justice system was concerned. With the fae, the courts had already demonstrated that when put to the test, fear beat out justice.

For us, right now, that was a good thing. As long as we could keep the villains off the defensive, Adam should be okay.

What Stefan had said was true. They were obviously waiting for someone, and Jesse, Ben, and I were the logical targets. I had to assume that they were prepared to deal with Ben and me. Stefan would throw a wrench in their plans, but I didn't know if it was a big enough wrench.

While I was debating, someone started speaking. The voices were coming from Kyle and Warren's bedroom on the second floor. I looked up and saw that the blinds weren't drawn—unusual for Warren, who was quite aware that there were things that could look in your window in the dark.

"They aren't coming," someone said. "We can't afford to wait until daylight. We need to find them. Orders are to get the information."

"Yessir," a second man said. "How far can I go?" The second man gave us a total of at least four. I could still hear the rumble of the other two down in Kyle's living room.

"Get the information," the first man said, and I heard the bedroom door shut and the footsteps of someone leaving.

"You hear that, Johnny?" There was a sick eagerness in his voice. "He said I could go as far as I want."

Another man, presumably Johnny—giving me a count of five bad guys—said, softly, "Only until we get the information, Sal. You hear that? Give us what we want, and I'll stop him. Sal was captured by the Afghanis a while back and didn't come back quite right. He likes torture. Tell us where they are likely to have gone to ground and everything stops."

Silence.

"So where would they go?" someone asked, and there was the sound of flesh on flesh.

Someone made a noise, and the hair on the back of my neck rose as my lips pulled back from my teeth. Kyle. They were hitting Kyle.

"Staying quiet isn't helping, son," said the soft voice. "I don't want to do this. Boss don't want to hold your lover any longer than we have to. Takes a lot of people to hold a werewolf pack—and some of them are going to get dead. If we can get Hauptman's daughter and wife, we can let the rest of you the fuck go."

I wonder if Kyle heard the lie.

"Fuck you," he said.

Maybe he had. A divorce attorney, I expect, would have a lot of practice telling when someone was lying.

They hit him again. Beside me, Ben was vibrating.

Stefan said, sounding hungry, "Mercy, there are only two of them in that room."

I shifted back to human so we could talk.

Ben nudged my knee, hard.

"I know," I told him. "Can we take them without alerting the others?" I shivered. The Tri-Cities wasn't Montana, but it was still too cold to stand around naked in November. Or maybe I was shivering with my coyote's desire to go kill someone.

The first man said something ugly, and Kyle made a noise.

Yep. It was the go-kill-someone shiver.

"We can," Stefan said. "And if not—I can kill them all."

That didn't sound like a bad plan, standing out here listening to them hurt Kyle. I *knew* it would be stupid to leave bodies, but his pain was putting paid to my good sense.

"Throw me up," I told him, and turned back into a coyote.

I looked at Stefan, and when he met my eyes, I jerked my chin to the balcony that came off the bedroom. He frowned at me doubtfully. I rose up on my hind legs and bounced once. Then lifted my muzzle toward the balcony again.

His eyebrows rose, but he picked me up and threw me. I cleared the railing but had to twist hard, so I landed in the middle of a planter instead of on top of the lawn furniture that might squeak under me.

Ben jumped to the top of the railing, and Stefan followed. Stefan hopped off and landed on the balcony with bent knees and no sound. Ben's ears flattened at me, so I moved off the planter and let the heavier werewolf use it as a stair so that he didn't have to land so heavily. Hard to land quietly on a hard surface with werewolf-sized claws.

4

The brocade drapes were an inheritance from the people who had built the house. Kyle loved the fabric but complained a lot about the way they left six inches between the bottom of the curtains and the floor.

I dropped to my knees and peered through the bottom of the sliding glass door that Kyle planned to replace with french doors next summer along with the drapes.

Kyle and Warren's bedroom was decorated in a minimalist and very civilized style. The blood on the carpet looked like the single contrasting note one of those designers on TV liked to recommend.

There was so little furniture that the villains had had to bring up a chair from the dining room so they had something to use to stage their interrogation. They'd tied Kyle to the sturdy chair naked. His feet were free, but it didn't matter because they were also bare. Unless you are a werewolf or maybe Bruce Lee, bare feet can't do much damage unless you have more of a strike opportunity than being tied to a chair presents.

From the looks of him this wasn't the first round of abuse he'd taken. I kept my growl to myself, though I could do nothing about the snarl that wrinkled my nose. Kyle's face was bruised, the aristocratic nose sat at an angle, and dried blood covered his chin and upper chest. A cut above one eye had bled, too, and that eye was swollen shut and purple. There were red marks on his cheekbone and stomach that were fresher, having not had time to bruise.

The two men in the room were dressed all in black, and they wore the same body armor the men who held Adam had worn. The taller man was bald, his skin tanned by a life spent outdoors. I put his age between twenty-five and thirty. The other man was heavier built and not so tan, his hair the shade of rust and cut tightly against his scalp.

The bald man's body language was relaxed, and that made the worry he projected in his voice even more of a lie than the words.

"I don't like letting him free to do as he wants, Mr. Brooks. It isn't good for him or you. He might do some serious damage. Things that can't be repaired. I can stop him if you just let us know where you think she might go. We'll get out of your hair, and you never have to see us again."

Kyle spat out blood. "You must be fae. I never heard so much truth built into a lie. Did your mother have wings and pointed ears?" he asked, his voice as cool as it was in the courtroom.

Hadn't Kyle ever heard that you weren't supposed to antagonize your kidnappers? Especially when they were beating on you?

At least he had their attention fully on him.

Taking advantage of their preoccupation, I changed back to human and reached up to the catch on the glass door, which was, luckily for us, unlocked. Hopefully, the heavy drapes would disguise the cold outside air now wafting into the room as I carefully, quietly slid the door open. It was good for us and for Kyle that he had not had time to replace either the door or the drapes.

As soon as I had it opened, Stefan dropped to his knees to get a good look through the gap between the floor and the drapes, and I shifted back to coyote. My four-footed shape might not be as impressive as one of the wolves, but it was more lethal than my human shape. I squeezed next to Stefan and looked again.

The bald man's face had lost its pleasantness, though he'd taken his time to answer Kyle's taunt. "Your mouth is dangerous to you, Mr. Brooks. I'd suggest you use it to give us the information we want, or you might not be able to use it at all."

"You're a dead man," Kyle said. "Warren doesn't take kindly to people who hurt me."

We had to get in there—and now the only obstacle was the curtain. If we could be quiet enough, the men downstairs would not hear us.

"Your Warren is our prisoner," said the bald man, back to his Mr. Nice Guy persona. "He can do nothing to help you."

Kyle smiled. "You just keep telling yourselves that."

The younger man bounced a couple of times on his feet and feigned a strike. Kyle pulled his head out of the line of fire and the man hit him in the shoulder with a spinning back kick that launched Kyle's chair over onto its side. If he'd hit him in the head with that foot, Kyle would have been dead.

On the floor, Kyle's face was aimed right at me. He blinked twice and shook his head. "Get the hell out of here."

"I'm sorry, Mr. Brooks, but we can't do that," said the bald man with mock sorrow, unaware that Kyle hadn't been talking to him. The other man put a foot on the chair and rocked it a little.

Stefan had stood up so there was room for Ben to put his head on the ground next to me and look below the curtain, too. When he saw Kyle, the werewolf went still.

Ben was not the largest werewolf in the pack—though he was big enough. But he was among the most dangerous. He was fast—and he wasn't bothered by the thought of killing someone, even when he was as human as he ever got. He had been abused, severely abused when he was a child. People, outside the pack and Adam's family, just weren't real to him. We were working on that, Adam and I, but I discovered right then that Ben considered Kyle one of the pack.

Better to aim my weapon than to let it go off half-cocked. I bumped him, and when I had his attention, I pulled my nose out from under the curtain. Then I looked up at the top of the curtain and back to him. Shapeshifting makes all of us pretty good at charades.

Ben stood up and kept going until he stood balanced on his good hind leg with a front paw on the side of the house next to the sliding door. I backed out of the way—and realized that Ben and I were alone on the balcony. Stefan had disappeared.

I nodded sharply, and Ben's free front paw slammed the curtain, rod and all, onto the ground, where it would not interfere with us. I'd gathered myself to leap, but what I saw made me pause because there was no one to attack.

Stefan was already in the room, lowering the bald man to the ground with gentle care. The first man, the man who'd hurt Kyle, was dead, his eyes starting to fog over and his body draped over

Kyle. Stefan had incapacitated both men without either making a sound. Pretty efficient, the coyote in me thought, and the rest of me was very, very glad that Stefan was on my side.

Despite my earlier stand, even knowing it could come back and bite us, I couldn't deny that I was happy that Stefan had killed Kyle's assailant.

I changed back to human and hauled the dead man off Kyle while Ben aimed himself at the bindings on Kyle's wrists that held the rest of him into the chair. Stefan touched Ben's nose and moved it out of the way.

He looked at the bindings for a moment. Yellow nylon rope wrapped Kyle's wrists and wove in and out of the sturdy wooden chair. "There is no way the police are going to believe you broke out of that."

And that was the first sign I had that Stefan really had taken what I'd told him to heart. We were going to call the police—and Kyle, very human Kyle, was going to rescue himself.

Stefan put a hand on the seat of the chair and the other on the back. "Brace yourself," he warned Kyle, then pulled the chair apart. The ropes fell away like magic.

Everyone but Kyle froze, listening for any sign that someone else had heard us.

"Sweats," Kyle whispered to me, rolling off the chair like it hurt. "Top drawer of the bigger chest of drawers. You can steal a pair, too." He looked at the chair pieces, and murmured, "The bedroom is supposed to be soundproofed. Doesn't work on Warren, but maybe we'll luck out with less gifted listeners."

The first drawer I found had underwear, so he must have meant the other top drawer. They were sorted and army neat, matching bottoms and tops folded together. I grabbed the top two sets.

No one came boiling up the stairs, so either they hadn't heard the chair go—or they thought it was part of the interrogation.

Stefan helped Kyle up and steadied him when he was a little wobbly on his feet. I handed over a pair of bottoms. Stefan continued to hold him upright while Kyle pulled the sweats on with great concentration. Once Kyle had the pants on and both feet on the floor to steady himself, Stefan took the rope and started to tie up the bald man.

"How often do the people downstairs come up?" Stefan said.

"The only time anyone has come up here was a few minutes ago," Kyle told him. "Could be back in a minute, or next week."

I handed Kyle a sweatshirt. He shook his head, and said, "That's the wrong top for these."

"Fashion princess." I rolled my eyes and gave him the other top, noticing only as it unfolded that it proclaimed, "I'm prettier than your girlfriend," in purple glittery script. I recognized it because I'd given it to him for his birthday.

"I have news for you, Kyle, it'll be a while before you are prettier than anyone's girlfriend. Bruises are not your best color. Are you sure you don't want the other top?"

He glanced at me and gave me a crooked smile. "You look worse than I do. These goons get to you, too?"

We were all keeping our voices as quiet as possible.

"Car accident." I pulled on the sweatpants. They were tight, but Warren's would have been tighter and left me with a foot of material to trip on.

"They have Warren," Kyle said, his eyes, briefly, looking as terrified as I was.

"I know," I told him. The top that matched the sweatpants I wore was a spiffy teal. "They have the rest of the pack, too."

"So I gathered." Kyle indicated with a tip of his head that his information had come from the bald man. "Are we on the side of the angels?" Kyle pulled on his top, though not without wincing.

Stefan looked up from the bald man, and said, "The first one I killed because I don't let people who hurt those I care about live. He is dead in such a way that a human could have killed him. Since Mercy has been so concerned with the body count, the second man is merely out—and I made certain he did not see me. If you choose to call in the police, there is nothing that can be used against us—werewolf or vampire."

"So our halos are nice and bright," I told Kyle. I looked at Stefan. "Is calling the police smart? Won't we be putting pressure on the bad guys to get rid of their hostages?"

"No." Stefan turned his gaze on me. "If this is a government operation, having the local police involved will force them out into the open, and they cannot afford the bodies any more than the werewolves can. If it is something spearheaded by renegade agents—which is what it sounds like—involving the police will alert the agency involved and bring us new allies. That's how we'll do this, Mercy. If we can, we trap them in their actions until the only move they have left is what we want them to do."

He took a breath—which he doesn't have to do unless he wants to talk, though he usually does if only out of consideration for we breathers who get distressed if the people we're around don't breathe for a few minutes. "You were right, Mercy. I was thinking like a vampire before. These people want to separate the werewolves from the protection of society. So we'll get society on our side instead. It helps that Kyle is human."

Kyle smiled like it hurt. "Quite human. I am a black belt—got it ten years ago and haven't practiced much since. But it could explain how I took down two trained men with Mercy and Ben's help." He looked at the dead man, and nodded sharply. "Thank you for that, Stefan. He's no loss to the world."

"Will you get in trouble for his death?" I asked Kyle. He was a lawyer—family law—but he should still know.

He shook his head. "Self-defense in a slam dunk." He looked at Stefan. "Do you know who is responsible?"

"Renegade Cantrip agents is our working hypothesis," I said. FBI agents would have had too much experience to react out of fear the way Mr. Jones had. Homeland Security, I didn't know enough about. But Cantrip—short for Combined Nonhuman and Transhuman Relations Provisors—had attracted a number of anti-nonhuman zealots. I knew that they had training but not much field experience—and they'd have access to as much information as the government could amass on the werewolves. For firepower, they'd have to have help. "And a hired troop of competent mercenaries for muscle. Here"—I jerked my chin toward the two men on the floor—"we have the mercenaries. There are at least three more downstairs. I didn't see anyone else, but they'd be dumb not to have someone out keeping watch."

"Mercenaries mean money," said Stefan. "A lot more money than most Cantrip agents make."

Kyle smiled briefly. "Follow the money. Fine. You're sure that the police would be helpful?"

"Wait." There had been a click. Everyone fell silent—and then air started to blow out of the registers in the floor. I'd heard the heat turn on. Stefan went to the door, cracked it open, and took a quick peek outside. He shut it noiselessly and shook his head.

But he was quieter when he talked than we'd been before.

"They only really need one person alive to blackmail Adam. The rest are just a precaution. If Adam and the pack are hostages, they need every one they can keep their hands on." He frowned at us both. "That doesn't mean they are safe—idiots are the hardest people to plan around, and anyone who captures a werewolf pack without killing every last one is an idiot."

"Okay," said Kyle. "Let's see if we can't make this a little uncomfortable for them." He walked to the side of the bed and picked up his cell.

I grabbed his hand and looked at Stefan. "What if they're listening to the phones?"

Stefan smiled. "Then they'll have warning and either run—or they will attack us up here."

A lot of things could have gone wrong. We settled down to wait, ready to defend ourselves if the men downstairs decided to check on Kyle.

Stefan left when the sun started coming up. Ben and I waited with Kyle, despite Kyle's protests that he could handle this on his own. We were safely out of it; if we left, we gave the enemy no one to follow . . . Kyle had a lot of arguments, which he delivered with the cell on mute.

I wasn't leaving Kyle alone in a house full of bad guys. I finally stole his phone, took it off mute, and introduced myself to the operator. I explained that I thought that these same men were responsible for launching an attack at my house—yes, I was married to the local Alpha. One of the pack had escaped and found me—and we'd figured out something was wrong. We snuck in through the upstairs window just after Kyle had managed to free himself. I told her about the blood we'd found in the backyard that belonged to Kyle's boyfriend, a pack member, who had been taken off the premises by these bad guys, presumably to be held by whoever had taken the rest of the pack.

Kyle listened hard, since it was the first time he'd heard a lot of what I said. I didn't give the police the whole truth. There were too many things the werewolves didn't want getting out, and I wasn't mentioning Stefan. But I stuck to it as closely as I could.

When I'd finished, it was not just the SWAT team who were headed our way, but a fair percentage of a number of different police departments—and, to my relief, someone was going to go check at the firehouse where Mary Jo worked as well as the houses of our married pack members who hadn't come to our Thanksgiving dinner but had been taken just the same. They'd make sure that there were no other hostage situations.

I handed Kyle back his phone. He shook his head at me but took it in one hand, put it against his ear, and opened the gun safe in his closet with the other. The safe held two handguns and Warren's rifle—it was a Spencer repeating rifle dating back to the Civil War. He'd let me shoot it a couple of times.

Kyle took Warren's .357 in hand and gave me his own 1911 because that fit my hand better than Warren's gun would have. My own gun was still in Marsilia's car. Kyle left the rifle in the safe when he closed it.

Warren's father had carried it during the War Between the States and at his death it had come to Warren, who was eight or nine at the time. That's as much as I knew about Warren's life as a human except that he considered himself a Texan and had spent a long time as a cowboy.

I agreed with Kyle's decision: the Spencer was too important to be risked if the police decided to take the guns. If we had to shoot someone, it was probably going to be within handgun range anyway.

"Stay quiet and find a good hiding place," said the 911 operator on the other end of the phone; she'd been giving us all sorts of good advice and updates.

"We are taking cover in the bathroom," said Kyle, and gave her the basic layout of the house—which took a while because it was a big house.

He was steady and cool while we watched the door between his bedroom and the rest of the house. The bathroom afforded us a little protection—the walls were marble slabs, and we weren't in direct line of sight from the door.

Kyle kept the phone tucked between his ear and shoulder, and I could hear the operator keeping him up-to-date on what was happening. I had a sudden sick thought that we really didn't know if we could trust the police. What if the government really was behind it all? What if the police were in on it, too?

Paranoia: the gift of the survivor and the burden of the overtired, stressed, terrified coyote.

I thought about the likelihood of the police being under the control of the bad guys and came up with it as being unlikely—but not as unlikely as a group of humans descending on pack HQ and abducting a pack of wolves—including wolves who were not out to the public. Since the latter had happened, it made me feel less paranoid for suspecting the former.

"Okay," said the operator. "The police are there and in position, just hang tight and wait for them."

As the sounds of rapid-fire orders seeped into our bolt-hole, I became more and more uneasy about trusting the police to be on our side.

About that time, there was a gentle tap on the bedroom door.

"Mr. Brooks? This is Kennewick PD, sir. Please put down your weapons. We have the suspects in custody and you are safe."

Kyle put his gun down on the floor—then noticed me not doing the same thing. He reached out toward me, and Ben growled. I was not alone in my paranoia—or else Ben was just picking up on how unhappy I was. Wounded and surrounded by the dead and terrified, he wasn't exactly Mr. Sane right now, either.

"Give us a moment," Kyle called out. "Mercy's pretty freaked-out. She's had quite a night, and it's not over. Let me talk her down."

There was a pause, then a more familiar voice called, "Mercy, drop the gun. We're the good guys. We'll find Adam, but you've got to put down the gun and let us in."

"Tony?" I called out, not releasing my grip on Kyle's gun. But my stomach muscles started to loosen. Tony Montenegro worked for the Kennewick police and he was on our side.

"It's me, *chica*. Let us do our job."

I engaged the safety and put the gun down on the floor next to Kyle's.

"Come on," Kyle said. "They'll feel better if we're not near the guns." And then he murmured, "I'll feel better, too. Ben, is there anything you can do to look less frightening?"

Ben dropped his head and tail, hopping on three feet to accompany us to the bedroom door. I wasn't sure his posture made him look less lethal—and that was before he ruined it by snarling at the bound kidnapper who had awakened at some point and was struggling.

The bald man froze, and I patted Ben on the head. "Sorry, Ben," I murmured. "No eating the bad guys when they are tied up, and the police are on the other side of the door."

I wasn't really kidding, though I didn't know it until I said it. Both Ben and Kyle gave me a thoughtful look.

"I'm going to have the werewolf lie down next to the wall," Kyle said loudly. "He's already been hurt by the guys who took out Adam. I don't want anyone shooting him by accident."

"Everything's been going smoothly," said Tony reassuringly. "We've got two guys, they surrendered peacefully enough, so no one is too trigger-happy except for Mercy. But lying down by the wall is a good idea."

There had been a third man downstairs, I thought. Or maybe one of the two from below had been the man who'd come up to give the men holding Kyle their orders. I listened to Tony explain that the wolf who was in the room was one of the victims and not to be shot. He was being very cautious, but then he'd seen the werewolves before.

Timber wolves are big and scary. Anyone who has ever seen one in a zoo or in the woods is in no doubt that they are in the presence of an apex predator. Werewolves are bigger and scarier than that. Sometimes they can downplay it, a little body language, a little pack magic, and they can pass for a huge dog if no one is looking for werewolves.

Ben was in no condition to play harmless, which wasn't his best thing anyway. That he was wounded meant that if someone got jumpy, Ben would take it to the next level. Lying down next to the wall ten feet from the door was as good as it got. I stood between him and the door.

"Okay," said Kyle. "No one is armed or—" I think he started

to say dangerous but stopped himself. He'd told me that no one should lie to the police; the trick was not to tell them much until you had a lawyer. "No one is armed."

The door opened, and the police cautiously entered, giving Ben a wide berth—which was probably smart. He might be tracking a little better than I was at that point, but not much better. And he didn't like being cornered by strangers in uniforms at the best of times. We all held very still while they examined the two men on the ground without touching.

"I killed the first guy," said Kyle, sounding shaky. I couldn't tell if it was an act or not. No one would believe a lawyer would confess to murder unless he was in bad shape, but Kyle didn't want them looking at Ben.

"No bite marks that I can see," said one of the officers, who was kneeling by the dead man. "I'm not a doctor, but I can't turn my head that far around. I'd say his neck was broken."

The tension in the room immediately dropped, replaced by a curious elation.

"No one wants a werewolf kill on their watch," Tony explained quietly to me when he saw my expression. "And Adam has been very helpful from time to time. And no shots were fired, no one died at our hands, none of ours was hurt—and we got to play heroes. This operation went down slick and smart. It is a very good day when we can say that."

Of course, it wasn't over then. They took us to the Richland Police Department—I didn't ask why they didn't use the West Richland office.

They interviewed Kyle and me separately; he'd told me that

would happen. I didn't know the policemen who talked to me, and at least one of them was terrified of Ben.

I had told them that Ben needed to stay with me, and they didn't argue after I pointed out to them that if I wasn't with Ben, I wouldn't be there to stop him if he got upset. I'd removed his bandages, and they'd taken photos of his wound—which still wasn't healing. I'd refused medical care for him (by that time he was in a foul temper—in pain, his vulnerability exposed and photographed, and *hungry*). Someone had found a first-aid kit, and I'd rewrapped his leg.

His presence made the police who were talking to me start out a little unfriendly. No one likes to be afraid, and only an idiot wouldn't be a little afraid of Ben in his current mood. They also seemed to be a little slow, asking me the same questions over and over again.

Then they went out for a bit and came back actively hostile.

Fine. I could be hostile, too. Adam was being held by crazy people with guns—and I was stuck arguing with a pair of officers I was beginning to think of as Tweedledumb and Tweedledumber. Maybe Ben wasn't the only person in a bad mood.

They were convinced that the attack couldn't have been unprovoked. What had the pack been involved in that got such a response? The attack on our house looked a lot like some of the drug cartel attacks. Did I know about the way the cartels were blackmailing the field hands at the paper-pulp tree farms to plant drugs between the rows of trees near Burbank?

About the fiftieth time we were going through the same old thing—they had a problem with me being unwilling to tell them where Jesse and Gabriel were hidden—a youngish man in a very well-tailored suit came in and introduced himself as Loren

Hoskins, my lawyer. He advised me not to say another word, so I shut up and let him do his job.

An unpleasant three and a half hours later, he escorted me outside, a firm warning to me that I leave the police work to the police ringing in my ears. Presumably that meant that they didn't want me out looking for Adam because the police are so well equipped to take on guys capable of taking out a whole werewolf pack. I might have said something to that effect as we were leaving. But they didn't have a werewolf's hearing, so the only one who heard me was my lawyer.

"They have training that you don't," said the lawyer in a very quiet voice.

That was true. But they didn't have a mate bond and a werewolf pacing beside them. Ben was limping, but he was putting weight on his bad leg. Either he was getting better, or he was so tired all of his legs hurt.

"Kyle called me," Loren-my-lawyer said, opening the back door of his car to let Ben inside without any apparent concern for his leather upholstery or the worry of having a werewolf sitting at his back while he drove. "He told me he thought that the both of you were at a point that a lawyer would be good—and heavily implied that if they were being so hard on him, it might be because there was some pressure from above. He also said, in so many words, that if they were giving him, a lawyer, a hard time, that they were likely doing worse to you—would I mind coming to your rescue and sending a lackey his way?"

He held open his passenger door for me like a gentleman. I was sweaty, bloody, bruised, and wearing Kyle's sweats. We were getting looks from people walking by—the nice-looking, well-dressed man and the psycho woman from hell. Inviting me into his car might have been a braver thing than letting in a werewolf he didn't know.

"They didn't have you under arrest," he told me. "So, theoretically, we could have walked out of there anytime. But I didn't like the vibe I was getting from them. If I'd pushed earlier, we might just have gotten you arrested—which is ridiculous under the circumstances."

I sat down and discovered that the relative safety of his car was enough to make me try to doze off as soon as the seat belt was fastened and the door shut.

"Kyle's free as well," Loren-my-lawyer said, waking me up from my doze. I don't think that he'd noticed I'd fallen asleep, as we were just turning out of the parking lot. I'd missed him getting in, starting the car, and backing out of his parking space. "According to my associate, who texted me, they released Kyle as soon as his lawyer appeared. While we were talking to the nice police officers, Kyle has been to his doctor, who has already checked him out and let him go. Kyle texted me as well. He suggests that I drop you by his place for lunch. He told me to let you know that he has hired a security team to watch the house to keep this from happening again."

I needed to find Adam and the pack. Before I could do that, I needed to contact Adam. My hands closed into fists, and I had to flatten them on my leg. I needed to check with Gabriel and Jesse, and I needed to check with Tad, who had expected me back a long time ago. Gabriel's sister's phone was in Marsilia's car, and so was my gun.

"What time is it?" I asked.

"Half past noon."

I'd been up for thirty hours and was stumbling stupid tired. I needed a safe place to sleep before I would be useful to anyone. Kyle's house was as good as any.

"Sure," I said. "Wake me up when we get there."

After that initial bit, I found I couldn't sleep with a stranger so near. I kept my lids closed, though, and it helped with the dry burn in my eyes from staying up too long. I directed him to turn a block later than Kyle's house, and he let Ben and me out by Marsilia's car.

He glanced at me and glanced at the car. Sure blood, bruises, and werewolves didn't make him turn a hair—but me driving Marsilia's car? That was worth a second look.

I'd left the keys in the pocket of my jeans, which were still in the back seat. Anyone could have sat down, pressed the ignition button, and driven off. There were some places—down by my garage was one of them—that you wouldn't want to do that. But here, in the wealthy area of West Richland, it was more or less safe. Besides, who would believe that someone would leave a key in a car like that instead of locking up?

I opened the back door of the car, and Ben, somewhat wearily, hopped in onto the bloodstained blankets. He was tired, or he'd just have run the block or so to Kyle's house. He looked thinner than he had earlier that night. He hadn't eaten since Thanksgiving dinner yesterday evening, and he was going to need a lot of food. Kyle would have red meat for Warren.

I should have thought of that. Loren-my-lawyer wouldn't have minded stopping at a fast-food place to get food for Ben. I needed to take better care of him.

I pressed my fingers to my cheekbones and let the pain from

my injury drive my tears away. I would cry when everyone was home—*everyone except for Peter.* Until then I had more important things to do.

I parked the car in Kyle's pristine driveway. When Kyle opened his door to let Ben and me in, he did a double take.

"Holy Hummer, Batgirl, where did you get a Mercedes AMG?" Kyle had changed out of his sweats and wore a black-and-red button-up shirt that complemented his dark hair and went with the black slacks that were so casual I knew they must have cost him a pretty penny. We all found our refuges where we could: I baked cookies, and Kyle wore expensive clothes.

"It's not my car," I told him. "Marsilia left it for an oil change, and I couldn't resist." Kyle knew who Marsilia was. So I added, "Ben's been bleeding all over the back seat. Do you think we can clean the blood out of the leather well enough that she'll keep it? Who do you think should pay for the damage? Ben for bleeding on it; the bad guys for shooting Ben so he was bleeding in the first place; or me for stealing it?"

"That is *Marsilia's* car, and you stuck a bleeding werewolf in the back seat?" Kyle said, ignoring my attempted humor. "I shouldn't have sent Loren—you'd have been safer stuck in the black hole of the justice system for a few months until something distracts the Queen of the Damned from killing you."

He'd picked up my name for Marsilia. I hoped he never used it around her. I noticed that the earlier red marks on his face had darkened to bruises to go with the other bruises he had. His nose had been reset, but both of his eyes were black and puffed up. I might have won the disreputable award last night, but with Kyle's new bruises, for the first time in a long time, someone looked more beat-up than I did.

He limped when he stepped back to let me in.

"It's a good thing for the guy who beat on you that Stefan killed him," I said soberly as I walked into the entryway. Ben also limped, and I found that since my knee decided to hurt, I was limping, too. That made three of us. Kyle's house smelled like gun oil and strangers. "Or he'd have to face Warren."

Kyle flinched, closing the door behind Ben. "I know. It's going to be months before I'm not explaining my face to everyone I meet. Hello. No, I was beaten by an army of muscle-bound men who didn't even have the courtesy to be cute. No, don't worry about it. I'm fine now. The nose just has a little bump—like Marilyn's mole, it emphasizes the perfection of the rest of my face."

He glanced down at Ben. "Both of you come into the kitchen. Ben, I've pulled out the remains of last night's turkey. There's also four pounds of roast I was going to cook tomorrow. I'll cook Warren another turkey so he can have turkey hash. It's on a platter on the table."

Ben rubbed his muzzle over Kyle's shoulder in a way that I think was supposed to be reassuring. Kyle sucked in a breath. Either it hurt, or the reminder that the werewolf was big enough to rub his shoulder without much effort wasn't exactly reassuring.

"Ben, when was the last time you brushed your teeth?" asked Kyle.

Or else Ben's breath was really bad.

Ben showed his teeth in a mannerly grin and started eating the food Kyle had left on the table with enthusiastic concentration.

I slumped in one of the breakfast-bar stools and blew out a

loud breath. "Did you find out if they found out anything about them?" I asked.

Kyle gave me a look, then busied himself making me a peanut butter and huckleberry jelly sandwich. "What really bothers me is that I understood that question. You will eat this and go to sleep, so your pronouns get their antecedents back. The *police* haven't gotten very far yet investigating the men who invaded my house. The bad guys have good lawyers, very good lawyers. Not as good as Loren and nowhere near as good as I am, of course, but top-notch, expensive, out-of-town lawyers. Loren tells me that he thinks the lot of them will be out on bail by tomorrow because of all the money floating around. Tough to keep them when the only dead body is one of theirs—and by my own testimony he was the only one guilty of assault."

I stared at him over the sandwich he put in front of me. "You're kidding, right?"

Kyle shook his head. "Eat that, Mercy, don't just stare at it. Dickens has it that 'the law is a ass,' and a lot of the times he is right. We have them on criminal trespass. Tony is incensed, he told me, but they can't get them for terrorist activity. Somehow, the two men downstairs were unarmed when they were arrested—so another man must have gotten away with their weapons, because the police turned my house upside down looking for guns while they were questioning us and all they found were our guns, the guns we took from the bad guys, and the Spencer in the gun safe." I thought about the man who'd given the orders, who might or might not have been one of the men in the living room and my vague suspicion that they would have left someone on watch.

"Then, mysteriously," continued Kyle, "the guns belonging to the two men up in my bedroom have disappeared from the evidence room. They are holding ours, Mercy, pending further investigation. So I'm doing some shopping today because I'll be damned if I'm going unarmed when people have kidnapped Warren." His manner had been as confident as always until he reached that last part, and his voice broke.

"He's alive," I told him. "You'd know if he weren't. The only one they killed was Peter."

Kyle jerked his head up. "Peter's dead?"

I nodded. It was too much trouble to stay upright, so I folded my arms and put my forehead down on them. "Peter's dead. The moron shot him because Adam let him see what Alpha meant. Now Peter's dead, and Adam . . ." I shook my head.

A hand rested on my shoulder, then Kyle's face buried itself in my shoulder.

"I called my father," he said, his voice muffled by the material of the sweatshirt I wore. "Told him that if he didn't want his friends knowing all about his gay son who was sleeping with a werewolf, he needed to release my trust to me today. In four hours, we'll have money to throw at the problem."

"I'll finish this sandwich," I told him. I knew how much it had cost him to call his family. The only one he talked to was an older sister. "Then I'm going to sleep. Do you mind if I sleep here?"

"Well, not *here*," said Kyle, pulling away from me. He wiped his eyes and covered up the emotion with brisk efficiency. "But in a guest room. A bed will be helpful when you wake up and feel like you are going to feel after tonight. I'm going to hit the hot tub and join you in the same room."

He gave me an apologetic smile. "The security people say it's the only bedroom in the house that is really securable. They've swept the place for bugs, and we have our own army surrounding the house. Jim Gutstein tells me this will be gratis—Adam is apparently a very good boss, and they are embarrassed to have lost him. He also expressed his desire to find Adam and assures you that the full power of the company is currently turned in that direction. They will let us know when they find out a bit more."

"You hired Hauptman security?" I asked. Jim Gutstein was the highest-ranking non-werewolf at Adam's office.

"Only the best," he said.

I filled him in on everything I knew that he didn't until he tapped me on the shoulder to stop me.

"Finish your sandwich and go to sleep in a proper bed. After sleep, we can go buy guns, then tear the Tri-Cities apart looking for our men, right?"

Kyle was a smart man, and I followed his advice.

I smelled him first: the musk and mint that said werewolf, the other unique scent that said *mine*. I was so relieved. I'd been sure he was hurt and alone and I couldn't find him . . . but, silly me. Here he was, right beside me.

"Adam," I murmured.

The wolf stirred and put his nose on my shoulder. He was lying on top of me and making it hard to breathe under his weight. I vaguely knew it was a dream because Adam was both human and wolf at the same time, but Adam was more real than that thought, so I discarded it.

You are alive, he said, and there was a relief in his voice that shook me.

"Of course I am."

Something stirred the ant's nest, he said, nuzzling under my ear. *What did you do?*

I didn't want to think about it because then I knew I'd remember that this was just a dream, and I wanted to be safe in our bed with Adam stretched out half on top of me, touching me as I allowed no one else to touch me.

This was a dream where he was safe, and there were no men in body armor armed with nasty weapons who were backed by someone powerful enough to put pressure on the police. Not powerful enough to suborn them entirely, or they wouldn't have ridden to our rescue. But there was a lot of money involved and some raw power.

Figure out who they are, ordered Adam, pulling his head back so he could look me in the eye.

"Follow the money," I agreed, pulling him back down. I needed his warmth against me more than I needed to see him. My body believed better than my eyes, which knew I was looking at a figment of memory. "Kyle already suggested it. Now if I can just work out a way to do that." I could set Adam's associate Gutstein on that, couldn't I?

Gutstein can look. You were talking about the police. What have you been up to that the police were involved?

"When the bad guys took Warren, they took Kyle, too. Held him at his house."

Adam growled, and so did someone else. I couldn't see him or feel him, but my nose told me it was Warren.

"He's okay."

Adam stiffened, and that other wolf who was Warren snarled.

"I said okay, not terrific," I grumbled at them. "I wasn't lying.

He got beaten up—Stefan killed the one who did it, though Kyle has to claim credit for it. He handled it, Warren. He's smart and tough. He'll be waiting, so you'd better survive this."

The snarl died, and Adam and I were alone in our bed in the huge house that served as pack HQ and as our home.

"Ben and I helped Stefan," I murmured to Adam. "They had Kyle alone and were trying to get him to speculate where Jesse and I would be likely to show up. Stefan killed the one and tied up the other. Kyle called the police, and they swarmed the house and saved the day."

Jesse.

He didn't have to say anything more. In this dream of mine I heard his terror, his fierce burning protectiveness.

"She's safe," I promised him. "I hid her with Gabriel and set Tad to watch over her."

Adam's body stilled, the stillness in a hunt that occurs just before something dies. *Tad?*

Here in my dream, safe with it just between us, I could tell him. "Zee told me that Tad could keep Jesse safe." Not in those words, but that was what the grumpy old fae had meant. Truths that you can read between the lines in a fae who is your friend are as far from a lie as a fae can get.

Adam's body softened, turning warm and melting into mine, the distance between us blurring into nothing. *Then she is safe.*

His mouth sought mine. He tasted of heat and love. But he tasted also of illness born of silver, and I was crying before he was finished. They were killing him, I could feel it. Much more silver, and he would no longer be able to link with the pack and he would die while the bastards who had him were still waiting for signs of weakness.

His chest rose and fell, and his heart stuttered against mine. I could feel how close his death hovered—too much silver, too much of the drug that slowed his reflexes.

Jesse is safe. You are safe. It's all right, Mercy. You didn't think I was going to die of old age, did you?

It was a joke, graveyard humor. Werewolves never died of old age because they didn't age. But he had no business making a joke like that. Not now, not ever.

Anger roared through me and carried with it a tidal wave of terror because Adam had given up.

No. He told me. *I haven't given up anything. But the pack comes first. While they concentrate on me, the pack is working to free themselves. When I die, I can take the poison with me, and our pack will be strong enough to protect themselves. I love you, Mercy.*

I absorbed what he said. He'd found something he could do. I'd seen him draw upon the pack to force silver out of his body. Apparently it worked in reverse. He was drawing the silver from that damned concoction Doc Wallace's son had created. When he was finished, he'd be dead—but the pack would be free.

I couldn't breathe, couldn't respond. Adam intended to die.

Are you not my daughter, whispered another voice, Coyote's voice, so quiet I almost missed it. Had I not been caught in that first moment of shock when everything goes quiet before the pain begins, I would not have heard it.

Coyote never loses, Coyote told me. *Because I change the rules of the games my enemies play. What are the rules of your game?*

Adam hadn't heard that other voice. I knew because he still hovered over me, his mouth soft with our kiss, a terrible good-bye in his eyes. He'd found a solution to the game that his enemies played, found a way to win, because Adam was competent like that. The cost was too high.

"Find another way to win," I said, my voice hoarse.

There is no other way, he said. *I love you.*

But I'd been talking to myself and not to him. I pulled him back down to me.

He cooperated because he had no idea I was changing the rules of the game on him. I was not Coyote's daughter, not quite. But that was okay because being almost Coyote's daughter in my dream would be enough.

Adam's lips came down upon my own and I opened my mouth. Looking into his eyes, I pulled the things that were killing him into me, swallowing down the silver that was poison to him and nothing to me.

He didn't understand at first, but when he did, he struggled, but it was my dream, not his. In this dream, I wasn't a coyote shapeshifter trying to hold a werewolf, I was Coyote's almost daughter, and I had all the strength of the world in my arms.

"Mine," I told him, though my mouth was still fastened to his. "Mine."

I meant that he was mine, but also that the silver he took from the pack to save them was also mine to bear, not his. I also used the word to call the silver from his body into my own, the silver and the ketamine and all the rest of the harm that had been done to him.

But he was an Alpha werewolf, and he was more than a match for me, even in my dream.

He roared, ripped free of my hold and off of our bed—in my dreams it was still our bed at home, not the one in Kyle's spare bedroom. It wasn't anger in Adam's voice when he spoke. *Mercy, you don't know what you're doing.* It was fear.

I started to go after him, but had to stop, kneeling on the edge of the bed because I was sick to my stomach. Either the silver or the ketamine wasn't sitting well. Heck. Maybe it was the DMSO for all that I knew. Adam . . . he was better, I could feel his strength, could feel the pack stir in alertness because they could feel it, too.

Don't do that, he ordered retroactively, coming to his feet. He knew how well I followed orders. He looked away, took a deep breath, and reached out toward me. *If you die . . .*

I didn't think it would kill me, no matter how much my stomach hurt. But I wasn't going to show him that it had affected me. "Not my day to die," I told him.

He stared at me, and I lifted my chin and stared back at him. There wasn't a pack around who needed to see me bow down to the Alpha. He could have made me drop my gaze anyway. I wasn't immune to his dominance, just stubborn. I could see the moment he gave up.

I remembered that there were other things I needed to know.

"Did you find out where you are being held?" I asked, then, seeing the answer on his face, I continued, "Any clues at all? Do you smell anything? The river? Sagebrush? Diesel?"

Dust, Mercy. His voice was quiet. Then he looked around himself. I don't think he was seeing our bedroom like I was. *Dust and Peter's blood.*

I'd heard that kind of rage in Adam once before. He'd torn the corpse of a man I'd already killed into small pieces. The men who had made themselves our enemy had no idea what they had done.

They are sending a helicopter to pick up Darryl and me. Soon.

"They're still sending you out after the senator?" I thought that our call to the police would have preempted the attack.

Yes.

We'd told the police about why Adam and the pack had been taken. They seemed to be taking our word seriously.

They know. They told me it would be more difficult now, but they didn't seem to be really bothered. Either the attack itself is what they want—or there is something else I am not seeing.

He sat back down on the bed and put his hand against my forehead. *Are you okay?*

I smiled at him. "Ariana is going to see if she can contact Bran. Maybe he can ride to the rescue."

Adam considered that. *What about the vampires?* he asked.

I stared at him. "Marsilia hates me, and Ben bled all over the back of her Mercedes."

The AMG?

Something distracted me. Something terrible. "What is that smell?"

I woke up with Ben licking my face as earnestly as a cat—which hurt. His breath made my eyes water—and I have a high tolerance for nasty odors.

"Jeez, jeez," I said, scrambling away from him. I hit something hard, then kept moving away from Ben when whatever it was fell to the floor with a thump and freed up some space on the bed.

My stomach hurt. Not like the flu or even bad food. More like I'd swallowed something that was eating me alive. The truly vile smell of Ben's breath didn't help. "Ben, your breath stinks. Have you been eating roadkill?"

"Ow. Ow. Ow," moaned Kyle from the floor where I'd knocked him. I'd forgotten he was in the bed with me—that he'd told me he'd be sleeping here—because even getting myself into the bed was a blur. "Remember, a guy who didn't even have the decency to be cute hit me a lot yesterday. And this room doesn't have a rug."

Ben laughed at me, and I covered my nose with both hands. But I was awake now and remembered where I'd smelled breath that bad before. "DMSO from the tranq, right? DMSO gives you bad breath." Then I saw the clock on the chest next to the bed.

"What time is it?" I asked, hopping out of the bed and stumbling over Kyle's feet. The room was dark, but there were no windows. The darkness reminded me that Adam had suggested going to the vampires. Maybe I ought to. But there was something . . . Tad. Oh holy wow, I'd forgotten about Tad. I'd told him that I'd get right back to Sylvia's as soon as I made sure Kyle was okay. If it was really dark outside, he'd been watching them for a whole day, expecting me to return soon.

I took a step toward the door, which was a mistake. Every muscle hurt, my face throbbed, and I almost blacked out from the sudden way my body informed me that it wasn't happy with me. My stomach, then the rest of my muscles, seized in the worst charley horse I'd ever had.

"Mercy?" asked Kyle, rolling onto his feet with a little less than his usual grace.

Ben whined.

And I threw up silver goo all over the beautiful stone floor of Kyle's guest room.

5

I stared at the floor—and Kyle did the same. Ben jumped off the bed and put his nose near the mess. He backed away quickly, his ears came up, and he looked at me. The expression on the wolf's face quite clearly said, "What the hell?" even if I hadn't been familiar with reading expressions on monster-sized wolf faces.

Kyle's floor was covered with silver. I licked my hand and looked at the result. My palm was gray where the saliva touched it. "I think," I told them, torn between triumph—because all that silver on the floor meant it wasn't in Adam—and terror. Having that place where Adam and I touched be something that I could drag something as physical as silver through was terrifying in its implications. "I think I'd better wash this off."

There was a bath attached to the guest room, and I staggered into it, washing out my mouth and scrubbing wherever the silver had touched. Kyle opened the sink cabinet and handed me a new toothbrush and one of those little travel toothpastes. I used it, twice. My lips were still black, like one of those thirteen-year-old goth girls who wore black lipstick.

"I used to know a couple of guys who painted their lips with silver nitrate to turn them that color," Kyle said. "I thought it was pretty stupid. Your lips weren't black when you went to sleep. What happened?"

"I'm afraid to guess," I said. Silver nitrate sounded familiar. I was pretty sure that was what Gerry Wallace had used in his tranquilizer concoction. "Give me a few minutes, and I might have something worked up that sounds vaguely coherent, okay?"

He looked worried but nodded. I looked in the mirror again and touched my lips. They felt just like they usually did. I grabbed a towel and went out to clean up the mess, but stopped when I got to it. The silver sludge was thickening. What if the towel stuck to it and made a bigger mess? And there was a lot of the stuff, more than I'd thought. If all of this had come from Adam, he should have been dead.

"Well," I said. "What do I do with this?"

"What? Never vomit on a floor before?" Kyle asked conversationally as he perched on the side of the bed. "Or never vomit silver?"

Ben, sitting far enough away from the mess that there was no chance he'd touch it, stared at me. He leaned toward me and sniffed before settling back, his eyes intent.

I lifted my arm and smelled it, smelled Adam on it. I suppose if I could suck silver through the mate bond, it made sense that Adam's scent could follow me, too.

"It's magic," I told them, and Kyle rolled his eyes.

"Look." I was speaking as much to myself as to him and Ben. "This shouldn't have worked. You can't do *this*." I waved at the mess. "*I* shouldn't have been able to do this. Pack magic, mating magic means that I can talk to Adam sometimes when we aren't near each other. It doesn't mean that I can suck the silver out of his body and bring it back with me." I looked at the mess again. "And if there had been this much silver in his body, he'd be dead—and look like the Tin Man."

Kyle blinked. I don't think I've ever seen him quite so . . . neutral.

"You can talk to Adam when he's not in the room, and you don't have a phone?" he asked.

I nodded.

He closed his eyes, and I could read his expression when he opened them again. "Thank you, dear Lord," he said with relief. "I thought I was going crazy."

In spite of everything, I couldn't help but grin.

"Warren's a little nervous about how much werewolf stuff you can absorb without running for the hills," I said half-apologetically.

He narrowed his eyes. "Warren doesn't get to keep me in the dark." Then the temper faded out of his face. "I'd put up with all sorts of werewolf shit if it meant he was back here and safe." His words were raw, and I felt them on my skin because I knew exactly what he meant.

"Yeah," I agreed with feeling. "But the silver? I think that was more about what *I* am than any weird werewolf magic."

"Being Native American made you toss up silver?" asked Kyle skeptically, but Ben gave me a look of sudden comprehension. The pack knew about Coyote.

The mess on the floor was definitely becoming solid. I was pretty sure it wasn't going to come off with a little soap and elbow grease—and heard Coyote laugh in my ear. A silver dollar, when they were still silver, was a troy ounce of .90 pure silver. I have a host of trivia in my head.

"How many troy ounces in a pound?" I asked because that wasn't some of the trivia I knew.

"I don't know," said Kyle soberly. "That looks like a lot of troy ounces to me."

Coyote magic, I thought, breaks rules. I looked at Kyle and decided that he could be trusted, just like the rest of the pack. "It's not Indian magic—or not just Indian magic anyway. It's Coyote magic."

"Coyote?" asked Kyle. "Are you talking about your other form or *the* Coyote?"

Ben just narrowed his gaze.

"My father was a Blackfeet bull rider from Browning, Montana, named Joe Old Coyote," I told Kyle. "But before he was Joe Old Coyote, he was the Coyote of song and story. After Joe Old Coyote died in a car wreck, he was Coyote again."

I understand from people who have seen him in court that Kyle is mostly unflappable until he chooses to be otherwise. Being in love with a werewolf had raised his ability to nearly supernatural levels.

He didn't blink, didn't pause, just said, "So the silver slime is because you are Coyote's daughter?"

"I'm not *Coyote's* daughter," I said firmly. I glanced at the floor. "And it's not slime, anymore. Joe Old Coyote *wasn't* Coyote." Because if he had been, my father hadn't just died, he had abandoned me, abandoned my mother, and I would have to hunt him down and hurt him.

"Okay," Kyle said. "You're rambling." He reached out and touched me. "Are you okay? You look flushed, but you're cold."

As he spoke, a shiver rolled up my spine. I crouched down and held my hand over the silver slab that covered a couple of squares of stone tile.

"That is the freakiest thing that ever happened to me." I nodded toward the mess. "And if you knew my life, you'd realize just how freaky that is. While I was sleeping, I drank the silver out of Adam, woke up, and threw it up on your floor—sorry for that, by the way—and now my lips are black."

Kyle took in a breath. "While you were doing *freaky* stuff with Adam—as fine as he is—did you figure out *where* he is?"

I shook my head, and he sighed. "That's good."

I raised my eyebrow. He grinned, tiredly. "That would have been useful, Mercy. And having something *freaky* and *useful* would have been too good and sent the spirits of evil gods on our tail."

I stared at him.

His grin grew less tired. "You might have been raised by werewolves, Mercy, but I was raised by a Scottish granny while my parents were out earning their millions. When the fae came out, she just harrumpfed, and said, 'There'll be trouble now.' And she was right about it, just as every doom-filled prediction she ever made was right."

I let myself fall down onto my butt because my knee was remembering I'd been in a car accident, and it had had enough of my kneeling. Ben steadied me briefly, then jerked away.

"Thanks," I told Kyle. "I'll keep the wrath of the dark gods in mind. Any more cheery thoughts?"

"Not until Warren is standing right here chipping up the mess you made," he said soberly.

I reached over and wrapped my hand around his ankle to comfort him just as the doorbell rang.

"What time is it?" I asked.

Kyle glanced at the watch on his wrist. "Too early for company. Four thirty in the morning."

His cell rang, and he picked it up.

"Mr. Brooks. There are two men on your doorstep. A white male, mid-forties, about six feet tall, in better than average shape who looks very comfortable in the suit he's wearing and extremely uncomfortable about his companion. The second man is shorter, younger, mixed-race, and in very good shape. Might mean he likes to work out—might mean he's a werewolf. Do you want us to intercept and send them away?"

"No," said Kyle. "We have backup in the house, right?"

"That's right, sir. And someone watching the porch."

"Then let me go see if these are allies or enemies. I'll give you a peace sign if they're okay."

Kyle hung up and changed his clothes to slacks and a polo he had folded up on the lone chest of drawers in the room. I had the choice of wearing his clothes that I wore all yesterday, or mine that I had worn the day and night before. Since the latter were still bloodstained, I pulled on his sweats, their pleasant teal color doing a fine job of emphasizing the bruises on my skin, and followed him down the stairs, Ben at our heels like a well-behaved guard wolf. He wasn't limping—which made one of us—so he must finally have started healing.

As soon as we were on the stairs, the doorbell quit ringing. Either they had given up, or they could hear us on the carpeted stairs through the door.

Ben and I hung back as Kyle opened the door to a pair of men, one of them unsurprisingly around six feet tall wearing a black wool coat that emphasized rather than concealed the expensive fit of the dark gray suit he wore. His face was slightly homely in the likeable way of a good character actor.

Next to him was a smaller man who looked vaguely Middle Eastern but darker-skinned. He wore jeans, scuffed hiking boots, and a long-sleeved gray silk button-up shirt. It was cold enough to bite, but he had no coat or jacket.

"What brings you to my door at this time of the morning?" Kyle asked shortly.

"Kyle Brooks?" said the taller man. "My name is Lin Armstrong. Agent Armstrong. I work for CNTRP—Cantrip, if you prefer—and I was wondering if you would mind if I and my associate come in to ask you a few questions about the men who broke into your house yesterday."

I sucked in my breath—Cantrip was the agency I suspected our villains belonged to. I don't know what I would have said except that when I inhaled, I caught their scents. I could smell dry cleaning fluid, wool, and some dog breed that clung to the complex scent of Agent Armstrong. I also smelled an unfamiliar werewolf.

Ben's posture changed. His ears flattened, and he crouched a little, but slid between me and the door anyway.

"What pack are you from?" I asked, stepping around Ben, so I stood next to Kyle. "Excuse me?" said Agent Armstrong.

But the other man, he smiled, a wicked white smile in his dark face. "What pack do you think I belong to, Ms. Thompson?" He had an accent: Spanish, but not the same Spanish as most of the people I knew who spoke Spanish as a first language in the Tri-Cities.

I frowned at him. "Hauptman. It's Ms. Hauptman. Who are you?"

"*Charles Smith* asked if I would come up here and find out why he couldn't contact anyone here when he tried," the werewolf said, emphasizing the name because he lied when he said it. I knew who he meant anyway. The Marrok's son Charles had recently worked with the FBI under the last name of Smith.

This wolf had just told us a number of things. First, he had been sent here by the Marrok—Ariana must have reached him. Second, he and Armstrong were not closely associated—otherwise, he would not have lied to him. He had not, however, answered my question, which made me think that it might be important to know.

"I asked," Armstrong said, "through channels if I might be able to grab a werewolf to work as a . . . liaison. Since I believe that it is a group of rebel Cantrip agents who are responsible for your recent—" He looked stuck for the proper word.

"Problems," supplied the strange wolf. I knew most of the Marrok's pack—having grown up in it. I had no idea who he was.

I didn't say anything because I didn't know what to say. Packs changed over the years—people move. The Marrok's pack tended to gain problematic wolves who couldn't function in a normal pack. This wolf's body language told me that he was dangerous, that he spent a lot of time on the edge of violence, that his wolf was very close to the surface.

The wolf in human-seeming spoke into my silence. "When word came to Charles to see if there was someone who could . . . play ambassador with you and Mr. Brooks, I was already on my way, sent here by the whispers of the fairies." He paused, and . . . preened a little, as if he enjoyed being the center of attention, then looked at Kyle. "Mr. Brooks, it is rather cold out here. Would you mind calling off the gentleman who is aiming at us from your neighbor's roof and letting us in?"

"Who *are* you?" I asked the werewolf, again.

He smiled again, though his eyes were cool. "Asil, Ms. Hauptman. You might also know me as the Moor, though I find the title overly dramatic and wouldn't have mentioned it, but that you would find it, perhaps, a little more recognizable."

I gripped Kyle's arm a little more tightly. I knew who the Moor was. The Moor was a scary, scary wolf who I'd thought was merely a story, like the Beast of Gévaudan.

"It's okay, Kyle," I said, hoping I was right. "Asil is one of Charles's wolves." Kyle would understand I meant the Marrok.

Asil smiled because he heard the lie in my first sentence. Maybe Kyle did, too, because he gave me a sharp look before he waved at the security team with the two-finger salute immortalized by President Nixon before either of us was born.

"I am not at liberty to tell you anything," Armstrong half apologized as he sipped his coffee. He glanced from my face to Kyle's, taking in the spectacular bruising Kyle was sporting and my own, more modest bruise—which started at my jaw and hit the top of my hairline. Kyle looked like he'd gone into a boxing match with his hands tied behind his back—which is sort of what he'd done.

Armstrong grimaced. "I know it's not fair. But I have to operate by my superior's orders."

We were sitting in a room I'd actually never been in before. It was decorated in cool tones and was in the basement, with only a small window. Presumably it was one of the rooms that Adam's security team had deemed safe—or else Kyle had some other reason to drag us down to a room that smelled of carpet shampoo and the lady who cleaned his house, with no hint of either Kyle or Warren.

"Don't tell me," Kyle said sourly. "A group of Cantrip agents who were unhappy with the limited power given them to combat the scary werewolves and suddenly scarier fae decided to go off on their own. Someone decided that they needed a really big event to turn the tide of public opinion in their favor—and they decided the murder of a popular anti-fae senator would be the torch they could use to inflame the public and get, at last, the right to shoot werewolves and fae on sight. They failed when Mercy, Ben, and I managed to call the police on them, and you've been sent to fix the situation however you can while also finding out where they got the money to hire a private army. How am I doing?"

For a moment, Armstrong's friendly face wasn't so friendly. The Moor smiled and lifted his own cup to his lips. If I wasn't looking at his eyes, he appeared too young, too urbane to be responsible for the violence he was famous for. He caught me looking, and I looked away—but not before I saw his pleased smile.

"Don't patronize us," Kyle said softly, his attention on Armstrong. "You need us to find your people before they do something even stupider. I'm not sure we need you at all."

"Your cooperation will be noted," Armstrong said. "That might become important for you if Bennet succeeds in making a bloodbath here that he can blame the werewolves for."

"Who is Bennet?" I asked, and Armstrong pursed his lips.

"Ah, excuse me," he said. "Let us instead say, 'our rogue agent' who is apparently responsible for recruiting other dissatisfied agents." The slip of his tongue that gave away Bennet's name seemed purposeful because he wasn't very upset. "It is imperative that we stop him, and you can help by telling me anything you know about how Hauptman and his pack were taken. Anything about the men who held you here. Anything might be useful. In return, I assure you that we will turn our resources to locating and rescuing your people."

He was sincere and truthful, which surprised me somehow. I'd expected him to lie his head off.

"We are on the same side," Armstrong said earnestly, and he believed that, too—I could hear it in his voice.

"Those men who broke into your house are all dead, Mr. Brooks," Asil said quietly—and Armstrong jerked his head around so fast it was a wonder he didn't kink his neck. He wasn't so much surprised about the dead men, I thought, but that Asil knew about their deaths.

I wondered if Asil had killed them himself.

The werewolf caught my expression and smiled, showing his teeth. "Not me. I was not sent here merely as a liaison, Ms. Hauptman, but as a useful tool in your arsenal. They were released on bail last night. Because they were scheduled to fly to Seattle, then off to South America by private charter, I thought it would be expeditious to talk to them before they left. But they were dead when I went to the hotel they had checked into, and I nearly interrupted a federal cleanup of the site." He smiled toothily, and I understood that the cleanup was of the sort meant to keep the men's deaths from the local police as well as the public.

If he knew all that, Charles had been busy, because he was more current than Ariana had been when she left. Armstrong was watching him with sudden wariness. Apparently he hadn't known how much Asil knew.

"Did *you* kill them, Agent Armstrong?" I asked. Most people didn't know that werewolves could hear lies, and those who did thought I was human.

"No, ma'am. But my people were responsible for the cleanup. There was an anonymous call to my superiors." He grimaced. "I've spent most of the last twenty-four hours playing cleanup, catch-up—and all sorts of other things that end in -up when things go to hell."

Asil nodded at me. Like me, he'd heard the truth in the agent's voice. Armstrong had not killed them and "unhappy" was a very small word for what he was feeling about their deaths and the involvement of Cantrip agents in the whole thing. My nose could sense more than just lies. Emotions, especially strong emotions, have scents, too.

"You told the police that they wanted your husband to go after Senator Campbell, Ms. Hauptman," Armstrong said.

I lifted my chin. "That's right."

He shook his head. "Doesn't scan. These guys were the real deal, Ms. Hauptman. They make a lot of money by not shooting their mouths off. There is no way that they told you that."

Asil met my eyes. He knew how I got my information. He tilted his head a little and gave a shrug.

He was the dominant wolf in the room. If he didn't care what I told a federal agent about how werewolf magic works, maybe I shouldn't, either.

I opened my mouth, then closed it again, visions of being locked up in a white room somewhere with someone asking, "What is Adam looking at, Ms. Hauptman? Is it a triangle or a square?" in my head. It was probably the result of too much *Mystery Science Theater 3000* at a young age, but there was also a real danger in telling people too much.

"You know how you told us that there were things you couldn't tell us?" I said. "It's like that. There are things I cannot reveal to you at this time. Need-to-know things."

Armstrong grunted, but he could hardly complain. "On a scale of one to ten, how sure are you that the threat was aimed at Campbell?"

"Zero," I told him, because I'd thought long and hard about this. "The threat was aimed at the werewolves. Campbell might be a secondary target—or maybe he was scheduled to be miraculously saved at the last moment. It's easy to thwart an assassination when you know the who, where, and when. I don't know why they picked Adam."

"He's become a public figure," murmured Asil. "People like him, and they trust him. When newspapers and magazines want to talk to a werewolf, they try for Adam because he's pretty and well-spoken. Three-quarters of the people interviewed on the streets of New York for a recent morning news story could pick Hauptman out of a lineup. Better than either of the last presidential candidates or the mayor of New York did."

"You think this was aimed at Adam specifically?" I asked.

Asil frowned at me. Maybe we weren't supposed to be talking in front of Agent Armstrong. "I think," he said slowly, "that we don't know enough."

"And our enemies know too much," I said. "They knew all of the pack—and there are a number of our members who aren't out. They came looking for Jesse and me. Where did they get their information?"

"Jesse?" Armstrong asked.

"Adam's daughter," I said. "She's not a werewolf. We'd gone out shopping, had a car wreck, and ended up at my garage, where Ben had come to tell us that the pack had been taken."

"Ben?"

I tipped my empty cup toward the werewolf stretched out on the floor near me, but not touching. Ben was pointedly not looking at Asil—though he was still keeping his body between us. "This is Ben. He was upstairs when the rent-an-army broke into our house and took out most of the pack in one fell swoop. He managed to get away and warn me."

There was a funny pause, and I looked up.

"I thought." Armstrong swallowed. "I thought that he was just a big dog. I like dogs."

I looked at Asil, then back at Armstrong. "You *do* know that Asil is a werewolf, too?"

The fed rubbed his face. "I'm too old for this. I've been up for twenty-four hours."

"Ben won't hurt you," I told him, just as Asil got up to put his empty cup on the low table between the chairs. Ben surged to his feet, growling—but with his head tilted so he didn't meet the more dominant wolf's eyes. Armstrong spilled his coffee, jerking away. The sudden move attracted Ben's attention, and he showed his fangs to the Cantrip agent.

"Armstrong, drop your eyes." Kyle's voice was calm and easy.

I reached for Ben's ruff, but as soon as my fingers got close, he slid away from my hand.

"It's my fault. We need to get this over with before someone gets hurt." Asil finished setting his cup down and looked at Ben, though he spoke to the rest of the room. "You will have to excuse us while this wolf and I have a talk." He reached down and snapped his fingers in front of Ben's face. "Come with me."

I stepped between them. Ben couldn't put himself between us again without knocking me over—so he nipped me on the back of my knee. A very quick nip, not enough to hurt, just a protest.

Asil tilted his head and smiled. "I do like you, Ms. Hauptman. You are not exactly what I expected, but I like you. By all means, come with us."

"What exactly are you going to settle?" asked Kyle, sounding a little hostile.

Asil examined him for a moment. "I won't hurt him, Mr. Brooks, but Ben is trying to protect Ms. Hauptman from me. There is no need, but he has to decide that himself. It will be a lot easier on him if we do this without an audience."

"It's okay," I told Kyle. "It's a good idea if we are likely to spend much time in each other's company." And I could question Asil without Agent Armstrong listening in—and he could question me.

"Guest room," suggested Kyle. "The one we were sleeping in. Apparently this house is low in rooms that are really possible to secure. Otherwise, you'll have to make do with a bathroom. Agent Armstrong and I can wait here."

I waved and took the lead out the door and up the stairs. Ben followed me as close as he could get without touching me, leaving Asil trailing behind us.

"Kyle Brooks is mated to your third," Asil said, as we hiked up the stairs, his voice thoughtful. "He is a lawyer. He was tied up and being tortured by a pair of professionals, and he managed to get himself loose and break one man's neck and knock out the other without killing him. Such an enterprising and ambitious thing for a human lawyer to do to a pair of men who make their livelihood from killing people. How wonderful that he managed it."

"Kyle Brooks has a black belt," I said very quietly. "He's in good shape and was rescued by a vampire friend of mine who killed the man who hurt Kyle and let the other live because I asked him not to kill everyone in sight."

There was silence on the stairs behind Ben and me.

"I believe I misheard," said Asil, who'd stopped on the stairs. "English is not my first, nor even my fifth, language. Did you say 'a vampire friend'?"

"I did." I half turned to look at him as I stopped, too.

"The world," he said, "is a very strange place, and just when I thought I'd witnessed all the wonders it had to teach—here is another one. This 'vampire friend' of yours did it for a price?"

"He did it because he is my friend and Kyle's friend," I said.

"Impossible."

There was something in his voice that sent Ben surging up against my legs, which wasn't so bad—but then he bounced away like a ping-pong ball, and I almost lost my balance because I'd braced for his impact. I did lose my temper.

"Maybe for you," I snapped at Asil, turning to finish the last four-or-five-stair climb to the second floor. "Me? I have friends."

There was another of those speaking silences, then he laughed. "Please tell me I won't end up with eggs in my pillowcase or peanut butter on my car seat."

I threw up my hands involuntarily and turned to him to face him again. Walking backward, I said, "I was twelve. Don't you wolves have anything better to gossip about than things that happened twenty years ago?"

"Mi princesa," he told me, his voice deep and flirty, "I was in *Spain* and I heard about the peanut butter. Two decades are nothing, I assure you—we will speak of it a hundred years from now in hushed voices. There are big bad wolves all over the world who

tremble at the sound of his name, yet a little puny coyote girl peanut-buttered the seat of Bran Cornick's car because he told her that she should wear a dress to perform for the pack."

"No," I said, getting hot about it again. I turned and stalked down the hall. "He said Evelyn—my foster mother—should know better, that she should have made sure I had a dress to wear. He made her cry." And that was the last time I consented to play the piano.

I opened the guest room door, and Asil paused until I looked at his face. "Yes," he said sincerely. "Such a one deserves peanut butter on the seat of his pants."

And that sincerity was the last straw. I put my hand over my mouth and leaned against the door and laughed. I was worried, tired, and it felt like every muscle in my body ached—and all I could see was the peanut butter on the back of the Marrok's elegant beige slacks and the expression on his face when he realized what had happened. I'd been hiding under bushes in my coyote shape downwind and everything—but he'd seen me anyway. Bran could always find me wherever I was hiding. He'd raised an eyebrow at me, and I'd run all the way home.

"He always knew when it was me," I said when I could speak.

Asil smiled; it was a warm and friendly smile. "He told me that gave you sorrow. You would scheme and plan so no one would know—and never realized that he didn't even have to investigate such an incident. 'Who else could it be?' he told me when I called him to . . . discuss the incident. 'Can you imagine any of the pack putting peanut butter on the seat of my car to teach me a lesson?'"

"Huh." Such simple logic had been beyond me—and it just seemed right and proper that the Marrok would know everything, like Santa Claus with big sharp teeth. "He made me clean the whole car. It was worth it, though. He apologized to Evelyn, brought her flowers, too."

"He apologized," Asil said slowly, and I laughed, again, because Asil said it like he was storing up information to use to torment Bran.

"I needed that." I waved him into the room. "Thank you."

He glanced around the bedroom and took in the unmade bed and, his eyebrow rising ever higher, the puddle of now-solid silver on the floor. Then he said, "One thing I have always wondered is how Bran did not notice the smell of peanut butter on his so-expensive car's lovely brown leather upholstery."

"I made a peanut butter and jelly sandwich. I put it on a paper plate with a little note that said, 'For the Marrok,' and set that on the dash of the passenger seat," I told him. "He was so busy looking at it that he didn't notice the seat until it was too late." I looked at the silver on Kyle's floor, too. They were probably going to have to replace the stone tile under it. "The eggs, though," I continued absently. "The eggs were a failure. They don't break when you want them to—the pillow cushions them too much, and they leave your victim with ammunition to use against you."

"Mercedes, tell me—" Asil walked around the end of the bed, which brought him closer to me, and Ben growled.

Asil stopped where he was. "Very well. Let's release your wolf from his predicament before we say those things that cannot be said in front of the government man." He looked at me and pointed back at the door. "Go stand in the hall so we avoid the situation where he is torn between what his instincts say and his need to protect you."

It sounded okay, so I did it, standing in the doorway so I could keep my eyes on them. That left Ben and about ten feet between me and Asil. Had he meant me any harm, the distance wasn't enough, but because he did not, it was enough to assuage Ben's need to see me safe.

Asil put his hand on Ben's nose and pushed down until the red werewolf's head was all the way on the floor. Ben gave a half groan, half growl.

"I pledge to you," Asil said, meeting Ben's eyes, "that I mean you and yours no harm. I recognize that you belong to Adam Hauptman, and I have no need for you to belong to me. I am an ally while Adam cannot be here, standing in for the Marrok, who has sent me to serve in his stead as lord over all the wolves as we are all his vassals. Do you accept me as such?"

Ben pulled his nose out from under Asil's hand and stood up without crouching for the first time since he'd laid eyes on the other wolf. His tail and ears were up for a moment until he deliberately ducked his head and dropped his tail to a more neutral position.

Asil smiled at him. "Good. We understand each other. Now Mercedes Thompson *de* Hauptman, I need you to tell me exactly what has happened and what you know. Quickly, please, we haven't much time."

So I told him everything I knew.

When I was done, he got up off the bed where he'd been sitting and looked at the metal on the floor again. It had lost its bright color while we were talking, and now had a faint patina of black.

"How is your stomach feeling now?" he asked after a moment.

"Raw," I admitted. "But it's been that way since I wrecked my car and Adam and our pack were taken. I have no idea if it is from the silver or not."

Asil crouched on his heels in silence of thought, and I considered reminding him that he'd been in a hurry. At last he said, "You are certain that Peter is the only fatality?"

"So far," I said.

"I find that very interesting in light of the murders of your attackers." His eyes were bright and merry as he looked at me. Apparently, murders were good fun. "The one who killed the hired men would not bother keeping all of the pack alive. Such a man would say, 'One werewolf is enough to keep Adam on the hook, and this many hostages are expensive and dangerous to keep.' Which would be right. They were bloody stupid to take down a whole pack—any commander who ever had charge of a host of enemy soldiers would have been happy to explain it to them." He lost himself for a moment, presumably in happy contemplation of the troubles our enemies had gotten themselves into.

"Two different people?" I said.

Asil nodded. "So it seems to me. Moreover, a man who knew to hire these men, a man they would work for, would not have killed these mercenaries out of fear of what they know. These are very well-trained, sought-after mercenaries often hired by governments friendly to the US, Charles tells me. The kind of men who stay bought and don't take kindly to being betrayed."

"The Cantrip agents had the contacts but not the money to hire them," I said slowly. "Federal agents are well paid—but not that well paid."

"Can you contact Adam right now?"

"I can try."

"Please do so. We need to let him know what we know—and see if there is any new information he can offer us about his location or the people who have taken him."

I sat down on the floor and closed my eyes—reached down the

rough golden rope that tied my mate and I together and—"Ow, ow, ow," I said, my eyes watering. "Owie, owie, owie. Damn. Damn."

Asil looked from me to the silver on the floor. "That will teach you not to use your bonds for things they were never intended," he told me. "Especially not silver. Werewolves and silver do not mix."

"Shut up," I said fiercely and very quietly because the sound of his voice sent sharp, arcing lightning rods of pain from my eyes all the way through my skull.

"That is quite a lot of silver," he observed. Then, sounding intrigued, he said, "And it is pure silver, though the substance that the tranquilizer dart uses is silver nitrate—which is a white powder."

Asil got up and moved around. Ben came close—I could smell him—but he didn't get close enough to touch. Werewolves are different when they are in their wolf shape, less human and less caught up in human manners. It would be wrong. But wolves are gregarious, far more so than humans or coyotes, for that matter. Normally, Ben would be pressing against me if I was in distress. Asil must still have been worrying him.

When my head quit feeling quite so breakable, I looked up—and Asil handed me a glass of water from the bathroom. I drank the whole thing and felt better.

"Don't worry," he told me when I handed him the empty glass. "I expect the effect is temporary. It'll probably go away once the silver is out of your system entirely." He touched my lips, a light, quick touch that didn't allow me time to react.

He showed me his fingertips—which were red, as if he'd put his fingers in a flame. I touched my lips, too, remembering how black they were.

"They used to use colloidal silver in nose drops for people with asthma or bad allergies," he told me. "People who used them regularly sometimes had their skin turn blue—there is a man who ran for the Montana Senate who is blue-skinned. I thought your lips were from lipstick—though you are a little older than most of the young ladies wearing black makeup."

I stared at him in horror. "It won't go away," I told him. "I'm not a werewolf, my body won't reject silver the same way yours does." Gabriel's little sister, Rosa, had done a report in school about a girl whose skin had turned gray when she was a teenager back in the fifties and nothing anyone had tried had made any improvement. I'd proofread it for her.

I scrambled to my feet and went into the bathroom to look at the mirror again. I took a washcloth and scrubbed at my lips, but they stayed black.

Asil didn't follow me into the bathroom, but he stood at the door.

"You told Armstrong that you think this was aimed at the werewolves."

"Don't you?" I asked.

Asil shook his head. "It doesn't matter what I think. Let's look at the world through their eyes a moment. If Adam did exactly as they asked him to, what would be the result?"

"They kill the pack anyway—can't have witnesses. They'd kill Adam, so he doesn't kill them. The senator's dead or wounded by werewolves. The people who think the only good werewolf is a dead werewolf would have more power." I ticked them off on my fingers, then said, "Kyle and I, Adam and I, and just I have gone through this a hundred times."

"Okay," Asil said. "The rogue Cantrip agents like the last part, the one that lets them go hunting werewolves. Maybe they like the dead senator part, too. Campbell has been standing between them and their kill-'em-all hunting license for a long time. But who is after Adam or the pack? You think they are the ones this is aimed at—so who benefits?"

"Shouldn't we do this part downstairs?" I asked, my throat tight. I didn't want to go over and over how much danger Adam and the pack were in—I knew. "We were discussing this with Armstrong."

Asil shook his head. "What happens if Adam and the pack are gone?"

I bared my teeth at him. "I go out for revenge—I don't do peanut butter much anymore. But if they aren't afraid of the pack, they aren't going to be afraid of me. Bran is scarier—but they probably don't know about Bran."

"Maybe they do," said Asil. "Maybe they're after Bran."

"They knew about Gerry Wallace's silver/DMSO/ketamine cocktail," I conceded. "They knew every wolf in the pack. Maybe they do know about Bran."

"Mercy?" Kyle called up from the floor below. "Are you through telling the werewolf all the things we mere mortals shouldn't know, yet? I'm making breakfast, and the sun's coming up."

"What were you planning on doing next before Agent Armstrong and I arrived?" asked Asil.

"I was going to go to get Adam's people, the ones who work for his company, to see if they can figure out where the money is coming from. See if they can tell if it is government money or private. I was going to the vampires to see if they knew anything about where someone might be holding a pack of werewolves—they run this town's supernaturals like the mob ran Chicago back in the day." There was something else. Something I was supposed to be remembering. "Damn it," I said, diving for my dirty, bloody jeans. "Tad. Damn it."

I pulled out Gabriel's sister's phone and saw that I'd missed calls—and had twenty new text messages. There were fifteen calls exactly one half hour apart from a number I didn't know. I didn't bother to read the text messages, just dialed the strange number. Tad answered.

"So," he said grumpily without waiting for me to say anything. "I take it you're dead? Because, otherwise, there is no excuse for guilting me into sitting outside in winter watching the most boring family on earth for more than a whole day. They started sending out the kids with cocoa yesterday about two in the afternoon. Dinner was homemade burritos with Spanish rice and refried beans—and almost good enough to forgive you for making me think you might be dead."

"How did they know you were there?" I asked.

"I knocked on the door to use the bathroom. Figured it was safer than leaving them to be slaughtered by enemy government agents while I went out to find the nearest gas station." There was a pause. "You all right?"

"No," I told him honestly, closing my eyes. "Not at all. Adam's still gone. They had a few men here at Kyle's—"

"That's Warren's boyfriend, right?"

"Right. Anyway Ben, I, and Stefan—mostly Stefan—got Kyle out of their clutches but spent the day at the police department answering questions."

"Good for Stefan."

I rubbed my eyes and thought. "I think the best thing to do might be to grab Gabriel and Jesse and bring them back here.

There are police keeping an eye out on Kyle's house, and Adam's team is running security." I looked at Asil, and asked—"Are you planning on staying here with us?"

He nodded. "Until Adam is found, yes."

"Okay, did you hear that, Tad? I have one of Bran's wolves here to help out, too."

"I don't have a car," Tad told me. "I hiked over. You'll have to come get them yourself."

"No worries. I'll be over in about fifteen minutes." I opened my mouth to ask if he would consider helping us further but closed it again because he'd been standing guard all day.

"If Kyle has an extra bed in his mansion," Tad said, "I'll catch a few winks of sleep there, and I'll help you until this is finished." He paused, too. "I'm sorry I've been a jerk. Life hasn't been a bed of roses lately, but I don't have to take it out on you."

"Sure you do," I told him. "Who else would listen to it? I'll be over as soon as I can."

I clicked the phone off.

"I'll come with you," Asil said. "They know where you are—which makes you the shiniest target."

"Fine," I said. "If we leave Ben here, there will be room in Marsilia's car."

Asil looked at me. "Your vampire friend is Marsilia? Mistress of the Tri-Cities' seethe?"

I snorted. "Don't be silly. Marsilia hates me and would love to see me rot in Hell. I stole her car so that the bad guys couldn't find me—and because I wrecked my car. Ben's already bled all over her Mercedes, though, so a few more miles on the odometer won't make her any madder." I caught sight of Ben. He was watching me intently and told me as clearly as he could without words that he didn't intend to be left behind.

"You need to change back," I told him. "You've been shot and dragged all over the place, and you've been wolf for nearly two days. Time to change back and rest up. All I'm doing is picking up Jesse and Gabriel and coming back here. Bran sent Asil over to be useful, so he will be and, unless I'm much mistaken, we'll also have an escort of Adam's finest trained professionals to make sure I make it back safely."

"I'll keep her safe," Asil told Ben solemnly.

"Besides," I said, "I'd like to leave Kyle with some real backup in case something happens."

It was the truth—and that one worked. Ben liked Kyle—and Ben didn't like very many people.

6

ADAM

Fear was a familiar friend. Adam sometimes thought that he'd been afraid since he'd stepped on the bus that took him to basic training all those years ago. And the older he got, the more he had to fear. Right now, he was afraid for Mercy, who didn't have the sense to be afraid for herself.

When he'd been a boy, he'd thought that if you were just strong enough, tough enough there wouldn't be anything to be afraid of—except for God, of course. His parents had been small farmers, patriots, and devout Baptist God-fearing Christians and raised him to be the same. But their best efforts had met the world, and, mostly, the world had won.

He'd left the farm first, and Vietnam had done its best to scour him of his patriotism. It hadn't succeeded entirely, though he reserved the right to think most elected officials could do with a little jail time to mend their ways. Vietnam had also taught him that the tougher and smarter you got, the more afraid you learned to be. It had also taught him that there were monsters in the world—and he had become one of them.

Then he'd come back home and found out that war didn't cause fear—love did. He loved Mercy with a fierceness that still surprised him.

Adam took a deep breath, and it didn't hurt. Silver didn't burn in his joints and dull his senses anymore. He tested his body, just to be sure. Someone watching would only see that he continued to sit with his back to the wall of the cold stone room where the pack had been imprisoned. He tightened and released muscle groups that responded with their usual quickness and force.

He didn't understand what Mercy had done. No, that wasn't quite true—she'd taken the silver poisoning his body into herself. He understood that was how the pack bonds worked for her, that she saw things in symbols and pictures while he smelled things. Samuel had once told him that he and Bran both heard music. What he didn't understand was how she'd used the pack bonds and magic to do the impossible.

And what really scared him was that he was fairly certain that Mercy hadn't known what she was doing, either. She could have killed herself. Silver wasn't poisonous to her. However, if someone had injected an average Joe human with the amount of silver that had been in his body, it wouldn't have been good for the human, either. He wasn't a doctor, but he was pretty sure it would have been fatal.

He could feel her, so she wasn't dead, but the link felt . . . off—and that really scared him. He had to control the urge to run, to bull through anything that stood between them so he could protect her. But he wouldn't waste her efforts, he would wait until the proper time, then he would go hunting.

Something changed in the room, and Adam pulled his head into the here and now. He listened. The almost constant soft clink-clink was the sound of his bound wolves moving restlessly, even drugged into almost unconsciousness because the pain of the silver in their bodies and in the chains that held them made it impossible for them to lie still. He could smell them, smell silver and sickness in spite of all that he could do for them.

Judging from their condition, the sacrifice he'd intended would not have helped the pack enough. Jones was afraid, and he'd pumped them all too full of silver. Adam, though, was now free of the effects of all those darts. He could do more for the pack, but he didn't want Mercy to deplete herself keeping him healthy. So he would wait until it was necessary.

Perhaps the soldier who moved like water through the densely populated room would give him other opportunities. The human stepped over Warren's still body and crouched, finally, in front of Adam. He settled in close, because Adam could feel the disturbance the man's breath made in the air.

"Alpha," said the man who'd reprimanded Mr. Jones after he'd shot Peter, the one who seemed to be in charge of the military or pseudo-military rank and file.

Adam opened his eyes. The other man was crouched so his head was level with Adam's, close enough to see the whites of his eyes. He was wearing the familiar black armor, and his face was blackened and mottled with a fresh application of greasepaint.

Warren was lying just behind him, and Adam saw the gleam of his eyes in the darkness. Darryl slid closer, his chains silent as the big man moved. Adam made a move with the hand away from his enemy observer, and Warren, then Darryl subsided.

Adam was in no danger. Free of the silver and drugs, Adam

could have crushed his throat before the man took his next breath. It was tempting. Very.

But this one wasn't the man who'd killed Peter, so Adam waited to see why he was here. Killing was easy. It could be done at any time.

"We are going," the other man said in a conversational voice. "Leaving our employment here."

Adam lifted his head and met the other man's gaze. After a brief count, his opponent turned his head.

"You aren't as foggy as my employers think, secret knock 'em out darts that work on werewolves or not," said the enemy soldier. "They don't affect you the way they are supposed to, I saw that right off, even if *Jones* chooses not to. So you might have picked up that I had some men waiting at Kyle Brooks's house with orders to capture your wife, your daughter, and Ben Shaw because our intelligence said that was where they would probably go. Early this morning, the police broke up the party—" He quit speaking for a moment and stared at Adam's face. "And how do you know that?" He shook his head and spoke to himself. "Freaking supernatural bullshit. I told them we should stay out of it, but the money was too good, and we always like to keep the government happy with us. Keeps us employed."

He sat there in front of Adam and thought some more. Patience, Adam counseled himself, there was more information here, and it would be easier if the man chose to tell him about it himself.

"So we ended up with one of ours dead and three in custody—and your wife is talking to the police about how someone kidnapped your pack and wants you to go kill the good Senator Campbell. I thought maybe one of my boys talked out of turn—which they wouldn't. But maybe she knew about it the same way you know what went down this morning, huh?"

He waited a moment, but both he and Adam knew that Adam wasn't going to respond.

"Now my outfit is pretty big news, and we make good money. With no civilians dead, it didn't take our lawyers long to get the rest out—and once out, they're all the way out. Too many eyes on them to make them useful for this operation. No worries, we have the resources to replace them with operatives with clean slates and redeploy the hot ones somewhere less worrisome—out of the country until certain people forget the ones who work for a paycheck and keep after the people who pay the money, you know what I mean?"

Adam didn't say anything, just waited for the man to get to the point.

"I'll tell you the truth," he said slowly, as if he had all the time in the world. Maybe he did. "I asked to be in on this. You are demon spawn, you werewolves and the fae and the witches. All of you need to die, and someday I hope to be one of the people called upon to rid your scourge from the earth."

And Adam smelled the fear on him for the first time, fear and eagerness for blood. Adam was sympathetic; he was afraid for his people, for Mercy—and hungry for blood, too.

"But I didn't get where I am by working against the rules," the mercenary said. "Rules keep people alive and keep the money flowing. Rules say that the people who hire us don't get to kill us when we've served our part or because we know things they don't want to get out. We don't talk—and we police our own if someone thinks about singing inconveniently." He met Adam's eyes briefly again. "You know about rules, you wolves. I've heard that."

The mercenary paused, waiting for a response that didn't come. When it was clear his invitation to talk had been turned down, he continued. "So these guys had a flight out of here for the morning, but Slick—one of the ones who got away—he went over to the hotel where everyone should be and surprised a government cleanup crew and the bodies of my men who should have been alive. He managed to get away and contact me. All casualties, no survivors but Slick. He's taking a roundabout way to a rendezvous, and I'm taking my boys out. The word to eliminate the men who were arrested didn't come from our company—no one who works for our company is that stupid. We're leaving; and then we'll deal with the betrayal."

Adam asked, "Why are you telling me this?"

"I don't like your kind," said the mercenary. He looked around and spat on the dirt floor. "But that's personal. Someone screws us over? That's business. They killed my boys because they didn't want them to talk. Don't know what we know that is so valuable, but I'm telling you what I know in hopes that it torpedoes their plans." He paused. "Those men took my orders, and that makes their deaths personal."

"I understand," said Adam.

The other man frowned at him. "I'd heard that about you, that you wore the uniform."

"Ranger," said Adam.

The man examined him, taken aback.

"Doesn't mean I'm not a monster," Adam continued. "But I do understand how a soldier works. You follow orders, and in return, you expect the men above you to have your back while you risk your life. When they don't . . ." Adam shrugged. "Something needs to be done."

The other man nodded, took a deep breath. "That's right. Okay. Folks pay us—we work for them all the way. We don't take better money, we don't talk. But our employers broke the rules. If they're afraid of something getting out—well, maybe I think that might be a start on teaching them not to betray the soldiers who work for them. The folks giving us the orders—they're regular government—Cantrip Agency. You know, the ones who are running around screaming that the fae and werewolves and all the rest are dangerous and need to be exterminated when their job was supposed to be learning about the supernatural world and acting as intermediaries between you and the government. The rhetoric they're spouting is that they want the power to go wolf hunting before some other agency gets it. They're tired of having to call the cavalry because they can't have their own army."

The mercenary frowned at Adam. "But you probably guessed that."

"Most of the competent people end up elsewhere," agreed Adam. "FBI, CIA, Homeland Security, National Security Administration, Secret Service, or one of a few other agencies. Cantrip has been a dumping ground for the screwups for years, and this has the same sort of FUBAR painted all over it that I've seen whenever desks try to run real operations."

The other man grinned at him. "What you said. I'm going to repeat that to my superiors."

"Okay," Adam said. "But where is the money coming from? I know what Cantrip's budget is; they don't have enough of a black-ops slush fund to work this. Maybe if they all gave up their salaries, they'd be able to hire something like your operation without alerting someone. You guys are more likely to be out protecting some drug lord in South America or fighting the war when the Geneva Convention is too restrictive for the home troops."

The other man put a finger along his nose and pointed it at Adam. "I could like you if you weren't a hell spawn, you know? No. Cantrip doesn't have that kind of money, though they would if a werewolf killed the Billionaire Senator, right? If his party didn't see to it, his very rich and very, very powerful family would. Word is that the head of this operation is cooperating with some money man, a rich son of a bitch anonymous puppet master who seems to have it in for you, Hauptman. He funded this operation, and the only stipulation was that it was your pack that got elected for assassination duty. Don't know who he is, but people are afraid of him."

And that was *very* interesting. Adam found himself settling in, ready to hunt. That it was personal made his enemy specific. Not people who hate werewolves, which was a very large group, but a man who hated him.

"Your intelligence was very good," Adam said. He needed to know where the information came from. "Traced cell phones for where the pack members who weren't at my house for Thanksgiving would be—that would have been Cantrip. But how did you find all the pack members?"

The other man nodded. "Right track. It's where I would have looked first. The list of pack members was provided to us—came from a different source. Same folks who provided the tranq. If I were to guess, I'd say it was someone high up in the military who doesn't like werewolves. But he wasn't the man funding this—just an interested bystander."

The tranq and information both could have come from Gerry Wallace before he'd been killed. Adam's pack hadn't changed since Gerry's death. Gerry's job had been to keep track of the lone wolves—and to do that he had a pretty extensive list of who was in which pack as well. Adam would have to warn Bran that someone had that information and was making it available.

"Did you ever see him?"

"Which him?"

"The money man or the information man."

The other man tilted his head. "Just the money man, once, I think. Said he was a flunky, guys with lots of money always have flunkies. He was soft-looking, looked like a civilian through and through. Dressed in a suit and looked like butter wouldn't melt. But he made the hair on the back of my neck crawl—and I always trust my gut. He looked soft, but he didn't move like a civilian, get me? Moved on the balls of his feet, and when he pulled a chair up, it didn't take him as much effort as it would have taken a civilian. He was stronger than a man who looked that soft should have been."

"You don't think he was a flunky."

"You read people, too," the mercenary said. It didn't sound like it bothered him. "No. I think he was the money man himself. I've trained a lot of men. Some of them are better at giving orders than taking them. He was one of those. But subtle about it."

"When and where?"

The other man shook his head. "Now, that is too much. More my company's secret than my ex-employers'." He pulled out a cigarette and lit it. Crouching for that long wasn't easy, especially if the one doing it was a human over thirty. But the mercenary didn't seem to find it uncomfortable.

"My doctor tells me if I don't quit smoking, I'll die of cancer someday," he said.

"If it ruins your endurance, it'll kill you sooner than that," said Adam. "Smokers don't run as fast or as long."

The man laughed. "Tell you what. A couple of days ago word came to me that these folk aren't Cantrip. Oh, they work for the agency all right. But they've gone rogue, and Cantrip has a group out looking for them." He looked at his cigarette, then put it back in his mouth and inhaled. "Cantrip's problem-solver got into town last night—just in time to do the cleanup on my boys."

A small red light flashed on his wristwatch. He tapped the watch and ground the cigarette out on the sole of his boot. "Son," he said. "If I have to depend upon running fast to stay alive, I'm already dead. Got to go now." He pulled out a key and frowned at it. "It's a strange old world, you know? Never know who you're going to find yourself in bed with."

He stood up and tossed the key toward Adam, who let it fall to the ground next to him.

"Good luck, now." The mercenary stepped over Darryl on the way to the door. "You aren't a bad sort for an abomination."

"I could say the same to you."

The mercenary glanced back and laughed. "Yeah. There is that." He opened the door, and said, quietly, "I heard one of them say that there's another assassin on the senator's security detail."

"Aimed at whom?" asked Adam.

The mercenary nodded. "I do like you. That is the right question. For you if you succeeded, for the senator if you didn't." He left without another glance.

As soon as the door shut behind him, Darryl and Warren both looked up at Adam. Darryl inhaled and gave a soft growl, too drugged from the ketamine to bring out words.

"Yes," said Adam. "I'm better." He didn't say why or how. They'd think it was Bran, and his legend would help them get up and on their feet.

He used the key to free himself and opened the shackles that held Darryl first, then Warren. When Warren sat up, Adam dropped the key into the old cowboy's hand. Warren was in the best shape next to Adam.

"Free everyone, but stay here until I get back or summon you," he told Warren. "Free Honey last, and be ready in case she really loses it."

Then he stood up and stripped out of his clothes. The final thing that he had learned in Vietnam, even before he'd been turned into a werewolf, was that he was good at killing.

Naked, he walked to the door and turned the knob—his mercenary visitor had left the door unlocked and unbarred. It opened into the small antechamber where Mr. Jones's desk was still in place. The room was dark, but they were underground—or so his nose told him, though the ceilings were higher than usual for a basement.

The steel bar that kept them imprisoned was lying on the floor. Adam bent down, picked up the bar, and set it on the ground next to Darryl, who closed his hand on it and tried to get to his hands and knees. Adam's second was functioning on instincts.

"Shh," Adam told him, and put a hand on his shoulder until he subsided. "Wait and protect. I'll be back. See if you can get them to change."

Warren's yellow eyes met his.

"I'll save Mr. Jones for Honey," he told Warren, then let the wolf take him.

By the time he rose on all four feet, most of the pack had been freed of their chains, but they were still unable to stand. Honey looked up into his face.

"Are you going to kill them all?" she asked him.

Murder, his father had taught him, was a sin.

Honey had been in his pack for nearly thirty years, she knew better than to ask if he *could* kill them all. He nodded once and loped out of the open door with an eagerness he made no attempt to check.

Adam had long ago accepted that he was not going to make it to Heaven.

He'd thought that they'd been stowed in some sort of government facility—there were a lot of places out in the Hanford Site near the nuclear facilities that were all but deserted. But as he paced through the long hall, he realized that this was some sort of commercial building rather than a government building. There was a sign leaning back-out against the wall. He pulled it away from the wall until he could see the front. TASTING ROOM, it said. He was in the unfinished basement of a winery.

That would explain the high ceilings and large, empty rooms. Their jail cell had been meant to hold racks of barrels of aging wine, as were the rooms on either side of the hallway he now paced down.

The winery had not been put to use for its intended purpose—he couldn't smell any grapes or wine. The half-dirt, half-tile floors and the hallway drywall *sans* tape and texture meant that someone had stopped while the building was still in the construction phase.

The basement was empty, though it was obvious that there had been people here fairly recently. They left behind the smell of body armor, gunpowder, and greasepaint as well as trails of footprints and marks where things had been dragged. Two of the rooms, identical to where they had been held, had been used as living quarters. The only difference was that the heavy wooden door that had been barred to keep wolves in was removed and set inside the rooms that had housed the mercenaries. Presumably so that no one could keep them in.

The mercenary commander who had talked to him had been right, Adam decided. Under other circumstances, Adam would have liked him, too.

In the distance, Adam heard diesel engines start up, the same engines, he was pretty sure, that had hauled the pack out to whatever distant proto-winery Cantrip had found to use as werewolf storage. The mercenaries had either parked a fair distance away from their temporary HQ, or—and he thought it more likely, given the dismantled doors—they had pushed the vehicles away from the building until someone deemed it safe to start them. The noise was faint to Adam's ears. He doubted a human would hear it even if he'd been listening for it instead of asleep.

He found the stairs and climbed them silently. They brought him to an empty room, designed to be open and airy. The walls were unpainted, but the floors were tiled in sandstone that was difficult to walk across without allowing his claws to click. A double door designed to open easily at a push led to the outside. He pushed one of the doors, and it opened. He went outside to take a recon of the layout and was unsurprised to find that they were out in the boonies somewhere. There were dead grapes everywhere—he'd been right about the winery. The building was surrounded by maybe a couple of hundred acres' worth of gray vines that had been dead well before winter hit. He could see the sad-looking dried-up starts of grape bunches.

He padded out onto what had been meant to be a grand wraparound porch, but it was missing the railing and several sections of flooring. A parking lot had been laid out, one big enough for ten cars or maybe a bus or two, but it hadn't been paved. There were four black SUVs and a Nissan with a plate frame advertising a national chain of rental cars in the lot.

The house/winery was about halfway up a hill from a two-lane highway that stretched in either direction and vanished around the wrinkled, hilly country. An orchard of apple trees bordered the would-be vineyard to the west and a rather better tended vineyard on the east.

Neither of the nearest properties looked to have a house on it. The closest neighbor was out of sight—doubtless it was the reason this place had been chosen by . . . whoever had chosen it. He'd find out who that was.

He considered crippling the cars, but decided against it. He turned back into the house. It was time to show these people why they should be afraid of werewolves.

He followed the sound of breathing to a hallway with rooms on either side, as if the original designs for the winery had also provided for a bed-and-breakfast.

The first room had the same unfinished walls as the public rooms did, but here the floor was also unfinished. The plywood squeaked just a little under his weight, but the man sleeping on the temporary cot didn't wake up. He was in his thirties, from the look of his face, which was . . . ordinary. He snored a little.

It had been nearly half a century since Adam's first kill. He'd like to have said that he remembered them all—a man should take notice when he killed another man. But there had been too many. Some of them had been sleeping peacefully.

He crushed the man's throat with his jaws and tried not to pay attention to the taste of his blood. Since he'd become a werewolf, he'd eaten a few people, but that was harder to live with than just killing them. So he tried to avoid it when he could.

The second man was older, in his fifties, but in decent shape. He had the good haircut of a bureaucrat planning on rising in the ranks of his profession. His hair was dyed, but it was a good dye job, leaving him with just a touch of gray.

Adam didn't remember seeing him—but he'd be the first to admit that he hadn't been at his best since his kidnapping. This one woke up before Adam killed him, but he didn't have a chance to cry out.

He continued down the hall. The next two who died were also easy kills.

He came to a room empty of people, but he opened the door anyway. He should have just kept going, but when he glimpsed a photo of Mercy, he shouldered the door further open and went in. One wall was filled with photos of his pack and their families, including Mercy and Jesse. Each labeled with a name so that people could come in and study the wall, get so they would recognize their targets.

It was a kill list.

Every single one of the pack was on it—and their immediate families, human and wolf alike, young and old. Sylvia Sandoval was there and so were her girls.

They were planning on killing the children.

Adam's next three kills weren't so clean after that, nor so silent. He let the fourth one scream because he was sleeping with a smile on his face.

They were planning on killing children, and this one was smiling.

When Adam got through with him, the man's corpse reeked of terror and pain. Adam needed to control himself better; he couldn't afford to lose control of the wolf because he might never regain it. He had a job that no one else could do to his satisfaction, a duty. The thought settled him; he knew about duty, both man and wolf.

The next bedroom was empty, though it smelled of a woman. He memorized the scent because if she'd taken flight, he'd have to hunt her through the dead vineyard. Part of him, the human part, knew he would have to give that hunt to someone less . . . eager than he was. Warren. Darryl, Adam's second, was still too much a gentleman to kill a woman without suffering for it. Warren was more practical.

The modern doorknobs designed for handicapped access were so much easier for a wolf to open than the traditional round ones were. The whole ground floor was designed especially for handicapped access, so he made no sound as he opened the next room to discover that there would be no need for him to hunt anyone yet. He'd found the woman from next door, and she and Mr. Jones had evidently found themselves too involved in each other to notice his last victim's cries.

He'd promised Jones to Honey.

It was harder than it should have been to leave them alone, but he closed the door as quietly as he could. There were three more people to kill—he could hear them. He was getting hungry.

He broke the next man's neck with a swat of his paw—like a grizzly. It was quick and clean. The second one was a woman, crouched behind her cot, which she'd knocked over to provide cover. He had a momentary thought that someone had been watching too much TV, because a cot is no kind of protection at all—and then the woman pulled out one of the dart guns and started firing.

The first dart hit badly and bounced off his shoulder. Warned, he dodged the second two and jumped the cot to crush her skull between his jaws. He shook her once to break her neck and make sure of the kill, then dropped the body. He didn't enjoy killing women.

He stopped where he was, the corpse on the ground halfway between his front paws, and fought off the urge to eat her. Woman or not, his wolf was hungry, and dead, she was just meat. He didn't have time for it—and the strength of the urge meant the wolf was gaining the upper hand. When he was certain he had himself under control he headed off to hunt down the next one.

That one had barricaded himself in one of the rooms Adam had visited earlier. The door was ironbound and thick, meant to look like the old colonial Spanish doors. It stopped the bullets that the man shot into the door as soon as Adam touched the doorknob—it must not have been a large-caliber handgun.

But the gunfire did one thing. Mr. Jones opened his door, a gun in his hand. Adam dropped his head and roared at him. It was a sound the lesser wolves could not make, more like a lion than a wolf. The woman behind Jones screamed and screamed. Jones shot twice before Adam hit him, but he hadn't stopped to aim, hadn't been able to control his fear. One bullet skimmed Adam's side, but the other missed him altogether—hitting a moving target isn't easy.

Adam deliberately bumped Jones with his shoulder and knocked him off his feet. The woman's screams intensified, and he pinned his ears at her. His father had taught him only a cowardly man would hurt a woman. But this woman had agreed to kill people because they were associated with his pack, to kill the children.

Still, Adam killed her quickly and as painlessly as he could. And when the silence of her death filled the room, his father's admonitions rang in his ears.

Jones made an incoherent noise and scrabbled with his gun, trying to get his shaking hands to work. Adam left the woman's body and grabbed the gun out of the human's hands and crushed it. He dropped it, now unusable, to the floor.

His jaws ached to finish Jones . . . but he'd promised Peter's killer to Honey, even if she hadn't been in a state to know it. Revenge was a dangerous thing, but a quick clean act sometimes allowed the victim closure. So he left Jones for Honey and went to deal with the only other Cantrip agent he'd left alive.

The door was solid wood and locked against him. Adam hit it with his shoulder and cracked the wood, breaking it free of its hinges. It hurt, and he stopped to tear it to bits. Only when the door lay in broken shards did he come back to himself.

The man was on the floor, blood pouring from a bullet wound—either Jones's gun had been a bigger caliber and gone through the door, or it had gone through the wall. His gun lay on the floor beside him, and his hand couldn't get a grip on it.

"Tiger, tiger burning bright," he stuttered, looking at Adam as he choked on his own blood. *"In the forest . . . in the forest."* He drew in a breath, looked Adam in the eye, and said again, quite clearly, *"Forest."* His body convulsed once more, then he lay still.

Did He who made the lamb make thee? Adam responded silently with the appropriate line. It was a question that he held dearly: Had God made werewolves? How could He have done so and still be benevolent?

Adam stared at the man until a stray sound reminded him that,

William Blake's poetry aside, all of the Cantrip agents weren't dead yet.

He called out to his pack, summoning them to the last of the hunt. They came, stumbling and slow, and mostly in wolf form now. The change would help them fight off the effects of the drugs. Warren, Darryl, and a couple of others held on to their humanity. They stopped when they saw him waiting at the top of the stairs.

Warren's nostril's flared, and Darryl ran a hand over his mouth. Adam looked at Honey, and the golden wolf swayed a little. He caught her eye, then glanced behind him to send her hunting.

Only when her impassioned snarl behind him signaled that she'd found what he'd sent her after, did he step aside and motion the rest of the pack on by. When the last of them had passed him, he started his change back to human. There had been a landline in the planning office. His change was faster than usual—whether due to Mercy's meddling or the killing field he'd made of the ground floor of the winery, he didn't care to speculate.

The phone worked, which was nice, because otherwise he'd have had to use one of the Cantrip agents' phones, and with the taste of the hunt on his tongue, that would have been unwise.

He called Mercy first. He needed to hear her voice to remind him that he was not entirely a killer, not entirely a monster. But her cell rang three times. And then a recorded voice informed him that her line was unavailable. He fought down instinctive panic.

She was smart, she would have destroyed her phone to keep them from tracking her. If she were dead, he would know.

Human form or not, he was still too close to the monster who had ripped a door apart for being a door, and that monster needed to hear his mate. He took a deep breath and thought human thoughts for a few minutes.

Adam called Elizaveta and got one of her grandsons, though he could hear her cranky voice in the background.

"Who is calling at such an hour?"

As soon as her grandson told her, she took the phone from him. "Adamya," the old witch said. "We have been so worried."

"I need a cleanup," he told her abruptly, so weary he leaned against the wall. "This is a landline, can you trace it?"

"*Da*, this is not a problem. How many bodies?"

He couldn't remember. Hadn't kept count. He looked at his hands and realized that they were black with blood.

"That many," she said into his silence. "We will come and do what is necessary."

"It has to be done before dawn," he told her. "They are sending a helicopter at dawn."

"Then they will find nothing," she told him.

"We need transport, too," he said. "For thirty wolves."

"This we can also do," she promised him.

"And I need to know where Mercy is," he said.

"She is at Kyle and Warren's house," Elizaveta told him. "I thought you would ask, so I sent one of my grandsons to follow her."

"Good," he said. "Come as soon as you can."

"Yes," she told him—and hung up.

Elizaveta was nearly seventy; she was powerful, but her body was beginning to fail her. In the last two years, she'd lost both of the people she'd been training to take her place, the people who should have been helping her carry the burden of her work. Both of them were killed in incidents involving his wolves.

She might have taken it wrong, might have blamed his pack, except that she liked Adam. His mother had been Russian; her parents had fled Moscow when she was a child. She had spoken

Russian as her first language, and Adam had learned it at her knee. When he'd first spoken to Elizaveta in Russian, she'd recognized the accent of Moscow, her hometown, and it had created a bond that he deliberately used. He was always very careful not to tell her that his mother had left fleeing the tide of revolution that had immolated Russia just after WWI.

He was at least as old as Elizaveta. She didn't know it, would never know it because Adam understood people. Oh, she knew in abstract, unlike the public, that werewolves could live a good long time, but she'd never made the connection to him. He knew that because if she ever processed what she knew, she would hunt him down and try to make him turn her.

He would kill her before he did that.

The vampires had a taboo about attempting to turn anyone who was not a normal human. It had happened. The local seethe had a witchblood—and a woman who had been brain-damaged while still human.

Adam knew of three werewolves who had been witchborn. They were the three most dangerous and powerful werewolves in the world, and he didn't think it was an accident. The idea of that much power in a woman so morally . . . ambivalent was disturbing.

The thought made him laugh. Here he stood dripping blood on Spanish tile, his naked body drenched with the blood of strangers, and he was judging other people's morality.

He could have let them all live, turned them over to the courts. But the courts had let a serial killer walk because his victims had been fae and werewolf.

Cantrip was a government agency—these people were not serial killers, and if he turned them over to the courts, only Peter's body and a kill list would stand as witness against them. Additionally, it would come out that they had a drug that worked on the wolves, a vulnerability that Bran had been trying to keep secret—and Adam agreed it was best not to advertise to everyone who might decide it was a good idea to rid the world of werewolves.

Probably the justice system would only slap the wrists of whoever was in command. He might even lose his job—to be hired immediately at ten times his salary by someone who supported his vision. Cantrip would hire another person with the same attitudes. The end result would be that the enemy prospered, and the wolves would lose a few more weapons in their struggle to survive.

But Adam could have done it anyway. Could have captured the enemy without killing anyone. He chose not to. And it wasn't because he was sure that the courts would not grant them justice; that was just an excuse, really. He clenched his bloody fist, then brought it up to his mouth and licked it.

They had attacked his people, and they had killed the one he most needed to protect. They threatened those under his protection, and for that, they could only die. The world needed to remember that it was a bad idea to attack a werewolf pack.

He picked up the phone again and dialed Hauptman Security.

"Gutstein." There were the sounds of a busy office behind him. It was very early in the morning, an odd time for busy.

"Jim." Adam closed his eyes.

"Adam. *Sir.* Good to hear from you." Behind him, the office noises ceased—and then someone cheered, followed by a whole lot of noise.

Jim Gutstein covered the speaker of the phone, but his whistle still made Adam jerk the phone away from his ear until it was over. When he put the phone back to his ear, Jim's voice was still muffled. "Can't hear a word he's saying. Shut up until we know what's going on."

Silence fell, and Jim said, "Sorry, sir. Brooks told us what he knew, and we've been worried."

It took Adam a half a second to connect "Brooks" to Warren's Kyle. He still wasn't at the top of his game. He needed food—and he refused to consider all the meat that was nearby.

"And shorthanded," said a whiny voice over Jim's line.

"Tell Evan—" Adam started, grateful for the routine that helped keep him human.

"There goes that promotion, Evan," said Jim. It was an old joke, and everyone laughed. In the noise, Jim said, "Are you okay, sir?"

"Never better," Adam said wryly, "considering the scope of the SNAFU. However, I have this situation under control. I need you to find out who is in charge of security for Senator Campbell and tell him that a group from Cantrip, at least one person in the military, and a money man in the private sector have it in for the senator and tried to arrange an assassination."

"The word is that they already know," Jim told him. "Mercy was pretty clear to the police."

"I'd rather know that they have that information for certain. You tell them that the people behind the attempt tried to blackmail me into doing it—and though that situation is under control, it is not certain that the senator is safe. I have taken a bite out of the Cantrip faction." He smiled—with teeth. "The military gentleman was probably aimed more at us than him—and that might be true of the money man as well, but they are still in play. They had alternate plans if they couldn't force me to act." The kill list hadn't been the only thing in their Ops room. Mostly just notes and scraps of paper, but he was good at connecting the dots. "Someone in their security team is prepared to assassinate him should I fail. I failed, and, hopefully, the money is gone, but I don't know if he or she has any way to know that."

"I'll find out who the senator's security detail is and tell them. I know someone who can talk to the senator directly. That will make the feds send someone official to talk to you."

"Tell them I won't talk officially." Jim had been with him nearly fifteen years. "There are bodies I won't claim, Jim, or lie about. My official story is that I woke up and the place they were holding us was on fire, so we escaped. Officially, I don't know anything except that they seemed to want me to assassinate the senator."

"Is it on fire?"

"Not yet," said Adam. The witch could do a lot with a body, but she wouldn't be able to erase the marks his claws had made in the tile or the doors he'd splintered. Fix the bodies and burn the house.

The blood was drying on his skin, and it itched. The smell was making his hunger worse. Time to finish this talk.

"Good," Jim said. "I want you to know that we are behind you, you and your wolves. We've got your back. And right now I've got all sorts of our most expensive equipment keeping watch on Kyle Brooks's house, and we have people following Mercy. We haven't been able to locate Jesse. Brooks told us Jesse was safe."

"Yes. Good. I'll stop in tomorrow, and we'll call a meeting to discuss how we should proceed."

"Do you want us to tell your wife that you're okay?" Jim asked.

Adam looked down at the dark stains on his hands. "No. I'll tell her when we're really out of here."

"All right. We'll keep her safe."

The pack had left the last kill finally and crowded into the previously adequately sized room as he hung up the phone.

Honey, nearly as blood-splattered as he was because her fur held on to it better than his skin did, came forward with her head and tail low. The closer she came, the faster she moved. When she reached him, she dropped to the ground and leaned against him hard enough that if he had not been braced for it, he would have staggered.

No, he thought as he bent down to rest his hand on the top of her head, and looking over his battered pack, he did not regret killing these people.

"Tiger, tiger, burning bright in the forests of the night," he told them in a burst of exhaustion-driven fancifulness. "What immortal hand or eye dare frame thy fearful symmetry?"

Warren leaned against the doorway, and said, "We're not tigers, we're werewolves, boss. God didn't make us, nohow. Just ask the dead guys where we come from." Despite the drawl and deliberately poor grammar, the exhaustion and pain turning his skin haggard, his eyes were sharp.

Darryl made a noise that might have been a growl if Adam hadn't heard his second's real growls. Darryl reached over and gave Warren's hair a rough caress, an unusual sign of affection from the pack's second.

"Dead guys don't get an opinion," Darryl told everyone. "We're the good guys. That we're scary doesn't mean we're the villains."

7

Dominant werewolves are control freaks and do not enjoy being passengers in cars. Asil was no exception. He put on his seat belt, closed his eyes, and sat tense and unhappy as I drove toward Kennewick.

We'd had a brief discussion about who would be driving, and he clearly felt my argument that I knew where I was going and he didn't was insufficient. He reluctantly agreed, however, that since Marsilia would hold me responsible for anything (more) that happened to her car, it was only fair that I drove. We couldn't take his rental because they came lo-jacked to the max, and I didn't want to lead anyone to Sylvia's home if I could help it.

"Don't worry," I told Asil cheerfully. "I already wrecked one car this week. I have no intention of wrecking another. Really."

He glowered at me—which was impressive since he didn't open his eyes.

The morning sky was dark and overcast, which actually doesn't happen all that often here. It wasn't much lighter than it had been last night. Rain started to splatter the windshield as I pulled onto the highway back to Kennewick. The car informed me that it was thirty-four degrees F outside.

About once a winter, we get a spate of freezing rain that is unholy scary to drive in. Rain turns to ice as it hits the road, and that turns the highways into frictionless surfaces that look no different than wet pavement—until suddenly steering and brakes quit working. I've seen semitrucks stopped at red lights start sliding without any impetus other than the weight of their load pushing eighteen wheels sideways across the road. Freezing rain makes auto-body men happy campers as they count the wrecks using all of their fingers and toes.

But at thirty-four degrees, we were safe enough, so I didn't have to worry about the rain.

"After you retrieve Adam's daughter, you really still intend to contact the vampires?" Asil asked when we were nearly at our destination.

"Can't do that until it gets dark," I told him, then took a good look at the sky. "Nighttime dark, not daybreak dark. I don't know what new delights this day will bring; however, if we all make it to this evening, then, yes, I do. Marsilia owes the pack. Much as she'd like to see me roast on a good hot fire for a long time, that's personal. Business is more important. Business means that she doesn't want to get on the bad side of the werewolves, especially right now. She's down four of her five most powerful vampires. Two of them betrayed her to a vampire trying to take over her seethe and were kicked out. Stefan left the seethe about the same time. The one powerful vampire left to her is mostly crazy as far as I can tell. She can't afford to offend us."

"What if the pack isn't a factor?" asked Asil, soft-voiced.

"What if they're all dead? Does she hate you enough to go after them? She cut her teeth in Italy during the Renaissance; a little sleight of hand is not beyond her now."

"She knows about Bran, knows I was raised in his pack and that he is fond of me. If it turns out that she was involved, he'd wipe her seethe from the face of the earth, and she knows it. No." I thought about it. "No, it isn't her. There are too many downsides and no profit in it for her. She actually likes Adam, I think, and he's pretty easy for her to deal with. Straightforward. Another Alpha might not be so accommodating."

Though without Adam, would there be a pack here in the Tri-Cities? He'd been brought in to deal with a lone wolf who had decided to build a pack, then started killing humans. Adam had stayed because the backbone of his business was security contracts with government contractors, and the Tri-Cities was full of them.

That wouldn't benefit Marsilia either, though, because weakened as she was, she counted on Adam to keep the nastier unallied supernatural creatures under control and keep others from settling here at all.

"Ah," Asil said, as I pulled into the apartment complex. He opened his eyes as we slowed. "Disappointing. I had hoped the responsible party would be the vampires. I could kill vampires, I think, without losing control. If it is humans who are our enemies, I shall have to find another means of stopping them." He showed his teeth. "Age catches up with us all, and I enjoy the kill too much to be allowed it. If we are to be allies in truth, Mercedes, you should know my weaknesses before they become an issue."

Most of the werewolves who belong to the Marrok's pack are there because they can't function in a normal pack. Asil, it seemed, wasn't an exception.

"Okay," I said after discarding several versions of comments that mostly boiled down to "please, please don't kill anyone, then."

I drove past Sylvia's apartment, still thinking about the likelihood that Asil would be put in a position of killing someone. There were no empty spaces to park anywhere. I guess most people were still home at seven thirty in the morning on a Saturday with rain coming down in sheets more common on the other side of the state. Go figure.

I finally found a place next to the Dumpsters a few apartment blocks down. The little Corolla that had followed us from Kyle's house, presumably full of Hauptman Security personnel, had to keep going. I gave them a little wave as they went by.

I opened my door and got out—and something hit me in the back.

The weight dropped me flat on my face on the pavement. The suddenness of it held me still more than any hurt—though pain came right on the heels of the realization that someone had landed on me. I'd hit the ground limp, raising my head just a little to protect my face—years of karate benefiting me yet again. It set my knee and cheekbone off again. "Don't fight me," said the woman perched on my lower back. "I don't want to hurt you." She put something narrow and hard around my right wrist and reached for my left, braced for me to pull at the trapped hand.

Instead, I rolled sideways toward the hand she'd already gotten, one knee under me to add additional force. The move knocked her against Marsilia's new car with a thump that wasn't hard enough to do real damage. At least not to her. Even as the sound of her head on the oh-so-sleek side of the car chimed my if-I-live-through-this-I'm-dead meter and raised it a few notches, I changed.

The odd little cuff that had been tight on my wrist dropped off my coyote paw, and I slid out from under the woman completely.

I also acquired an additional opponent—clothes. I slid out of Kyle's sweatpants when I slid out from under the woman. I leaped with my back feet and rolled in midair, pulling my head and front paws out of the sweatshirt and left it behind. My panties clung to my left foot and my tail, but the real trouble was my stupid bra.

I landed, took two more running leaps, and tumbled head over teakettle when my bra fouled my front legs—which meant that her first shot slid along my fur instead of wherever she'd meant the bullet to go.

I focused on her as I rolled on the ground maybe fifteen feet out, fighting the too-stretchy-to-break straps. Leaping away had been the wrong thing if she was shooting. At least if I was rolling around tangled in clothes on top of her, she couldn't *aim*.

I had a blink of time to see her rise to a shooter's crouch, a dark-skinned woman with white hair in a waist-length braid and a young face. She would have looked more at home in an anime convention than holding a big gun made bigger by the silencer on the barrel. "I didn't want to do it this way." She took aim at my wiggling body. "Dead doesn't pay as much."

And then something dark, shadow-quick, passed over the roof of the car and landed on her. I heard the snap of bone before my eyes registered that Asil crouched on top of her, his face eerily calm with eyes the color of citrines.

"Half-breed fae," he grunted, examining her face as I changed back to human. It wasn't an epithet, just an observation. "That gun has too much metal for a full-blooded fae to handle even with leather gloves."

I opened my mouth to argue with him instinctively—Zee had

no trouble with metal—but the dead woman kept the words in my mouth. My head caught up with events and I realized that, although he seemed to be calm enough, his bright eyes said differently. I'd been raised among werewolves and I'd never seen anyone, not even Adam, who was pretty damn fast, move that quickly. Just a feeling of motion, then she was dead, and Asil was there.

I pulled the bra all the way off to give myself time to think—and the scary werewolf time to calm down. Realizing I was standing naked next to a very full parking lot that might soon be filling with people, I put the bra on correctly and pulled up the panties. The sweatshirt lay between Asil and me and I had to force myself to walk toward him and pick it up.

"She is also truly gone," he said impersonally. "Full-blooded fae are usually harder to kill than this." He patted down her body with a speed that indicated long familiarity with the process. His voice was a little darker than it had been before, a little more strongly accented.

"She didn't see you in the passenger seat," I said, glancing at the Mercedes. The windows were darkened beyond strictly legal limits, especially the glass on the back and side of the car. For Marsilia it was a safety measure—if she happened to be out too long, the sun would be kept at bay. For me it meant that the fae woman hadn't noticed that there were two of us in the car. The passenger door was opened where Asil had exited.

"Careless," Asil agreed, standing up and looking at me. I pulled the sweatshirt over my head and carefully didn't look up to his eye level as I pulled the shirt down.

There was subtle tension in his body to match the predator's gaze, and I thought of his warning not two minutes earlier. I wondered if killing a half-blood fae was close enough to human to be an issue. He seemed to be handling it okay so far—but with the wolves, that could change awfully fast. And that calm of his was ringing all sorts of bells in my hindbrain.

"We need to hide her before someone walks out to dump their garbage," I told him, approaching him and kneeling. It was a submissive posture—even if I did it to grab the sweatpants that lay at his feet.

He didn't say anything, just watched me. I didn't look up to see him doing it, but the back of my neck felt his eyes. The ground was really cold on my butt, and I pulled the pants on with more energy than usual. I'd kept one sock on—I try not to think about how ridiculous I must look in coyote form when I have to change without losing my clothes first, but I couldn't help but wince as I looked about for the other sock.

I didn't find the sock, but my shoes were next to the driver's side door of the Mercedes. The sight of the door put the search for my sock, the dead woman, and the werewolf who'd just killed her, momentarily right out of my mind.

"Damn, damn, damn," I said, putting my hand on the dented metal. When I'd knocked her into the car, the would-be assassin/kidnapper's head had left an impression in the driver's side door—cars aren't as tough as they used to be. My old Rabbit could have taken a blow twice that hard without even noticing it. I took another step closer, and my cold bare toes bumped into warm flesh.

I looked down and met a pair of eyes that had been dark before death fogged them over. The half-fae woman had been stunning, but now, her magic gone, she looked merely ordinary. I glanced at the werewolf who had taken himself away from the body and now stood with his back toward me, facing the nearest apartment building, an apartment building with lots and lots of windows.

"We've got to get the body out of sight," I said.

I had to pull the body out of the way to open the driver's side door and pop the trunk. Asil didn't move, and I didn't ask him to. He wasn't in the way of the door—and he was still scaring me.

She jerked a little when I moved her. I was a coyote, a predator—I've killed before. I knew it was only the air left in her lungs, knew that her floppy head meant a broken neck. But her abrupt motion made me jump and drop her anyway. At least I'd moved her far enough so that I could get into the car—and I hadn't squeaked.

Only when the door was open did it cross my mind that there was a button for the trunk on the key fob in the hip pocket of the sweats. Guys' sweatpants have neat things like pockets in them.

Asil hadn't helped me move the body the first time, but as soon as the trunk was open, he picked her up without my saying anything, grabbing the gun and the cuffs she'd used on me when he bent down. Body, gun, and cuffs gave him no trouble. She was locked safely out of sight in the trunk nearly as quickly as he'd taken her from alive to dead. He stared at the trunk for a moment and flexed his hands while I stared at him, hoping he wouldn't look back at me.

I've seen a lot of wolves in human form with those bright wolf eyes. A lot of them. And none of those eyes scared me as thoroughly as Asil's had. There was something else at home in Asil's head and it had enjoyed killing the woman and would have been happy to continue the little spree. Bran's son and chief assassin, Charles, scared me, but I was confident that if Charles wanted me dead, it would be quick and painless. Asil's beast enjoyed playing with his victims.

Oh, yes, it would not be a good thing if Asil had to kill again, but I was pretty sure it would take something bigger than me to keep it from happening. After Asil's little speech in the car, I would have thought he would have tried harder not to kill anyone all by himself.

I opened my mouth to say something, and the bland little Corolla rolled past us again; the driver waved and shrugged. No parking for Hauptman Security. If I waved and shouted, would they come running or just keep looking for an empty parking space?

Empty parking space.

She'd been waiting right here for us, I thought. Right next to the only parking place, which, conveniently, had a garbage container for her to lie on top of—she'd jumped on me from above. I wondered if she'd glamoured the spot so no one tried to park in it. I wondered if she'd known Tad was here. I wondered . . .

"What if she had a partner?" I asked, and started not quite running, but moving rather more briskly than a walk toward Sylvia's apartment without bothering to put on shoes. A case of frostbite I could deal with—not so much dead Sandoval girls. She'd been looking to take me alive, but hadn't hesitated to pull the gun. How did that play into our villains' plan? And if they were willing to kill me, what about Jesse? Had she already visited the Sandovals?

The only reason that I didn't flat-out sprint was Asil. If his wolf was that close to the surface, there was a chance he'd decide I was prey if I started running away.

"Why do you think there might be another one?" he asked, sounding entirely normal.

"Because so far these guys have worked in teams of more than one." But that wasn't it, not really. My instincts were chattering unhelpfully—conclusions without evidence.

He caught my not-quite lie. "The group that took Adam were

human, yes? Fae and human do not work well together. Yet, you are sure she is involved."

I glanced at him. His eyes were dark again, and I was relieved.

"Mercedes? Why do you think she is part of the kidnapping plot and not of some other thing? Adam is Alpha, and you are his mate—that makes you targets for all sorts of people."

It struck me that Asil was perfectly okay with the fact that there might be two separate groups out to kill us. "I think," I said, "that adding another"—and remembered that he already thought there was more than one gun aimed at my pack even if they were all, mostly, working together—"adding *yet* another enemy who wants to kidnap or kill me to this soup pushes my belief in the ultimate fairness of the universe too far to one side. I just wish I knew how she knew we were coming here."

I looked up at the back windows of Sylvia's apartment. She was a smart woman who worked at a police station: her apartment was on the third floor. There was nothing to hint at a problem within. No bodies flying through the air, no broken glass, no little pink-clad Sandoval girl screaming as she ran from scary people with guns.

Maybe I was wrong. Maybe my dead assailant had been on her own.

"Add to that," I continued almost absently because my instincts were screaming at me. Asil's eyes were still dark, so I risked breaking into a jog. "I haven't ticked off any of the fae lately. It's not the vampires in a separate attack. If *Marsilia* had decided to put me out of my misery today, she would have succeeded. I wish I knew how our dead fae knew to come here. Either they overheard Tad and me talking or they somehow knew to look here—" My voice trailed off because I realized how stupid I'd been.

Someone who didn't know the soap opera of my life from close up might not realize that Gabriel's mother and he were estranged. Sylvia's apartment would be the last place *I'd* have looked for the kids. But someone from the outside, someone who only knew that Gabriel had gone missing with Ben and Jesse and me, someone like that might very well check out his nearest relatives. I'd over-estimated our enemies, and they'd found Jesse. That's what my instincts had been telling me.

"Mercy?" asked Asil, who had sped up to keep pace with me. His beautiful accent made him sound like someone's lover instead of a man who had killed a woman with as little thought as I gave to opening a jar of mayonnaise. Maybe less thought.

Not that he scared me anymore. Not now when I was pretty sure we were going to need him soon. "I—"

The back wall of Sylvia's apartment blew out, spitting stucco, plaster, glass, insulation, and a man's body down on the sidewalk below. Some of the debris must have bounced because nearby car alarms went off. The body rolled when it hit the ground, got up, ran back at the apartment building, and did a Jackie Chan up the side. I was really happy to see him moving because I'd recognized him on the way down.

"Tad!" I hadn't intended to yell or run, but I was doing both.

Asil paced me, but we split up as we reached the apartment building. He went in the same way Tad had and I, not blessed with supernatural strength, had to run up the stairs instead.

I ran up those steps as fast as I've ever run. The door opened, and Jesse and Gabriel spilled onto the stairs with various Sandovals clinging, pushing, and sobbing. I counted and came up one short—no Sylvia—even as I slid over the guardrail to stand on the outside of the bars on the edge of the stairs to let the youngsters by.

"Your mom?" I said, as they passed.

"At work," Gabriel said.

I tossed him the keys to Marsilia's car. "Take the car, it's over by the garbage bins three buildings that way." I pointed appropriately. "Get to Kyle's house but don't speed. You have a body in the trunk and no child car seats."

"Body?" said the oldest of Gabriel's sisters. If I weren't clinging to the stairway while there was a lot of noise coming from above where someone who might as well have been my little brother had gotten tossed through a wall just a few seconds ago, I could have remembered her name. Right now I could barely remember my own.

They were tough, those Sandoval kids. They'd be okay with a body in the trunk of the car.

"Bad guy," I said. "Tried to kill me and got taken out by my backup."

"Cool," said one of the littler ones—Sissy.

They hadn't paused in their downward trek, and once on solid ground, Gabriel rearranged everyone so the littles were carried. Jesse took advantage of the lull to mouth, "Dad?" at me.

"He's alive," I told her. "But that's all I know. Get out of here."

And then I rolled back over the railing and up the last set of stairs and headed into the apartment—only then remembering that I'd left my gun in Marsilia's car. I stripped out of my clothes and let my coyote out.

In the distance, I could hear sirens. The police department wasn't too far from here, and there was no way anyone could have ignored the noise coming from Sylvia's apartment.

As human, I stood no chance against something that could throw Tad through a wall. As a coyote, I was definitely outmatched—but I could be distracting, and I was just that much faster on four legs than on two. Fast enough to outrun most werewolves, anyway.

I skulked into the living room—the only room I'd been in before. On top of the scent of the Sandoval family I could smell werewolf, Tad, and . . . something fae. The fae smell mostly like the old philosopher's division of the world to me—earth, air, fire, water—with the addition of green growing things. Ariana smelled like forest, and so did this fae.

The noise was coming from a room farther into the apartment. Someone screamed, and I couldn't tell who it was. I set caution aside and bolted down the narrow hallway and into the master bedroom at the end.

The dead woman's partner was nightmare hideous. His head was misshapen and too large for his body. One large eye, emerald green and liquid, stared off to the side, while the other was only half as large and solid black. Two odd lumps that looked like nascent antlers emerged from his temples. His nose was two slits above a mouth too large for his face and filled with uneven, spade-shaped, yellow teeth. A black tongue flicked out and across his nose slits as he fought.

For all his horribleness, he wasn't more than four feet tall. His body was slender, almost delicate-looking, with wrists smaller than mine, in human shape. His outsized, four-fingered hands gripped a sword made of some sort of black metal that was nearly as tall as he.

Asil had a baseball bat and was using it like a katana—turn and turn and never let the bastard get a good hard strike on your weapon. The Japanese had had lousy steel and had learned to compensate. Tad had a pair of kitchen knives and was keeping the fae from getting into a good rhythm with them—unhappily, it was interfering with Asil, too.

The fae fought well. Like someone who had learned the sword when it was the weapon of choice.

Not all fae were long-lived. Some had lives comparable to insects'—a few seasons, then gone. Most of those, Zee had told me once when he was a little drunk, were gone in truth. Their more fragile lives incapable of dealing with the steel and concrete that was conquering the earth.

Others lived nearly human long—twenty years for some, a hundred and fifty for others. Originally only a small percentage of fae were nearly immortal. The rise of humans and technology had selected for those tougher fae, and they now accounted for a far higher percentage of the fae than they ever had before.

A human lifetime was long enough to become an expert swordsman—my own karate sensei was accounted quite good in various weapon forms, including the sword. But Asil was a famous swordsman with centuries of practice, and this fae was more than holding his own. He was old.

Tad wasn't doing badly—his father had taught him, he'd told me once. If Tad had had something bigger than kitchen knives, if he and Asil had fought together before, they could have worked together. As it was, they had difficulty staying out of each other's way.

I slunk down low and, keeping to the outside edge of the room, slowly moved closer to the fight. I slid under the bed. Under *my* bed, dust bunnies, underwear, and a random shoe or two were common residents, but Sylvia was more organized than I and all she had under her bed was one of those thin plastic containers full of wrapping paper. I crawled from the head to the foot of the bed and, with my nose under the bedspread, watched for a chance to be of use.

The fae, leaping back to avoid Asil's baseball bat, hit Sylvia's desk and rolled over it, sending monitor and keyboard crashing off the top, along with a small clay jar filled with writing implements. Several neat stacks of rubber-banded papers escaped the hit. The fae hissed and damn near levitated off the desk like a cat thrown in a swimming pool and all but crashed into Asil to get away.

In the Tri-Cities, whose population has largely been employed by the government in one way or another for more than half a century, there is an abundance of those old, clunky steel desks straight out of the 1950s. I've seen them at rummage sales and every other kind of sale—and once, memorably, a good friend went to a government sale and thought she was bidding on a pallet with two desks and a dozen broken chairs, but ended up with a row of pallets—nearly fifty desks, three hundred and fifteen broken office chairs, a nonfunctional electric pencil sharpener, and four boxes of pink erasers. My office chair at the garage was actually four of those chairs, all Frankensteined into one that worked.

These industrial-strength desks were painted various shades of gray and institutional green or yellow. Sylvia's desk was of the yellow variety and, like all of them, made of steel.

Which meant that unlike the dead woman, and despite the big sword he was waving around so skillfully, this fae could not bear the touch of cold iron—or steel.

Tad dropped his knives and lunged—but Asil had just pushed the fae directly in front of me, so I didn't wait to see why. I sprang out from my hiding place and buried my teeth in the fae's left calf.

I don't have jaws like a bulldog, but I locked my jaws as best I could anyway. Asil swore at me in Spanish—I knew it was me because he ended it with "Mercedes." I knew it was swearing because, even in lyrical—if to me mostly unfathomable—Spanish, swearing sounds like swearing.

Asil also struck the sword on an upswing to keep the fae from hitting me with the pommel. The sword, edge against the wood of Asil's weapon, sliced the bat in two, leaving Asil with eighteen inches of wood to fight the fae's magicked blade. It hadn't felt any different to my senses than any other sword until the edge touched wood—and then it tasted like Zee's magic.

The fae laughed as my weight caused him to stumble. He said something in Welsh that in less dire circumstances I might have been able to translate or at least guess at. He aimed the sharp end of his sword toward me as he caught his balance.

"Let go," yelled Tad—and the steel desk hit the fae with a boom that would have done credit to a cannon. Papers, bills, bits and pieces of computer parts, and office detritus flew out the previously made hole in the wall, along with the fae and me. Landing jolted me enough that I lost hold of his calf, only then realizing that Tad's "let go" had been aimed at *me*.

The desk landed right next to my head before rolling onto the fae, leaving me half-stunned on the grass.

The fae shrieked, a pain-filled, rage-filled sound that hit my ears like a blow. If I'd heard it from a mile away, I'd have known it didn't come from a human throat. I smelled burning flesh, and he lifted the desk off and tossed it into the road, where it bounced once and cartwheeled into a battered truck.

He started to reach past me for his sword, which lay a dozen feet from us where it had fallen, but someone else got there first.

The fae hesitated for a bare moment, his eyes on the sword, but the sound of sirens up close and personal—or maybe it was the face of the man holding his sword—made him turn on his heels and run. Tad called insults from the open hole in the wall of Sylvia's bedroom.

The man who stood over me tossed the fae sword aside and dropped down to sit beside me. Gentle hands moved over me, but I couldn't focus, couldn't breathe—hoped so hard that it took longer to regain my ability to pump air into my lungs. As soon as I did, I shifted back to human and squirmed into his lap.

"Adam," I said, clutching him like a ninny while something tight in the middle of my chest softened. Tears slid down my cheeks. It would have been humiliating if he hadn't been clutching me back just as hard.

I wiped my eyes and pulled away to look at him. He was a little the worse for wear, his beard at the scratchy stage, and his eyes were . . . It had been bad. However he'd escaped, it had cost him.

He kissed me, and it was a hard, possessive kiss. He pulled back, and said, "So I went hunting you and got here just in time to see you flying out of a hole in the third story of an apartment attached to a man's leg."

There were burns on his lips, and I reached up to touch them.

"Silver," I said. It was important, because I didn't want to hurt Adam, but I lost track of what I was saying.

"Hey, you two lovebirds," said Tad dryly. "I couldn't help but notice that Mercy is buck naked and we have police arriving. So I fetched her clothes."

Adam looked up and smiled at Tad, but he spoke to me. "Better get dressed, Mercy. Tad's right."

I bounced out of his lap and grabbed the clothes from Tad and pulled them on with more speed than grace. Everything hurt and—I looked at Adam, who was rising to his feet—nothing hurt at all.

Tad strode over to the blade on the grass and looked at it assessingly. "Come here, then," he told it, and held his hand up. The sword flew into his grip, then . . . disappeared. He closed his hand over a small bit of metal and shoved it into his pocket.

"That will make it a little hard to explain the bat it cut into two, but it's too dangerous to allow it to get put into police custody," he told me. "Dangerous for the police."

My head felt fuzzy, but then I'd just been tossed out of a third-story window and discovered Adam was safe. And here. And that meant I didn't have to be in charge anymore.

With Adam here, I had no worries left at all. None. Something happened, some magic that smelled like fae had just been waiting for that moment, but I was too happy to worry about that, either.

I tied the drawstring at my waist, and asked Tad, "Your father made that sword, didn't he? Out of something that isn't iron or steel so that the fae could use it."

Tad nodded, looking at me closely. "I think there were five of these swords, each a little bit different from the other. Dad has one. All of them are bad news. If someone's not using them to slaughter a crowd of people, then some damned Gray Lord is blathering about how such a fae treasure needs to be protected. The Gray Lords are amassing fae artifacts like dragons amassing gold. And if this is too dangerous for the police, it's way too dangerous to be putting it into the hands of the Gray Lords. I'll give this one to my dad, and he can worry about dealing with it." He looked at me carefully and tilted his head. "Touch your nose, Mercy."

I put my hand on my nose, but it felt like my nose. If there was some smudge or something, I couldn't tell.

He looked at Adam and started to say something, but a police car stopped next to the desk in the road, lights flashing but siren thankfully silent. As if it was the signal everyone was waiting for, people started boiling out of their apartments. Two more police cars followed, and the middle one disgorged Sylvia. Tony got out of the driver's seat and followed her.

"Gabriel and the kids are okay," I yelled over the sounds of people talking and exclaiming over the damaged building. "I sent them to Kyle's."

Sylvia stopped and closed her eyes, crossed herself sincerely if briefly. She strode over to us, Tony in her wake. She looked up at the hole in the wall of her apartment.

"Tad stopped them," I told her. "And Gabriel made sure all the kids got out safely."

"Who did this?" asked Tony carefully; he was looking at the hole in the wall, too.

Tad made a noise, and Adam moved behind me and wrapped his arms around my shoulders. I leaned my chin on his forearms, content in his hold. "They were professionals. Mercenaries." There had been no fire in the woman who attacked me. No anger. No sorrow. This had been a job and nothing more.

"I know who this one was," said Tad unexpectedly. "Not that it'll help us any. Hey, Tony. Long time no see."

"Good to see you, *chico*," Tony told him. "What happened?"

"Mercy stowed Jesse and Gabriel—you know Gabriel, right?"

Tony looked at Sylvia and nodded. "I introduced Gabriel to Mercy in the first place."

"Don't think I haven't forgotten that," said Sylvia, and he winced a little, looked at me, and winced again.

Sylvia gave me a look that would have sent vampires running for cover—she was rather pointedly ignoring Adam. "You are sure that the children are safe?"

"I sent them to Kyle's house," I told her. But she didn't know Kyle. "He's the boyfriend of one of the wolves, a lawyer. He's got security people guarding his house, so the kids will be safe there. I'm sorry, Sylvia. If I had thought that they would know to look here, I never would have brought Jesse."

"You also sent this one." She tipped her head toward Tad. "Though he looked like a boy no older than Gabriel."

"I'm tough," Tad said soulfully, looking more puppylike and not very tough at all.

I couldn't tell what Sylvia was thinking, but she bent down and started collecting the paper that littered the ground.

"Right," said Tad breezily, to Tony. "So Mercy left Jesse and Gabriel with Sylvia, thinking they would be safe here from whoever was trying to grab them. But she was worried about them, and asked me to keep an eye out."

I saw comprehension dawn on Tony's face. "You're Zee's son," he said. "I keep forgetting that makes you half-fae." It was easy to forget. Tad looked human, just like the purebloods do most of the time. I never have known whether Tad's appearance is a glamour like the one his father wears or if he really does just look human. Half fae, I am told, can go either way—and some of the half fae who don't look human also don't have enough magic to hide what they are. A lot of those don't make it to adulthood. The fae are a very, very practical race as a whole.

Tad nodded at Tony. "Mercy knew I have enough oomph to

cause a big ruckus if someone came calling. And someone did." He looked up at the apartment ruefully. "If we can't catch the bastards who did this, I suppose I'll have to pay to get it fixed."

"Not your debt," said Adam. His voice was different, darker and harsher than usual, but he was so warm against my back. "We will take care of the expense of fixing your apartment, Sylvia."

I waited for her to explode, and I couldn't blame her. No one looking at the wall that lay mostly on the postage-stamp lawn next to the apartment would think that her children had been safe.

"It was my fault," I told her. "These guys knew the identities of all the pack members, even the ones they shouldn't have. I assumed that they would also know that you and Gabriel hadn't been talking. But I think they just hunted down Gabriel's nearest relative."

Sylvia stood up, tapped the handful of bills she'd gathered on her leg, and looked at the hole in her apartment. Then she looked at me. "No," she said slowly. "It isn't your fault. It is the fault of the people who came into my home intending to harm innocents."

"You are right," Adam told her, but then added with Alpha firmness, "But the pack will still pay for the damages. They were hunting my daughter."

She frowned at him but couldn't look at his face for too long. "All right," she said, her voice a little softer than it had been.

She looked at Tad. "You are a good young man—and, it seems, just as tough as you told me you were. Thank you for the care you took of my children."

"Hey, Sylvia," a young man wearing a WSU shirt called out. "You need some help? Me and Tom can get your desk back up to your apartment and maybe some of these looky-loos can pick up the mess." He tugged the braid of a cute girl a few years his junior, who was standing next to him.

"Stop it," she said, batting his hand away. "Yeah, sure, Ms. Sandoval. We can do cleanup."

An anxious middle-aged woman with a clipboard ran out to join the festivities.

"I'm Sally Osterberg," she said to one of the officers who was taking down notes. "I'm the apartment manager. Can you tell me what happened?"

"We're just getting to that, Sally," said Sylvia, still unnaturally calm—maybe it was that she had all that training for working dispatch, or maybe it was just being a single parent to a herd of kids whose ages spanned the school system.

"Do you prefer to do the repairs yourself and submit a bill, or would you rather we hire contractors to fix it?" asked Adam.

Sally turned to him and paused before her face lit up. "Adam Hauptman? You are Adam Hauptman? Oh my goodness. I thought . . . I saw in the news that you had been kidnapped by some kind of paramilitary group? Did you have to fight your way out? Are they—" She stopped, and not because she'd run out of words.

I tipped my head so that I could see Adam's smile as he told her, "I am. I did—and this seems to be connected to whoever has it in for my pack and me."

"This is so exciting," she said. "Wait until I tell my sister we had a werewolf crash through a wall—and not just any werewolf, either." She caught herself and blushed bright red. "I sound like a dork."

"No," Adam said, not bothering to correct her misapprehension about who had done most of the destruction. "You don't.

You sound like anyone would when caught up in *Twilight Zone* events. Can you get someone to board that hole up so Ms. Sandoval's possessions don't suffer from the weather?"

"Oh yes," she promised, "right away."

"Thank you."

He gave her another smile, which she returned until her eyes met mine. She cleared her throat. "I'll just go do that."

Tony looked at her trotting off, then looked at Adam. "Next time we have a domestic disturbance, I am taking you with me."

Adam smiled, and I could see how tired he was. "That only works sometimes—on violent men I often have the opposite effect. Unless you want bodies on the ground, you'll want to leave me home."

"So," said an officer standing beside Tony, "is there someone here who wants to tell us what happened? Without bodies or injured, we're not in emergency status, but the lieutenant does like us to get enough for an accurate report."

I opened my mouth, but Tad gave me another of those sharp looks he'd been sending me. He turned to face the policeman who'd asked, and at the same time put his body between me and the officer as his best "aw shucks" smile lit his face. "I'd spent most of the last day sitting on that fence." He nodded toward the eight-foot concrete block fence that encircled the apartment complex. Then he saw the cop's face. "I know, right? You're wondering why I pulled guard duty when I look like the before picture on a gym advertisement. My dad is fae, though, and I'm stronger than I look. Anyway, Jesse was making—"

"Jesse?"

"Adam's daughter, the one we were trying to keep safe from the bad guys," said Tad, moving behind the officer so he could see his notes. "She spells it J-E-S-S-E. And I'm Tad—like 'tadpole'—short for Thaddeus, but don't go there, and my last name is Adelbertsmiter." He spelled that for him, too. Twice.

The officer turned to force Tad to give him some space, but Tad just followed him around.

"Thank you," the officer said firmly. "What happened to the wall?" He looked at me, but Tad answered that, too.

"I was eating Jesse's brownies when someone rang the doorbell. I sent Jesse, Gabriel, and the kids into one of the bedrooms and went to answer the door."

"So you let him in?"

"Do I look like I'm five?" asked Tad indignantly. "No. I asked who it was and he said he was UPS and had a package for us. I told him to leave it on the porch 'cause I was naked, just out of the shower."

"I thought you were eating brownies," said the officer, who seemed to have resigned himself to having Tad hanging over his shoulder.

"I was." Tad shook his head. "I lied to the guy. I was there to keep the kids safe, no way was I opening the door to some stranger. There are things out there who can take it for an invitation—and you don't invite evil into your home."

"No," said the officer faintly, "I can see that you wouldn't."

Tony rubbed his mouth to hide a smile. Tony had seen Tad in full-blown Look-At-Me mode before. It wasn't that Tad was lying to the police officer, but, like a good stage magician, he'd keep the police looking where he wanted them to look. I didn't know what Tad was trying to cover up, but with Adam here and safe, I didn't really care.

"I thought you fae couldn't lie?" said one of the kids who was supposed to be cleaning Sylvia's stuff off the ground.

Tad nodded at him. "Yeah, that's only the true fae and some of the halfies. All that kind of stuff doesn't apply to me. 'Cause I lie and"—he spread his arms to invite everyone to admire—"I'm still here."

Behind me, Adam laughed quietly.

"Anyway," continued Tad, now talking to the crowd instead of the police, "the supposed UPS guy, he said he needed a signature. I told him to leave a form and we'd pick the package up at the UPS office—and that's when he unlocked the door with some kind of picklock or magic, I wasn't paying attention because he tried to hit me with a stun gun. When that didn't work, he drew a freaking sword and tried to take off my head."

"A *sword*?" said the officer, who was starting to look as though he was having trouble keeping up.

Tad nodded. "I know, right? Weirded me out, too. I guess he was pretty old, 'cause he knew what he was doing with that thing. I took two years of aikido at school, and he made a monkey out of me." I wondered if anyone would notice that although Tad was pretty banged up, there were no sword cuts. "I drew him back farther into the apartment to give the kids a chance to escape. Sometime in there, he tossed me through the wall."

All the people who were cleaning up the mess near him and the policemen and policewoman who were listening to his story looked at Tad—because he didn't look like he'd been tossed through a wall. Tad wasn't good-looking, his ears were too big and they stuck out and his nose was flattened as if he'd gone three rounds with George Foreman, but when he wanted people to watch him, they did. It wasn't magic; it was force of personality.

"Half fae," he told them again. "Sometimes it helps." He looked up at the hole, too, and shook his head and winced.

"Doesn't mean it didn't hurt. I ran back up and kept him occupied while the kids escaped. I tossed the desk at him, knocked him out the same hole he'd knocked me through, and by then you guys were pretty close. He picked himself up and ran."

Apparently we weren't going to talk about Asil. I glanced around, but didn't see Bran's wolf anywhere. Maybe Asil was responsible for Tad's look-at-me-not-at-what-I'm-hiding performance.

"Adam, what can you tell me about your kidnapping?" Tony wasn't as caught up in Tad's performance as the other cops were.

Adam gave him a tired smile. "I'm going to get some rest. I'll have my lawyer get in touch with you, and I'll give a full statement tomorrow. Okay?"

Tony gave him a reluctant nod. "Fine. Get in touch before ten tomorrow or I'll give you a call. Mercy, your turn."

I thought about the body in the back of Marsilia's car and tried to decide where to start.

"She didn't see much," Tad said, and this time I could feel his magic push past me, focusing Tony's attention on him. "How about she takes Adam home, and they both talk to you tomorrow. I know who this guy was because he's a spriggand—that's a kind of fae and fairly rare, thankfully, because they are nasty, bitter mischief-makers one and all. This one is a pureblood, and that makes him a renegade because he's not holed up in the reservations with the rest of the fae. There's only one renegade spriggand. He goes by the name of Sliver and usually hangs out with a half-fae woman called Spice. They hire out as muscle or assassins. I didn't see any woman, but she might have been keeping watch."

Spice must be the dead woman in the trunk of Marsilia's car. It would have been a good time for me to tell the police about her—her death was self-defense. If I told them right now, it would look better than if they found out about it later. But I was content just resting against Adam and couldn't find the impetus to say anything.

Tony frowned at Tad. "And why do you know the names of assassins for hire?"

Tad's brilliant facade soured. "Because even though they don't care a fig for the half-bloods, the pure-blooded fae send us lists of fae who did not answer the Gray Lords' call. We, the rejected, are to watch out for these fae and turn in any purebloods we see."

Tony nodded slowly. "I see. And if you don't turn them in?"

Tad's smile left entirely, and he looked very adult. "Nothing good. The Gray Lords don't have much use for half-bloods."

Tony blinked a couple of times and bit back whatever homily had come to him. Finally, he looked around at the destruction that was getting cleaned up. It was a crime scene, so probably no one should be cleaning yet—but it was also Sylvia's private papers flying in the wind.

"No bodies on the ground," said the officer Tad had cornered. "No one bleeding. No lawsuit because Mr. Hauptman is paying the damages—though we'll need to do a report just in case. We can let them clean up, Tony." He looked at Adam. "Mr. Hauptman is coming in tomorrow to make a statement about his kidnapping. That works for me—Tony?"

Tony frowned at me, and Tad's magic lit up again. Finally, Tony said, "Okay." He looked at Sylvia, and his face softened. "Why don't you give your keys to one of your neighbors so they can lock up after they're done cleaning the mess? I'll take you to Kyle's house, so you can look in on the kids."

8

ADAM

Adam kept his mouth shut and left his arms wrapped around Mercy so that he was anchored and didn't snarl at the nice policemen.

He kept his eyes off her face because he was having a hard enough time with all the noise and people as it was—the bruise that covered half her face would not help. His instincts kept shouting that something was *wrong*, and had ever since he'd seen the desk land, and he couldn't tell if it had missed her. He'd stopped breathing. The thought of his world without Mercy in it . . .

Well, that didn't help him calm down, either. He had the feeling that enemies were watching, that no one was safe. It was just the aftereffects of battle, dealing with his kidnappers last night and interrupting Mercy's fight this morning. That on-edge feeling had been familiar even before he was a werewolf.

Adam politely refused to answer any of Tony's casual questions as they waited for Sylvia to converse with her neighbors. The policeman finally gave up prying. He was a good cop, Tony, and knew that there were things they were hiding; but Adam had scrubbed in the shower of the unfinished winery while they were waiting for Elizaveta to show up. He knew that the only stains left of his killing spree were invisible ones, and he knew how to hide those, even from a good cop's instincts.

Tony picked up a fluttering paper that had attacked his shoe and looked at it. A bill from the power company, Adam saw, with a lot of red on it. Tony clenched it in his hand.

It was no secret that Tony loved Sylvia—or that she had put him off firmly. But, Jesse had told Adam, that had been a couple of years ago, when Sylvia's husband had been dead only a year. Tony had respected her wishes and backed off then, which was the right thing to do. But, maintained Jesse, someone should kick Tony and make him try again.

Or else, judging by the expression on Tony's face while he shoved the crumpled bill into his pocket, maybe a fae should destroy her home, threaten her children, and leave her unpaid bills floating in the wind. Sylvia was tough, smart, and could survive on her own—she didn't need a handsome prince to ride up and rescue her. But that didn't mean such a man might not want to protect her from everything he could, anyway.

Adam tipped his head down to see if Mercy had noticed Tony's epiphany, but as soon as she realized he was looking at her, she turned her attention to him and smiled.

Her lips were outlined in black that faded to gray. If it had been lipstick, it would have been an interesting effect with her coloring. But he knew, from the way the silver had burned his skin when he'd kissed her, that it wasn't some new color of lipstick. He was also sure that the silver impregnating her lips had something to do with the way she'd taken it from him through their mate bond. He just hoped to Hell that she hadn't been harmed any other way from that. It might mean they weren't going to be able to kiss without giving him blisters for the rest of their lives, but he could deal as long as that was the worst it had done.

There were a lot of things to worry about tomorrow. Today he was good. He waited until Sylvia was secured in Tony's car. Then, when he was satisfied the people he felt responsible for were safe, it was time to leave.

He kissed Mercy's temple, and said, "Wait here." Then he headed off at a jog to find his people.

He found both identical Toyota Corollas, the one he'd arrived in and the other manned by Mercy's surveillance team, parked near the Dumpster. He had the man who'd driven with him hand over the keys and ride back with the other two. By the simple expedient of combining them, he gained a car to take Mercy back to Kyle's. He opened the door—but realized, as he bent to slide in, that the pair of shoes on the ground next to his car were Mercy's—as was a sock just under the Dumpster.

He smelled Mercy, death, fae—*and* a strange werewolf. It was that last scent that made him growl. He'd forgotten that Mercy had gone off with a werewolf Bran had sent to help. A werewolf who was making himself conspicuously absent.

It appeared that more had happened than just the part of the fight he'd seen.

He gathered up sock and shoes and drove the car back to where he'd left Mercy. She waited for him just where he'd told her to, and waved to him cheerfully as he drove up. Beside her, looking at the ground, stood Zee's son; his face—now that there was no one to perform for—looked worried.

As Adam pulled up, Tad turned to him, and said, "Is it okay if I come along?" He looked at Mercy and frowned a little. Adam was unhappy about all those bruises, too. "Before all this happened, I was going to go to Kyle's with Mercy and the kids."

"Fine," agreed Adam. If Tad hadn't asked, Adam would have insisted. He wasn't leaving any of his people vulnerable, and Tad belonged to Mercy and thus to Adam. Adam glanced at Mercy, and said, "I'll drive."

He knew that he looked nearly as rough as he felt. He'd seen himself in the bathroom mirror after his shower, and Mercy was better at reading his face than most people. Even the half beard he wore wouldn't protect him from her scrutiny.

He waited for Mercy's response. He enjoyed their arguments because very few people argued with him at all. Mercy would argue until she won, he convinced her he was right, or it was clear that she was not going to win no matter how right she felt she was. If she was cranky enough about it, she'd get him back—that damned junker Rabbit was still cocked up on one wheel where he could see it out their bedroom window. He kind of liked it—not the leprous Rabbit, the Rabbit made him crazy—but that she cared enough to make the effort.

This was a battle he wouldn't lose, though he probably shouldn't drive. His concentration was as shot as his temper. Nothing like lack of sleep and battle fatigue to give him fuel for a really nasty case of road rage. Even so, there was no way that he could relinquish enough control to let anyone else take the wheel, not even Mercy, who was a good driver.

Instead of arguing, Mercy just smiled and got into the passenger seat without a word. Inexplicably, that sent his temper flaring worse than if she'd argued.

He bit his tongue because he'd look like an idiot if he yelled at her for *not* arguing with him. Tad hopped into the back and fastened his seat belt.

As Adam drove out of the parking lot, Tad said, "We should pick up the other werewolf over by the high school; just turn down Tenth."

"Why did he run off?" Adam asked, then looked at Mercy.

"He was worried that his presence would just complicate things." In the rearview mirror, Adam noticed that Tad was tapping his fingers and watching Mercy as if he was worried about her.

"Who died over by the Dumpsters?" Adam asked.

"The other half of the fae team who tried to take Jesse," Mercy said, sounding as if she were talking about something mundane . . . like grocery shopping. "She jumped me when we parked, and Asil killed her. By the time it occurred to me that it would be smart to tell the police about her, the kids had already taken off in the car with the body."

Adam damned near stopped the car. On any other day, he'd have been upset about a body in the trunk of the kids' car. But that was before he'd heard Asil's name. "Bran sent *the Moor*?"

"Asil," Mercy agreed, so he knew he hadn't misheard. "He said Charles sent him, but he was talking in front of Agent Armstrong of Cantrip."

Armstrong must have been the fed who was at Kyle's house, the one who'd tried to get him to wait when Adam had hustled out to find Mercy.

Mercy was right, *Bran* had sent the Moor to take care of Mercy and Jesse. The Moor, who was so crazy his own son had sent him to Bran to be put down. Except that Bran, for his own reasons, had decided not to do it.

Asil. Maybe he had recovered from being crazy.

"He kept that bastard from wiping the floor with me," said Tad. "I was overmatched—and that's an understatement. I might have been able to slow the spriggan down long enough for Jesse and Gabriel to get the kids away, but it would have been a close thing, and I would have had to pull out my big guns to do it." He looked out the window, and continued blackly, "My control of the big guns isn't what it should be. So I'm glad Asil showed up."

College had changed Tad. It was supposed to, Adam knew. But looking at Tad for a moment longer than was really safe while he was driving, Adam was afraid that he'd gained the sort of knowledge that a chick learned from being pushed off a cliff rather than the low branch of a tree, and had taken damage from the fall.

Adam had grown up that way, too.

The Moor was waiting for them, leaning on a lightpost and looking bored. Adam had never actually met Asil, but he looked Moorish, wolfish, and dangerous. Who else could he be? He didn't have a mark on him from the fight, though it would be hard to see a bruise on his skin from a distance. People were looking at him as they drove past in their cars, mostly, Adam thought, because Asil was wearing nothing more than a summer-weight shirt. It took a more experienced eye than most people had to see exactly what Asil was.

As he pulled the Corolla over to the curb, Adam met Asil's eyes briefly, and the old wolf gave Adam a commiserating smile, which Adam found himself returning. This trip was going to be rough. Probably worse for Adam, who was still wound up tight with the aftermath of this morning's killing. But if half the stories Adam had heard were right, Asil was wobbling precariously between human and beast, so it wouldn't be easy for him to be cooped up in the car with an unfamiliar dominant wolf, either.

Asil opened the door behind Mercy and slid into the back seat. As soon as the door shut, the urge to tear out the strange wolf's throat tightened Adam's hands on the wheel. He should not be driving feeling like this. But without the task of getting to Kyle's in one piece to focus on, he was certain to do something regrettable.

"Adam," said Tad, clearing his throat, because he doubtless could read the uncomfortable atmosphere in the car, "we need to go to my dad's house before we go anywhere else."

"Why?" It was almost a growl rather than a real word. Adam needed to keep his time in the car with the other wolf to a minimum, and that didn't include a side trip. Asil's presence behind him was an itch between his shoulder blades.

"Because that damned sword isn't the only fae artifact that Sliver and Spice ran around with, and Mercy is acting strange."

Yes, howled the beast that lived in his heart. *There is something wrong with Mercy. I've been trying to tell you, but you thought it was just from the fighting. It isn't. This is like what happened to her before, when we couldn't protect her.*

Adam looked at Mercy, who looked back at him with big eyes and a half smile on her face. "I'm fine," she said, which if it had been true, she would never have said, not in that tone of voice. She'd have been arguing with Tad or making smart-ass quips about strange people.

"Rub your nose," Tad told her.

She rubbed her nose.

"Pat your knee."

She did that as well.

"Cough twice."

She covered her mouth and coughed.

"Have you ever seen Mercy take three orders in a row without arguing?" Not being psychic and able to hear Adam's inner beast, Tad thought he had to convince Adam.

"Not even when Bran is the one giving the orders." Adam put his foot down on the gas. If the tension in the car had been strong before, it was nothing to the current conditions—and it had nothing to do with the Moor.

Adam wanted to kill something, anything to make Mercy all right. Under his hands, the wheel of the car groaned, and he loosened his fingers and fought not to lose control.

The other werewolf was doing his best to make this easy, keeping quiet and keeping his gaze focused out his window, so Adam couldn't meet his eyes. Adam appreciated it and tried to reciprocate as well as he could when anger was a tide that threatened to blind him.

"What did they use? And how do we fix her?" He spoke between gritted teeth, trying to keep his human form and stay between the white lines on the road. His hands tightened again, and there was a pop as something gave way in the steering wheel of the little car. When it didn't seem to affect his ability to turn, Adam ignored it.

"I don't know how to fix her," said Tad. "But my dad will. He can't use phones anymore—Mercy called him yesterday, and the powers that be took away his phone privileges. I have a way to reach him at home."

Okay. Zee was good. Adam sucked in a deep breath and tried to make his wolf realize that changing right now was a genuinely bad idea.

"What was it that got her?" He knew squat about fae magic but couldn't help but ask. Maybe it would be something that wore off.

"An artifact—a set of bone wrist cuffs," Tad said. "It's supposed to make prisoners easy to control. Before Asil killed her, did Spice put a set of cuffs on you, Mercy?"

"Just one," Mercy said in a chipper voice. "I changed to coyote and stepped out of it. Asil threw the cuffs into the trunk with the body."

"If this is true," Asil said, "why didn't it show up until after the battle was over? She wasn't being compliant when she threw herself at the fae in the apartment."

"I don't know," answered Tad. "Maybe because she only wore one of the cuffs. Maybe because she only had it on for a short time. But you see it, don't you, Adam? It took me a while to be sure."

"Yes." His beast had noticed immediately and become frantic, but Adam hadn't wanted to see anything wrong.

Zee's house was less than a mile from Kennewick High School, a small Victorian nestled in a small cluster of houses that dated from the time that Kennewick was a tiny transportation hub connecting railroad and river traffic. The house needed paint and a little work on the porch. The yard was tiny, as was common in the days when the use of horses meant that the distance between places mattered more. House and yard were surrounded by a wrought-iron fence that was suitably elaborate for an iron-kissed fae's home.

Adam put his hand on Mercy's shoulder and brought up the rear of the procession to the house. Even through the sweatshirt she wore, he felt the silver that coursed in her blood.

Tad didn't unlock the door when he turned the fancy brass

knob, but Adam had the feeling that he'd unlocked it in some other way. Mercy would have known because Mercy could sense magic a lot better than Adam could.

Zee's house was furnished sparsely and none-too-fancily despite its Victorian appointments, which included the original light fixtures and fine woodwork. The living room had a matching couch and love seat that were comfortably worn. A small flat-screen TV adorned the wall between two built-in bookcases filled with paperback books. A handmade rug softened the hardwood floor.

To the right, a door opened to an eat-in kitchen that had a 1950s-style table for two that had passed shabby and hit antique. On the wall next to the table was a large photo of a serious, young-looking man who looked a lot like Tad. The man was dressed in a suit and standing next to a good-looking woman in a wedding dress with her brown hair in a poofy style common a couple of decades ago. Her smile lit up the room even from a photograph.

Mercy lingered, looking at the photograph.

"Come on, Mercy," said Tad, and she immediately complied.

"You've made your point," growled Adam, unable to hold back his anger, though Tad didn't deserve it. "That's enough."

Asil hadn't spoken a word, just took everything in. He didn't protest when Adam hung back so that the other wolf was never behind them.

Tad took them up the typically Victorian narrow and steep stairs to the second story and from there to a hallway. At the end of the hall was a half door—two feet wide by three feet tall, the kind of door that would have hidden a linen closet or a dumbwaiter. Since it was next to the bathroom, Adam would put his money on the linen closet.

Tad put a hand on the door and closed his eyes. Mercy stirred, staring at the floor and moving closer to Adam, away from the wall. Adam could smell her unease, and he put his arm around her. Her feelings were clearly written on her face, too—and she'd never have shown fear to anyone if she could have helped it. She watched the walls as if something dangerous were crawling up from the floor beneath them.

"Whatever they did to her is more than just following orders," Adam said.

"Yes," agreed Tad, his hand still on the door. "I think it steals her will. That way, she'd answer questions, follow orders—and not try to hide it when something scares her. It's okay, Mercy," he told her when she took another step back from him. "This is old magic, but it knows me, and it won't hurt anyone here and now."

"Carefully worded for a fae who doesn't have to tell the truth," said Asil.

Tad turned to the old wolf coolly. "I am always careful with the truth. It is a powerful thing and deserves respect."

"Of course," answered Asil. "When you are old, you will find yourself assuming that everyone else is careless with important things, too. My comment was not meant as censure; you merely surprised me."

"What do you see?" Adam asked Mercy, who was looking at things he couldn't perceive.

"Magic," she told him. "Fae magic, old magic, and it's crawling from the basement up to Tad's hand like a cat seeking a treat." She looked at Tad, and for a moment Mercy looked more fae than he did. "It likes you, but it isn't very happy about us."

Tad smiled at her. "It'll behave itself."

The white milk glass knob on the door turned without help,

and Adam liked that no better than he liked the description Mercy had given. Magic was outside his ability to sense unless it was very strong, and he did not like things that he could not perceive.

When Tad pulled his hand off the door, it opened and revealed dark wooden stairs that were even narrower and steeper than the ones they'd just come up. They twisted as they rose so they took up only the same amount of room as the narrow linen closet had, and Adam could only see four steps before they were out of view.

Tad stepped in, and Adam heard the fabric of his shirt catch on a rough spot on the wood at the top of the doorway. Asil followed, and Adam urged Mercy up as soon as the old wolf's feet disappeared from his sight.

The passage was tight, even for Mercy, and she banged a knee on a step, winced, and stopped climbing.

"Are you all right?" he asked, his hand on her ankle.

"No," she said without heat. "Not really. That was the knee I hurt in the car wreck, and there's a ghost."

"A ghost?" He knew Mercy saw ghosts, but she usually didn't tell him when she saw them. She'd once explained to him that most ghosts were only sad memories. The ones that were closer to alive were often better off if they didn't know she could perceive them. He had a feeling that there was a story there, but he hadn't pressed.

"Mmm," Mercy said. "Right in front of me. I think she's the same one that looks out of Zee's dining room window sometimes."

Adam couldn't see anything except for Mercy's back because of the stupid spiral staircase, but he'd probably not be able to see a ghost even if they were in an open room. "Can you get her to move?" he asked.

"She's a repeater, I think," Mercy replied hesitantly.

A repeater, he'd learned from her, was a ghost that she could see but who did not react to the real world at all, just did a certain action over and over again, usually in the same place and sometimes at the same time every day. More an impression than a remnant of a real person.

"What is she doing?"

"Crying." Mercy's voice sharpened a little, making her sound more like herself. "That's what she does in the window, too. I wonder if she was that much of a wet blanket in real life?"

Peripherally, Adam had been aware of Tad and Asil talking somewhere above them. But he'd been paying attention to Mercy, and so he didn't react quickly enough when Tad called out, "Mercy, what's the holdup? Get up here."

She scrambled up the stairs, heedless of the ghost. It was too late to do anything, so Adam hurried behind her. He saw nothing unusual and didn't feel so much as a shiver. He emerged right on her heels to find Mercy tight-lipped and shaky.

"Mercy, are you okay?" he asked, and she looked at him and solemnly shook her head.

"I was wrong. It wasn't a repeater." She rubbed her hands and glanced behind him. "But she can't get in here."

"Who is she?" asked Asil.

"What does it mean that she wasn't a repeater?" Adam didn't like the way Mercy looked—too pale, and there was sweat on her forehead.

"It means that she tried to hitch a ride." Mercy hugged herself and bounced on the balls of her feet.

"*Who* is *she*?" Asil asked again.

"Give us a minute," snarled Adam, though he stopped himself from looking at Asil and escalating matters further.

The other wolf's chest rumbled warningly.

"Sorry," Adam said with an effort that cost him. "Mercy. Is there anything I can do?"

She shook her head. "No. I'm okay. I've just never had that happen before. She just clung to me, and I couldn't tell her to go away." She shivered. "But Zee has this place barricaded with magic, and she couldn't follow me here."

She'd been in danger, and Adam had been right there and helpless. He had been leaving her alone because she didn't like "cuddling in public" much, and in this state, she had no choice. But when her teeth started chattering, he hugged her to him. She was icy cold and leaned into him. She was all muscle and bone—and she'd be offended if she knew he thought of her as fragile. Without the formidable will that drove her, she was . . . small.

Her teeth quit chattering almost right away. She looked over Adam's shoulder, and said, "She's a ghost, Asil. I've seen her a few times hanging out around this house."

"Our house is haunted?" Tad sounded taken aback.

"She doesn't bother you," Mercy said defensively. She stepped away, and Adam let her go. "I'd have told you about it if she were bothering you."

Crisis apparently averted, Adam looked around. The room was narrow and long, wide enough, if barely, for three people to stand shoulder to shoulder. The floor was carpeted with layers of Persian rugs that were worth a not-so-small fortune.

Unmatched bookcases lined the wall on one of the long ways of the room, ranging from hand-carved museum pieces to boards separated by cinder blocks. The top two shelves of each held a selection of unpainted metal toys. The rest of the shelves were filled with various sharp-bladed weapons. The books, and there were a lot of them, were piled on the floor on the other side of the room. The wall directly across from the doorway they'd entered was entirely covered by an enormous mirror.

"Could you shut the door, Mercy?" Tad asked, walking up to the mirror. "I don't activate the mirror without the door closed."

Adam got to the door before Mercy could and closed the ghost out. He didn't like it that she was still obediently following orders, although this time, he thought, Tad hadn't meant it like that. Tad would know that giving Adam or Asil orders, under these circumstances, might be a bad idea, and so he'd told Mercy.

Mercy touched the door after Adam shut it. "There's some kind of magic," she said.

"Protections," Tad agreed, without turning from the mirror. "Useful to keep out ghosts and spies."

He knocked three times on the mirror, and said,

Spiegel spieg'le finde,Vaters Bild und Stimme,
in der Tiefe Deiner Sinne, seiner Worte seiner Form,
meiner Worte meiner Form, führe, leite, führ' zusammen,
deiner Wahrheit Bindeglied,
verbinde unsere Wirklichkeiten,
Wesen und Natur im Lied!

"Mirror, mirror, on the wall," Asil murmured when Tad quit speaking.

"Shh," said Tad. "This isn't that mirror. That mirror broke, and good riddance to it. Let's not give this one ideas, please."

Adam couldn't tell if he was serious or not.

After a few minutes, during which the mirror did nothing more interesting than reflect everyone present back at it, Asil started to look at the toys on the shelves, though he kept his hands to himself. It gave him an excuse to keep his back to Adam, which Adam appreciated.

Mercy bent down to get a better look at the books—most of them were German and old. But Adam noticed that there were a couple of newer mysteries, too—and what looked like a complete *Doc Savage* series, numbered one through ninety-six, in paperback. Mercy reached out to touch one old book, and Adam's instincts made him block her hand. "It's not smart to touch a grumpy old fae's things," he said.

"It wants me to touch it," she explained earnestly.

"All the more reason not to do it," Adam told her, keeping a hold on her hand.

A compliant prisoner, he thought, has to do whatever she is told by who—or whatever—tells her to do something. He wondered if that ghost would have given her trouble if she had been able to exert her will. He glanced at the mirror, but there was still nothing more interesting than their reflections in it. "Tad, what's the holdup?"

"Shh," the young man said. "Not so loud. Someone on the other side of the mirror might overhear. He'll come as soon as he can."

"There's a lot of metal in here for a fae's den," murmured Asil. "And enough magic to make my nose itch."

"Zee is a metalsmith," Mercy explained, leaning against Adam. Like Asil, she spoke quietly. "Iron-kissed. Siebolt Adelbertsmiter."

"The Dark Smith of Drontheim?" Asil was suddenly a lot more tense, his voice half-strangled.

"That's right," said Tad, looking away from the mirror because Asil was more interesting. At least that was why Adam was looking at him. Fortunately, the other wolf was looking at Tad.

"Your father is Loan Maclibhuin, the Dark Smith of Drontheim?" Asil turned to Adam, averting his eyes at the last minute. "Are you sure you want to contact Maclibhuin? Do you know what he is?"

"He's mellowed with age," Mercy assured Asil before Adam could say anything. She sounded like herself. "No more killing people because they annoy him. No more making crazy weapons that will inevitably cause more problems than they solve because he had a bad day and wanted to destroy a civilization or two."

Tad snorted. "He likes Mercy. He'll help us."

Suddenly exhausted, as much by keeping a tight rein on himself as by the events of the past few days, Adam sat down on the rug and pulled Mercy onto his lap, where she couldn't get into trouble.

When Mercy squeaked in surprise—though she didn't fight him—he said, "No telling how long it will take the old fae to answer. No sense for you to stand the whole time. Your knee is bothering you." He'd noticed that she was keeping her weight off it.

"Car wreck, then that step," she said, relaxing against him. "But it's my cheekbone that really hurts. Falling from Sylvia's apartment didn't help."

"Wait a moment," Tad said, and left them in the attic by themselves as he ran downstairs for something, closing the door behind him.

"He left us alone in the heart of his father's power," said Asil.

"That's because I would kill you before I allowed you to do anything," Adam assured him with an easy voice. "Tad knows that we stand with him, Mercy and I. And if you think this is the center of Zee's power, you are very much mistaken. This is a cache, he probably has fifty of them around somewhere. Paranoid old fae." Adam understood paranoia. It was a useful attribute if you were trying to keep the people you loved safe.

Asil didn't reply, which was probably a good thing. They needed more space between them before they could deal with each other safely. Tad came pounding back up the stairs with a deck of cards and a poker-chip carousel.

Mercy drew in a breath, and Adam looked at her. There was nothing Mercy enjoyed so much as complaining to people about the idiosyncrasies of werewolves; he had always found it charming—and useful. He waited a moment, but she didn't say anything.

Adam put his hand on her face and turned it, gently, toward Tad. It would be better if she explained the problem to him. Until Asil and Adam had been properly introduced on Adam's territory—such things had a very well-established protocol so that no blood was shed—Asil would be easy to offend. He and Adam had both been very careful not to pay too much attention to each other.

"Mercy, would you tell Tad why poker is a bad idea?" he asked her.

"Asil and Adam don't know each other," she said amiably. "And even if they did . . . poker isn't really a good werewolf game." She appeared to consider that a moment. "Or rather, it is too good a werewolf game. It would end with bodies."

Tad glanced at both wolves, one after the other. "Seven-up?" he suggested. "War? Gin rummy? I know you play gin rummy because Warren taught me to play it when I was a kid."

"Tell him," Adam said to Mercy.

"No games between two dominant wolves unless they know each other very well and have established their dominance. There was a very nasty chess match that happened in the Marrok's pack when I was six or seven. Bran put an end to it, but not before one of the wolves ended up with a pickax in his leg." Mercy continued instructing the uninitiated in her Mercy-matter-of-fact fashion. "Adam and Warren could play, for instance, because, though they are both dominant wolves, Adam has firmly established himself as more dominant in both their eyes. One lost game won't make any difference. Darryl and Warren, though, are second and third in the pack hierarchy. They play CAGCTDPBT during pack gaming days, but they play on the same side. Always."

Tad gave Mercy an assessing look. "No poker. No gin rummy, and especially no chess if you don't want to end up pickaxed. And I didn't know you played CAGCTDPBT."

"Werewolf games," Mercy said solemnly, "play for keeps, or go home." She was so cute sometimes it made Adam's heart hurt. She was also a killer CAGCTDPBT player. The pack made Mercy and him play on opposite sides to keep it fair.

"I threw out my Go-Fish cards a long time ago." Tad's voice was dry. "I'm going to play some solitaire and leave the rest of you to twiddle your thumbs."

Exhausted, worried, and unhappy, Adam leaned against the wall and let his eyes half close in an old soldier's trick. He wasn't really asleep but not really awake, either. Any break in the current patterns of sound, sight, or scent would attract his attention.

Tad sat down in front of the mirror and laid out a game of spider solitaire. He played three or four games and lost all of them—no cheating for Tad.

Asil seemed happy to occupy himself studying Zee's little toys as far away as he could get from Adam. The Moor wasn't exactly what Adam had expected. Much less crazy, and also much better at the dance that kept everyone alive in a small room with two dominant wolves who were strangers to each other than a wolf of his reputation ought to be. Bran usually knew what he was doing, and that seemed to be true when he sent Asil as well.

Mercy wasn't sleeping, but she lay quietly in his lap. She liked to cuddle when they were alone. He decided to enjoy it because it settled the beast inside him a little. The wolf was convinced that as long as he held her, nothing could touch her.

Neither could he. Not for long.

Mercy put her hand on Adam's, and he could feel the silver go to work on his skin. He didn't react because he craved her touch more than he minded the burn—and she'd taken it for him, hadn't she? So maybe part of it was guilt, feeling that he deserved to hurt because he'd brought harm to her.

She leaned forward, reading the titles on the books again. He opened his eyes a bit more to make sure she didn't try for that book that called to her again.

Zee had a modern college text on metallurgy right next to a very old book bound in leather with a title that was nearly indecipherable, between the faded gold embossing and the old German script. And just out of easy reach was the little green linen-bound book with the warped cover that had fascinated her earlier. Mercy shifted restlessly then froze, jerking her hands away from him.

"I've burned you," she whispered, horrified.

Tad looked up from dealing another round, and Asil glanced their way—and then returned his attention to the fae weapons on the shelves.

"I'm a werewolf," Adam said softly. "It won't kill me."

She frowned at him, and he closed his eyes again. "It's all right, Mercy. It's already healed." He wanted to tell her not to worry, but then maybe she wouldn't. Not because she chose to follow his advice but because of the damned fae artifact that made her obedient. An obedient Mercy because she had no choice—that was an abomination.

She curled up, tucking her hands in where they couldn't accidentally touch him. She closed her eyes, too—he knew because he had only *mostly* shut his.

The better to see you with, my dear, said the Big Bad Wolf.

He also saw something else. Adam had a habit of keeping track of things in his environment—situational awareness. It had saved his butt more than once. He was especially aware of things that could be used as weapons.

One of the blades on the shelves was moving. He didn't catch it in actual motion, but when they'd first come into the room, it had been in the back corner of the bottom shelf of the bookcase nearest the mirror. Now it was in the middle of the shelf and had slid nearly off the edge.

He wondered if it might be chasing Asil, if only very slowly.

It was a hunting knife with a dark blade that showed just a touch of rust. The hilt was some sort of antler. When he closed his eyes a little more and turned his gaze so that the knife was in the corner of his vision, he could tell that there was some sort of runic lettering down the blade. But as soon as he looked directly at it again, the runes disappeared.

Because Adam was carefully not-watching the blade, he noticed something was happening to the mirror.

The corners were darkening until, gradually, it quit reflecting the room and looked more like a huge photo of a heavy, gray, silk curtain than a silver-backed glass mirror. Adam lifted his head to see it more clearly. As soon as the whole of it was dark, frost bloomed. It started in the very center of the mirror, as if it were very cold and someone was blowing on it with a warm, wet breath. A fog of ice spiderwebbed out in a crystalline sheet across the glass.

As soon as the ice covered the entire surface, a darker line dripped down the middle of the mirror and dark, callused, long-fingered hands slid out of the glass and pulled the gray aside, sending a light snow to the rug that butted up against that end of the room.

Zee stepped through the mirror. Tad looked up and started gathering his cards together, though his game wasn't half-finished yet. Asil's eyes slitted, and he rolled to the balls of his feet, ready for whatever would come. Mercy turned her head, and said, "Hey, Zee. Long time no see."

The Zee that stepped through the mirror wasn't the one Adam was used to. Gone was the glamour that he'd presented to the world. He was no slender, balding old man—his sharp-featured face was both unaged and ancient, with skin the color of fumed oak. His body showed the musculature of a man who spent his days before a hot fire bending metal to his will—wide shoulders and taut flesh that knew hard work.

"Mercedes," he said. "What have you done to your lips?"

Mercy touched her lips but didn't say anything. Adam found that a hopeful sign.

White-gold hair slicked down over Zee's shoulders like a waterfall of pale wheat. He wore, incongruously, a pair of black jeans and a gray flannel shirt with a motor-oil stain on one cuff. On his feet were his old battered, steel-toed boots.

Asil's lips curled back, and he snarled softly.

"Peace, wolfling," said Zee in his usual impatient and crabby fashion. "It's been a long time since I hunted your kind. And, as I recall, *you* got away cleanly anyway. You have no axe to grind."

The old fae frowned at Tad, who had set the deck of cards on the poker caddy and gotten to his feet.

"What's wrong, Tad, that you've called me here?"

"What isn't is a better question," said Tad. "I'm really glad to see you. I don't know exactly where to start."

"If it helps," Zee said, "I'm caught up to where someone has apparently taken most of the wolf pack captive. Last I heard, Mercy set you to guard Jesse and Gabriel while she went off to see how Kyle fared. I see that you managed to recover at least one of the wolves, Mercy."

"Adam recovered himself," Mercy told him. "The lips are from the silver."

Zee frowned at her and took a couple of steps nearer. Adam stood up and pulled Mercy to her feet beside him, unwilling to let this stranger with Zee's eyes and voice approach him when he was in a vulnerable position.

"Silver?"

Mercy explained how Coyote told her to change the rules and so she'd drunk the silver out of Adam's body. Adam intended on having a word or two with Coyote the next time he saw him—not that it would do any good. Mercy backtracked and began again with Stefan's helping her free Kyle and ran all the way through to escorting Asil to Sylvia's house.

"So I sent Jesse and Gabriel to take the kids to Kyle's house," Mercy said.

"In Marsilia's car, which now has a dent and a dead body in the back," said Zee.

"It sounds worse than it is," she assured him.

"No," Adam disagreed. "It is exactly as bad as it sounds."

"You know these assassins?" Zee asked Tad.

"It was Sliver and Spice." Tad leaned against the bookcase nearest him and caught the hunting knife before it fell on the ground. He frowned at it and set it back in the corner it had started in. "You stay there," he told it.

Zee smiled, and his face suddenly looked a lot more like the Zee Adam knew. "I wish you better luck than I have with that." He nodded toward the knife. "It doesn't like to stay in one place when interesting things are going on. How do you know it was Sliver and Spice? They are both skilled at hiding who and what they are."

"Here," said Tad, taking out the small bit of metal that the fae man's sword had turned into. "This is yours. Sliver was using it on Asil—who fought him off with a baseball bat from Walmart. And Sliver had to drop the glamour to keep up with him." There was a bit of hero worship coming off Tad.

"The Moor doesn't need a pesky magic blade to triumph over evil," Mercy murmured, and Adam gave her a sharp look.

Zee took the object from Tad, and in his hands, it formed once more into a blade. This time, though, it was black as pitch but only two feet long.

"Of course he did," Zee said, sounding a little put out that Asil had triumphed over one of *his* blades. But his face smoothed out, and he said, "He outsmarted me for three weeks in high winter in the Alps. It stands to reason that a spriggand would have no chance at all, even with such a blade as this."

"Sliver got away," Tad said. "But not before Adam showed up out of the blue and stole that sword from him."

"You didn't bring me here to tell me this," Zee said. He didn't look at Mercy, but Adam could feel his attention.

"Right," Tad said. "Mercy, touch your toes, then turn around three times."

Adam understood why Tad had to do it, but he couldn't help the unhappy sound he made. "You need to quit giving her orders," he warned Tad. He wasn't angry, not at Tad, anyway. But her easy compliance made his wolf want to jump out of his skin. The last time she'd been caught in this kind of magic, she'd been raped, and he remembered it, both wolf and man.

"Peace and Quiet, also known as the Fairy Queen's Gift," said Zee, in a contemplative voice that made Adam think that he wasn't the only one who was bothered by Mercy's obedience. "I had heard that it had surfaced again. Did Sliver and Spice get away with it?"

Adam caught Mercy's shoulders and stopped her before she finished the second turn. "You don't have to listen to him anymore, Mercy. Stop."

"No," Asil said. "The cuffs are in the trunk with the dead woman—who it is probably safe to assume is Spice." He grimaced. "Did she pick the name from the singing group?"

Tad smiled. "Not unless they were around a couple of centuries ago."

"Sliver is alone?" Zee sounded for a moment like a hunting wolf. "Interesting." Then he looked at Mercy again, and some of the inhumanity slid away from him.

"Stealing someone's willpower was always a rare and difficult fae gift," Zee said. "It's a spell easier to work on someone who is asleep or happy."

Mercy shivered, as if she were suddenly cold, again. "I don't like being obedient." Adam hugged her and wished he could go back and kill the man who'd done this to her last time *before* he'd hurt her. Wished, at the very least, he could protect her from her memories because if this was making him remember, it had to be doing the same to her. Rage choked him—and Mercy patted his arm in reassurance.

Zee caught his eye and nodded grimly, and Adam knew he wasn't the only one unhappy that such a spell had caught Mercy again. "Peace and Quiet was made as a gift for a fairy queen who collected the wrong fae's son into her court."

They'd run into a fairy queen before. They weren't fae royalty precisely but had a gift that allowed them to enslave humans and fae alike. Almost like a honeybee queen, they set up courts designed to both feed their power and entertain them. Not Adam's favorite kind of fae.

"She didn't last long," Zee continued, "because the cuffs only work for a short period of time on the fae, though it can be more permanent on humans."

Zee put his hand under Mercy's chin and looked into her eyes. "The woman who gave the fairy queen the gift wanted her son back. Once the queen died, all the humans and fae went back to their old lives."

Without the glamour, his slate gray eyes were brighter and odder-colored.

"Beware of fairy gifts," Mercy said.

"And Greeks bearing gifts," agreed Zee without a pause.

"How do we break the spell?" Adam asked. "Killing the woman didn't seem to work."

"Love's true kiss," Mercy said, though Adam had been asking Zee. "But I can't kiss Adam because it hurts him. Too much silver."

A kiss?

Adam looked at Zee who shrugged. "Actually, a kiss from someone who loves you is an effective remedy for a number of the effects of fae magic."

All right then. Adam lifted Mercy's chin and kissed her. He'd kissed her at Sylvia's apartment, too. But this time he didn't let the burn of the silver distract him.

He pictured his Mercy in his mind. Mercy holding a plate of cookies in the hope that they would make her neighbor feel better after his wife left him. Mercy baring her teeth at him because he'd annoyed her by trying to make her stay safe. Mercy pulling the damned tires off the wreck in her backyard because she was mad at him. Mercy shooting Henry before the cowardly wolf could challenge Adam while he was hurt.

And his lips first bled, then blistered against hers.

He accepted the pain and put it behind him, letting his body feel only the softness and warmth of hers. He took in a breath through his nose and let her scent surround him. This, this was his Mercy, and he wanted her—mind, body, and soul, she was his. And he was hers. The kiss warmed up, and he pulled her tighter into his body and let the heat of their kiss spread through his body in hopes it would catch flame in her.

She returned his kiss, her body softening—his partner in this as in so many things. She fit against him well—all muscle with just a hint of softness, smelling of burnt oil, harsh orange-scented soap, and Mercy.

Then every muscle in her body tensed, and she started to struggle. He held her just a little longer, to relish her fight, which told him the spell had been broken. But Mercy knew how to break the grip of someone who was larger and stronger than she was. That he didn't want to hurt her was of more use to her than his strength was to him. She twisted her wrists to break his hold and ducked out and away.

"Damn it, damn it, Adam," she raged at him, while Adam

caught his breath. "*You* don't let me hurt you like that. You haven't eaten since God knows when because I can see your ribs. You've lost twenty pounds in two days. Too much shapeshifting, not enough food—and having to heal yourself every time you touch me just makes it worse. And then you let me hurt you, you stupid, stupid . . ." She was so mad, the words wouldn't come out of her mouth.

"Or you could try to force her to do something absolutely against her will," said Zee casually. "That works more often on this kind of magic than love's true kiss."

9

Adam's lips were blistered, and his face looked like he had a bad sunburn. I'd done that to him.

"You don't ever do that." My voice, my whole body shook from the shock of the magic breaking, from my momentary inability to stop hurting Adam. "I just got you back." The coyote inside me wanted to take a bite out of something, anything in a frenzy of . . . in a frenzy. "I can't touch you without hurting you. Don't let me hurt you." The last sentence came out as a whine, and I realized I was babbling. I shut up.

Instinctively, I backed away, so I was in no danger of touching anyone. I didn't want to contaminate anyone with the remnants of that magic—filthy magic—on me. Didn't want to hurt Adam again. *Didn't want to touch him with my filthy skin, I was dirty, dirty. That was wrong.*

I knew that was wrong. An echo of trauma that never quite

left me, though its hold was not as vicious as it had been. I tried to collect myself and center on the real issue here. On Adam.

A trace of blood trickled down Adam's chin, but the red flush on his skin was disappearing as I watched. Silver burns. I touched my lips. It was from the silver and not some weird taint of the magic that had robbed me of my will, or a taint that lingered from that long-ago rape. I *knew* that, but it still felt like the two were entwined—the fae magic and the marks on my mate's face.

"That silver," said Zee, "is something I can help you with, Mercy."

I looked at him, my heart still pounding—with anger at Adam, with the release of a magical spell I hadn't really believed in until it left, and with a shadow of memory. I remembered listening to Tad tell us that I'd had my will stolen away, and I had been . . . uninterested. I'd felt that way before.

"The silver," Zee told me, his eyes sad as if he knew where my thoughts were dwelling. "Just the silver. The rest is over and done."

"Okay." My throat was tight, and I didn't want him to touch me. Didn't want anyone to touch me ever again, but I knew that made no sense.

"Mercy."

Adam waited until I looked over and met his eyes. "You broke the spell the minute something happened that you didn't want. You were never really in its power. Not once you didn't want to be."

His voice gave me an anchor, and I drew my unruly thoughts back in line. He'd be okay. His lips were healing a lot more slowly than usual, but as I'd yelled at him, he'd had a rough few days. He needed to eat something soon.

"Mercy."

I nodded, so he'd know I'd heard him. I wasn't ready to risk talking right away. Too many things were raw, and Adam and I weren't alone.

"Why didn't the cuff act right away?" asked Asil. Maybe he'd done it to take everyone's attention off me, but I didn't know him well enough to be sure. "The coyote that jumped in and attacked that fae, magic sword and all, was not without willpower."

"It was when Adam came back," Tad said. "It isn't easy to steal someone's will. With Huon's Cup . . . before . . ." He made an unhappy sound. Looked at Asil, who might or might not know about that incident. Before. When I'd been raped because I could not resist the magic of the cup I'd drunk.

Tad cleared his throat. "The cup that worked on Mercy before used the act of drinking out of it to imply consent, *and* it was a more powerful artifact in the first place. Peace and Quiet is a two-part spell, each lesser. The first is spelled to make the wearer happy and relaxed. Sort of like the best marijuana ever. That leaves the prisoner vulnerable so that the second one can work to make the person wearing it compliant. The magic continues to work after the cuffs have been removed, so they could be used to subdue more than one prisoner."

I rubbed the wrist the cuff had been on. I hadn't felt anything from it—though I'd been busy at the time. If she'd used the other cuff first, would I just have let her take me? Instead, the magic had snuck up behind me and taken me without giving me a fair chance to fight it. It had waited until the euphoria of having Adam back had left me defenseless, then stolen my will.

"Will the magic come back if I relax again?" I asked, swallowing bile. I was safe. Adam was here, had been here the whole time.

Nothing bad had happened—though I remembered the feel of the weeping ghost's attempt to take control of my body. What would have happened if Zee hadn't built wards into the doorway that I could cross and the ghost could not? The walls of the room confined me when the coyote inside me wanted to run until I focused my eyes on Adam again. In his steady regard, I read my safety—as ridiculous as my need for it was. If the ghost had gained control, he'd have dealt with it—as he'd dealt with the fae magic that had turned me into a helpless doll.

"No," said Zee firmly. "It isn't so easy to work magic upon you, *Liebchen*. One chance was all it had. Probably you'd have recovered on your own after a few days. The Fairy Queen's Gift is weak, a designed weakness that brought about the downfall of the fairy queen who depended upon it too much."

I nodded, and the tightness in my belly eased.

Zee looked at Tad. "It also isn't so easy to destroy an artifact, powerful or not. I would never advocate it because it would put me in trouble with the Gray Lords." He looked at the black blade and smiled a little, handing it back to Tad. "*Hier, mein Sohn*. You take this for a while. You might find it useful. Be careful, though, it is a hungry sword and likes best to eat magic—and it has a habit of betraying its wielder."

Tad smiled, worked whatever magic was necessary to turn it back into a steel grip with no blade in sight, and tucked it into the pocket of his jeans. "I understand," he said. "And I know the stories about this sword."

"Good." Zee looked at me. "Removing the silver isn't going to be pleasant, Mercy." He glanced at Adam. "But we have to do it now or maybe never. I don't know if I'll be able to use the mirror gate again." He frowned. "Ariana could attempt it, but her magic is not what it once was. Tad has the magic, but he doesn't know enough to ad-lib such a spell."

"Is magic ever pleasant?" I asked. "I'd rather you did it." I'd been hoping the old gremlin could do something about my little silver problem, and I wasn't going to let a little PTSD moment stop me. I braced myself, closed my eyes, and made sure I had control of my face.

Zee laid his hands on my cheeks and filled me with his magic. It didn't hurt at first. Zee's magic had a flavor, one that spoke of oil, metal, movement, and red heat. I could feel the call of his magic, and it felt very different from the way I'd called the silver out of Adam. Gradually, my feet started to tingle, but as soon as that tingle started to travel upward, the sensation in my feet changed to a sizzle like the bite of a red ant or two that rapidly increased to a thousand. The sensation followed the tingle all the way up my body.

"Ow, ow, ow," I chanted.

"It didn't hurt when she took the silver from me," Adam said, sounding unhappy.

I shut up. I could deal with a little stinging; okay, a lot of stinging. I didn't need to upset Adam.

"Not being Coyote's child with a mystical connection to a werewolf, I have to follow the rules of magic," Zee told Adam. He pulled his hand away from my skin and frowned at the disk of silver he held while I caught my breath. "This is a lot of silver to have scattered in your body, Mercy—and we are not finished yet. And you said that you already rid yourself of some of it?"

Adam nodded. "I saw the bedroom floor." He must have gone to Kyle's first, then, and followed me to Sylvia's. "More silver came out than went in. They gave me five or so good shots of the stuff, but nowhere near the amount on the floor."

"Conservation of matter," said Asil, "would indicate that perhaps she pulled the silver from more than just you. How bad is the pack?"

"Conservation of matter," said Tad astringently, "is a funny concept when expressed by a werewolf. Who knows better that magic makes science blink than a 170-pound man who turns into a 250-pound werewolf?"

"They are not as bad as I'd feared," Adam said slowly, though he acknowledged Tad's comment with a smile. "I hadn't considered that she might have helped the lot of us. Most of them are still pretty sick—but Warren and Darryl are almost back to normal. Still, if there had been that much silver, even scattered through all the pack, we would all be dead."

"But there are still some sick from the silver?" Zee asked.

"Yes."

Zee waved to Tad. "Come over here and put your hand over mine, I'll show you how to do this so you can heal Adam's pack."

"Cool," I said without enthusiasm, but my hackles had smoothed out again. "I get to be a teaching exercise."

Like a dog with a face full of porcupine quills, I found it harder to stand still and let silver be drawn out a second time. But the pain did focus my attention on the present, as did Adam's grim face. I gave him a cheery smile, and his frown deepened.

Zee taught magic the way he taught mechanicking—by making Tad do all the work while he stood behind him and made acerbic corrections. He did it in Old German, and though I can get by in modern German, the old stuff sounds a bit like Welsh spoken by a Swedish man with marbles in his mouth.

In the end, Tad held a dime-sized bit of silver, I rubbed the cramps out of my thighs, and Adam stalked back and forth like an enraged baboon I'd seen once at a zoo. Asil had retreated to the far corner of the room with a book, to keep his presence from inciting Adam further.

"If Tad intends to do this to the werewolves," I said through gritted teeth because every muscle on my body was cramping with equal insistence, "then Adam will have to hold them down."

Adam stalked over to me and began kneading my shoulders. I sighed in relief and let him work on them while I turned my attention to my left calf.

"It won't be so difficult with the wolves," said Zee. "Their bodies are already working to get rid of the silver, and all it will require is a little assistance. They also heal faster."

"I'll keep watch," Adam promised me. "Tad won't take any harm."

"So are the fae planning on taking over the world?" I asked Zee.

He laughed so hard, he couldn't speak for a few minutes. "The short answer is yes," he told me cheerfully.

Asil set aside his book and quit pretending he was not interested.

"But?" I said, and he laughed again.

"Liebchen," he said. "*If* they could all point their swords in the same direction for more than ten seconds, they just might manage something scary. The reality is that everyone is tired of merely surviving and is looking for a way to thrive in this new world of iron." He shrugged. "I don't know what will happen except that things are changing."

"I heard someone"—Coyote—"say that change is neither good nor bad," I told him.

Behind me, Adam made a wolfish noise that meant disagreement. "The older you are, the more you fear change, even if you think you are in charge. *Especially* if you think you are in charge. There are a lot of very old fae."

Zee inclined his head to Adam in a move that looked a lot more royal in his own shape than it did when he'd done it while wearing his human-seeming. "As you say. I would tell you that there is nothing to worry about except that there is. There are a lot of fae who hate the humans, Mercy. Some fae hate them for the iron encircling the world, some hate them for the loss of the old Underhill even though we have replaced it, and some hate humans for their ease of procreation." He sighed and looked old. "Hatred is not a useful thing."

"To hear you say *that*—that is a thing I never thought to hear no matter how old I became." Asil laughed and Zee raised an imperial eyebrow and someone who didn't know him might not have seen the wry humor in his eyes.

"Not useful," Zee said, then looked as though he was listening to something, though my ears didn't pick up anything strange. "But it is powerful. Someone is knocking at my door, I must return." He put his hand on his son's shoulder. "Stay safe."

"And you," Tad said.

And Zee walked through the blackness that filled the mirror's frame as though it were just another doorway. He said something that I heard with my bones and not my ears, and the frame was filled with a mirror once more.

"That is one I thought would never change," said Asil thoughtfully.

"He loved my mother," Tad told him. "Love is more powerful than anything, even an old grumpy fae who knows how to hate."

Asil gave Tad a thoughtful look. "Indeed?" And then he looked back at the mirror. "Love is both useful and powerful—but seldom convenient."

"I don't know about that," Adam said. "I've found it pretty convenient."

"That's not what you told me," I corrected him, and he laughed.

The ghost tried to give me trouble again on the way back down the stairway from Zee's mirror room. But I wasn't stoned by fae magic this time.

"Go away," I told her.

"Mercy?" Adam was just behind me, and he put his hand on my back.

"Not you," I told him. "It's the ghost." He growled, and it made me smile.

Proving that she could do something other than cry, the ghost screamed at me, her face all but pressed to mine. No one else reacted. It was really ear-piercing, so someone would have reacted if they could hear it. It was just another one of those things that only I could perceive—lucky me.

For a long time I'd thought that was the only thing I could do with ghosts—observe them. Then I'd met a vampire who could steal the power of those he consumed. He'd taken the power of a walker like me, and he'd been able to do more.

I focused my attention on the ghost, borrowed a little Alpha from Adam, though I didn't really need it, and said again, *"Go away."*

She disappeared abruptly, and there was a crash somewhere below. I heard Tad, who'd preceded us, run down the stairs to the main level. Asil, like a lot of the older werewolves, didn't make any noise when he ran.

When Adam and I got down there, Tad was sweeping up glass in the kitchen while Asil watched. It looked as though the ghost had managed to dump all the dishes that had been in the drainer by the sink onto the floor.

Tad looked at me as he dumped the shards in the garbage. "I thought you said all that she did was cry?"

"I think," I told him apologetically, "that when I walked through the ghost without my usual mulishness, although she didn't quite manage to take me over, she did succeed in pulling herself a little closer to this world. She's probably going to be a little more of a presence here until the effect wears off."

"We have a ghost."

"I told you that already," I said.

"Cool." He set the dustpan on the counter and grinned at me. "Haunted houses are nifty."

"Tell me that when she keeps you up all night with her sobbing," I told him. "But if she gets too obstreperous, just let me know. I might be able to make her leave you alone." I hadn't done a lot of experimentation on that front. Ghosts had so little self-determination—bound as they were by the rules of their existence—taking any control away from them seemed like a crime. As long as they didn't try to possess me or bother my friends, they were safe from me.

"'Obstreperous,' huh," said Tad. "I see you've been using that Big Word of the Day calendar I got you last Christmas."

"That is irrefragable," I told him solemnly.

Silverless, de-magicked, and vowing never to play word one-upmanship—or even Scrabble for that matter—with either Adam or Asil (What exactly was a quicquidlibet, anyway?), I drove to Kyle's, where we would meet with the Cantrip agent and everyone else.

Adam only raised his eyebrows when I told him I would drive—which meant he was really exhausted. He closed his eyes as soon as I got the car on the road, and no one said much on the trip. Probably, with two dominant wolves who weren't in the same pack, it was just as well.

Marsilia's car was parked in Kyle's driveway. I had to park the Corolla a block away because there were a lot of cars on the street—including a short bus that was covered with quotes from the Bible—mostly from Romans, but there were a few Revelation quotes and a lot of Proverbs. Most of them I recognized, but the chapter and verse were helpfully spelled out on each just in case. When I paused to read, Adam gave a quiet laugh.

"Elizaveta," he told me. "I told her we had the whole pack to transport, and she showed up with a couple of vans and that. She said that one of her nephews borrowed it from his church. He told them that he needed to move some things. They left it here for us to use until we get everyone all sorted out."

"It's a good thing that Kyle's old neighbor is dead," I told him. Adam hadn't called me; he'd called the witch who hadn't even bothered to answer my phone call. "Every time I parked my poor old Rabbit in front of Kyle's house, Kyle got a letter of complaint taped to his door. I can't imagine what he'd have done in response to this bus."

"Hey," Adam said, quietly into my ear. "I called you first, but your phone was dead. *Then* I called Elizaveta."

It shouldn't have made me feel better. Elizaveta was more useful; he *should* have called her first. She could destroy evidence and had minions who could borrow vans. But he'd called me first instead. Impatient with myself for having been so jealous about something so stupid, I looked around for a distraction, and my eyes found the bus again.

"'Thou shall not suffer a witch to live,'" I told him, pointing at the front quarter panel. "I wonder if Elizaveta saw that. It doesn't say werewolves, but I expect it is implied."

"'Wives, be subject to your husbands,'" Adam deadpanned without looking at the bus. "'Let your women keep silence in the churches.'"

"Ah, Paul. He has so many useful things to say. 'It is well for a man not to touch a woman,'" I replied sagely, and Adam laughed and kissed me.

I stiffened, irrationally worried that Zee might not have gotten all the silver, but Adam made a sound closer to a purr than a growl. So I relaxed and participated.

"Do they always flirt with biblical quotes?" Asil asked Tad.

In long-suffering tones, Tad said, "They can flirt with the periodic table or a restaurant menu. We've learned to live with it. Get a room, you guys."

"Quiet, pup," said Adam with mock sternness. He gave my butt a promissory pat as he said, "Respect your elders."

At Kyle's house, I took time to take a better look at the dent in Marsilia's car. It wasn't as bad as I remembered it, but it was bad enough. She was going to be furious, and I couldn't blame her. I just hoped she kept it between us and didn't try to involve the pack—the pack had sustained about as much damage as it could handle right now.

"Don't worry," Adam said. "We'll get it fixed."

"It can't make her hate me any more than she already does," I said, willing to look on the bright side.

"It might make her hate you more *immediately*," offered Tad, and I laughed even though he was right.

"She won't hurt Mercy," said Adam softly. "She knows better than that."

Asil trailed past the trunk, nostrils flaring. "The dead woman is still in the car." He glanced around as if he was looking for something. "Armstrong's rental is gone. He said he had some more coordinating to do with his people. He'll be back, though. Sooner rather than later."

"Tell me about him," said Adam. "I only had time to shake hands and go."

"I'm not your wolf," warned Asil, his voice suddenly harsh.

Adam took in a breath of air and shook out his shoulders. "Sorry," he said, looking at the car and not the other wolf. "Habit. We need to get ourselves ironed out before there's bloodshed. You've been very courteous, and I thank you for it. I'll try to do better. Would you share what you know about the Cantrip agent with me?"

There was a pause, and I kept my eyes on Asil, watching for a sign that he'd decided not to take Adam's apology. His eyes were yellow—that they'd shift back and forth so easily told me as much as his earlier warning had about how little control he had over his wolf.

"Charles vouches for him," Asil said at last, letting the apology lie—which was the safest way to play it. "Lin Armstrong is a troubleshooter for Cantrip and has the power to make things happen. Charles told me to tell you that he can be trusted. As long as we're following our own rules, he won't rock the boat."

"Even with the blood of Cantrip agents hot on my hands?" asked Adam softly.

"Tell him the whole truth," I said impulsively. "Better yet, wait and catch Tony when he comes with Sylvia and tell the whole herd. We're in the right here, and they are the ones who benefit from lies."

"Talk to the lawyer first since you have one immediately available to you," cautioned Asil. "Then give the others as much truth as the lawyer tells you to, and not one word more."

"If you do that, we'll need time to get the story straight," I said.

"We'll tell him the truth," Adam said heavily. "I'm tired of playing games. Maybe it's time to spread a little fear. If they had been a little more afraid of us, Peter would still be alive."

Adam opened the front door, and we were hit with a wave of noise and motion that only got louder when people realized who was at the door.

"Quiet," said Adam—and everyone—the wolves, security personnel, and what looked like two dozen little girls (though I knew that there really weren't that many, they just moved fast) shut up and stood still.

"Good." He looked around. "Where is Kyle? I need to talk to him and get y'all organized." He was tired if he was drifting back into Southernisms.

"I'll get him," said Mary Jo's voice in the back of the crowd. I caught a glimpse of her before she disappeared up the stairs. She was dressed in sweats that were too big for her, and her skin tone was greenish, like she'd just woken up after spending the night at an all-you-can-drink orgy.

Jesse, with the littlest Sandoval on her hip and her hair mussed and damp, waded through the crowd and kissed her dad on the cheek. She rested against him for a moment. "Welcome home, Dad."

He hugged her hard, then relaxed his hold to ruffle Maia's hair.

Maia said, "I rode in a car with a dead body."

Adam gave me a laughing glance. "I guess we might as well tell everyone the whole truth and nothing but the truth."

"It's a secret," Maia explained.

He ruffled her hair again. "Yes. But not a secret from your mom. You shouldn't keep those."

"I tell Mamá everything."

"Good for you."

"So," Jesse said, backing up a step, "I hear that you managed to survive without Mercy to rescue you this time."

He smiled. "Brat. Remember who's paying for your college."

She grinned at him. "Maybe I'll just get pregnant and work at fast food for the rest of my life." She turned and trotted off the way she had come before he could formulate a reply.

Amid laughter that had as much to do with relief we were safe as with Jesse's humor, Adam went to work ordering the chaos. I waited for a while, watched various members of the pack come and go. They needed to check and make sure he was still okay, and I understood exactly how they felt.

When he and Asil disappeared together to take care of the who-was-the-biggest-baddest-wolf issue, I slipped away to the kitchen to look for food for Adam—werewolves need to eat, and from the looks of him, wherever they'd held him, they hadn't fed him at all.

Kyle's kitchen was a mess. Dirty dishes everywhere and one whole counter was covered with trays of sandwiches that looked as though someone had called out a caterer at some point. I took a few minutes to unload clean dishes from the dishwasher and start the next batch running—dominance displays take a little time. Then I snitched a heavy-duty paper plate from a stack on the counter and loaded it with four sandwiches thick with near-bloody roast beef.

When I emerged from the kitchen, Adam was the only werewolf in sight, and the total volume of the noise in the house had dropped an appreciable amount. He was trying to push his security team gently out the door.

"We don't think that the house is secured. And with all due respect, Mr. Brooks hired us."

I had never met Jim Gutstein, but I recognized his voice from several phone conversations. He was in his fifties and still in the kind of shape primarily limited to professional athletes and werewolves. His dark gray eyes and jutting chin proclaimed his resistance to leaving despite the tiredness even I, who did not know him, could see. Exhaustion, I knew, only made stubborn people more stubborn.

"Here," I told Adam, before he could say something that put Jim's back up even further than it already was. I had experience dealing with dominant personalities, most of them werewolves. A human had no chance. I put the plate in Adam's hand. "You eat this."

I turned to Adam's man. "Jim, I'm Adam's wife, Mercy. It's very good to meet you." I opened the door and stepped into him, forcing him to back out the doorway. He'd have had to get more physical with me than he was comfortable with to stop me. The rest of his team followed me out.

"Thank you," I told him sincerely. "Go home so Adam will sit down and eat. He's fine, he's grateful, and he'll talk to you on

Monday. Leave a couple of people here, and he'll never know—but you, Jim, need to sleep."

Jim Gutstein frowned at me, but another one of the men put a hand on his shoulder. "She makes more sense than you do right now, Gutstein. Sleep. Then you can give him hell. Chris and Todd have the house covered, and it is chock-full of werewolves. You heard the boss man, the likelihood of another mass attack is slim to none."

"Good night," I said, while they were still talking. I went back into the house and shut the door before Jim could bull or argue his way back in.

Adam was alone in the foyer, holding his plate and looking at me with a bemused expression on his face. I decided I was on a roll and pointed toward the kitchen.

"You need to go eat that right now, mister," I said.

He laughed, and I could see again how tired he was. "Yes, Madame Alpha Coyote, I do. Would you join me? I think everyone else will keep for now."

He meant for more than food. Only a blind woman could miss it. It was a gentle invitation, and I could pretend not to see, could escort him into the kitchen and get started on the dishes while he ate.

"This is a big house," I said, instead. "But there is a pack of werewolves lurking somewhere as well as your daughter, her boyfriend, a police officer, a federal agent coming back shortly, and a pack of Sandoval girls. I'm not sure there's a spare space anywhere."

Adam smiled, and I was glad I hadn't just taken him to the kitchen. "Leave that to me."

We ended up sneaking out to the garage and up a rope ladder into the attic space above. Sunlight illuminated the room from a pair of skylights. The walls were finished and painted a light teal that complemented the dense cobalt carpet, but there were no lights or furniture.

"How did you know this was here?" I asked. I pulled up the rope ladder and pulled the trapdoor up until it latched. No sense giving obvious clues about where we were if we were going to sneak off alone.

Adam set his plate down on the floor.

"Warren. He said he and Kyle could keep everyone out of their bedroom, but that stealth might work better for us."

He looked at me and his warm brown eyes had a touch of gold and his voice was a little hoarse. "Let me see your skin, Mercy. I need to know you are okay."

I stripped, feeling a little self-conscious. I didn't mind being naked, but a woman likes to be pretty for her mate and I was covered with bruises, cuts, and bumps. My bad knee was swollen and probably purple to boot. At least my lips weren't silver anymore.

I didn't cover myself up, but I turned my back to him as I slid Kyle's sweats down my legs.

"Mercy," he said.

"Yes?" I glanced back at him to see that he was pulling off his shirt.

"A bargain for us," he said. "I will not hide from you if you don't hide from me."

The idea of Adam's hiding from anything left my mouth open while he made short work of the rest of his clothes, so I had to hurry to catch up. He was right. I didn't feel quite so naked when he was naked, too. He didn't say anything, just touched my bruises with light fingers.

When he paused at my cheek, I said, "That was the car wreck."

He frowned at me. "Okay. The car wreck and then it hit the ground when the fae assassin jumped on my back."

We went on like that. Him touching a cut, a bruise, a bump, and I'd tell him what happened.

When he was finished, he put his forehead on my shoulder and pulled me hard against him. "You'll be the death of me," he told me. "I could wish you less bold, less brave—less driven by right and wrong."

"Too bad for you," I commiserated. "I know it's rough. My husband tried to kill himself to save the pack, you know. And earlier today, he faced down a fae he knew nothing about—and some of the fae are forces of nature."

"My wife was going to fight him," explained Adam. "I had to protect him from that."

I laughed.

"You know what Jesse's mother would have done if the feds came and took the pack while she was my wife?" he asked.

"Filed for divorce," I hypothesized.

It was his turn to laugh. "Point to you. And then she would go to everyone she knew and tell them how awful her life was, how people expected too much of her. Do you know what my second wife did?"

"Got beaten up and ran in circles mostly while you rescued yourself," I told him.

"She cared for the pack that was left," he said. "She got my child to safety. She got word to Bran—who sent help. She stepped between my child and those who would harm her."

I snorted. "Sounds like a paragon."

"She saved my life and gave me strength to save the rest of the pack." He heaved a sigh and pulled back so he could look at me.

"And I have this urge to turn you over my knee and bruise your butt so that you do exactly what my first wife did."

I narrowed my eyes at him. "You ever lay a hand on me and you better never go to sleep again."

He laughed, sat down on the carpeted floor more as though he just couldn't stand up anymore than as if he'd actually made the decision to sit, and laughed some more. He was very, very tired—but he had just threatened to spank me, so he got no sympathy from me. I folded my arms.

He wiped his eyes with his thumb and looked up at me. His laughter had died altogether. "You don't know how fragile you are, Mercy. The last time we got into trouble, you spent months in a wheelchair. You fight as long and as hard as any werewolf, without any of the weapons we've been given. You are smart. You are careful. And you've been very, very lucky. And that scares me more than any spriggand carrying one of Zee's swords or a Cantrip zealot armed with silver. Luck runs out."

"I tell you what," I said, sitting beside him and biting down the urge to feed him the line he'd given me: did you think I'd die of old age? I hadn't found it funny at the time and didn't think that he would, either. "Think of me as Coyote's daughter, if that helps you. Coyote is lucky."

Adam shook his head. "No, Mercy. Coyote isn't lucky. Coyote is rash, and everyone around him dies—including him. But when the sun rises, he's all better and he goes out to look for new friends. Because Coyote is immortal." *And you are not.* He didn't say it, but we both heard it.

I tapped on the floor and then leaned forward. Time for a distraction. "This coyote is all better right now. Are you and I going to be friends, wolf?"

He canted his head and touched my chin with his hand. "I don't know. Are you going to keep doing your best to get yourself killed?"

It hadn't been I who had been trying to commit suicide—I hadn't realized I was still mad at him about that. I turned my head and nipped his finger. I'd meant it as chastisement, but he didn't take it that way. Gold lit his eyes with fire, and he left his finger where it was.

"I guess so," he said, sounding resigned, but his lips were soft on mine.

Both of us dozed a bit afterward, not really asleep but too content to get up. I buried my nose under his ear, where his scent could wrap around me. I licked tenderly at the warm skin of his neck.

"Peter is dead," he told me suddenly.

I put my weight on his chest, so he wouldn't feel so alone. "Yes."

"It was my job to protect him."

"The average werewolf lives ten years after he is changed," I reminded Adam. "A human has seventy years or so upon the earth before his time is done. Peter was older than that, four times older than you are. His was not a short life, and his death was quick." It wasn't enough, and I knew it. But it would count for something later, when his death wasn't so . . . near.

"My fault," Adam said. Someone who didn't know him would have thought his voice was calm. "There were not so many of them. If I had attacked them when they came to take the pack . . ."

"You thought they were feds," I said. He knew all of this, but if he needed to have me say it again, then I would. "If werewolves start killing federal agents, soon there won't be any werewolves. It was the right thing to do. I was there when Peter was killed, and it could have been any one of you. Jones had decided to kill someone, and nothing would have stopped him."

"Jones is dead." But his body was relaxing underneath me. Adam wasn't stupid. This wasn't the first time bad things happened that he couldn't control.

"I'm not surprised."

He huffed a laugh. "I didn't kill him."

I lifted my head so I could see his face. "That does surprise me."

"I killed the rest of them and let Honey kill Jones." He watched my face closely. He'd hidden what he was from his first wife, who had been entirely human, and she'd still run away from what little she'd glimpsed.

"Good," I said. "That way, I won't have to."

He laughed again, and his body softened as much as it ever did—there just wasn't much soft about Adam. "I love you," he said.

"I know," I told him seriously. "How could you help it?"

He laughed again and rolled over until I was on the bottom, and flexed his hips against mine. "I tried," he whispered in my ear. "But it didn't work."

I breathed into his ear for the pleasure of feeling him shiver against me. "Of course not." He smelled like home, like safety, like love. "Of course not."

"I promise I won't spank you," he told me, his voice rough and low as he added, "not unless you ask me to."

I let him feel my laugh against his shoulder. "That's because you aren't genuinely suicidal."

We loved again then, the short nap of the rug soft under my skin and the warmth of him surrounding me.

Afterward, he fell asleep while he was eating, between one bite and the next, like a toddler. I don't think that he had slept since the pack was taken. He didn't even stir when I pulled away from him to go put my clothes on.

The room might have been finished, but it was not heated. Adam was a werewolf, which meant the colder the better for him—not so for me. Fully clothed, I sat down next to him to watch over him while he slept.

The quiet time didn't last.

The door between house and garage opened no more than twenty minutes after Adam dropped off. Warren called, "Sorry, boss. You're needed if you don't want Kyle to shoot the rest of the pack."

He didn't speak that loudly, but Adam's eyes opened up anyway. He smiled at me, and said, "Good to know. Tell Kyle to hold up, and I'll be right down."

Warren steadied the rope ladder when Adam tossed it out of the trapdoor. "We've put the pack downstairs in the big room to create some space apart from the Sandoval girls." The big room was the largest room in the house, and it had a pool table and a stairway leading to an outside door into the backyard. Kyle's house was bigger than ours, but not set up for groups of people quite this large.

"They wouldn't do anything on purpose," Warren said, as I climbed down the rope ladder behind Adam. "But we're all on edge."

"Silver-sick doesn't help," I said. "Tad can help with the silver."

"And then we'll send most of them to their own homes," said Adam. "Even if our enemy has teeth left, it will take them a while to regroup. For the short term, we should all be safe enough."

Warren grunted, and, with my feet safely down on the cement floor, I took a good look at him. Warren was my first friend in Adam's pack—he'd been my friend before he'd joined the pack.

"You look better than I expected you to," I said, and, to my surprise, he flushed.

"Food," he said with a shy smile.

Adam snorted. "Kyle."

"Well, yes," agreed Warren, then his eyes went cold as he tossed the rope ladder back up into the hole in the ceiling. "Mercy, next time you see our favorite bloodsucker, you tell him I owe him one."

"I'll tell him, but he did it for Kyle."

Warren nodded and hopped on top of the metal shelving that lined the wall so he could close the trapdoor properly.

There were no digs, humorous comments, or even sly looks when Adam, Tad, and I joined the pack in the great room in the basement. I took that as a sign of how bad everyone was feeling.

Some of the wolves were notable by their absence.

"Darryl and Auriele went to their home," Warren told us. He glanced at Adam. "They seemed mostly recovered from the silver, and he is supposed to participate in a conference call with some Chinese scientists on Sunday."

"All the most dominant wolves seem to be pretty well clean of silver," Tad said.

"He told us it's because you used your mate bond to pull the silver out of Adam, and through Adam, the pack," said Honey. She was sitting on the pool table with her legs crossed underneath her. She was pale, and her mouth was tight, but other than that she looked mostly like herself. "I didn't believe him until Kyle showed us the silver on the floor." She frowned at me. "What kind of freak are you?"

Any other time, I'd have said something cutting. I felt Adam stiffen beside me, and I put my hand on his arm to forestall whatever he wanted to say. Honey had never liked me much—and since I had forced the pack to take a new look at their hierarchy, particularly the way women's ranks were awarded, she'd liked me even less.

Honey was as dominant as Peter had been submissive, and a female wolf is supposed to take her rank from her mate. She *wanted* the role she'd been assigned as his mate rather than the one that should have been rightfully hers as a dominant wolf. She didn't want to be who she was; she wanted to be delicate and ladylike and feminine. She resented me for challenging that.

I wasn't afraid of her. She wasn't the type to take her dislike to the next level and try to kill me. Normally, I'd have given her as good as I got, but she'd just lost Peter. We all had just lost Peter.

"I am Adam's freak," I told her. "Get over it."

"Kelly," Adam said, ignoring Honey altogether. "Come here."

I didn't know Kelly well; I'm not sure anyone did. He was a big, quiet man who worked at a local yard and garden store. He usually had an air of vitality, but now half crept, half stumbled to Adam.

Warren grabbed a chair that another wolf vacated without being asked and set it down next to Tad. He pulled Kelly onto the chair and stepped behind him. He reached across the big man's chest and grabbed Kelly's opposite wrist and pulled it tight as he trapped Kelly's free arm, too.

"This might hurt," Tad said.

"*Will* hurt," I told Kelly. "But I survived it."

Kelly's eyes went gold, and he showed me his teeth. "Coyote."

There were still some wolves who resented having a coyote in the pack.

I smiled toothily back at him.

"Coyotes are tough," he said. Apparently he wasn't one of the coyote-haters. Good to know.

"So are wolves," I told him.

"And both of you talk too much," Tad said. "Brace yourself."

He didn't put his hand on Kelly's face—which was smart. Even in human form, werewolves have strong jaw muscles. He touched his forearm, just above where Warren held it. Tad's eyes drooped to half-mast, and his nostrils flared and power burst into being where there had been none a moment before.

The scent of fae magic seared my sinuses; Kelly roared, and his whole body arched off the chair. Adam dove to help hold him and so did Honey, who grabbed both of Kelly's legs in her arms.

Tad jerked back—and there was a popping noise when his hand came away from Kelly's arm.

"I'm sorry, I'm sorry," he said hoarsely. "I didn't mean for that to happen."

Kelly went limp.

"Did you get the silver out?" asked Adam, releasing his hold cautiously, but the werewolf didn't move.

Honey dropped Kelly's legs like they were hot and scooted away until she reached the pool table. Warren let go as well.

Tad showed him a scant handful of whitish gray powder.

Adam smiled. "Good. Kelly?"

The big man shook out his shoulders, took in a breath, and let it out. "I'm good." He glanced at me. "Thanks for the warning."

"No trouble," I said. "Mine took longer."

He leaned his head to the side without smiling. "Coyotes *are* tough. Good to know."

Tad drew the silver out of the wolves who needed it—including Ben. Kelly got the worst of it, as Tad's skill improved with practice. When Zee's son was finished, Adam sent most of the werewolves back to their own homes, where they could protect their families and rest. Honey stayed because he didn't want her too far away from him for a while. Werewolves can get volatile in extreme emotion and, as her Alpha, he could keep her from losing control. It was not uncommon for wolves who had lost their mates to have to be killed shortly thereafter. She had changed to her wolf but otherwise seemed okay.

Warren stayed, of course, because it was his home. Ben stayed because he wouldn't go home when Adam told him to. Adam talked to him in private and then let him stay. I think it had something to do with the way Honey watched me when Adam wasn't looking.

Once everyone left who was leaving, the house felt like it heaved a sigh of relief; I know I did. Kyle ordered pizza for all who remained, and we were in the middle of eating it when the doorbell rang and a tired-looking Agent Armstrong came in.

Jesse and Gabriel took charge of his sisters and hauled them out to the hot tub after determining that Kyle and Warren did indeed have swimming suits of all sizes. Kyle was a divorce attorney, and sometimes his clients and their children needed a safe place to go for a while. That was why his house was so big and why some of the rooms were Disney-themed and sized for people under ten years old.

Honey was given the job of making sure nothing happened to them. I asked Jesse and Gabriel to make sure that Maia didn't try to ride Honey the way she'd done with Sam. Wide-eyed at the idea, Jesse promised sincerely to do her best. She knew Honey as well as I did, and even on the best of days, Honey wouldn't make a good horsey. Everyone else, Adam called to a meeting in the upstairs theater room. When Armstrong protested all the civilians, looking at Tony and Sylvia, Adam said, in a voice that could have frozen a volcano, "Their presence is nonnegotiable."

It wasn't, I thought, so much that Tony and Sylvia's participation was important to Adam, who knew neither one very well—it was that Armstrong had tried to take control of the meeting, and Adam, fresh from being held captive, was not in the mood for it.

Adam moved one of the two love seats around so it was in front of the TV before sitting on it—at the head of his impromptu council. He didn't bother with his usual charade of human-only strength, having lifted the heavy piece of furniture and carried it by himself with obvious ease. I sat down next to Adam and worried over Armstrong's pale face. We didn't need more enemies.

Warren gave Adam a cautious look and settled in the other love seat, pulling Kyle down beside him. Tad had been planning to go out to the swimming pool, too, but Adam had asked him to come after Armstrong protested Tony and Sylvia. At Adam's direction, Tad sat rather uncomfortably on the couch with Tony and Sylvia. There were no more seats in the room.

Ben—human again and wearing a set of Kyle's sweats that said, "Taste *This* Rainbow"—glanced around and sat on the ground at Adam's feet without a quibble or change of expression. That left Armstrong standing alone.

The lack of seats was on purpose, I thought, glancing at Adam's face. He was not happy with Cantrip, and poor Agent Armstrong was the only representative present.

Asil came in late. He glanced at Ben and at Agent Armstrong, who was contemplating the reason for his seatless state. Asil raised an eyebrow at Adam—though he didn't really look him in the eye—and headed back downstairs. He brought two of the dining room chairs and pointedly set them on either side of Warren's love seat. He took the side that left him as far from Adam as he could get without leaving the room and, at his gesture, Armstrong took the remaining empty chair.

"You all here know everything Mercy told the police, right?" Adam said as soon as everyone was seated. "So let me begin with last night."

For all that we'd talked about the whole truth and nothing but the truth, Adam's story was edited a little. He was quite clear on the point that he killed the Cantrip agents responsible himself—while I and all the werewolves in the room knew he lied. He wasn't the only one who had killed, but he was the one responsible. I understood that just fine.

"I considered holding them for justice," Adam told us, told me, really. "But they had a kill list that included all of the humans associated with my people—children not excepted." He looked at Sylvia. "Gabriel was on that list. You were not wrong to tell him that his association with us put him in danger."

"Maybe not," she said, "but I was wrong to expect that to matter to him." She looked at me, and her lips quirked up. "A friend in danger is not someone who should be deserted. Safety is not always the right path."

"They were willing to kill children?" Armstrong asked, not as if he were questioning Adam but as if he couldn't quite wrap his head around it.

"Like Joshua at Jericho," said Adam. I put my hand on his leg and squeezed it. "They felt that they needed to dig us out plant, root, and seed so that our corruption was truly destroyed. You'll have to accept my word for it because the whiteboard went up with the winery where we were held."

He paused. "There were three fresh graves in the vineyard that held some of their own people. Maybe they objected—maybe they just got in the way. We didn't kill them, we didn't kill anyone until our escape. From the state of the bodies, the Cantrip agents in the graves died a couple of days before we were taken."

"How *did* they get you all?" asked Asil.

"We thought they were government agents, so we did not initially respond with lethal force." Adam breathed deeply, but it must not have helped because he got to his feet and began to pace. "That is a mistake, Agent Armstrong, that we will never make again. You might pass the word along." For a moment, his menace was such that no one, not even me, dared take a deep breath. He shook his shoulders loose and spoke more moderately. "At any rate, we did not kill or harm anyone when we were taken. So two dead women and the dead man are the responsibility of either the Cantrip agents or the mercenaries they hired."

"If you please, Mr. Hauptman," said Armstrong. "*Renegade* Cantrip agents. My agency was not responsible for their actions, and both officially and unofficially, we find this business appalling."

"I just bet you do." Warren's voice was heavy with rage. Warren was usually the voice of sanity in the pack.

"Warren," said Adam—and Warren looked up, then away. "Do you need to leave?" It was a real question, not a reprimand, and Warren took it the way it was meant.

"You need Kyle here," he said, his voice low and his head tipped slightly away from Adam's. "In his legal capacity."

"Not as our lawyer," Adam said. "Not yet. But his presence is useful, yes. I'd like him to stay."

"Then I'll stay, too. I can deal."

Adam looked at Tony. "I asked Sylvia to come because Gabriel was endangered. I asked you to stay because I do not want to keep the police in the dark about what happened. You are safer if you know everything. However, we cannot afford to let this go to trial in human courts. We . . . *I* will not allow it."

Tony narrowed his eyes. "I am a servant of the law, Adam."

"There will be hearings, just not in the human court system," Adam told him. "I answer to a higher power—that power that kept werewolves from being the monsters Cantrip is afraid we are for all the years that humans knew nothing of us. If my actions are deemed excessive, I will pay for them with my life."

"Those werewolves who killed that pedophile in Minnesota this past spring—they died within a few days of it. All of them. Natural causes, we were told, though their bodies were cremated very quickly and no autopsy was performed," Armstrong said neutrally, his eyes on me rather than Adam.

"A force of nature, anyway," I said obliquely. Charles was a force of nature, right?

"I'm a servant of the law, too, Tony," Kyle said too hastily to be as smooth as his usual redirection. "And no one knows better than I how the law and justice do not, can not, always coincide. I swear to you now that werewolf justice is swifter and more *just*, if more brutal, than our court system can manage." He leaned forward earnestly. "We humans are not equipped to deal with a werewolf fairly. And if the police had tried to arrest those men in Minnesota, some of them would have died. I am content that justice will be served in this case."

There was a long pause.

"Even if *I* agree it was self-defense," Tony said, "you have just confessed to killing federal agents. I am not qualified to give you a pass on that, Adam."

"Agents who attacked law-abiding citizens without provocation," murmured Kyle. "Adam is a security expert. I imagine that he has the attack on his house on camera somewhere."

Adam grunted. "With nice face shots of several of the Cantrip agents, Gutstein informed me tonight. And we have Peter's body."

"Where is Peter?" I asked.

"Safe," Adam told me. "They'd buried him in the vineyard next to their own dead. We dug him up, and arrangements are being made."

"Suspicious deaths require autopsy," said Tony.

Adam looked at him and nodded. "Yes. We'll talk. There is nothing suspicious about his death. He was murdered right in front of me. He has a bullet hole in his forehead."

No one said anything for a moment after that. The expression on Adam's face might have accounted for the silence.

"I have the power to say that Cantrip and the federal government is satisfied that Adam acted in self-defense when he killed those people," Armstrong said. "Mr. Brooks is right, it would be a political nightmare for Cantrip if the actions of these men were to come out even though they were not acting in any kind of official capacity." He took a deep breath. "It would be a similar disaster for the werewolves. In the current climate, I don't know that you could get a judge to declare self-defense, Mr. Hauptman. If the trial went to a jury, a decision either way could lead to riots and unrest that might break out into open fighting in the streets."

Armstrong looked at something none of us could see, then he met my eyes and held them. "I am a federal agent, sworn to uphold the interests of my country. I am a patriot. I have seen fear and hatred cause men and women who have likewise so sworn to forget their oaths and give in to their hatred. I don't want this to go to court."

Tony threw up his hands. "I agree with you," he told Armstrong. "Both about the self-defense and Adam's chances in court—though if the case is kept local, I think he would do better than you think. Still, there are bodies."

"The buried Cantrip agents were shot execution style, with the same gun that killed Peter," Adam said.

"You run ballistics?" asked Tony.

"No."

Tony frowned at him. "Then how—" Then he shook his head. "Never mind. But those aren't the only bodies."

Adam's face became even more expressionless. "There will be no other bodies. After we escaped, there was a fire at the winery."

Another silence followed.

"I can accept a separate justice," Tony said, finally. "I've known you. I and my department have called you for help, and you have never failed us. I've seen you meet violence with soft words. And I've never seen you lie. I'm in agreement with Agent Armstrong.

I have a few ideas, and I think if Armstrong is willing to help, we can sell this to the department."

"You said there was a fire at the winery?" asked Armstrong.

Adam sat down and rubbed his hands over his face. "Yes. We are used to cleaning up our own messes. We've found fire to be very effective."

"Teeth and the denser bones," said Tony with extreme neutrality, "tend to show up after a fire."

"I'd be very surprised if there are any teeth or bones," I told him half-apologetically. Adam had left Elizaveta out of his explanation. "You don't have to worry about that."

Armstrong gave me a sharp look, but he didn't say anything further. Instead he asked, "What about the mercenaries the renegades were working with? Did you identify them?"

"No," Adam said. "They're out of it, and of no more concern to me. I think there are only three players left."

Asil held up a finger. "The money man." He held up another finger. "The turncoat in Senator Campbell's security detail." And a third. "The person who gave the Cantrip agents the contact information for the mercenaries and the dossiers about your pack and werewolves in general."

"I have a friend looking into the information man," Adam said. "He's pretty sure that he can find the contact name from the mercenaries without causing an international incident."

On Kyle's landline, Adam had been able to get in touch with Charles. Charles was scary good at finding out things no one wanted anyone to know. Charles was just plain scary in general.

"But," Adam continued, "I think the damage the information man can do is done. So there is no great urgency in running him down."

"Let's be clear here, in this room," said Armstrong. "Are you talking about killing him?"

Adam shook his head. "Killing him is a lot more problematic than just keeping an eye on him. The past few days aside, we try our best not to go around killing humans, Mr. Armstrong."

"You don't consider yourself human?" asked Armstrong.

Asil raised his eyebrows at Adam, who shrugged, and said, "'Humans who are not werewolves' is too wordy to say more than once. We are as human as we can be."

"So we're left with the money man and the potential assassin in Senator Campbell's security team." Tony was leaning forward intently.

Adam leaned back and stretched out his legs. The tension in the room ratcheted down four notches, proof that werewolves aren't the only ones who can read body language. "Let's deal with Senator Campbell's problem as the more manageable evil. I've sent word to Senator Campbell through people I know in the security industry, but it might be better, Agent Armstrong, if you warned the senator yourself. Keep in mind that whoever this traitor on his security detail is, he is not necessarily driven by any agenda other than money. If he is only a gun for hire, taking out the Cantrip people who wanted to kill Senator Campbell might be enough to stop him. If he is a zealot, of whatever stripe, he's likely to get impatient and try on his own." Adam paused and raised an eyebrow. "You can tell the senator that I am happy to send a couple of trained security professionals who are werewolves to ensure his safety if he would allow it. No charge."

Armstrong's mouth quirked. "Have you ever met the senator?"

"No, sir."

"I have. He might just take you up on your offer. He is not as anti-werewolf as he is painted. He just doesn't like it when they go around eating people."

Put like that, he didn't sound so bad. But I'd heard some of his speeches.

Adam nodded, but his voice was reserved when he said, "It would please me if he accepted. If something happens to him at this point, it will cause people to blame the werewolves. I'd rather he and his family be safe and sound for years to come."

"And that leaves the money man," said Kyle.

"Yes," said Adam. He looked at Armstrong. "Do you have any idea where the money is coming from?"

"No. Alexander Bennet—he was the man in charge, and probably the one who shot your man—Bennet's financials show nothing unusual and neither do those of any of the people who were likely associated with him. FYI, identifying those people is going to be a nightmare. Looking for people in Cantrip who have problems with werewolves and the current legislation is like looking for cheese in Wisconsin. Bennet just didn't show up for work one day, and there are two more like that. One of them had a heart attack and is in the emergency room of a hospital, the other is likely to be ashes here—unless she ran off and got married or something. We have to check out everyone who is working from home, on leave, on vacation—or used to work for Cantrip at some point in time. If you had left the bodies, it would have made that part of my job much easier."

Warren, who until that point had been silent, said, "I have driver's licenses for you—though we don't have any ID for the people that were buried next to Peter. You'll be able to figure out who they are from their bodies."

Adam looked at him.

"If you'll pardon me, boss, you weren't in any condition to be thinking of things like that. But it occurred to some of us that we might find it useful to know who our enemies are." He looked at Armstrong. "I'll give you copies and keep the originals."

Armstrong looked as though he'd like to argue, but under Warren's scrutiny, he subsided.

"Okay," said Tony. "One more thing. Adam, you are going to have to come up with a story to tell the press that will fly with my superiors."

Adam nodded. "Jim Gutstein is going to call in a few favors, and tonight I'll talk to the press out of Kyle's office. I'll take Mercy's story and run with it."

"Let me help," said Armstrong. "I have some experience in taking scary things and making them ordinary."

"This is all well and good," said Sylvia. "But you need to explain to me why Maia told me she rode here with a dead body."

"That is *my* fault," Asil said.

"More bodies?" said Armstrong.

"I thought there weren't any bodies at Sylvia's?" Tony was frowning.

"Someone sent a team of assassins after Jesse and Mercy," Tad said, and looked at me. "They were waiting for you, Mercy. Now that I've had time to think about it, I think they were in place before I even got to Sylvia's to watch over the kids."

Tad cleared his throat and gave me a sheepish smile. "I felt them when I got there. It's one of the reasons I got close enough that the kids spotted me. After a while, when nothing happened, I figured that there was someone like me living in the apartment complex—half-fae and not required to be in the reservation."

"I thought all fae were required to go," Armstrong said. "That was our briefing."

Tad shook his head. "No. Only those deemed powerful enough to be of use. But these assassins, like Agent Armstrong's people, were renegades—"

The door popped open, and a wet and bright green swimming-suit-clad Sofia Sandoval flew in. "Mercy, *Mercy*. Gabriel says come quick. Someone hit your car. Smooshed the trunk."

I was dead. Marsilia was going to kill me for killing her car, and I didn't really blame her at all.

Everyone in the meeting boiled out to look—as much to get out and move than because anyone else was concerned. It wasn't quite five o'clock, but this late in the fall, the sun had set while we'd been talking, and the rear of the car was beyond the streetlight. I have good night vision, but even my eyes need a minute to adjust between indoor artificial light and darkness.

But it didn't matter, because I didn't get to the car before Gabriel snagged me and pulled me aside with some urgency.

He spoke quickly and quietly. "I think we are in real trouble. We'd just finished getting the kids out of the hot tub in the backyard. Jesse and Mary Jo took everyone else upstairs to dry off and change, but Sofia stayed out to help me put the cover back on the hot tub. We heard a crash and came out front to see what happened. I thought at first someone had just done a hit-and-run on the car."

He gestured, and I could see the top of the trunk, which had a reverse dent rising from the middle. "I sent Sofia in for you so I could shut the trunk before she saw the body. I didn't see anyone driving off. Just a woman on the street. Looked like she was jogging, you know? Making good time, too. I thought about heading after her to see if she'd seen anything, but then I noticed just how odd the trunk was, so I took a better look." He leaned in, and said, very softly. "The body was gone, Mercy. And the sound we heard was her hitting the lid of the trunk so she could get out."

All of the werewolves—Asil, Adam, Ben, and Warren who had been looking down the street, presumably for whoever hit the car—turned to look at Gabriel and me. Asil opened the trunk.

"She was dead," he said. "I swear to it. I know she was fae, but I have killed them before. She was dead. When we walked by here earlier, I could smell the body starting to decompose."

I couldn't help it, I laughed. "Zombie fae. That's all we needed. I don't know about you, but I'm going to get a *really* good night's sleep with zombie fae running around. I'll go see if I can track her."

"Mercy," Adam said.

"I won't approach," I promised. "I'll just see where she's going and come back and get you. By the time any of you wolves can change, she'll be long gone."

Since young Sandovals were beginning to filter out of the house to see what the excitement was all about, I didn't strip before changing into my coyote. Adam helped me get the sweatshirt off when my coyote-self got stuck in it—and only then did I remember that I'd shifted right in front of Armstrong and Tony, neither of whom had known what I was.

One of my foster father Bryan's favorite sayings had been, "No use crying over spilt milk." Besides, Tad must have used the distraction to get the fae cuffs out of the trunk because I caught a glimpse of him slipping Peace and Quiet under his shirt, so something good came out of it anyway.

I put my nose down and was off and running. Asil was right—she'd begun to rot, and she left a very clear trail.

Adam ran beside me in his human form. Apparently he didn't want me out zombie hunting on my own. Coyotes run a great deal faster than people can, and I run faster than most coyotes. Werewolves are good runners, but even a werewolf can run only so fast in their human form—four-footed travel is a lot quicker than two. He was keeping up with me, and moving faster than any human could have—and maybe I wasn't running at my top speed. Not even close, really.

Having Adam beside me if I had to confront a zombie fae assassin was worth slowing down for.

10

I thought we were going to catch her. It hadn't been five minutes since Sofia had broken into the meeting—and how fast could a zombie fae assassin run?

But when we got out to Bombing Range Road, the nearest main thoroughfare (so named because the area had been a bombing range back in WWII), the trail disappeared at the edge of the road. It was full dark, though it was only 6:00 P.M., but dark doesn't bother me much. I had a clear view in either direction for several miles, and there was no dead woman running along the side of the road. There were, however, a number of cars traveling both directions.

"She got into a car," Adam said, trying not to appear winded, as I cast back and forth with my nose to the ground. "Someone picked her up—or she hitched a ride."

Disturbing to speculate about either way, I thought, but there was nothing we could do about it now. "Disturbing" was a good word. Of all the things that had happened over the past few days, a dead fae getting up and running off might just be the *most* disturbing.

Still—a zombie. Maybe it would intrigue Marsilia enough she'd forget about her car. Not likely, but maybe. I wasn't sure I should feel responsible for the damage to the trunk. How could I have been expected to know that the dead fae would break out on her own?

Adam stared down the road. "If you hadn't slowed down for me, you might have caught her."

Maybe I would have—and maybe that wouldn't have been a good thing. Warren's truck pulled up, and Warren leaned over and opened the passenger door.

"No luck?" Warren asked, as we hopped in. I took the middle seat.

"No. Looks like she got in a car. Could have gone either way."

Warren turned the truck around and headed back before he said anything. "That's disturbing," he said.

Zombies or not, the press needed to be appeased.

Tony had checked in with his boss and given him the official story that Adam and Armstrong had come up with—which was basically to leave out Cantrip's involvement completely. The conveniently out-of-sight anonymous mercenaries took the majority of the blame. They had been hired to force the werewolves to act in violence and attack Senator Campbell, to get rid of the senator and to make the werewolves appear to be monsters.

Adam didn't look like a monster. He looked like a handsome, charismatic man. He was very good on camera.

The person behind the plot apparently panicked when some of

his mercenaries were captured while holding Kyle Brooks prisoner. He had them killed to keep them from talking.

Armstrong had done some *un*cleaning to reveal the deaths of the men caught kidnapping Kyle because it was now a useful part of the story.

When they heard about the killings, the other mercenaries left, burning the winery and letting Adam and the pack break free. Officials were trying to find the mercenaries (with an implied fat chance) and the man behind the plot (also fat chance). And hopefully, everyone would leave satisfied with nothing but the truth—if not quite the whole truth.

So Adam, Tony, Armstrong, Kyle, and Warren headed for Kyle's office in Kennewick by way of Adam's house so he could dress appropriately for a press conference, leaving the rest of us to hold down the fort. The good news was that between the runaway dead woman and the upcoming press conference, no one had said anything to me about the fact that I'd changed into a coyote. Maybe they all assumed I was a half-blood fae like Tad.

When Ben came up to tell me that there was a messenger from Marsilia for me at the front door, I was in one of the upstairs bedrooms reading *James and the Giant Peach* to the youngest three Sandovals. Kyle's stash of emergency family-in-need supplies included a big box of books designed to appeal to a wide range of age groups.

"It's just getting to the good part," said Sofia. "We're almost to the giant bugs."

"Can you keep reading?" I asked Sylvia.

"Who is Marsilia?" she asked, taking the book from me.

"The woman who owns the car I've been driving around," I told her.

She winced—she'd seen the car.

"Is that the vampire, Mercy?" asked Sissy, who was nearly seven going on thirty.

"Vampires?" Sylvia asked. "There are vampires, too?" And then she said, "You stole a *vampire's* car and trashed it?"

I winced, too. "Officially, there are no vampires. If you don't believe in them, they will leave you alone. So it's best if you don't believe in them."

Maia nodded solemnly. "My best friend Penny asked me if there were vampires, and I told her, no. I did tell her I rode a werewolf, and her mama told me that lying wasn't good. I wasn't lying that time, but sometimes lying is good, right? Mercy, will you come to my house when they come over again and tell them I'm not lying?"

Maia was either going to grow up to rule the world or loose a planetwide plague upon the land. Maybe both. She had started kindergarten this year, or should have anyway, so we had a little time before we had to look for a place to hide from her.

"You *stole* a *vampire's* car?" Sylvia said again.

"Stole is a strong word," I told Sylvia. "It was at my shop for an oil change when trouble hit, and I needed a car that no one could track. It'll be okay, trust me—as long as you don't talk about vampires. They take their secrecy very seriously."

"Mercy," said Maia.

"Okay," Sylvia said. "I'll make sure the children understand."

"Mercy." Maia's eyebrows lowered, and her voice rose. "You need to tell Penny's mama so she won't think I'm a liar."

"I will speak to Penny's mama," said Sylvia. "Now hush so I can read about big bugs and rotten fruit."

They hushed.

Ben followed me down the stairs. Asil and Honey, in her wolf form, were waiting at the base of the stairs. Ben must have told them before he'd gone upstairs to get me. That was okay, it saved me time.

I pointed to Honey, and said, "Stay out of sight, please. Too many guards says I'm scared of her—which I am—but I don't have to advertise that. It would reflect badly on the pack. Ben and Asil can come to the door with me, because no guards says I don't respect her." Which was also true but not useful.

I patted the lamb necklace around my neck to make sure it was still there. Objects of faith worked against vampires, and for me the lamb worked as well as a cross. Adam had given me a gold-with-emerald-eyes replacement for my silver lamb because wearing silver is problematical when you are the mate of a werewolf. It was just the right size to stay around my neck when I changed, and it was sturdy enough to stay on when I ran. On the same chain I wore one of Adam's army dog tags. Wedding rings are dangerous for a mechanic. I took a breath and centered myself as if I were about to enter a match at a dojo.

The man waiting on the porch step was a complete stranger, though my nose told me he was a vampire. I didn't know all of Marsilia's vampires by name, but there weren't that many, and most of them I knew by sight.

Marsilia was low on powerful vampires. Maybe she'd been recruiting. Though I had no way of telling which vampires were more or less powerful than others, this one did not seem like a new vampire. They had less control of themselves.

He was Asian—Chinese, if I wasn't mistaken—with a lean build. He wore black jeans and a gold silk shirt with a mandarin collar. With the porch light shining directly on him, I could see that it was embroidered with dragons in a gold just slightly darker than the cloth of his shirt. The temperature had fallen with the sun, and if he'd been human, he'd have been shivering in the cold.

He'd been changed young—not as young as Wulfe, who still looked like a half-grown teenager, and had since the Middle Ages. But if the vampire on Kyle's porch had been over twenty when he'd been turned, it hadn't been by much.

He bowed his head in greeting—the kind of bow I made before beginning a karate match, with head up and eyes on your opponent rather than the way some of the older European vampires and werewolves do it. I returned his bow the same way he gave it.

"I am Thomas Hao, Ms. Hauptman," he said without inflection of accent or emotion. "It is my great pleasure to issue you and your mate an invitation to meet with Marsilia, Mistress of the Tri-Cities' seethe. You may, of course, refuse. I am asked also to inform you that if you come tonight, certain matters may be quickly resolved. She has some information regarding the recent regrettable incidents that she believes would be interesting to you."

"Oh, that's too easy," said Ben, looking at me. "What does she want?" He spoke quietly, and both he and Asil had stayed a step farther back in the foyer than I was, so Hao didn't have a clear view of them. That didn't mean he couldn't hear them clearly.

"Do the wolves speak for you, mate of the Alpha of the Columbia Basin Pack?" Hao asked, his voice exquisitely polite. No, this was not a new vampire.

"I agree with Ben," I said half-apologetically. "I've all but totaled Marsilia's new, very expensive car, and she's just going to forget about it and give me information to top it off? If that's so, why not just a phone call?"

Hao studied me, then looked over his shoulder and took a step back to stare at the Mercedes. He stood there motionless for a few seconds, and when he turned back to me, I was sure I saw amusement on his face, though there was not even a hint of it around his mouth.

"Ah. I do not believe she is aware that the car had been damaged, Ms. Hauptman." Yes, that was amusement.

I folded my arms; last night I'd have jumped at the chance. Having Marsilia invite me would have given me a slight advantage over inviting myself, as I had planned. But with Adam and the pack back safely, we didn't need the vampires anymore. "I think I'll play it prudent. Tell Marsilia that I'll have the car repaired to her satisfaction and give her a few months to get over it before I visit."

Hao looked at his feet and pursed his lips. "Marsilia is worried, Ms. Hauptman. We know about the abduction of the pack. The one behind the incident is a danger to everyone in the Tri-Cities and not just to the Columbia Basin Pack. At a different time, the damage to the car would, I am certain, have just the effect you are concerned about. But Marsilia is old and very, very wealthy. A car is as nothing given what she sees coming."

Beside me, Asil came subtly alert, and I felt it myself. This was a twist I hadn't seen.

"Why doesn't she just use the phone?" I asked.

"Or let you tell us right now," murmured Asil.

"Because one may be overheard on the phone, and this is dangerous information," said Hao, choosing to ignore Asil, "information that may prevent more deaths in your pack." He paused, and again I got the impression he was amused, but no sign of it crossed his face. "Also, because Marsilia dislikes using phones or"—he glanced at Asil—"surrogates when she can make you dance to her bidding."

That sounded like Marsilia, all right.

Vampires do not breathe except to talk, they do not perspire, and their hearts race only with stolen blood. So it's very difficult to tell when they are lying and when they are telling the truth. I cannot reliably do it.

"Can it wait until tomorrow night?" I asked.

"*I* believe that you would regret it if you waited," Hao said. It struck me as odd that he ventured an opinion. I might not be able to tell how old or powerful a vampire was, but I could read subtle cues. This vampire was not anyone's minion. He caught the mistake himself and was more careful as he continued to speak. "I was to tell you that you should bring Adam and however many of the pack you choose to."

Adam's welcome put a different slant on things. For one thing, it made it less likely that she was setting me up—unless she knew Adam wasn't here right now. It also meant that she probably had a use for the whole pack.

"She wants the wolves to deal with this person, so she doesn't have to," I said.

"No," he answered. "No. She will act against him, but matters are more likely to be successful if she and the pack can coordinate their efforts."

She was worried, I thought, and so was Thomas Hao.

"Adam is not here at the moment," I told him. And he wouldn't be for hours.

Hao's mouth tightened. "That is regrettable."

I was having to rely on body language instead of my nose, but either he was very good at lying with his body (and very few people, vampire or not, are aware enough to do that) or he was dismayed that Adam would not be coming.

"It would still be a good idea," Hao told me. "If you came, Mercy who is a walker."

A walker is the name given to those of us who are descendants of Coyote, Raven, Hawk, or any of the other archetypes who once walked this land. Vampires do not like us. First, I see ghosts, and ghosts congregate around the daytime resting places of vampires, betraying the presence of the monster who killed them. I am also resistant to a lot of magic—and almost entirely resistant to the standard magic of vampires. When vampires came to the New World, they were met by my kind and nearly destroyed. I think that if disease and war had not decimated the Indians—and thus the walkers—there would be no vampires in the Americas.

Of course, being resistant to vampire magic didn't mean I was a match for a vampire in any way, shape, or form.

This vampire stared at me with black eyes and waited. Marsilia wasn't going to hurt me—she couldn't afford to because the werewolves would destroy her if she did. She was just playing games. If I didn't accept her invitation, by werewolf rules, which weren't so different, really, from vampire rules because both are predators, it would be a coup for Marsilia and a black eye of cowardice for the pack.

Being seen as strong and scary kept the monsters at bay. If I showed the world that I was afraid of Marsilia, it made those wolves who belonged to the pack that much less safe.

I could insist on waiting until Adam got back. That might make me look weak, but it wouldn't reflect, much, on the pack. Adam had had less than an hour's worth of sleep since he escaped, and

I was pretty sure he hadn't slept otherwise since before the pack was taken.

I was tired, too, and wanted nothing more than to go back upstairs and read about giant squishy fruit with the Sandoval girls. We had lost Peter, and I didn't want to lose anyone else, no matter how much the vampires scared me. Waiting for Adam, when I *knew* Marsilia wouldn't hurt me, really was cowardice. Adam was exhausted, and this was something I could do for him and for the pack.

"All right," I said. "I'll come. I have matters to arrange first if I'm going to go. I can find my way to the seethe."

Hao shook his head. "The Mistress asked me to make sure that you made it there safely. I will wait here."

"It might take me a while," I warned him.

He bowed again. "I am used to waiting."

"Your decision," I told him, then closed the door. I looked at the werewolves and waited for their reactions.

Asil gave Dick and Jane—the nude statues that adorned Kyle's foyer—an amused look.

"I like the hat," he said.

"Which one?" I asked.

Jane had a new hat this month, a straw cowboy hat with an ostrich feather pointing jauntily up, just like the first ten inches or so of the ski hat Dick wore somewhere south of his belly button. The long tail of Dick's hat drooped down until its pompom end hung just below Dick's knees.

Asil's amusement turned into a real smile, an open and beautiful smile that made him look twenty-five instead of how-many-hundreds of years old.

"Kyle has Christmas wear for them," I told him. "He usually

dresses them up the day after Thanksgiving. But he's been a little too busy to get them rigged out."

"You aren't really going to go, right?" asked Ben.

"Marsilia isn't going to hurt me," I told him.

He rolled his eyes. "Have you seen what you did to her car?"

"Peter died," I told Ben. "Go find Tad, and tell him that you two will be watching this house tonight."

His chin rose.

"I'm not taking Tad into the vampire den," I told him. "And Honey . . . Honey should not be left guarding the kids, not tonight." Not when Peter had just died and she might lose control of her wolf.

Honey padded into the foyer, graceful, golden, and beautiful. She snarled at me.

"I *am* the boss of you," I told her as I headed for the stairs. "You're coming with Asil and me, so put a sock in it."

"Does the whole pack follow your orders so well, little coyote?" Asil asked, amused.

"Yes."

He laughed again.

I gave him a cool look. "Or they regret it for a long time."

We hadn't had a chance to resupply on cell phones yet, and that left me with no direct way to contact Adam. The first rule of being married is to communicate where you are going and why. I called Tony, and Sylvia answered—Tony had left his cell phone with her. Kyle's phone went straight to voice mail. I left a message on it and stopped to think. Armstrong probably had a cell, but I didn't have his number.

I called Kyle's office from the landline and told the recording that I was "going to meet with Marsilia" but didn't dare to get more specific than that. I called Stefan. He didn't answer his cell phone, and no one answered his home phone. I left more-detailed messages both places. When I set the phone on the counter, Asil and Tad were both in the kitchen.

Tad looked at Asil. "Mercy needs clothes to wear if she's going to face Marsilia. Stay here because I want to talk to her." Asil gave me an amused glance, Tad a less amused glance, but didn't protest waiting while Tad escorted me up the stairs and into the bedroom that he'd been sleeping in. He took out the odd chunk of metal from his pocket and invoked the sword his father had made.

"I already destroyed the cuffs," he told me, holding it out. "So I don't need it. I'm not a swordsman, and you're going into enemy territory dangerously unarmed. I don't know Asil, and Honey doesn't like you. You may need something."

"Asil is Bran's, he will defend me," I told him. I didn't take the sword. I've had some weapons training in karate classes, but I've also read the stories about the Dark Smith of Dronheim.

"Which is more than you can say about Honey," Tad groused. "Maybe you should take me."

I shook my head. "I don't want to leave either Honey or Asil with the kids. Honey might lose it and kill someone—I'd rather it be the vampires than the kids. Asil . . . is not entirely stable. If something does happen here and he had to kill someone, it could be worse than Honey losing it. This visit with Marsilia shouldn't be dangerous." If Hao was not lying. "Can you discern lies?" Some fae could, some couldn't—though they themselves could not lie.

"Not with vampires," he admitted.

"Vampires are tricky," I agreed instead of saying, "Me either." "But I think Hao was serious about Marsilia taking action—which makes me suspect that we are dealing with something that directly threatens the vampires after all. She wouldn't stir herself on our behalf unless there was something big in it for her." That "I think" kept it from being a lie. If he thought I could read Hao's truth, he'd be less likely to argue. But I was pretty sure Hao had not been lying.

Who gains, Asil had asked me, if the pack is gone from the Tri-Cities? Not Marsilia, I'd assured him. Because Marsilia benefited from our pack. No one wanted to take on Adam—and because Marsilia and Adam had cooperated a time or two, people thought that we cooperated more with the vampires than we really did. Adam didn't object because he felt it kept the riffraff out.

But that meant one of her enemies might come after the pack in order to weaken *her*. She'd already withstood one attempt to take over her territory—and we of the Columbia Basin Pack had supported her. "I should be safe enough," I told Tad. "Honey might not like me much, but she is loyal to Adam, and she is impressive. And of the werewolves we have here, she's the single best fighter. I need you here—you'll take care of the children, first and foremost. Ben is good for defense if you need it, but I don't know how he'll be around kids." With his four-letter vocabulary and his anger problems, I'd have normally avoided leaving him with children or undefended women. But he was loyal to Adam, and I was confident that he wouldn't hurt any of the kids even if he might expand their vocabulary in unfortunate directions.

"All right," Tad said. "All right. But you take the sword." He held it out again. It looked wicked and wrong in a room filled with Thomas the Tank Engine's cheery presence.

I made no effort to take it. "I know about your father's swords."

Tad laughed. "Yeah, there was a long period of time when Dad was pretty angry with the world. This one is called Hunger, and it needs to taste your blood; then it will serve you—until it tastes another's blood it likes better. I know you've done some weapon forms in karate, but, you're right, it's still better not to use it unless you have to. You'll never know when it might prefer someone else—and since you aren't fae, it will be even less inclined to stay with you. However. It will kill vampires in a way a normal sword cannot. It will also eat magic—items or spells, though from my experience it is pretty slow." He looked at me. "And there's still that fae assassin running around when she should be dead. I don't know for sure that this sword will do anything to her, but it's more likely to incapacitate her than a knife, a bullet, or even a werewolf is."

He held the sword out again, and I took it gingerly.

"Use it to cut yourself to bind it to you. I'd recommend forearm or calf—and be careful, it's really, really sharp."

So I touched my left forearm to the blade—and it zapped me a good one as it sliced into the skin. It felt like magic turned to electricity—like touching a hot wire on a fence.

Tad frowned. "That's not supposed to happen. Let's try this."

He pulled out a pocketknife and cut his index finger. He got a few drops of blood flowing, then pressed his finger on the still-bleeding cut on my forearm. I winced and winced again when he took hold of my hand that held the sword and guided it to taste of our mingled blood.

This time there was no zap of magic but a gentle dance of power through my body.

"That's better," he said. "Now you should be able to sheathe the blade just by thinking about it."

He was right. In an instant, the blade had vanished, leaving what looked like a random lump of pitted metal.

"If the Gray Lords were mad about the walking stick—" I said—the lump of metal's residual magic made my forearm buzz all the way to my elbow.

"Let's just say that it would be better if you give it back to me as soon as you return—and I intend to give it back to my father at the earliest opportunity. This isn't like Peace and Quiet; Hunger is a major artifact, and the fae lords won't be happy to find that it is in your hands—particularly as you gave another fae artifact to Coyote."

I jerked my head up to look him in the eyes, and he grinned. "Dad told me. He had to tell a few of the fae because they knew you had the walking stick, and they wanted it back in the worst way."

I started to put it into the pocket of Kyle's sweats when Tad stopped me. "You aren't really going to wear those to meet with Marsilia are you?"

"Right," I said. "I'll go look in Kyle's closet."

Kyle's closet yielded a pair of jeans that were tight but not unbearably so and a blue sweater that Tad picked out. I hoped I wasn't stealing Kyle's favorite clothes. I got downstairs, and Honey, still in wolf form, and Asil waited for me.

Asil handed me a coat.

It was a good coat, and it fit. More importantly, it had a pocket big enough for the fae artifact that was sometimes a sword, so I didn't have to keep it stuffed in the too-tight jeans.

Asil drove Warren's truck, with Honey beside him—she wasn't happy about that, but I didn't like her any more than she liked me. That she was mourning Peter, whom I liked very much, just made me more uncomfortable around her. Let Asil deal with her and vice versa.

I drove Marsilia's Mercedes. We'd take the truck back and leave the car with Marsilia. That would get it out of my hands, and anything else that happened to it would be her fault. Tad had had to bend the trunk more to get it to latch. Now the trunk looked like a tree had fallen on it, which didn't improve the car's appearance at all. I'd moved my gun from the car to the truck, but I planned on leaving it there. If I was reduced to shooting at the vampires tonight, I might as well shoot myself and get it over with.

Thomas Hao led the procession in an inconspicuous white Subaru Forester with California plates. I thought we were going to the seethe right up until he turned in the wrong direction at the Keene roundabout, taking us away from the Tri-Cities.

I hesitated, driving an extra round on the roundabout. If he was from out of town, as the California plates indicated, he might have gotten lost. When I could see him again, the vampire had pulled to the side of the road and was waiting for us.

If he'd taken a wrong turn, he'd figure it out when we ran out of town and ended up out in the countryside, I decided. If not—then I'd guess we were meeting Marsilia somewhere else. It didn't make me happy, but I wasn't unhappy enough to turn back to Kyle's.

I pulled out behind Hao, and Asil followed me. When he drove past the big hayfields without slowing, then turned to take us farther out into West Nowhere, I figured that we weren't going to the seethe and took out Gabriel's sister's phone—which I still had—and called Sylvia on Tony's phone.

"We're not going to Marsilia's," I told her. "We're out on Highway 224 headed toward Benton City. I'll give you another call when I know more."

"I'll keep the phone nearby," she said.

Twenty minutes later, we were through Benton City and headed up on the bluffs that overlooked the Yakima River, surrounded by orchard and vineyard. I hadn't seen a house in miles when Hao turned up a gravel road between rows of orchard trees.

I'd spent the entire time thinking about vampires. Old vampires had money. Marsilia had been going through a fugue—old-vampire version of depression, from what I'd gathered. She had sat around not doing much for years, and that made her look weak, which is why Gauntlet Boy had attempted to steal her seethe. Marsilia would never so much as blink unless it benefited her.

She wouldn't arrange a meeting with the pack unless *she* needed help. This, *all* of this, had begun with the vampires. The more I thought about it, the more sense it made.

Of course a vampire would kill the mercenaries who might know too much. He wasn't scared of what they might say to the police; he was scared of what they would say to Bran or Charles. If the pack died—and he'd intended them to die, probably couldn't believe that they'd let themselves be taken by a handful of mercenaries and Cantrip agents—then the Marrok would hunt down the responsible parties.

The trees fell away first, then the gravel, and we crawled through what seemed like acres of grapes that looked deader than could be attributed to the season alone. Marsilia's car was a city car and wasn't too happy with the rocks and ruts that had replaced the gravel.

Vampires gained powers. Stefan could teleport—and that was a real secret because it made him a target. James Blackwood, the Master of Spokane, could steal the abilities of the supernatural folk he fed upon. Maybe this vampire could create a zombie from my assassin. *Why* anyone would want to was another matter.

I was so lost in my thoughts that it wasn't until I got a good whiff of smoke that I figured out where we were going. The smoke itself wasn't unusual—this time of year a lot of places burned agricultural rubbish. But this smelled like a house fire and not just burning plant matter.

Hastily, I called Sylvia again. "Tell Adam that we're going to the place where he was kidnapped and held."

"Is something wrong?" she asked.

"Not necessarily," I said, though I was suspicious that Hao had been so careful not to tell me that we were meeting at the winery Adam and Elizaveta had burned to ash. "She might have something to show me here."

Or maybe not. Maybe I'd just been really, really stupid.

I took a breath. "Tell Adam that I didn't recognize the vampire who brought us here. He says his name is Thomas Hao, and he drives a Subaru Forester with California vanity plates that say DAYTIME." I spelled it for her. On a vampire's car, the plates could mean anything from irony to hope.

"Could be this isn't Marsilia's gig at all," I said, not liking that thought, either.

"I'll tell them."

I hung up the phone and continued to follow the vampire.

We came upon the burnt remains of the winery from the back side, the final confirmation of my suspicions. The fire had burned hot, leaving only stone, cement, and just a few shards of very black wood behind. Elizaveta had been thorough in this as in everything else she did.

The waxing moon, three-quarters full, gave the remains a horror-movie eeriness. As did the ghost waiting next to the vineyard on the opposite side of the dirt track we were following. Seeing ghosts was not unusual, and that one wasn't the only ghost hovering about. I would not have paid any attention to him except that he looked familiar. I sped up until I was close enough to get a good look.

It was Peter, our Peter. He was standing next to one of the angled posts set into the earth to support the wires that the grapevines cling to. He was hugging himself and looking toward the—I checked—mostly empty parking lot in front of the building-that-was.

I stopped, turned off lights and engine both, and got out of the car, forgetting my worries about whether or not I'd been summoned here by Marsilia, by Hao, or by some unknown enemy.

Ghosts are the remnants of the people they had once been. Most of the ones I've met don't have much, if any, intelligence. There was no reason to stop. This wasn't Peter, not really. He didn't need me—but that didn't matter. He *looked* like he needed someone, and I couldn't leave him alone and vulnerable.

As I rounded the front of the Mercedes, the backup lights of Thomas Hao's car turned on, Warren's truck pulled in behind me—and Peter turned and saw me.

"Get out of here, Mercy," he told me earnestly. "There is someone very bad here." He tipped his head toward the burnt-out building. He was as coherent and aware as I'd ever seen.

"Peter?" I asked, conscious of Honey and Asil getting out of the truck.

"He can't get me," Peter said, sounding more hopeful than

certain. "He's calling me. Can you hear it? It's like when Adam calls, but different." He shivered and took a step toward the parking lot.

"Who is calling you?" I asked.

Peter shook his head. Sometimes ghosts appear in their dying state—complete with blood and gore. But there was no bullet hole in Peter's forehead, nor was he wearing the slacks and dress shirt he'd been wearing when I'd last seen him at Thanksgiving dinner, the ones he'd worn when he'd died. Instead, he wore the jeans, steel-toed boots, and flannel shirt that was his more usual garb.

I hadn't noticed at first because his presence had been too faint, but he'd become more real as he talked. If I hadn't known him, hadn't known he was dead, I might not have figured out he was a ghost—he was that solid to me.

Hao got out of his car and approached, arriving about the same time as Asil and Honey.

"Mercy?" asked Asil. "Who are you talking to?"

Honey whined very softly, staring at me intently, and Peter looked at her.

He fell on his knees, his face raw with pain, sorrow, and need, tears sliding down his face. "Honey. *Min prinsesse.* Oh, Honey, I am lost." He reached out and touched her, his fingers making her fur move. She shook and tried to get closer, though I don't think she could see him. Her movement only pushed her body through him.

Even when people don't know that there is a ghost present, they don't tend to stay intermingled with them for very long. Honey was no exception, and she took three quick steps back until she stood next to Asil, who put his hand on her head.

"Peter," I said.

Honey whined again and let out a little yip. Peter reached out, leaning until he touched her nose and looked at me. He started to say something, then jerkily grabbed his ears.

"I'm not going to him," he told me, wild-eyed. And suddenly there was a wolf where Peter had been—and that wolf was a submissive wolf. Peter the man might have been able to resist longer, but his wolf obeyed orders. Ears and tail drooping, he looked at Honey and turned to leave.

"Peter," I said harshly. I was getting better at stealing Adam's thunder. When I spoke, I pulled on the pack ties that, somehow, still held the dead werewolf. Something bothered me about that, but I was too concerned about keeping Peter from responding to whatever was calling him.

The pack bonds were gossamer-thin, but as I pushed my will through them, they grew more dense. He stopped, quivering—obedient still to the commands that had bound him in life.

"Peter." And this time I called him with the part of me that could see ghosts, the part that had sent the ghost at Tad's house away, that had forced obedience on the ghosts that had once belonged to James Blackwood, the Master of Spokane, who was now dead by my hand. I reached out to him, and said, "Come here."

Peter turned and sat next to my feet, his eyes on my face as though he were a herding dog and I his shepherd. Waiting for me to save him.

There were more ghosts here. They had been standing sentinel between the parking lot and the front of the house, and, although I'd noticed them, I hadn't paid attention because they weren't mine as Peter was. But when Peter had come to me, when I'd called him, they had all turned in my direction. Slowly, as if it were very difficult as well as imperative, they were coming toward us, too.

I bent down and took Peter's head between my hands. I breathed into his nose because it seemed like the right thing to do. Long-ago words spoken to me by Charles rang in my head.

Vision quest is opening yourself up to the world and waiting to perceive what it wants to show you, he'd told me. Then, almost absently, he'd said, *Magic is like that. It wants to use you, and your only choice is yes or no.*

So I followed my instincts, my magic.

"Peter," I told him, using Adam, using the pack bonds, using that other part of me—using everything I had. Stone-cold logic told me that what stood before me right now wasn't a ghost the way I knew them. I'd remembered why Peter shouldn't be bound by pack ties anymore.

Ghosts didn't look at me with intelligence and need, didn't respond to pack bonds. I looked, as I'd been learning how to do, I looked for the pack bonds and saw them, tinsel bright still, strengthened by my will. Pack bonds were soul binding soul—Adam had told me that. Though I could not perceive souls—pack bonds were another matter. Those bonds were firmly set in Peter's soul, and that soul was still here in his ghost, where it had no business being—here, where it was in danger from whoever it was who called him.

My senses were still expanded to their fullest, which is why I saw something else, too—a cloud of darkness that surrounded Peter and tried to slice through the pack bonds and take him from me. Asil touched my shoulder and abruptly lowered his head to stare at Peter. Honey leaned against my hip and froze, her body tightening until it felt like stone.

"Peter," I said, "you belong to us, to the pack. You are *mine.*" The touch of pack, of Honey, helped. I brushed at the cloud of darkness, and as I touched it . . . it dissolved under my hands, but not before I caught the tingle of magic. Vampire magic.

"Leave this place, Peter," I told him. I needed to do something about the way his soul lingered when it should have gone on after his death, but instinct—and I trusted what my coyote knew—my instinct said it was more important to get him out of here. Away from whatever had been trying to claim him.

He glanced at Honey, who was watching my face.

"She loves you, too," I said. "Peter, *get out of here*. Go somewhere safe."

And then he was gone, and some of the life died in Honey's eyes, too.

"It's all right," I told her. I felt down the pack bonds to be sure, and Peter was still there. He didn't feel alive, didn't feel like the others, but we still held him safely. I straightened and felt a buzz of relief that left me dizzy. "He's safe."

Hao watched me. "They are right," he said. "You speak to the dead."

"Who is binding the ghosts?" I asked Hao.

The dead were all around us, looking at me urgently. Their mouths were moving, but I couldn't hear them. The net of darkness surrounding them was thicker than the one that had tried to capture Peter. Maybe it prevented me from hearing them, or maybe it was just because I was tied to Peter by the pack bonds.

Hao looked around. "Are they bound? Perhaps he has anticipated us. Are you finished here?"

"Who is it?" asked Asil, his voice a low, menacing rumble.

Hao was not intimidated—but then he didn't know who Asil was. "That is not for me to say. If you are done, we should go."

I looked at the dead here, three women and fourteen men. One of the women wore a black cocktail dress, but the rest of them were in power clothes like real-estate agents or business people. Suits and ties for the men, skirts and jackets for the women. If they were here, caught like Peter had been caught, then they, too, were not merely ghosts. But I was not bound to them the way I was bound to Peter; I didn't know how to help them.

Then I recognized Jones, from when I'd seen him through Adam's eyes—Armstrong had called him Bennet, I remembered, Alexander Bennet. I don't know why it surprised me to realize I was staring at the ghosts of the other people who'd been killed here. I suppose it was because I was so used to seeing ghosts everywhere that I'd quit wondering who they'd been when they were alive.

Alexander Bennet had killed Peter.

"Yes," I said. "I'm done." I felt no need or obligation to save these people from whatever had caught them. They had killed Peter and would have killed our friends and their families—down to Maia Sandoval, age five, who had ridden a werewolf and tried to feed him cookies.

These people could hang in limbo for all eternity for all I cared. "I'm done."

They watched us as we returned to our cars. They'd quit trying to speak. I closed the door to the car, pushed the button to start it, and followed Thomas Hao to the parking lot, driving through several ghosts to get there. But this time I wasn't weakened by fae magic as I had been when the ghost tried to possess me in the secret stairway in Tad's house. All I felt was a slight chill as I passed through them. And then they were behind me.

I knew I was going to have to do something about them later, no matter how angry I was now. It wasn't a matter of what they deserved—it was a matter of who I was and who I wasn't. At some point, everyone had to draw a line in the sand over which they would not cross.

I almost turned the car around right then, but Marsilia—presumably—was waiting. There would be time enough to put things right if I *could* put things right with these ghosts who were not also pack.

There was only one other car in the lot when we pulled in—and I knew it because I did the maintenance on the seethe's cars in lieu of making the "protection" payments required of all supernatural creatures who couldn't defend themselves from the vampires. I suppose as the mate of the Alpha of the Columbia Basin Pack, I could have refused service without encountering trouble. But I felt like the interaction, as little as it was, gave both the vampires and the wolves a meeting place where we could interact without a lot of drama. I hoped that would help make the Tri-Cities a little safer for everyone.

The presence of the seethe's car meant that Marsilia *was* behind the meeting. It should have reassured me, but I was worried about the "he" who had bound the ghosts and tried to do the same to Peter's.

I drove to the far side of the empty parking lot. The formerly sleek Mercedes slid into the space and purred to a halt. I got out of the car, zipped up my coat, and turned to walk over to the winery.

Marsilia stood by my rear left passenger door as if she had been there all along, though I knew that space had been empty when I pulled in. I managed not to jump.

The Mistress of the seethe was a beautiful woman. The night robbed her gold hair of its richness, but the moon kissed her even features and made her dark eyes mysterious. She wore the most practical clothes I'd ever seen her in: a formfitting, long-sleeved, dark, rib-knit shirt and khaki pants that were probably green—I can see well in the dark, but colors are tricky, and there was no helpful porch light here. Her shoes were combat boots that looked like she'd worn them a lot—and that didn't fit in with the Marsilia I knew at all.

I took the key fob to the car out of my pocket and handed it to her. She looked at me, looked at the dent in the driver's side door, and paced slowly around the Mercedes, saving the trunk for last.

"Remind me not to leave an expensive item in your care again," she said. And that was the Marsilia who despised me, the one I felt just fine hating right back.

"You haven't shown yourself to be all that wonderful at taking care of your treasures, either," I said coolly. "At least the car can be fixed." She'd hurt my friend with her carelessness, and I wasn't sure Stefan would ever recover. "Besides, if what I suspect is true, this damage"—I waved at the car—"as well as the death of my wolf Peter Jorgenson is a result of vampire politics."

She didn't say anything, which meant my speculation was accurate.

"An assassin attacked me," I continued. "Her head hit the driver's side door during the fight and left the first dent. She broke out of the trunk—still quite dead." I tapped my nose. "I could smell it on her."

Marsilia gave me a tight smile. "Perhaps you are right," she said, and her hand went to the damaged trunk.

"But the bloodstains and claw scratch marks in the back seat are my responsibility," I told her, stepping off my high horse. "I took the car without asking you because I needed one that could not be traced to me. Adam and I will foot the bill for repairs."

Asil and Honey came up to flank me.

"No," said Marsilia with a sigh. "You are right, this was vampire business." She patted the trunk as if it were a living thing. "Especially this. Perhaps you can recommend a good repair shop."

She looked at my face and laughed. The subtle wrongness of the sound set the hair on the back of my neck rising. Marsilia was really old, and did not do emotions quite right. The effect was disturbing.

"Really Mercy, what did you expect? I can be civilized, too. It is only a car. Come inside." She waved her hand at the ruins of the winery behind her. "Come inside, and learn why your pack was targeted."

"Because someone saw us, saw the werewolves as your allies," I told her. "They wanted you weakened." The rest of the explanation hinged on that first part. "They hired mercenaries and dissatisfied Cantrip zealots so that Bran would go hunting for federal agents and hired guns—and miss the one who was behind it all. Personally, I think they underestimate Bran, but a lot of people do. He likes it that way. The bottom line, Marsilia, is that someone, some vampire, wants your seethe."

"Yes. And you, cunning little coyote," she purred affectionately, so I knew that my accuracy had displeased her, "you have been so clever as not to die." She reached out suddenly, and her face loosened with lust as she ran her fingers over Asil's face. "And look what you brought me. A new toy."

Marsilia had a thing for werewolves.

Asil smiled wickedly and deftly avoided her gaze—dominant werewolf instincts to stare down everyone they meet are all wrong when it comes to vampires. Vampires can capture most people's minds with their gaze. That is what allows them to hunt people and not get caught. The Moor was apparently aware of vampire eye tricks.

"I like you," Marsilia said to him. "You are pretty."

"I like you, too," said Asil. "Vampires are an acquired taste." He smiled, with white teeth showing.

She frowned.

"Marsilia," said Stefan, stepping out of the darkness. "You distract yourself."

She didn't look at him, didn't take her eyes off Asil, just angled her head a little toward Stefan. "And if I do? What is the harm?"

"Mercy might kill you before anyone else gets a chance." Stefan sounded bored.

Marsilia flashed her fangs at me with sudden rage. "Do you think you can kill me, little coyote?" Her voice deepened, and her eyes no longer looked black. "Do you think I am so easy?"

"Hey," I told those brilliant red eyes. "I'm not the one making threats. But if you try to do something to my wolves, you'll have to go through me to do it."

Out of the corner of my eye, I saw Asil smile, just a little.

"Your wolf would enjoy it," Marsilia said, evidently dismissing Asil's earlier remark as admiration rather than a threat. More fool her. "You should let him make his own choice."

I stepped between her and Asil. "Leave him alone, Marsilia." Not that Asil couldn't defend himself. Until that moment, I hadn't realized that I'd quit fearing Asil somewhere along the way and started liking him. Not that he couldn't still go crazy and kill me—but I grew up with werewolves. Any werewolf can kill you if you are stupid and quit respecting him. The trick is not to be stupid.

"She takes care of what is hers, Marsilia. You should learn from her," Stefan said silkily.

"Are you *trying* to get me killed?" I asked him coolly, as Marsilia hissed. "We were actually almost having a conversation before you stepped in to help."

He laughed, sounding a lot more like himself. "Is that what you thought you were doing? I heard Marsilia trying to take your new wolf from you."

Asil smiled again, with teeth, but he didn't say anything.

"No," I told Stefan. "She wasn't. She just thought she was."

Marsilia shook her head—and changed before my eyes. Not physically, not a change of shape, but a change of personality. Gone was the sex goddess, the vicious woman who hated and despised me. Instead, she looked—ordinary, tired, and . . . and maybe a little scared.

"You are right, Stefan," she said. "I am sorry, Mercedes. Tonight, we need to be allies."

Marsilia had just apologized to me. Hell must have been experiencing some climate change.

"So," I said, "are you going to tell me what you know? Or are we going to spend another hour on drama and one-upmanship?"

11

"Come on inside, then," Marsilia said, though she didn't sound angry. "Come inside, and we will talk."

I followed her, and everyone else followed me. If Stefan hadn't been there, I wouldn't have let Hao trail behind. I didn't really have a lot of confidence in Honey, and I didn't entirely trust Asil, though I liked him. But Stefan I trusted to watch my back against the strange vampire.

Marsilia walked to the edge of the burnt-out shell of the winery and stepped up until she stood on the rim of the foundation, then jumped the ten feet or so to the floor of what had been the basement. I jumped after her and landed with loose knees and ankles to take up the strain of landing. The hard floor still made my feet sting. I was macho, though, and didn't whine about it. Posturing like a werewolf, I thought with some amusement. Probably I wouldn't have yelped in front of Marsilia even without the wolf pack's reputation to worry about. Honey hopped down like the ten-foot leap was nothing, and Asil, Asil didn't make a sound when he landed.

Marsilia continued across the floor toward the center. Above us, twin steel I-beams loomed dark and menacing. I didn't like them because something could stand on them and attack us from above when we weren't looking. The vampires, the night, and the ghosts were making me paranoid. The moon had disappeared behind clouds, and only a few stars peeped out at us.

I could tell from the way the floor felt under my feet that we walked across tiles, but there was a good inch or more of black ash on top. My toe caught an uneven spot, and I realized that debris was scattered across the floor, large and small, hidden by the soot and the shadows. Unburnable bits of the building had fallen into the basement. I watched my footing and followed Marsilia, who had no more trouble than if she'd been walking across a ballroom floor. I could see in the dark, but maybe vampires could see better. Asil stumbled over something, which made me feel less clumsy.

Somehow, I expected there to be more vampires in the building, but, except for us, it was empty. In my experience, Marsilia did everything with an audience. But the only vampires here were Marsilia, Hao, and Stefan.

In the semi-enclosed basement, the acrid smell of the fire was much worse than it had been in the parking lot. The stink of it burned my sinuses, clogged my throat, and made me impatient. "Is there a reason we can't talk outside?"

"Yes." It was Hao who answered. "But it needn't concern you yet."

I didn't like the sound of that "yet," nor the subtle, patronizing feel, so I stopped where I was.

"It seems to me that it might concern me very much." I turned to look at him even though it left Marsilia behind me. Asil and Honey were keeping an eye on her—and it was a coup to have the guts to turn my back to the Mistress of the City. "Who is it that has Marsilia running scared? Who is it that keeps the dead from moving on?" Accusing her of being scared while my back was to her wasn't the smartest move I'd ever made—but smart coyotes don't fall in love with werewolves or go to meetings with vampires.

"You've met him." Stefan could smile and keep his voice totally serious. He wouldn't have smiled if Marsilia was coming up behind me, so I relaxed that little bit more. "Do you remember the vampire who was pulling Estelle's strings, who talked Bernard into rebellion?" When Stefan had been driven from the seethe with unpardonable brutality so that he could be an impartial witness.

"Gauntlet Boy?"

Marsilia laughed. One of those horrible not happy laughs. Like the Queen of Hearts in *Alice in Wonderland*. And on that thought I had to turn around so I could keep an eye on her. I noticed as I moved around that Honey's ruff was up, and Asil had stiffened.

"Gauntlet Boy?" She knew she'd creeped me out. I could read the pleasure of it in her expression. "Gauntlet Boy. Yes, Mercedes, Gauntlet Boy. He started amassing power five years ago, taking over one city after another. He sees himself as the vampire's version of Bran."

"Bran is not a bad thing." He might rule with sharp fangs, but life was better for everyone, werewolf and human alike, because he did so.

"A vampire's version of Bran is not Bran." Stefan spoke from right behind me. I hadn't heard him approach.

I moved casually so that I had my back to empty space, with Honey on my left and Asil on my right—and all of the bloody scary vampires (Stefan included) in front. I knew they saw me do it—but they were willing to let me get away with it without commenting. Maybe Marsilia was serious about working together.

"Not Bran," agreed Hao. "He goes by the name of William Frost. We do not know how old he is or where he came from. I first heard of him when the Master of Portland disappeared. For three weeks his seethe searched for him. As you know, Ms. Hauptman, because I am told that you do, vampires who are not powerful cannot live without feeding upon a vampire strong enough to maintain them. This is the most powerful hold that the master or mistress of a seethe has over their fledglings. The vampires of Portland were dying without their master, and so they called upon me. When I got there, though, they had already been . . . saved." He said the word with a twist of his lips. "William Frost had them in hand, he said. Then he invited me to join him. He was quite forceful. I did not, however, wish to join his seethe. I refused, but because I also did not want to command a seethe, I left him unharmed. Mostly."

Hao was not one of Marsilia's minions. He'd told me that she'd sent him to get me, but if he went, it had been because he wanted to. Both of them were acting as though he was her equal.

Stefan put a hand on Hao's shoulder. "You couldn't know."

Stefan liked Hao. I hadn't known that there were any vampires left that Stefan liked.

Hao shrugged. "It is past and done. I cannot do it over. I did not want a seethe, and I was happy to leave Frost to it—though he made my skin crawl."

He met my eyes, started to drop his—and then left them where they were. A vampire's gaze didn't affect me the way it does everyone else, but he tried anyway. When he failed, he gave me a solemn nod.

He looked away, and his gaze traveled to Marsilia and Stefan. "We are not good people, Ms. Hauptman. Good people don't become vampires. I knew he was evil, and I left the vampires of Portland to him." Hao smiled, and I knew that when he was really amused, he did not smile. "You have heard, I think, that the police are having . . . difficulties in Portland. Too many of them are dying as they go about their jobs. Bran moved the Portland pack to Eugene, Oregon, where they would be safer. I believe he was more worried about the police than the vampires, and he was right. Frost is not ready to take on Bran just yet."

I'd heard about the move out of Portland. It happens that packs move. Not often. Usually it is just a matter of the Alpha switching jobs to a place where there is no pack and bringing the rest of his wolves with him. I hadn't asked why the Portland pack moved to Eugene. At the time, it hadn't concerned me.

"Bran is watching him?"

Hao shrugged. "I do not know Bran, Ms. Hauptman—that is your area of expertise. If he is watching William Frost, he isn't doing anything about him. I suspect, though, Bran has enough on his mind without dabbling in—how did you put it earlier—vampire politics."

"I am sorry if I offended you." Nope. Not a bit, but it seemed politic to say so—or might have, if I'd used a different tone of voice.

He caught my lie and gave me an amused half bow. "Frost moved south from there instead of north to Seattle. I think it was because the werewolves in Seattle have a very strong hold on their territory, and the seethe there is small and weak. He would have had to import vampires from Portland to really control the city."

I couldn't remember who the Seattle Alpha was offhand. I'd have to ask Bran.

"He hit Los Angeles next. The vampires there are . . ." Hao's voice trailed off, presumably because he was looking for the proper adjective.

"Barbaric," supplied Marsilia. "Stupid. Weak. The Master of the Los Angeles seethe surrendered to Frost, practically gibbering in terror after seeing a demonstration of Frost's power. William Frost, whoever he is, wherever he came from, has one of the rarest of vampire powers—he is a necromancer."

"Not necessarily. Perhaps he was a necromancer before he was turned." Hao's nonexpression looked thoughtful, and I suddenly realized why I could read him. Charles had nonexpressions like that when his wife Anna wasn't in the room. "A witch with an affinity for the dead. If so, he is very old, because the witch family who had those spells, that affinity, was among the first destroyed in the wars in Europe."

He wasn't talking about human wars, but about the vendettas and feuding that killed off most of the witch families in Europe and sparked the Inquisition and its softer, gentler brother, the witch hunts.

"By necromancer," I said carefully, "you mean he controls the ghosts here. And he somehow reanimated the body of the fae assassin?"

"Yes," Hao agreed. "At the very least, he can do such things—and there is no reason for anyone else to do so."

James Blackwood, the Master of Spokane, had been able to control ghosts because he could absorb the powers of the creatures he fed from, and he had drunk the blood of a walker. Even the other vampires had been afraid of him—though not because he could control ghosts. He was just that crazy.

But a witch was different from a walker. A lot more powerful—

if I could judge by the kind of power Elizaveta had. A necromancer witch would control the dead—and ghosts and zombies weren't the only kind of dead. That was why Marsilia was afraid.

"Can he control vampires?" I asked.

"He is not strong enough to take us over," Hao told me, motioning to the vampires present. "Though younger or less powerful vampires would be at risk."

Was that why Marsilia hadn't brought any of her other vampires? Why we had met here instead of the seethe? Did she worry that Frost would interrupt us?

"He has control of Oregon," Marsilia said before I could ask her if she was expecting Frost. "The Master of Portland was the only one he killed, the only one who might have stood against him—the rest being weak of will and cowards. He has Nevada, not that there were ever many vampires in Nevada. He has California except for San Francisco. Frost is still afraid of Hao, and Hao is the only vampire in San Francisco. Like Blackwood, Hao prefers not to have encroachers in his territory."

"Your lieutenants, Estelle and Bernard," I said. "He suborned them to weaken you and take over your seethe. He didn't do anything like that with the other seethes? Why not?" I asked.

"He has to be careful with Marsilia," said Hao. "She held the Master of Milan in thrall for centuries, and any vampire with two pennies' worth of common sense is terrified of attracting the attention of the Lord of Night."

A small smile ghosted across Marsilia's face and was gone. "The Lord of Night might be angry with me, but he would enjoy avenging me." She made a noise, and I couldn't tell if it was happy or unhappy. Maybe even she didn't know. "But he would enjoy mourning my death twice as much."

"Only great love can inspire such heated rage," agreed Stefan, and there was a glimmer of affection in his voice. "But Frost is right to be afraid. Even now, the Lord of Milan talks of you to his courtiers."

She ignored Stefan, which made me think that what he was saying was very important to her.

"Only if I violated our laws could Frost steal my vampires by stealth," Marsilia told me. "If Bernard and Estelle had instigated a rebellion, Frost could have claimed he was coming to my 'aid.' But I rid myself of his tools, and he was forced to look for another way."

"In the meantime, he continued to take over seethes." Hao looked at Marsilia. "To my shame, I ignored him until one of my making came to me. She had been in Shamus's care."

"Reno," Stefan told me. "Shamus was a tough bastard, but fair and smart."

"As good a master as a vampire can be," Hao agreed. "Constance . . . Constance was strong. Frost broke her. She escaped him, or he let her go—it's hard to tell and ultimately not important. She came to me and told me I was a fool to keep ignoring Frost. Eventually, he would amass enough power that he could destroy me."

His face tightened, and he spoke very softly. "She said it over and over. It was the only thing she could say. She was afraid of the dark, afraid of small spaces and large. Afraid of rats and quite mad."

His nostrils flared slightly. When Charles did that, it was either a sign of high emotion or it meant he smelled something interesting. I had no idea what it meant when a vampire who did not need to breathe did it.

Hao looked up at the night sky as a drop of moisture fell on his face. "Constance couldn't be trusted to feed without killing, and she was always hungry. I was fond of her, and I had to kill her. But even if she had said nothing, her death would have caused me to look at what was going on outside my city."

My jaw had dropped when I thought he was crying—but then moisture fell on my face, too. It was starting to rain. I blew out, and my breath fogged. It wasn't going to stay rain for long. The good news was that it was only the barest drizzle, so maybe it would stop soon.

"I could have killed Frost without help or much effort when I first met him," Hao told me. "But like your Alphas, a master vampire gains power from those who serve him. Frost has many who serve him now."

"I'm the only one left in Washington before he goes after Seattle." Marsilia wiped a drop of rain off her forehead.

Stefan took a deep breath. "It's not just about Marsilia. It's not even just vampire business at this point, Mercy. He intends to bring us out the way the werewolves have come out, the way the fae have come out."

I envisioned every town in the US finding out that there were vampires—and not the seductive lovers in the paranormal romances Jesse bought, either. The Inquisition would look like child's play. Asil, who had *lived* through the Inquisition, gave me an unhappy look but didn't say anything. He was playing my second for all he was worth. Another werewolf might have read the lies of his body language, but the old vampires didn't have a chance.

Asil was my ace in the hole, and my instincts were telling me I might need one. Though anytime I was anywhere near Marsilia, my instincts screamed, "Run away, run away."

"Not quite the same way the fae and the wolves came out," said Marsilia, her voice dry. "Bran hides the monstrous side of the werewolves, and the Gray Lords would have had the world believing that the fae were all like Tinker Bell. The Necromancer wants the world to know exactly what a vampire is, reveal ourselves in our full glory to completely terrify our prey, let the humans know once and for all who is the dominant species. He doesn't just want to rule the vampires, he wants to take down the human government. He wants to *rule*."

I had nightmares about vampires sometimes. There was the particularly nasty vampire who I'd heard speak longingly of the "before times" when vampires killed every time they fed, and they fed where and when they pleased. Vampires still kill their prey—but they don't kill every time they drink. When the people in their menageries die, it is usually accidental.

I didn't want to live in the "before times"—and neither, I could tell, did Marsilia. The slaughter would go both ways.

Hao said, "I called Marsilia and spoke to her of what my Constance had told me—as it turns out, Frost had just talked to her. So I came to see what I could do to help. Having failed to kill him once, I feel that he is my responsibility."

Marsilia tapped her foot and grimaced. "I called Iacapo. He was *intrigued*." She probably wouldn't be happy to know how lost she sounded. "The problem with living so long is that one grows so bored that even disaster seems a good thing. And so I told him. He hung up. Oh, he'll come avenge my death, but he will not bestir himself before then."

"Iacapo?" I asked.

"Iacapo Bonarata, the Master of Milan, the Lord of Night." Stefan paused, and said in an odd voice, "I wonder if he has anyone left in his court who knows his given name."

I wondered if Asil was the Moor's first or last name. From

what I'd heard about him, he was old enough not to have a last name.

"There will be no vengeance if Frost has his way," said Hao. "If he wins this challenge, Iacapo will be handicapped by his own rules."

"It won't stop him," Stefan said with an odd smile. It made him look young for a moment. Then he continued thoughtfully, "But you are right. Frost might not know how free and easy our former master is with his own rules because when people think of the Lord of Night, they are more interested in the scary and very dramatic things he does to people who break them."

Marsilia nodded. To me she said, "Frost cannot take my seethe by murder or he risks the Master of Milan's remembering that his job is to destroy vermin—even all the way across the world. Frost was not skilled enough to take over my seethe by stealth. So he is left with a frontal attack—and this is a problem. He is not entirely certain that he can take me."

"Marsilia is no fledgling." Stefan looked at her, and his face was . . . pensive. "She has a well-deserved reputation that followed her here. She is powerful and dangerous, too dangerous even for the Necromancer to fight alone. The werewolves have dominance fights, fights to the death for the position of Alpha, yes?"

"Bran frowns upon them," Asil murmured. "But yes."

"We have the same, but with more rules and variety. Frost would not challenge her alone—he brings two more with him, a triad. Marsilia is allowed to bring two others to the fight as well."

"Except that he can bring two former masters," Hao said. "And none of the vampires Marsilia has are capable of acting against him. Constance was strong, and he forced her to do his will. She was not quite his puppet, not quite, not even at the end. But Constance was stronger than any vampire Marsilia has to call except for Stefan and Wulfe."

"And Stefan is not hers to call," I said. Marsilia narrowed her eyes at me, narrowed them further when I held her gaze.

"And Wulfe would be a mistake." Marsilia looked away. "He is strong enough in power and a vicious fighter when he chooses, but . . ."

Stefan broke in. "He is less stable now than he ever was."

"I have never been certain," Marsilia said, speaking to Stefan, "that he wasn't smack in the middle of the conspiracy that Estelle headed up. I know she thought so." She hugged herself and looked about fifteen. "To tell you the truth, I did ask him if he felt up to the fight. He said he felt that it would not be a good idea." She gave Stefan a gamine grin, an expression I've never seen her wear. "He called Iacapo and yelled at him. Said he was getting old and lazy if he couldn't bestir himself to 'squish' Frost."

Stefan snorted. "That sounds like Wulfe."

"I have heard it said that Wulfe made Iacapo," Hao said.

Marsilia shrugged. "Wulfe is the older—and Iacapo could never get Wulfe to obey him any better than I can. But that means nothing."

"Iacapo couldn't get Wulfe to obey him at all," said Stefan—which for some reason made both Marsilia and Stefan laugh. Stefan stopped laughing first. He rubbed the thigh of his jeans and looked away.

I followed his gaze and realized that he was watching for something. For Frost.

"Tonight," I said, feeling stupid because I'd been evaluating the basement as a fighting ground since I'd jumped in after Marsilia. "He's coming to fight you tonight. Here."

"Yes." Marsilia's eyes were dark again. And she still looked like a college student, young and vulnerable. I knew some of the people in Stefan's menagerie whom she'd tortured to death. She was not some helpless girl but a sociopath who had outlived most of her enemies.

I was her enemy. Stefan was my friend—and he wasn't Marsilia's anymore.

"You wanted Adam for your second," I said.

"How long has your fight been scheduled?" Asil asked.

"He picked the time, I chose the place," said Marsilia. "He challenged me two weeks ago."

Which gave Frost time to set up the attack on the wolves.

"They were supposed to hold the werewolves until the fight was over," I said, working it out. "Then what? He would come in to rescue the wolves and kill the humans? Vampires and werewolves unite?" I'd thought he wanted the wolves dead. But if he allied himself with Adam . . . Not that Adam would ever be that stupid. If Frost came in as the rescuer, it would take Bran longer to understand that he had a new enemy. Maybe too long.

Asil growled, a subsonic sound that jangled my nerves. Then he echoed the gist of my thoughts. "At least until he feels strong enough to take on the werewolves as a whole—because Bran would never allow Frost to do as he wishes."

"That was probably part of Frost's plans," said Marsilia. She sounded like I was amusing her. Maybe it was supposed to irritate me—but I thought it was just habitual; she seemed too distracted to be her usual nasty self. "But he had something else in mind as his real target. Whom does the pack protect, Mercy? Who would be vulnerable if the pack were gone?"

There was a dramatic pause while I stared at her. I understood who she meant, but for the life of me I couldn't figure out *why*.

"He wants *you* dead," Stefan told me. "When his mercenaries failed, he sent a pair of half-fae assassins after you."

He'd known that someone had been sent after us?

Stefan made an impatient sound. "Don't look at me like that, Mercy. Remember, I'm not a part of the seethe anymore. How do you think Marsilia got me to come here?"

He'd been sounding pretty chummy with her, I thought uncharitably.

"We only heard about the assassins earlier tonight," Hao said, half-apologetically. "After they had already failed."

"They were supposed to kill *me*?" I said. "That makes no sense at all. Why go after me?"

Marsilia's lips turned up as if she'd had a pleasant thought, and her voice was velvet-soft when she said, "*I* would kill you if you didn't have the pack."

I made a frustrated sound. "I mean someone who didn't know me. I'm a lightweight."

"Clever coyote, to survive so many attempts to kill you." Marsilia sounded somewhat bitter.

"Really, why me?" I looked at them. "I get the whole vampires-hate-walkers thing, I do. But we're not talking about sending me out on a hunt to find where he sleeps. I'm just not that—"

"Like Coyote, you just keep staying alive," said an amused voice from outside of our makeshift, ash-coated arena. He'd been standing on one of those damned I-beams watching us for Heaven knew how long.

He hopped down and looked around, laughing silently to himself, a man no one would ever look at twice. At least not unless he were wearing metal gauntlets that looked as though they ought to be part of a torture museum display—as he had been the last time I'd seen him.

William Frost turned around and clicked his tongue against his teeth. "You chose the oddest location for this, my lady fair. We shall all look like chimney sweeps when we are through here. And—no audience? Marsilia, my love, you disappoint me."

Marsilia drew herself up like a cat that someone had tried to pet without permission, and he smiled. "That's what the Lord of Night said when he sent you away, isn't it? 'Marsilia, you disappoint me.'"

Stefan cleared his throat. "I've heard that version. But . . . actually not." He sounded apologetic. "It was in Italian, which is a much more beautiful language, but I can translate for those who don't speak Italian." This last was aimed at Frost, with just the right amount of veiled contempt. "He said, 'My beautiful, deadly flower, my Bright Dagger, you dare more than I can allow. I will die of sorrow and boredom without you, but it must be done.' I was there for that part. The rest I have from an acquaintance in his court. The Master of Milan composed a love song in her honor, as beautiful as his pain, that all who listen to it are moved to tears. The painting the Lord of Night created on the evening when she was banished is still on the wall above his bed so that he can show his lovers that none can compare with his Bright Dagger." He smiled, showing his fangs, and his voice was nearly as sharp. "He will not be pleased with thee, William Frost. But you won't have to worry about it, because you'll be dead."

Frost had quit smiling.

"It's like that bit in *The Princess Bride*," I told him. "When Vizzini says, 'You fell victim to one of the classic blunders.' Never go in against an ancient Italian vampire when *death* is on the line."

Stefan laughed. I think he might have been the only one who had watched the movie. Or no one else thought I was funny.

"I have brought an audience for us," Frost said, ignoring me entirely. "So the display will not be ruined."

He clapped his hands, and the upper edge of the north side of the shell of the basement of the winery was suddenly lined with the shapes of people—like Indians on the ridgetop in one of those old Westerns. It should have looked hokey—and it did, sort of—but it was also worrisome. Then, in a simultaneous motion that raised every hair on my body, they all jumped into the basement. They were so close in sync that they made one sound when they landed. I'd seen vampires do that kind of thing before, responding to the dictates of their master or mistress. But repetition didn't make it seem less *wrong*.

A black cloud formed around their feet and rose as far as their knees before the ash settled back down on the ground. Maybe a little more rain would be a good thing—but the water that was coming down so far was still just a drop here and there.

"These are mine," Frost told Marsilia, raising one arm theatrically. "I have bound them to me in such a way that if I die tonight, they will all die. I thought it only fitting that they witness this."

He looked around again. "So it is you and the Soldier who will fight me, then? Who is your third?"

Marsilia just smiled at him—and I realized we were missing someone. I tried to remember when I had last seen Hao, and it was a long while ago. Long before Frost had done his sudden-appearance act. The sharp smell of the burnt building, so much more sour than true woodsmoke, made it impossible to pick out one vampire from so many. If Hao was somewhere nearby, I couldn't find him. I wanted to turn around to look, but controlled the impulse. If he had disappeared, it was for a reason. The broken-cement remnants of walls stuck up waist high in places. Maybe he was hiding behind one of those.

Frost laughed again, and all of his people laughed in unison. They all had exactly the same expression as he did on their faces.

Unable to help myself, I snarled. Frost looked at me with a sudden intentness that told me he'd been paying attention to me all along.

"Don't tell me that you're going to pull the coyote girl into this? What exactly is she supposed to do—besides die?" The words were a chorus spoken by all of his vampires in time with his lips. I could tell from Stefan's careful expression that I wasn't the only one who was getting creeped out by it.

"I've been good about not dying so far," I said. "You should quit concerning yourself with my health."

I didn't say it very loudly, and the vampires were too busy talking to each other to pay attention to me. But Asil frowned at me and made a motion with his hand. I recognized the soundless instructions because Adam used the same ones with our pack. Asil thought we should leave.

But I had a feeling that leaving was not an option. For some reason, Marsilia had wanted *me* here.

"I have heard about you, Frost," said Marsilia, sounding bored. "I had disregarded it as vindictive gossip, but I see that it is true. You are a show-off who wastes resources making himself look impressive. You talk and talk, and it is empty talk. You will bring in a new era of vampire freedom and power, and blah blah blah. And yet you have only puppets. When their strings are cut, you have nothing."

The other vampire's lips flattened, and he said silkily, "Marsilia, raise your right hand."

Her lips tightened and both of her hands fisted.

Pay attention, coyote, whispered a voice in my ear. *Can you see what he is doing? How he is doing it?*

Stefan, to whom the voice belonged, was several feet away. My stomach clenched. He wasn't supposed to be able to do that anymore. The blood bond between us had been broken when Adam brought me into the pack.

Stefan glared at me and tilted his chin toward Marsilia.

"Marsilia," said Frost again, focusing his attention on her. "*Raise* your right hand."

I felt it then, the thread of power he used—it was sort of like the power of Adam's voice when he'd roll it over the pack and bring them to heel. I could almost see . . . I squinted at Frost and tried to *look*, as I'd learned to see pack bonds without meditation. I had used that method to *see* Peter. But this needed some of the part of me that ran on instinct. The same part of me that ran on four paws gave me a little push and left me using coyote's eyes while still my human self.

And I could see magic.

Frost pushed his power at Marsilia. To me, his magic appeared to be a black spiderweb of nastiness that tried to stick to her. Greasy threads of power slithered from him to his puppet vampires. I wondered how much of the way I viewed his magic had been dictated by Marsilia's comment about puppets, because Frost's vampires had strings of his will tied around each hand and foot and a whole slender web around their heads. Or maybe Marsilia could see his magic, too. The vampires weren't the only thing he was controlling. Fainter threads of power dripped from his hands to the ground, glistening faintly where they snaked across the floor and climbed the walls surrounding us, disappearing over the edges.

Frost was a Puppet Master. I actually thought the name in capital letters, which meant I'd been hanging around the vampires too long. Marsilia had called him the Necromancer, and that was worse than Puppet Master. Names have power and I refused to give him any more than he already had. "Frost" would do, "Gauntlet Boy" if he got really scary. I looked at the threads trying to crawl up Marsilia's body and thought that I might be able to destroy them the same way I had the ones that ensnared Peter. And as if she read my mind, Marsilia's brilliant red eyes met mine. She jerked her hands and the Puppet Master—the Gauntlet Boy—stumbled forward. The strings with which he'd tried to capture Marsilia were broken on the ground in front of him, and they faded to nothing after a few seconds.

He was able to control every move of his vampires with very little effort, but he couldn't get Marsilia to move one hand. It was true that she fought him, and his minions had given up, but he still had thirty vampires dancing to his tune. That Marsilia had resisted showed everyone here that Marsilia wasn't just the Mistress of the City—she was a Power.

And the way she'd met my eyes made me think that she could have put a stop to it earlier. She had wanted to give me a chance to see what his magic looked like.

Marsilia knew more about walkers than I did. When she'd come to this country, banished from Milan, there had been no Europeans here. I wasn't sure how long she'd been in this area, but it was a couple of centuries. She'd seen walkers kill other vampires, lots of vampires.

This summer, on my honeymoon, I'd met other walkers for the

first time. I'd been exchanging e-mails with them ever since, trying to learn more about what I was. They knew more than I did, but they still suffered from the same problem I had. Too many walkers had died before they could pass on their knowledge to their heirs, and much of it was lost.

She'd had Stefan contact me deliberately. He'd never have shown me he could still talk in my head because he knew I would hate it. So did she. She hated that Stefan and I were still friends. She was teaching me what I could do to fight a necromancer—and doing her best to drive me away from him. I thought that she was wasting her time with that last, because Frost had been right.

She was going to pick me to fight with her. I was pretty sure that Frost was right about my chances of survival, too. She wouldn't have to worry about Stefan being my friend because I was going to be dead.

Frost was worried about fighting Marsilia, the vampires had told me. That's why he'd chosen a challenge of three. He didn't like the odds of going against her by herself, but he thought he could come up with two other vampires stronger than hers. Likely he was right—so she'd chosen a different way.

If Adam had come with me, maybe she would have used him instead. He was a werewolf, and necromancy would have no effect on him. But she would work with what she had.

"Yours is the challenge and the manner of challenge," Marsilia said coolly, as if she hadn't just jerked his chain. "You chose now, and a three-way challenge. My choice is the place and the official. I choose here. It is large enough and remote." She smiled at him. "Since it is in my territory but owned by you, I thought it appropriate."

Owned by Frost. That made sense if he was the money man.

Marsilia paused for a moment and looked around. "Almost symbolic since one of my colleagues destroyed it yesterday."

Adam would be surprised to find out he was her "colleague." But I kept my face still.

"And for the officials, as the Master of Ceremonies tonight, I call upon Stefan Uccello, also known as the Soldier."

One of Frost's vampires said, "That is unacceptable. He is yours. The Master of Ceremonies cannot be yours."

I'd quit looking at the magic threads that bound Frost to his vampires. It produced an eye strain, like those bizarre patterns that showed a 3-D picture when observed through unfocused eyes. I couldn't tell if Frost was making the vampire talk or if the vampire in question was doing it on his own.

"I am not Marsilia's," said Stefan. "I do not belong to her seethe."

"He speaks truthfully," Frost told his people. "I witnessed this myself. Marsilia treated him so shamefully that he left her seethe, and she was too weak to prevent him. A real man, a real soldier, would never serve such a one. We can accept him—in all ways."

Rat bastard. He was right, but that didn't make him any less of a rat bastard. I could see, even if no one else did, that those words had hurt Stefan. Here he was, helping her again as if his menagerie mattered not at all to him.

"It is my place to remind you of the rules," Stefan said, his voice even. "You, William Frost, have chosen three against three. Two fighters, with you as the captain of yours, and Marsilia as the captain of hers, with the other two participants on either side yet to be chosen. The fight is to the death of the captains."

"Excuse me," I said diffidently. "But both the captains are already dead."

Everyone looked at me. The vampires with cold, unfriendly

gazes, and Honey as if I were crazy. That was okay—because I was utterly crazy. I knew Marsilia was planning on making me fight a bug-nuts vampire. The more scared I get, the faster my mouth moves. I was a smart-ass because I was terrified.

Asil smiled. He was supposed to know all about crazy.

"The fight," said Stefan gently, because he knew me that well, "is to the *permanent elimination* of one captain or the other. Does that satisfy you, Mercy? As soon as that elimination takes place, the other members of the teams may quit fighting—or not, as they choose.

"The captains can call upon anyone to be on their team and those persons cannot refuse. The only stipulation is that they must be present—which for our purposes means within five minutes—of this room. Though I caution you both that an unwilling team member will not fight for you as well as one who chooses to fight. After the teams are chosen, you will each retreat to the farthest corner opposite each other and take five minutes to confer before the battle begins."

Asil caught my eye and quite boldly repeated his earlier gesture. Five minutes away was doable, I knew it as well as he did. Especially if Honey and Asil worked to slow down the vampires.

I looked at William Frost—Gauntlet Boy—and thought about what he planned. All of the bloodshed and chaos, and the people who lost the most would be the humans who lived in those cities. At first. Then those humans would gather their weapons and give battle. Then they would destroy the vampires, the fae, the werewolves—and it would cost them dearly to do it.

I would not, could not allow Frost to do as he planned. I could not let him win. I would do anything I could to stop him. I shook my head at Asil. He gave me a respectful bow.

Stefan walked between Marsilia and Frost, his posture military straight. "For the duration of the fight, the participants may use anything, any power, any weapon that comes to their hand. People who are not participants may not fight. This means that I must caution the audience—and more directly you, William Frost, that no vampire other than those requested by each of the participants, may join the fight. Even if they do not do it of their own free will. Violators will be killed—by me—and if such violation, in my estimation, leads directly to a victory, that victory will be overturned by the Lord of Night."

"You are drawing a very fine line," said Frost, but not as if it made him unhappy.

Stefan bowed his head in acknowledgment. "The rules are the Lord of Night's. My job is to make those rules clear. The first call for comrades belongs to the challenged—Marsilia?"

"I call upon Mercedes Athena Thompson Hauptman, mate of the Alpha of the Columbia Basin Pack," she said, not unexpectedly.

Beside me, Honey growled, her voice low and threatening. I'm not sure whom she was growling at—possibly me. Asil just stared at me. He knew I'd seen this coming.

"Yes," I said coolly.

I was no match for a necromancer, though I was beginning to think that I might actually be an asset along those lines. I worried Frost enough that he had tried—twice, if Stefan was right—to eliminate me. Fear like that can be as much of an asset as actual power.

"Mercedes," said Asil in a cheerful voice. "You are going to get me killed at last. Bran would not do it, but I believe your mate will have no trouble."

I frowned at him. "I make my own decisions. Adam knows that."

He smiled at me. "He may know this in his head, Mercedes.

But his heart will feel differently. You are a woman, and this is a thing of men."

"Asil," I said. "You heard. You want me to turn down this fight?"

He closed his mouth and looked away.

"Touching," said Frost. "But not germane. She is *required*. She cannot refuse."

Honey snarled at him, and he drew back involuntarily. She looked at me and snarled again, louder.

"He hired the man who killed Peter," I reminded her. She quit growling and looked at him, again, and this time she showed him her very large white fangs. Werewolf fangs are more impressive than vampire fangs. They are more impressive than coyote fangs, too.

"I've accepted already," I told Stefan. "Get on with it."

He looked at me a long moment. I couldn't read his face. "Don't get killed," he said.

"Awfully late to be worrying about that, vampire," snapped Asil. "You should have made certain that Adam could be here. He at least would have stood a chance."

"Werewolves," said Marsilia, "are specifically forbidden from participating."

I stared at her. "But you invited Adam, too."

She smiled at me. "He is not what you are, Mercedes. Do you think that I who beguiled the Marrok's son would not be able to beguile your mate so that he would allow you to fight?"

She'd caught Samuel, but she'd never have caught Adam. Samuel might be more dominant and a lot older, but Adam was more wary. He'd never have let her trap him in her gaze—and if he had, I could have freed him. But that part she probably didn't know. Mating bonds are one of the things we didn't talk to the public about, and they are idiosyncratic.

Mating bond or not, that she was so certain of her ability to incapacitate Adam made me reevaluate her intelligence—and not upward.

"She couldn't have asked Adam," Stefan said, meeting my eyes forthrightly. "Werewolves are specifically excluded from this kind of fight for territory." He wasn't just repeating the rule Marsilia had already stated. He was telling me he'd known what Marsilia planned and had not warned me.

For a moment I was hurt. But only for a moment. If Marsilia was right, that I was useful, more useful than Stefan would be—and I wasn't forgetting the way she'd misjudged Adam's vulnerability—then bringing me here had been the right thing to do. Frost had to be stopped.

I gave Stefan a faint nod.

"Your first pick, Frost," said Stefan in a "let's get this done" tone of voice.

"Shamus," Frost announced grandly. "Shamus, former Master of Reno and now my right-hand man."

We waited, but no one appeared.

"He will be here in plenty of time." Frost smiled genially. "He has always been a ferocious fighter. Under my tutelage, he has only improved—especially the ferocious part."

"Marsilia? Your second and last choice."

"I choose Thomas Hao, Master of San Francisco."

Out of the shadows, not three feet from Frost, Hao sort of coalesced. "Of course," he said. "I am delighted to accept the invitation."

Frost hissed, stumbled back, and for the first time, his eyes flashed ice blue with shock. He recovered himself almost immediately, giving Marsilia a small salute.

"You have been busy, I see. Well then, I have a surprise, too. Let us finish the preliminaries. I call for my last companion—Wulfe. Better known as the Wizard." He smirked at Marsilia, who was *not* happy. "Keep your enemies close, Marsilia. You have kept him so close to you all these years—but you failed tonight. You might have called him to your side, but you chose to summon this filthy walker instead." He spat. On the floor. Toward me.

I guess I was supposed to feel insulted or impressed. "Sticks and stones may break my bones, but words will never hurt me," I chanted tunelessly and quietly, as if to myself, except that everyone in the room could hear me. If Frost wanted to be childish, I could do it, too—and do it better.

Stefan turned his head away, and I was pretty sure he laughed.

But no one was laughing when Wulfe dropped in from behind me so I didn't see him jump, only heard the sound of his feet hitting tile. I turned so I could see him and still keep an eye on Frost.

Vampires scared me. I even had a mental list of the vampires who scare me the most. Some of those were dead. More dead. Not ever moving again. On the very top of the list of the still moving was Wulfe. I didn't know why, exactly, he was so much worse than other vampires. Maybe it was the way that every time I met him, he seemed to know just exactly how to freak me out. Maybe it was the "nobody home" look in his eyes.

The Wizard looked like he should be worried about how to ask a girl out on his first date, checking the mirror for acne spots, deciding if he should get an ear pierced and if so, how he could hide it from his mom. He wore ripped-up, red Converse basketball shoes, blue jeans, and a thick cable sweater. His hair had been shaved boot-camp short. He held a thick chain that was attached to a metal collar wrapped around the neck of another vampire.

The second vampire was huge. If he'd been standing upright, he would have been the tallest person in the room . . . the grungy basement. He must have weighed nearly three hundred pounds.

He wasn't standing upright, though. He was crouched on hands and knees, and he clicked his teeth together in a weird rhythm.

He saw me looking at him—all of the vampires had looked away from him almost immediately. If I had known him when he wasn't this . . . monster, I doubt I could have kept my eyes on him, either. He roared at me, then launched himself like a junkyard dog and hit the end of the chain hard.

Physics said that he should have been able to drag Wulfe across the floor. But physics had only a nodding acquaintance with Wulfe. He had no trouble holding the vampire—who must have been Shamus—with one hand. His other rubbed the stubble of his hair, which looked more white than blond in this light.

"Hey, Mercedes," Wulfe said lightly. "So they succeeded in roping you into this? I've always wanted the chance to taste your blood from the source. Walkers have this lovely bouquet. Like daffydowndillies in the spring, my old ma used to say."

"Wulfe," said Marsilia. I think she wanted to say something else, but didn't know exactly what. So she was just quiet, but her quietness had a quality of sorrow to it.

"Don't be mad, Marsilia," he said earnestly. "But us badass vampires must stick together, you understand." He paused. "Maybe not. How about if I put it this way? It grievest me, dear heart. But in sooth, it is for the best, as you will see anon."

"Five minutes," said Stefan. "Starting now."

12

We huddled in our corner. I huddled, anyway. Asil looked faintly bored. Honey never took her eyes off Frost. Hao lurked—which he did very well for such a compact man. Marsilia? Marsilia was all business.

I was going to fight vampires, and my name wasn't Buffy—I was so screwed.

"Did you see his magic?" Marsilia asked me briskly. "I had Stefan tell you to watch closely."

"I saw."

"Your job is to stop him from doing it. Any way you can. Walkers are immune to vampire magic—even vampire magic that has its origins in witchcraft."

She sounded a lot more confident than I felt.

"You didn't seem to have much trouble stopping him," I said.

She grimaced. "Yes. But he wasn't trying very hard—and he

exaggerated his reaction when the magic broke. He's trying to get me overconfident." She glanced over her shoulder at Frost, who was talking at Wulfe. Wulfe was watching Marsilia and not paying any attention to Frost that I could see. He noticed I was watching and winked at me.

"It is a tactic that Frost takes," Hao said. He paused and looked at his hands. They were smudged black, and he had black ash smears on his gold shirt. Marsilia's black outfit showed no wear and tear. I didn't bother looking down at myself. My foster mother maintained that I could get dirty in a swimming pool, and getting older hadn't helped much.

"There were only a few witnesses to his other fights who were willing to talk to me. Some of them were in the same shape Shamus is." He didn't look at the collared vampire, but I could feel his attention. "Shamus was a fine guitarist, and he liked Tennyson poems. He could and would quote them by the hour."

"Why aren't there other vampires here?" I asked. "He doesn't have all the seethes under his control, right? Aren't any of the other powerful vampires trying to stop him? Why are you and Hao the only ones here?"

"Vampires do not work well together—any more than Alphas work well together. And the Masters who are farther east feel Frost is at the limits of what he can control. An illusion Frost has done his best to foster," Hao answered me.

"And most of them think that Frost's desire to bring out the vampires and allow them to feed where they will is the best idea they've ever heard," said Marsilia. "Stupid. I hate stupid people."

"You don't seem to be in a hurry to plan anything for the fight," said Asil. "And you have two minutes left."

Marsilia looked at him—and for a moment I saw lust in her face again.

Hao bowed to Asil. "Marsilia and I have spoken about this much so our plans are already laid. She will take on Frost. I will take both Wulfe and Shamus. Ms. Hauptman's job is to keep Frost from bespelling either of us. It may be that Frost will be so busy that he has no time for tricks and your . . . Alpha's mate can sit on the sidelines and cheer."

I was going to have to come up with a rank for myself besides Alpha's mate. In the pack, I was just Mercy—but if ten more people called me the Alpha's mate, I was going to hit someone. It sounded like a chess move.

"More likely, he has tricks up his sleeves," said Marsilia. "He knew coming to this that he had failed to kill Mercy."

"He has a bunch of ghosts trapped here," I told her. And I remembered Peter brushing Honey's hair. Ghosts who could manipulate the physical world were few and far between. "They could be a problem."

"Ghosts are not problems," said Marsilia dismissively. "They moan and scare silly people."

"Ghosts who can throw rocks and debris are a problem," I told her. "And there's that dead but still-moving-just-fine fae assassin, too. If he animated her, it was because he had a job for her to do. If she is a real zombie, then my understanding of the rules says he can call her to fight with him. Zombies aren't living creatures, they are animated dead with no willpower or thoughts of their own. A zombie would come under the heading of his 'power' right?"

"You take care of the ghosts, then," said Marsilia. "And keep him from trying to control us. We will do the fighting."

Hao smiled and rolled his shoulders to loosen them. I'd been wrong. He did smile when he was happy.

"This should be an interesting fight," he said.

When the fight started, I was about fifteen feet behind the two vampires on my side with orders to stay as far away from the action as possible. My knee hurt, my cheekbone throbbed—and I was as scared as I've ever been.

"Dear God," I murmured earnestly. I'd quit worrying about who could overhear me when I prayed a long time ago. When you live with werewolves, there is no such thing as a private conversation even if you are talking to God. "Please don't let me end up in a wheelchair again. No broken bones would be a happy bonus, but I'm not expecting you to make up for my stupidity quite so completely." And then, even more sincerely, I said, "Whatever happens, you don't let that vampire make it out of here still moving. If he wins, it will be bad news. Any help you can give us will be appreciated. Amen."

Stefan heard me. He didn't look, but his mouth softened, and he shook his head.

"Go," he said, and stepped back against the wall where the spectators had been allowed to watch. He stood next to Asil and Honey, which I had a bare instant to appreciate—if something happened to me, I knew he'd do his best to get the wolves out of here. Not that Asil would need much help.

Vampires are loud when they fight. I don't know why that took me by surprise. I've been in a lot of sparring matches, and they get noisy. Maybe it was because werewolf fights are quieter, the silence imposed by the need to keep hidden. Though people know about the wolves, public fighting is still forbidden.

My job was to watch Frost, and that was what I'd do. The basement was "in," Hao had explained. I couldn't go outside the basement without forfeiting my place in the battle. That didn't mean I'd get out of fighting. It just meant that Stefan would have to kill me. That's why they had to have a powerful Master of Ceremonies. He would enforce the rules during the fight and declare the winner.

I found a perch on top of a broken section of walls with my back to the outer wall. Probably Frost wouldn't try anything too soon. Unlike human fights—or even werewolf fights—vampire fights could take a long time. Not breathing, not needing a beating heart meant that a vampire was dangerous long after a werewolf would be unconscious. It takes a great deal of damage to make a vampire lose consciousness.

The soot, disturbed by the violent action of the fighters, flew in a foot-high miasma of blackness. The footing was made worse because only part of the floor was tiled. Not even Marsilia was immune to inconvenient stumbles.

I was very grateful for Asil's perspicacity in grabbing a coat for me. Once I stopped moving, I quickly grew chilled. Tucking my hands in my pockets, I encountered Zee's abbreviated magic sword. Tad's warnings rang in my head, so I had no intention of drawing it under anything but the most dire circumstances. But it gave me something to fiddle with—and that actually helped me focus on something besides how terrified I was.

The action was so quick it was difficult to split my attention, and I was trying to watch Frost. Even so, I caught glimpses of Hao fighting and wished my sensei could see him.

I have to admit that Shamus attracted my attention first. Vampires usually look pretty human. I've only seen their true faces, what the monster inside looks like, a couple of times. Once would have been enough, but Shamus wore his monster on the outside.

His eyes glowed—not like a flashlight. It was more like a small Christmas tree light or a Siamese cat's eyes in the dark if the cat's eye actually lit up instead of catching and reflecting light. In a cat, it was cool—in a vampire it was just freaky. His lips were pulled back until his face looked as though it had been created to be a canvas to hold fangs and those faintly sparkling eyes. His fingernails lengthened until they were nearly as good a weapon as a werewolf's claws. There was nothing human left in Shamus at all.

Wulfe had released him from his chain, though the collar was still on. If Shamus wasn't twice Hao's weight, he was very near to it. He was fast—and, as promised, utterly ferocious. After Hao hit him once, Shamus was totally intent on reducing Hao to a pile of sludge.

But Hao was never where Shamus thought he was.

"Flow like water," Sensei Johanson often said, usually in a tone of exasperation. And he came pretty close. But I'd never seen anything like Hao.

Hao flowed like water. Sharp claws passed harmlessly by—and so close that a quarter of an inch more would have had Hao's skin sliced like a prisoner rolled in razor wire. He twisted, stopped, leaned back, and nothing touched him. It was beautiful.

I was supposed to be watching Frost, I admonished myself sternly. But I kept sneaking glances at Hao.

Then the ghosts came. I knew they were here before I saw them, their presence something the coyote could feel, a prickle down my spine and a tingle on the tip of my nose. I trusted the coyote's senses, tried to open my vision the way I had before, and took a good look around.

The dead spirits clustered against the wall, as far from the vampires as they could get. Ghosts, like cats (excepting my own Medea), don't like vampires. They didn't seem to be doing anything, though I could see the greasy spider-silk magic that tied them to Frost.

Despite the distraction of Hao and the ghosts, I was keeping my eyes on Marsilia and Frost. Who knew that Marsilia was a bruiser—and a trained boxer, from her tidy and agile footwork? Frost had been trained in some sort of hand-to-hand, too. It looked to be a relatively effective if piecemeal style, like the techniques the army teaches its new recruits—a style adjusted for vampiric strength and speed.

Just beyond them was a group of four of Frost's vampiric audience and with my vision changed because I'd been watching the ghosts, I about fell off my wall.

I couldn't see souls. Besides, vampires don't have souls. But something was wrong with Frost's vampires. Something was twisted and shredded that should have been straight and whole. I looked at my vampire then—at Stefan. He was standing a little in front of Honey, ready to grab her if she gave in to the drive that kept her intent on Frost. I still couldn't see his soul, but he looked *right*, just as he always did.

I found Marsilia. And she was different from Frost's vampires in the same way Stefan was. Hao had said his informant had been broken. I wondered if she would have looked like Frost's vampires.

But I wasn't here to check out Frost's vampires. I was supposed to watch him.

Both Marsilia and Frost were bleeding. Marsilia had found a metal bar somewhere, the kind someone might use to bar a door, and she hit him in the chin with it like Babe Ruth might have hit a ball out of Yankee Stadium.

He flew backward, and when he hit the ground, he fell like a wet washcloth. She pulled the bar back into batting position and watched him. He didn't move—but vampires don't need to breathe, and they can hold very, very still.

One of the ghosts of the Cantrip agents drifted closer to Frost. I thought for a moment that it was just chance. Throw a dozen ghosts into even a sizeable basement, and they have to go somewhere, right? There were ghosts drifting aimlessly all over the basement now—though only the one nearest Frost was anywhere near a vampire. The longer I watched them, the easier it was to see the binding Frost had netted them with.

It struck me as odd that in that dark basement, where every surface was blackened from the fire, I had no trouble seeing the web that held the ghosts captive. But the darkness of the net was different than just the lack of light.

The ghost that approached Frost had one of his sticky strings of magic wrapped around his neck, and that string was pulsing. Marsilia had started to relax, her hand on the bar less tense.

I stood up, but it was too late. Frost struck, his jaw hanging at an odd angle, but he moved so fast it was difficult to track. He grabbed the ghost and ate him. Not with his physical mouth. It was as if his body turned into a giant mouth and engulfed the ghost. To my sight, Frost's body flared—and then he stood up, wiping his own blood from his mouth with the back of his hand. The damage Marsilia had done to him was just gone.

She struck again, but he was faster than he'd been. As if the ghost had more than merely repaired him. He grabbed the bar and ripped it from her hands—and she was the one in retreat.

The fighting had started out loud. Shamus roared and screamed. Bodies make noise when they are flung on the floor. Not just the sound of floor and flesh, but grunts and cracks as bones broke. The metal bar added a new dimension to the noise. There was a rhythm to it as he drove Marsilia back toward me, and I realized he was just playing with her.

I couldn't help her with him. I had to trust that she was strong enough, good enough to protect herself, because I had another job—there were thirteen more ghosts in the room. And I had to figure out a way to keep Frost from eating them all. One of them was right next to me. I grabbed her by the wrist. My hand started to pass through, but I focused my *sight* on her and she became more solid, just as Peter had.

"Tell me your name," I said to her, giving my command that borrowed-from-Adam Alpha wolf push.

"Janet," she told me, her voice vibrating up my arm.

"Janet," I told her. *"Leave."*

She tried, but Frost's net held her. Her eyes were terrified. I tried stripping the net from her with my hands, but it didn't work. She wasn't pack, so I couldn't use pack magic to free her.

I pulled Zee's sword out and invoked its larger form. For Zee and Tad, Hunger had been a black long sword. For me, it turned into a plain-bladed katana with a gaudy red-and-purple hilt.

It didn't do anything to the net, though I had the feeling that in sunlight, when a vampire's magic would be at its weakest, it would have been able to eat the magic that bound the ghost. I even tried stabbing her with it. I felt it taste her briefly, and she looked even more terrified, if that were possible. But when I pulled the sword back, she was still there, encased in Frost's trap. I talked the reluctant sword back into its smaller form and stuck it back in my coat pocket.

The clank, clank, clank of the iron bar stopped suddenly, and I looked up to see it arc over the wall of the basement and safely out of useful range. Marsilia popped her shoulder back into joint without so much as a grimace and reengaged Frost. Without the bar, he was not so overwhelming—but she was still hurt. And then he reached out, almost casually, and ate another ghost. It was quick, and I was too far away to do anything about it—even if I could have figured out how. He smiled at me before he hit Marsilia in her damaged shoulder.

Desperate, I pulled my lamb-and-dog-tag necklace off my neck. Armed by my faith, the symbol of the Lamb of God had defended me against vampires. Maybe it would work against vampiric magic.

"Please, dear Lord," I said. "Let this work."

Then I pressed it against the net—which shrank away from the little golden lamb, twisting, curling, and lessening until the ghost stood free. I touched the lamb to her forehead, and said, "Janet. Be at peace."

She vanished in a bright flash of light.

"Yes!" I shouted in triumph and more than a little awe. My little lamb had outperformed Zee's sword.

From across the room, Stefan smiled at me.

"*Holy symbols*, Batman," I told him. "We have *help*."

I went after the ghosts, trying to avoid the fighting. It was more difficult than it might have been because Frost had heard my exclamation as well, and he kept trying to get to me. Marsilia redoubled her efforts to keep him away. I had to give up on two of them because Frost got too close. I was under no misconception about how fast Frost could kill me, not after seeing the damage he and Marsilia had been exchanging.

I had just freed a man wearing a dark blue suit and a Gryffindor tie when Asil's shout made me turn to see Frost right on top of me. Then Wulfe smashed into him like a freight train, if a freight train had been thrown by a Chinese vampire.

"Sorry, sorry," said Wulfe calmly to Frost as I sprinted across the room away from them. "But you need to watch what you're doing, or you're going to get hurt by your own teammates."

I pulled another ghost around and asked him his name without looking at his face because I was using the lamb to destroy Frost's magic.

"Alexander," he said.

My gaze jerked up, and I looked at Peter's killer. Why couldn't he have been one of the ghosts Frost had eaten? "You killed my friend," I told him.

"Yes," he sighed. "Werewolf, you know. Dangerous and evil."

"No," I told him. "Alexander Bennet. Dangerous and stupid."

"Are you arguing with a ghost, Mercy?" asked Wulfe in an interested voice from somewhere on the far side of the basement from me. "Good for you."

Wulfe was a mess, and in the darkness it was hard to tell what was soot and what was blood. Though he was not as obviously hurt as either Shamus or Hao—even water can't avoid being hit by two opponents forever. Hao was letting Shamus chase him toward a wall at breakneck pace. Wulfe had left them to it, evidently so he could watch me, though he made no move to stop what I was doing.

Hao stripped out of his golden shirt and ran at the wall. The shirt seemed to hover for a second, held in Hao's hand, which stayed where it was while his body pivoted on that axis as he ran his feet up the wall. The shirt ended up on Shamus's head at about the same time that Hao did a quick in-the-air somersault and landed with both feet on Shamus's back, driving the other vampire's head into the wall.

If I survived this fight, I was going to forever regret not having a DVD of it. Not that recording devices ever captured vampires correctly. They weren't that much faster in general than werewolves or me, but they could make very small movements incredibly fast, and it gave modern cameras fits.

The drizzle of rain earlier in the day had stopped for a while. But as the ghost started to tug on my hand, the one with the necklace in it, the rain began to fall again in earnest.

"Please," said Alexander, who had killed Peter. "I am so tired."

Me, too. I was also wet and cold and fiercely regretting I knew what the right thing to do was. But I finished the job I'd stopped in the middle of—cleaning off Frost's magic.

Instead of making soup of the ash on the floor, it was so cold the rain hit and turned to ice—freezing rain.

"Alexander," I told him forcefully. "Go." And I added the next bit because it was the right thing to do, too—even if I didn't know if it had any real effect. "Be at peace."

Like the others, he disappeared in a flash of light. If I had secretly hoped that the awful darkness that swallowed the bad guy in *Ghost* would come and haul him down into the abyss, well, that was a disappointment I'd just have to live with.

Fingers numbing, I went back to catching ghosts. I'd lost count somewhere—or maybe Frost had gotten another one when I had been preoccupied. But when I finished with the woman in the cocktail dress and turned to find the last one, there were no more.

The fighting had gotten more uncontrolled and violent as the combatants lost their footing on the ice and slid into spectators, debris, or walls with equal force. I slithered, slipped, and twice fell off my original perch after I finally reached it.

Shivering miserably, I shoved my hands in my pockets. I'd take forty degrees below zero any day over this miserable, wet, slick stuff. I could dress for forty below, but the wet went through whatever clothes I wore. My jeans were clinging to my thighs like an icy lover, and my coat, shoulders soaked through, was losing the war to keep me warm.

Something grabbed me by the back of my coat and tossed me onto the ground. Taken totally unaware, I tumbled over and landed flat on my back. My head slammed the floor hard, and I saw stars and little birds. I rolled anyway, tasting blood as I tried to get out of easy reach of my attacker.

Above me was the dead fae assassin I'd all but forgotten about. Her head bobbed at an unnatural angle, and weirdly, there were two of her crouched on the place I'd been perched. She jumped at me, and I pulled my cold hand out of my pocket and Zee's sword slid into her like a hot knife through ice cream. I was nearly as surprised as she was because the move had been instinctual and not planned—and I hadn't called the sword out.

Her body landed on me hard, and she was a lot heavier than she looked. Thankfully, impaled by the sword, she was also a dead weight. Only her head seemed to still be mobile and she couldn't turn it. The odd double image was making my head hurt. If I hadn't been worried about her doing something like biting my throat out, I might have closed my eyes. I got my left arm up and between her mouth and my neck.

But she didn't try to attack again.

"Hunger"—her voice sounded lost—"you have the sword. Where is my Sliver if you have his Hunger?"

She kept talking, but she'd forgotten to breathe, and I couldn't see her mouth, just feel her jaw moving against my arm. She could have been cursing me or telling me she loved me for all that I understood. I bet on the first rather than the last.

As she tried to say something, I'd realized that the strange double image I was seeing wasn't the result of a concussion. I was seeing her ghost, almost completely severed from her body but still connected to the dead body with greasy ties.

My left arm was busy keeping her off me; my right, holding the sword, was stuck between us. Since she wasn't doing anything immediately violent—and because I really was more afraid of Zee's sword than I was afraid of her—I wiggled my left arm down and tried not to pay attention to her cold, rotting flesh moving against my bare cheek as she vainly tried to talk. I also attempted to breathe shallowly, but it didn't help the smell much.

My left hand found the pocket of my jeans where I'd shoved the necklace. The jeans were wet and fought me, but I managed to snag the chain of my necklace with the tips of my fingers. The jeans had the last laugh, though. The lamb snagged on my pocket, and I gave it a hard pull. The jeans released the necklace, but my icy-numbed clumsy fingers lost their hold. The necklace flew with the force of my pull, and I heard it land well out of reach.

I tried to move, but as soon as the sword wiggled, her arms and legs began to twitch again. "Okay, Hunger," I told it. "Can't you do something about this?"

I tried it in German because, after all, it was Zee's sword. *"Also, Hunger. Können Sie nicht etwas tun?"*

I felt it listening to me. Goose bumps broke out on my skin, and magic thrummed in my chest and along my body where the dead woman's flesh pressed against mine.

In my hands, the pommel of the sword warmed. Spice's body began to vibrate about the time the warmth became heat.

I had a terrible thought. What if the sword liked the dead fae better than the live coyote and chose to switch allegiance? I'd been warned about Hunger's reputation for deserting its wielder. So I held on to the sword past the point where the heat became pain.

If the pommel was hot, though, it was nothing compared to the sword. The fae's body turned to ash on top of me between one moment and the next, mingling with the ash of the winery fire and the wet ice. I rolled and scrambled frantically to my feet, dropping the sword as I did.

There was nothing left of the zombie fae woman. I tried to wipe her ash off my coat and jeans, but I was so wet it just smeared. When I dropped it, the sword had burned down through the thin layer of ice on the ground, but it had cooled rapidly to the point where it was gaining another coat of ice from the freezing rain. It lay there in the muck, and the magic it had sent spinning through me was gone.

I didn't want to touch it—but I wanted even less to leave it here, where one of the vampires would get ahold of it. When I touched the hilt, it was so cold it burned my blistered and reddened hands again.

It fought me when I tried to shrink it down. That's why it was still in my hands when Frost hit me and knocked me a dozen feet away. I rolled to my feet and used the sword the way I'd practiced once a month for years when Sensei chose to have us work on weapon forms. Adrenaline meant the ache of my cheek and knee, the misery of being wet, cold, and afraid, was no more than a shadow upon my awareness. All the rest of me was caught in the blade and the dance of martial combat.

I'm not strong by vampire or werewolf standards, but I am fast, and armed with a sword, I fought with as much speed as I could summon. I didn't manage to hit him—but he couldn't get close enough to hit me, either. I was focused on him, but I caught a glimpse of the rest of the building here and there.

Marsilia was down. Her body was too broken for her to stand although she was trying to keep her promise because she was crawling toward our battleground.

Wulfe was down as well. He lay in the sludge, covered with ice, not too far from our dance, and I took care not to end up too close to him.

Hao and Shamus were somewhere behind me. I could hear them fighting, but I couldn't see them.

Stefan had a wrestler's hold on Asil, and he was yelling at him. "Stand down. *Stand down*, wolf. I don't want to have to kill you." Honey just watched my battle with yellow eyes.

But all of this, like my accumulated aches and pains, was peripheral to the rhythm of the battle dance. Frost couldn't afford to let the sharp edge touch him, and I was a hair faster than he was. The reach of the sword meant that he couldn't get close enough to use his strength against me. I was slowly, slowly backing the damned vampire across the floor.

I leaped sideways, and the edge of the sword caught on the vampire, then it broke free. When I landed, Frost was bleeding from his arm. It was a shallow cut. But it made me smile anyway.

I attacked again, but a noise distracted me—a wolf's howl in the distance—and I landed badly. It was enough to give Frost an opening, and he hit me with his body, like a linebacker. I folded over his shoulder and tried to roll, but he grabbed my wrist and flipped me to the ground and pinned me. I still had the sword in my hand, but it was useless because I couldn't move my wrist.

"If you had cost me this fight," Frost told me, his face pressed to mine like a lover's, "I would make your death slow." He slid his cheek against mine in a caress as he pressed his body against mine. "But Marsilia underestimated me—she has grown old since she was the Lord of Night's Bright Blade."

I changed to a coyote and bit his face. My teeth slid against bone, and he screamed. I opened my mouth again and caught his eye, ripping it away. Still howling, he retreated, and I changed to human before my clothes became an issue. I did not want to chance slowing myself down—or worse, let the vampire get his hands on Zee's sword.

I grabbed the sword again as I staggered to my feet. By instinct and training, I pulled the sword up as Frost leaped toward me. The blade slid through ribs as though they were cheese and lodged in his heart.

He started to say something, and my brain caught up with my senses just about the time a dark wolf hit him and ripped out his throat. The wolf looked at me, once, then went back to the slaughter.

I sat down on the ice-covered ground because I was too tired to move. Beside me, Adam ripped into Frost's rib cage with his front claws and his fangs. The sword had freed itself from the vampire when I sat down. I turned my head and watched Adam tug and wrench until the vampire's heart fell on the ground beside me. Vampires taste bad—very old flesh and blood just tastes wrong. I wiped my mouth hastily with the bottom of Kyle's shirt—I hoped it wasn't a favorite.

But the taste didn't stop Adam. He moved up to Frost's already torn neck and did more damage until the vampire's head rolled on the floor next to his heart.

Finished killing Frost for the moment, Adam crouched over the dead body, a silver-and-black killing machine.

"Adam?" said Marsilia. She was up on her feet again but not moving right.

Adam lowered his head and roared at her. It was a rumbling bass sound that vibrated my chest and hurt my ears at the same time. I could smell his rage.

I'd had my ten seconds of rest, and there was no more fighting to be done. I rose to my knees—and Adam turned to me and roared at me, too.

"I couldn't help it," I said to him. "He was going to destroy the world."

Adam snarled and snapped his teeth at me.

My cheekbone was hurting again; sometime during the fight, Frost had hit it. I was going to have the world's worst black eye. My shoulder hurt, my wrist hurt—my burnt hands hurt a lot, now that the battle rush was gone. I was cold, miserable, and tired.

Adam had every right to be mad. I'd have been outraged if he'd gone to battle without telling me. Without explaining himself.

"By rights, as the Master of Ceremonies, I should kill him for interfering," Stefan told me. I jerked my head around to look at him. I'd forgotten about that, forgotten, truth be told, that there was anyone but Adam and me there. "But I suspect that the Lord of Night won't stir himself to come punish me for a result that he himself desired. And"—he toed Frost's body—"he was as good as dead when you stabbed him. Adam was overkill." He bumped the body again. "Hmm. I thought he was older—but those of us who are really old turn to dust when they die. The sun will do the job."

Asil knelt beside me with a wary eye on Adam. "You okay?"

I wiggled my toes and fingers. The fingers hurt. A lot. But they moved. "Look," I said brightly. "No wheelchair. Last time I battled immortal monsters, I ended up in a wheelchair."

I heard Wulfe giggling. He was propped up on the remains of a wall that had taken more damage in the fight. The broken areas showed pale cement against the blackened surface of the rest of the wall. I had been trying to lighten the atmosphere, but I hadn't been as funny as all that.

Asil ignored Wulfe. "I like you—but I'll say it for him"—he tipped his head toward Adam—"because he can't. You aren't a monster, and if you insist on fighting them with toothpicks because it's the right thing to do, all the magic in the world isn't going to be enough to save you."

I looked him in the eye, ready to defend myself hotly—who did he think he was? And then I looked at Adam, who had quit growling. He was panting with effort—more effort than what he'd used to finish off Frost. How had he known? How far had he run?

My throat was raw, and my eyes were burning. It wasn't because of the remains of the fire.

"I understand. I really do. But I can't—" I swallowed. "I just *can't* sit and do nothing when you and the other people who are mine are in trouble. It isn't in me." Cautious, yes, I *did* cautious. I tried my best not to be stupid—and hey, I was still alive, right? "I called and let people know where I was. I brought backup. I can do that. I am careful." I wasn't talking to Asil anymore. "But Adam, good and evil are real—you know that better than anyone. I have to do the right thing. If not, then I am no better than that—"

I jerked my chin toward Frost's body. "'All that is required for evil to prevail is for good men to do nothing.'"

Hao said, "Life is not safe. A man might spend his whole time on earth staying safe in a basement, and in the end, he still dies like everyone else." Half-naked, covered with the same filth we all were, he still gave the impression of being in control of himself and his environment.

Adam sighed. He picked his way through body parts and lay down beside me. He was wet and cold, too, on the surface, but underneath the top coat of his fur, he was very warm.

"How touching," said Marsilia, then Shamus was on her.

There was a loud sound—and it was Wulfe standing over Marsilia instead. Shamus lay in two pieces, and Wulfe had Zee's sword in his hand. I had to look at my hands to make sure I wasn't still holding it. My skin still held the memory of the cool metal against it. Wulfe glanced at the sword, then met my eyes as Shamus slowly dissolved into ash that blended with the wet soot on the floor.

"You feed this fae artifact your good blood, Mercy, and you won't share with me?" Wulfe asked me wistfully.

Everyone stayed motionless—and Wulfe laughed and tossed the sword in my direction. I caught it before it hit Adam. This time when I willed it to diminish itself, it did so, as if it was scared of Wulfe, too. I tucked it into my pocket while Wulfe helped Marsilia back to her feet.

"I did want to go back to the time when we could freely become lost in the blood of our prey," Wulfe said, sounding a little sad. "I guess it won't happen now, but that might be for the best. Here, let me carry you, it will be easier." He picked Marsilia up in his arms.

His look took in Stefan and Hao. "You'll have to kill Frost's vampires. He overestimated his hold on them because they didn't die when he did, but they have no ability to direct themselves anymore." He sighed. "And then I suppose I'll have to go hunt the other vampires he broke in his cities." He looked at Frost's body. "You've made a lot of work for a lot of people. If you weren't dead, I'd kill you myself."

To Marsilia, he said, tenderly, "I'm taking you back to the seethe. You need to eat and bathe and rest." Then he walked to the side of the basement and jumped out, still carrying Marsilia.

"Was he on our side all this time?" I asked.

Stefan shrugged. "Who knows. I've seen him be a lot more lethal than he was tonight. There were no firebombs, for instance. But he doesn't always remember how to perform magic—that's what he tells us anyway. And Hao is well-known for his ability to fight."

Hao shrugged. "Frost is dead. If Wulfe were mine, I would kill him, but Marsilia's seethe is no concern of mine."

When we left the remains of the winery, Hao and Stefan were killing the vampires who had collapsed against the wall of the basement. Marsilia's Mercedes was gone, though the seethe's other car was in the lot. There was no sign that Adam had brought a car, so we all piled into Warren's truck—the werewolves in the back. We went home.

We gave the Rabbit a Viking funeral.

She sat a battered warrior—or a decrepit pile of junk—perched on a pile of wood three feet high and a foot bigger around than the car. I'd drained her fluids and stripped her of any parts that were usable before the pack had lifted her to her final resting place.

Those parts were now tucked in and around the junker Rabbit that still graced the space between my old home and my new one. Sure, I could have found somewhere else to put the parts, but Adam had yelled at me about fighting the vampire one too many times.

I know I'd scared him—I'd scared me, too. I also remembered how mad I'd been at Adam when he'd hurt himself kissing me because he thought it would break the fae's magic that held me. He'd been right to kiss me, though it burned him, and I'd been right to help Marsilia with the vampire. I'd yelled at him anyway.

Which was why the old junker only got to wear a pair of tires on its trunk instead of getting something rude painted in fluorescent pink or (and I was saving this one for something serious) a solar-powered blinking red light that I'd found at Walmart on the ill-fated Black Friday shopping expedition.

The fire burned hot and long past the time when the last of the marshmallows and hot dogs were roasted. Even with the heaping mounds of firewood, the car wouldn't have burned to ash without Tad's help.

It had been two weeks since Frost died.

Adam's appearance on TV had cemented (if it needed cementing) his reputation as a hero and a pillar of all that was good and civil. It was a fortunate thing that no one had gotten a picture of him tearing into Frost's body. Tony assured me that the police were satisfied with the abbreviated story Adam and Agent Armstrong had given them.

Kyle forgave me the shirt I'd destroyed, and he'd helped us look for his car without a word of complaint. He was, I think, happy we hadn't found it that night and covered his buttery leather upholstery with soot and blood.

Warren told me, as we drove through nameless dirt roads through seemingly endless vineyards and orchards, that Adam had just suddenly gotten out of the chair he'd been sitting in at Kyle's office and sprinted out the door, leaving the rest of them to soothe the reporter who'd lingered to get a few more details.

Adam had taken off in Kyle's Jaguar and left the rest of them to call a taxi to get home.

Adam had explained, a little sheepishly, that all he knew was that I was at the winery with the vampires—but he hadn't been really certain how to get there. He could feel me, but the roads kept turning the wrong way. Finally, he'd abandoned the car and taken off on four feet.

It took us three days to find the Jaguar—and then only because someone called the police and reported an abandoned car in their vineyard.

I gave the sword back to Tad as soon as I saw him again, a couple of days after our adventure.

"What did you do to it?" he asked me. "It feels . . ."

"Frightened?" I suggested.

He grimaced. "Subdued."

"Wulfe—you know the crazy vampire? Wulfe used it to kill another vampire."

He grimaced. "That would do it. You should ask Dad about Wulfe sometime. It'll give you nightmares."

Tad was living at his father's house still, but he quit being a hermit. He's helping me at the shop again. I hadn't realized how much I'd missed working with someone I liked. I might still have to close down the shop eventually, but not for a while.

Peter's funeral, held as soon as we could manage, had taken place in sunshine, though it was still cold. The pack mourned, as was fitting. It was a quiet affair without the usual speeches because Honey didn't want them. I agreed with her; speeches weren't necessary. We all knew what we had lost.

Asil went home directly afterward. As did Agent Armstrong, who had stayed for the funeral, though he'd never met Peter.

"It is a good thing to remember the victims," he told me at the grave site. "It gives me perspective."

Adam made Honey stay with us for a couple more days before moving back to her house. Mary Jo planned on giving up her apartment in the next few weeks and moving in with her. Mary Jo, firefighter, and Honey, princess, seem to me a disaster in the making—but neither of them like me for a lot of reasons that boil down to my being a coyote and not a werewolf. Maybe that will give them enough in common to let their roommate situation work out.

The last of the flames under the Rabbit died down just as the snow began to fall in earnest.

"Come inside," Adam suggested. "Everyone's gone except Jesse, and she's asleep."

His gruff tone and the touch of his lips on my ear told me that he had something more in mind than sleep.

"I am," I told him, as we walked back to the house, "feeling very lucky tonight."

"Oh? Because you didn't die in the crash, when the assassin

attacked you, or when you fought the vampire?" His voice had sharpened.

"You've yelled at me enough about that," I warned him. "Your quota is now full. Besides, that's not what makes me lucky."

After we had left the burnt-out winery and the vampires behind us, we went home—to our home. It was battered (the front door was so bad they had to replace the frame and resurface part of the house), but the bad guys were all dead.

I tracked blood, mud, and ash across the white carpet and up the stairs. I used to feel bad when I bled all over that carpet—but tonight I didn't care so much. Besides, Adam, still in wolf form, was even dirtier than I was.

"I'm going to shower," Asil said. "Then I'll sleep in the living room where I can keep an eye on the doors, just in case."

"There's a shower in the bathroom in the basement," I told him. "Get something to eat. There's food in the kitchen."

He smirked. "Yes, Mom."

Honey hopped onto the living-room couch with a sigh. It was white, like the carpet, but it was leather, so we could clean off anything that got on it. Probably.

Adam trailed beside me, up the stairs.

"You should eat, too," I told him.

He gave me a look, and I let it lie. If he really needed food, he'd get some. As soon as we made it into the bedroom, he started to change back to human. He was tired, and there was no urgency, so the change was very slow.

I peeled off everything I was wearing and threw it into the dirty clothes. Then I walked into the bathroom and turned on the shower. It took a long time to get clean. The ash clung with surprising tenacity, and since at least some of that ash had once been a person—a zombie person—I had to get it all off.

When I finally came out, Adam was stretched out on the bed, naked and asleep. He was clean, and his hair was wet, so he'd used the other upstairs shower.

I watched him while I towel dried my hair. Peter joined me. Dead or alive, he was a werewolf, he didn't care that I was naked, so I didn't bother covering up.

"He's a good man," he told me, looking at Adam.

"Yes," I agreed.

Peter tilted his head down to look me in the eye, and he smiled. "You know he doesn't believe that. He thinks he is a monster."

"It's all right," I said. "What he thinks doesn't change the facts."

"I told him where you were," Peter said. "You sent me away. Sent me here. But I found Adam, and I told him where you were and what the vampires had you doing."

"You left before I knew what they were going to ask me to do."

"You're a walker," he said. "And they were facing a necromancer who could bind the dead. Of course they wanted you."

See, even a dead man was smarter than I was.

"Peter," I said, "it's time for you to go. I know how to fix what Frost did to you."

Asil had given me back my necklace in the car.

"Good," Peter said. "But I would like to sleep beside her one more time."

"Yes," I told him. "Okay."

He changed into his wolf one last time and left the room without a backward glance.

I walked over to the bed and slid my sore fingers across the damp skin of Adam's shoulder. What if we had only one more time to sleep together? One last time.

He could have died instead of Peter.

I pulled the covers out from under him, and he was so tired he didn't even move. But when I got in bed beside him, he reached out and tugged me close.

"So," said Adam, holding the back door open for me as the snow smothered the last of the Rabbit's funeral pyre. "Why are you lucky?"

"Because." I leaned into him instead of going inside, pressing him against the doorjamb. His lips tasted like smoke and hot dog, with a touch of chocolate. He tasted warm and alive.

"Just because."

AUTHOR'S NOTE

Once upon a time I proved that I will quit because I don't like something, but I won't quit because I can't *do* something. That's how I ended up with a degree in German—which I didn't speak well when I graduated in 1988, and it didn't get any better from disuse. When I decided Zee would be German, I threw in a few German phrases here and there in the first two Mercy books. I kept it simple—how hard could it be?

Then I got this lovely e-mail from a nice man in Germany who told me that he liked the books—but my German was pretty bad.

I said, "Thank you, and you know you have a job now, right?"

So from that point on, Michael Bock and his lovely wife, Susann, have given Zee's German its authenticity. That doesn't mean I'm right all the time; even they can't prevent me from transferring things from his e-mail to my manuscript incorrectly. I know just enough to get it wrong.

When Zee needed a good spell to use in *Silver Borne*, Michael and Susann gave him voice. When Tad needed a spell in this book, Michael came through for me again. He and I worked on the English translation together.

Mirror reflect, find father's image and voice
in the depths of your senses.
His words his form, my words my form, lead, guide, drive
together in a connection of your reality.
Bind our realities, our being, in nature and song.

Best,
Patty Briggs

extras

www.orbitbooks.net

about the author

Patricia Briggs lived a fairly normal life until she learned to read. After that she spent lazy afternoons flying dragon-back and looking for magic swords when she wasn't horseback riding in the Rocky Mountains. Once she graduated from Montana State University with degrees in history and German, she spent her time substitute teaching and writing. She and her family live in the Pacific Northwest, and you can visit her website at www.patriciabriggs.com

Find out more about Patricia Briggs and other Orbit authors by registering for the free monthly newsletter at www.orbitbooks.net

if you enjoyed

FROST BURNED

look out for

ARALORN: MASQUES AND WOLFSBANE

also by

Patricia Briggs

Prologue

The wolf stumbled from the cave, knowing that someone was searching for him and he couldn't protect himself this time. Feverish and ill, his head throbbing so hard that it hurt to move, he couldn't pull his thoughts together.

After all this time, after all of his preparations, he was going to be brought down by an illness.

The searcher's tendrils spread out again, brushing across him without recognition or pause. The Northlands were rife with wild magic—which is why other magic couldn't work correctly here. The searcher looked for a wizard and would never notice the wolf who concealed the man in its shape unless the fever betrayed him.

He should lie low, it was the best defense . . . but he was so afraid, and his illness clogged his thoughts.

Death didn't frighten him; he sometimes thought he

had come here seeking it. He was more afraid he wouldn't die, afraid of what he would become. Perhaps the one who looked for him was just idly hunting—but when he felt a third sweep, he knew it was unlikely. He must have given himself away somehow. He'd always known that he would be found one day. He'd just never thought it would be when he was so weak.

He fought to blend better with the form he'd taken, to lose himself in the wolf. He succeeded.

The fourth sizzle of magic, the searcher's magic, was too much for the wolf. The wolf was a simpler creature than the mage who hid within him. If he was frightened, he attacked or ran. There was no one here to attack, so he ran.

It wasn't until the wolf was tired that he could gather his humanity—that was a laugh, *his* humanity—well then, he gathered *himself* together and stopped running. His ribs ached with the force of his breath and the tough pads of his feet were cut by stones and an occasional crystal of ice from a land where the sun would never completely melt winter's gift. He was shivering though he felt hot, feverish. He was sick.

He couldn't keep running—and it wasn't only the wolf who craved escape—because running wasn't escape, not from what he fled.

He closed his eyes, but that didn't keep his head from throbbing in time with his pounding pulse. If he wasn't going to die out here, he would have to find shelter. Someplace warm, where he could wait and recover. He was lucky he'd come south, and it was high summer. If it had been winter, his only chance would have been to return to the caves he'd run from.

A pile of leaves under a thicket of aspen caught his attention. If they were deep enough to be dry underneath, they would do for shelter. He headed downhill and started for the trees.

There was no warning. The ground simply gave out from under him so fast he was lying ten feet down on a pile of rotted stakes before he realized what had happened.

It was an old pit trap. He started to get up and realized that he hadn't been as lucky as he thought. The stakes had snapped when he hit them, but so had his rear leg.

Perhaps if he hadn't already been so sick, so tired, he could have done something. He'd long ago learned how to set pain aside while he used his magic. But, though he tried, he couldn't distance himself from it this time, not while his body shivered with fever. Without magic, with a broken leg, he was trapped. The rotting stakes meant no one was watching the pit—no one to free him or kill him quickly. So he would die slowly.

That was all right because he didn't want to be free so much as he didn't want to be caught.

This was a trap, but it wasn't *His* trap.

Perhaps, the wolf thought, as his good legs collapsed again, perhaps it would be good not to run anymore. The ground was cold and wet underneath him, and the flush of heat from fever and the frantic journey drained into the chill of his surroundings. He shivered with cold and pain and waited patiently . . . even happily, for death to come and take him.

"If you go to the Northlands in the summer you might avoid snowstorms, but you get mud." Aralorn, Staff Page, Runner, and Scout for the Sixth Field Hundred, kicked a rock, which arced into the air and landed with an unsatisfactory splut just ahead of her on the mucky trail.

It wasn't a real trail. If it hadn't led from the village directly to the well-used camping spot her unit was currently stopped at, she'd have called it a deer trail and suspected that human feet had never trod it.

"*I* could have told them that," she said. "But no one asked me."

She took another step, and her left boot sank six inches down into a patch that looked just like the bit before it that had held her weight just fine. She pulled her foot out and shook it, trying unsuccessfully to get the thick mud off. When she started walking again, her mud-coated boot weighed twice what her right boot did.

"I suppose," she said in resigned tones as she squelched along, "training isn't supposed to be fun, and sometimes we have to fight in the mud. But there's mud in warmer places. We could go hunting Uriah in the old Great Swamp. That would be good training and *useful*, but no one would pay us. Mercenaries can't possibly be useful without someone paying us. So we're stuck—literally in the case of our supply wagons—practicing maneuvers in the cold mud."

Her sympathetic audience sighed and butted her with his head. She rubbed her horse's gray cheekbone under the leather straps of his bridle. "I know, Sheen. We could get there in an hour if we hurry—but I see no sense in encouraging stupid behavior."

One of the supply wagons was so bogged down in mud that it had broken an axle when they tried to pull it out. Aralorn had been sent out to the nearest village to have a smith repair the damage because the smith they'd brought with them had broken his arm trying to help get the wagon out.

That there had *been* a nearby village was something of a surprise out in the Northlands—though they weren't very deep into them. That village had probably been why the mercenary troops had been sent to practice where they were instead of twenty miles east or west.

The mended axle was tied lengthwise onto the left side of Sheen's saddle, with a weighted bag tied to the opposite stirrup to balance the load. It made riding awkward, which was why Aralorn was walking. Part of the reason, anyway.

"If we get to camp too early, our glorious and inexperienced captain will be ordering the wagon repaired right away. He'll send us out from a fairly good campsite to march for another few miles until the sun sets—and we'll be looking for another reasonable place to camp all night." The captain was a good sort, and would be a fine leader—eventually. But right now he was pretty set on proving his mettle and so lost to common sense. He needed to be managed properly by someone with a little more experience.

"If I don't arrive with the axle until it's dark, then he'll have to wait to move out until dawn," she told Sheen. "With daylight, it won't take long to fix the wagon, and we'll all get a good night's sleep. You and I can trot the last half mile or so, just enough to raise a light sweat and claim it was the smith who took so long."

Her warhorse jerked his head up abruptly. He snorted, his nostrils fluttering as he sucked air and flattened his ears at whatever his nose was telling him.

Aralorn thumbed off the thong that kept her sword in

its sheath and looked around carefully. It wasn't just a person—he'd have alerted her to that with a twitch of his ear.

The scent of blood might have called her horse's battle training to the fore, she thought, or maybe he sensed some sort of predator. This was the Northlands, after all; there were bear, wolves, and a few other things large enough to cause Sheen's upset.

The gray stallion whinnied a shrill challenge that was likely to be heard for miles around. She could only hope that her captain didn't hear it. Whatever Sheen sensed, it was in the aspen grove just uphill from where they stood. It was also, apparently, in no hurry to attack them since nothing answered Sheen's call: no return challenge, not even a rustle.

She could go on past. Likely, if it hadn't come out yet, it wasn't going to. But what was the fun in that?

She dropped Sheen's reins on the ground. He'd stand until she came back—at least until he got hungry. Aralorn drew her knife and crept into the thicket of aspen.

He heard her talking and smelled the horse without moving. He'd heard them come by earlier, too—or he thought so anyway. The horse put up a fuss this time because the wind that ruffled the leaves of the aspen would have brought him the wolf's scent.

He waited for them to leave. Tonight, he thought hopefully. Tonight would be the third night he'd spent here, maybe it would be the last. But part of him knew better, knew just how long it took for a body to die of thirst or of hunger. He was too strong yet. It would be tomorrow, at the soonest.

He'd distracted himself with the hope of death, and only the sound of the woman's feet told him that she'd approached. He opened his eyes to see a sturdily built woman, plain of face except for her large sea-green eyes, leaning over the edge of the pit. She wore the uniform of the mercenaries, and there were calluses and mud on her hands.

He didn't want to see her eyes, didn't want to feel interest in her at all. He only wanted her to leave him alone so he could die.

"Plague them all," she said, her voice tight and angry. Then her voice softened to a croon. "How long have you been here, love?"

The wolf recognized the threat of the knife she held as she slid down the far side of the pit to stand, one foot on either side of his hips. He growled, rolling off his side in preparation to get up—because he'd forgotten he wanted to die. Just for a moment. He shook from exertion, sickness, and from the pain of moving his leg. He lay back down again and flattened his ears.

"Shh," she crooned, inexplicably sheathing her knife in the face of his aggression. "Not so long as all that, apparently. Now what shall I do about you?"

Go away, he thought. He growled at her with as much threat as he could, feeling his lips peel back from his fangs and the hair rise along his spine.

The expression on her face was not the one that he'd expected. Certainly not one any sane person would turn on a threatening wolf she was standing over. She should fear him.

Instead . . . "Poor thing," she said in that same crooning tone. "Let's get you out of this, shall we?"

She dropped her gaze away from his and knelt to examine his hips, humming softly as she moved closer.

She didn't stink of fear, was all he could think. Everyone feared him. Everyone. Even *Him*, even the one who searched. She smelled of horse, sweat, and something sweet. No fear.

He snarled, and she wrapped one hand over his muzzle. Sheer astonishment stopped his growls. Just how stupid was she?

"Shh." Her voice blended into the music she was making, and he realized that her humming was pulling magic out of the ground around and beneath them. "Let me look."

He was as surprised at himself as he was at her when he let her do just that. He could have torn out her throat or broken her neck while she examined every inch of him. But he didn't—and he wasn't quite certain why not.

It wasn't that killing her would bother him. He'd killed a lot of people. But that was before. He didn't want to do that anymore. So perhaps that was part of it.

He knew she was trying to help him—but he didn't want help. He wanted to die.

Her magic swept over and around him, cushioning him. The wolf whined softly and relaxed, leaving the mage in him fully in charge for the first time since the illness had hit. Maybe even longer ago than that.

Her magic didn't work on the mage because he knew what it was—and, he admitted to himself, because it wasn't coercive magic. He was mage enough to read her intent. She didn't want the wolf to become a lapdog but only to relax.

But the woman's helpful intent wasn't why he didn't kill her. Not the real reason. He hadn't been interested in anything in longer than he could remember, but she made him curious. He'd only ever met a practitioner of green magic, wild magic, once before. They hid from the humans in the land—if there were any still left. But here was one wearing the clothes of a mercenary.

She could pick him up—which surprised him because she didn't weigh much more than he did. But she couldn't hoist him high enough to reach the edge of the trap, so she set him down again.

"Going to need some help," she told him, and clambered to the top. She almost didn't make it out of the pit herself; if it had been round, she wouldn't have.

When she departed and took her magic with her, it left him bereaved—as if someone had covered him with a blanket, then removed it. And only when she left did he realize that her music had deadened his pain and soothed him, despite his being a mage on his guard against it.

He heard the horse move and the sound of leather and something heavy hitting the ground. The horse approached the pit and stopped.

When the mercenary who could do green magic hopped back into his almost grave, she had a rope in her hand.

He waited for the wolf to stir as she tied him in a makeshift harness that somehow managed to brace his bad leg. But the wolf waited as meekly as a lamb while she worked. When he was trussed up to her satisfaction, she climbed back out.

"Come on, Sheen," she told someone. Possibly, he thought, it was the horse.

The trip out of the hole was not pleasant. He closed his eyes and let the pain take him where it would. When he lay on the ground at last, she untied him.

Freed at last, he lay where he had fallen, too weak to run. Maybe too curious as well.